SHOTGUN WOMAN

A NOVEL

BEAU BERNSTEIN

SHOTGUN WOMAN
Copyright © 2024 Beau Bernstein
All Rights Reserved.
Published by Unsolicited Press.
Printed in the United States of America.
First Edition.

No part of this book may be used or reproduced in any manner whatsoever without written permission except in the case of brief quotations embodied in critical articles or reviews.

Attention schools and businesses: for discounted copies on large orders, please contact the publisher directly.

For information contact:
Unsolicited Press
Portland, Oregon
www.unsolicitedpress.com
orders@unsolicitedpress.com
619-354-8005

Cover Designer: Amanda Weiss
Editor: S.R. Stewart

ISBN: 978-1-963115-19-2

"L'audace, l'audace
T'jours l'audace"

Georges Jacques Danton

SHOTGUN WOMAN

CHAPTER I

DUST TO DUST

1953 Wheaton, Texas

In the slow quiet hours of a late summer Sunday morning, Eudora Burleson sat parked in an old white work truck beneath the outstretched limbs of a mighty oak tree.

She'd arrived early, long before the sun had risen in the sky. But upon seeing the cemetery gates, shrouded beneath a misty blue dawn, she'd trembled at the thought of going inside. So instead, driving along the perimeter of the high stone walls, she had followed a dusty gravel road past the groundskeeper's tool shed putting as much distance between herself and those gates as she possibly could. Then, once certain that she wouldn't be seen, she'd racked the old pickup into park.

And there she'd sat for hours now. Passing the time doing nothing much in particular. Thinking about things while at the same time not thinking much at all. Just watching the red sun rise through the rearview while smoking cigarettes and wishing she were anywhere but here.

Of course, Dora knew all that wishing didn't really count for shit. But given the circumstances, she reckoned she would afford herself the luxury, if only just this once.

Anything to get her through what was coming next.

With the windows rolled down, she gazed motionless at a pair of blackflies dancing just above her driver-side mirror. Black, like the color of her dress. And the veil drawn back atop her head.

Black like her heart, hardly beating.

Already the day was sizzling with an insufferable heat. Yet before her, the dark stone walls of the cemetery cast a terrible shade. Dora's eyes were long and weary. Outside a lazy breeze shuffled its way through the switchgrass. At last, the blackflies zipped off into the sky. Left alone with her thoughts once again, Eudora reckoned there wouldn't be any harm in just one more cigarette.

All the while, the clock in the dashboard ticked on to its ceaseless tune. As Dora took up her lighter, her eyes steered far clear of those steady hands for fear of what they'd tell her.

Because if she looked, she'd have seen it was time. If she looked, she'd have seen she was well over half an hour late to her own husband's funeral.

But, as it was, she still couldn't bring herself to look.

Because she still wasn't ready to go in.

Not yet.

Not that she wasn't prepared to suffer the burden. The indignity of arrivals whose presence only served to rub salt deeper into her wounds. From far and wide they'd come. Like vultures around a corpse. Like they always do in this nowhere town. Eager for their scrap of conversation. Their pound of flesh.

Every second spent among that carnivorous congregation was going to be downright miserable and Dora knew it. She only bore the weight and soldiered on because it was what Barett would have wanted.

He'd have wanted the good ones to get their chance to say goodbye.

That was just his way.

At this point, Eudora couldn't spare the strength to argue otherwise. Her mind was a mess. So recently he'd been here and now, he was gone - forever. Torn from her in an instant, irrevocable moment. The wound was so fresh she'd hardly had time to stifle the bleeding, but already that hurt could have filled a hundred lifetimes. Like some terrible record stuck on repeat, the realization would return in her mind.

How strange it was, the thought that she'd never see him again. In her memory she could still trace every sun creased wrinkle upon his face. Like canyons carved into clay. Even the truck still carried his scent.

He seemed so close Dora reached out to touch him.

But he was gone.

That thought would come in waves. Each one crashing stronger than the last. Like the savage undercurrent of the nearby Colorado River, it drug her down, until she found herself drowning in the thought.

Her hand trembling with a sick quiver, Dora slid another unsteady cigarette from the pack. In fits she shook her head, wrestling back the darkness closing in. As the tears came tumbling down, she wiped her eyes with the back of her black gloved hand. She pinched the filter between her lips. In the dashboard ashtray the smoldering remains of the dozen or so she'd smoked before still gave off a radiant heat.

Then, just as she swore upon lighting the first, she swore this one would be the last.

Just one last cigarette, then she'd head in.

But this time, as the lighter chimed to life, Dora paused, staring transfixed into the flickering flame. Suddenly, she wasn't sure she could bring herself to go in there and face them at all. The damn snakes and hangers-on. Crooks the lot of em. Small town politics can be a grisly battlefield. She and Barett had learned that awful quick. Suppose that's just what honest folk get for doing right these days.

But no matter how much Eudora despised what was coming, no matter how many exits she considered, no matter how many cigarettes she smoked there in the cab of that truck, the one thing she could not avoid was that still, despite all her objections, she could hear Barett's voice. As though he were right there next to her, speaking warm and low, with that half-cocked grin he'd get when he knew he was right.

"Shouldn't let a couple bad seeds spoil a good crop," he'd have said, with that chuckle that made him bounce all up and down. "Just g'on. Won't take but a minute."

"Oh, alright godammnit," Dora groaned to the emptiness beside her. "Have it your way."

Snatching the unlit cigarette from her lips, she tucked it safely behind her ear. A reward for when the deed was done.

"But I tell ya right now…" she grumbled, turning the keys in the ignition, "I ain't stayin in there but a goddamn minute."

As Barett's old work truck sputtered to life beneath the great oak tree, the rearview mirror rattled in place. Wiping away any trace of tears, Dora checked her shattered reflection and found herself damn near unrecognizable. Her bare face was swollen and red. Her lips, drawn down into a snarl. She reckoned she looked like some demon set forth from hell and somehow found the thought to be quite comforting.

"Alright you sons a' bitches," she muttered, drawing the black veil down atop her face. "Here I come."

Inside the cemetery walls, Rita VanBuren sat fanning herself to no avail as she checked the time on her wristwatch. On her right, Margie Watson's makeup was running in streams down her cheeks. On her left, Susan Bertram was still prattling on about some nonsense she'd long since tuned out of. Though Betty Schneider had arrived with them she was off standing beneath the shade of a tree like a mule escaping the midday sun. In a town like Wheaton, funerals were about as good of an excuse for socializing as you could hope to get. But even that seemed to be spoiled because the only thought on Rita's mind was the rather disagreeable sensation of sweat trickling down the small of her back.

The cemetery walls radiated the Texas heat like an infernal oven and with every new arrival the temperature seemed to spike by degrees. It was too damn hot to talk. Too humid to breathe. Stewing in silence, Rita's eyes scanned the cemetery grounds searching for some clue as to when they were going to get this show on the road. Not long after, she got her answer.

"Ready!"

Curious to the commanding voice suddenly shouting behind her, Rita turned in her chair. But before she could place where the sound had come from, she heard another -- three heavy bolts racking forward into position.

"Oh, shi--," Rita began.

"...Aim, Fire!" the booming voice continued.

Beneath the vast blue curtain of the Texas sky, three thunderous cracks rang out over the Wheaton County Jewish Cemetery.

"Jesus Christ," Rita cried, ducking for cover, "Are they doing that already? People are still coming in!"

"What?" Susan squawked beside her, both hands clasped tight to her ears. "Gah bless darlin, I can't hear a damn thing!"

"Honestly, is there no program for the ceremony?" Rita huffed, shielding herself with her purse, "No schedule of events? Speakers, sermons... rifle salutes? I mean they're out here just shootin rifles off over our heads, without any warnin at all!"

"What?" Susan repeated, rubbing her ears. "The turnout, you say? Oh, I know, just look at all these people who showed up!"

Though completely off-topic, for once in her life it seemed Susan Bertram was not exaggerating. In what became widely regarded as one of the largest turnouts in Wheaton County history, the funeral of Barett Burleson was nothing short of spectacular. Of course, as expected, the usual suspects had arrived for the event; a collection of small-town big shots starved for any form of social occasion. Each one of them a bit too eager to see and be seen.

Already among the gathering congregation were some of the town's most recognizable faces. A veritable who's who of the Wheaton County elite: Patty Nielsen of Nielsen's Pastries; Frank DuMond from the Diamond Diner; Jeb Ferguson, the oil baron; Jack Benson, the high school football coach; Hank and Gina Henigan of H&H Ranch; and former State Senator Davis Farriday to name a few. Even the esteemed author James Perkis had made a rare public appearance from his reclusive garden enclave. And yet, more arrivals continued their steady stream into the cramped confines of the cemetery gates. Within the high stone walls, black clad groups gathered amongst themselves exchanging handshakes and quiet conversation, huddling like cattle beneath any shade they could find. Already, there were too many people and not enough chairs. The rifle salute had started at least twenty minutes too early. The honor guard, meanwhile, was half an hour late.

And perhaps, most alarming of all, Eudora Burleson was still nowhere to be found.

Everywhere bothered moans and groans were beginning to make their rounds. At the great iron gates of the cemetery, Herman Appelbaum, the frail, grey undertaker, maintained an air of quiet calm. But inside, his nerves were fraying at the seams. Doing his best to remain in control of the situation, he hid his misgivings behind a flimsy smile and continued to greet the long line of visitors bottlenecked at the gates.

To each passerby, he extended his hand, and kindly relayed the same message. Just as he'd been instructed.

"Welcome, welcome. Mrs. Burleson mighty appreciates your attendance and asks that all condolences and sympathies be saved until the end of the ceremony. Please appreciate that this is a time of great anguish for the Burleson family, and we simply ask that Dora's privacy and wishes be respected. Now, if you please, right this way, thank you kindly."

As he ushered in yet another family, Herman's composed disposition broke for a moment as he waved over his son and assistant, Adam. Excusing himself from his duties at the gate with a gentle bow, Herman led his son aside, then yanked him close.

"Oy vey iz mir, I've never seen so many people," he muttered, wiping the sweat from his brow. "Now, listen boychik, I need you to take over at the gates. People are beginning to get restless. They're asking me what's going on and to be honest I haven't the slightest idea of what to tell them."

"Just tell the truth," Adam replied. "It's not your fault she wouldn't let you do your job. She didn't pick the casket, didn't pick speakers, didn't even pick the paper for the programs. Couldn't even be bothered to write an obituary!"

"Oh, I'd say the obituary is the least of our concerns at the present time," Herman sighed, wringing his hands in prayer.

"How do you mean?"

But the old undertaker did not hear, for his eyes were lost among the ever-growing mass of townsfolk milling about the grounds.

"Tatti!" Adam shouted, snapping the old man back to attention, "What do you mean that's the 'least of our concerns'?"

"Well," Herman managed, adjusting his glasses with another heavy sigh, "She's had the body...cremated."

"She what?" Adam gasped, "She can't do that!"

"Quiet," Herman commanded, pulling the young man further aside. "Quiet now. She's already done it. No sense arguing it; it's done. When the body didn't arrive for the preparations, I... well, I called up the residence and that's what she told me. Said she'd had a change of heart."

"What are we gonna tell all these people then?" Adam hissed through pursed lips. "This is a Jewish cemetery, Tatti! We don't bury ashes! How can we get on with a funeral if there's no body?"

With gentle hands Herman begged his son to settle. Then, drawing a deep breath to fortify himself, he spoke with a renewed sense of calm.

"I informed Mrs. Burleson that the faith does not allow the burial of a desecrated corpse, and thankfully, she has agreed to keep the remains in her personal care until we can find another avenue."

Then, after ushering a group of mourners by with a showman's smile, Herman continued. "That said, as strange as it may sound, Dora wishes to proceed with the funeral as planned."

"Wishes to proceed?" Adam snorted, his face twisted with confusion. "What does that...I mean...she means to bury an empty casket in front of all these people?"

The silence on his father's lips spoke volumes.

"Oy, I can't believe this," Adam scoffed. "This woman is twice as crazy as they say!"

"Stop," Herman commanded. "We do not disrespect our people. This is a painful time for everyone involved. Most so for Mrs. Burleson. Now as you can see, many people have come out to pay their respects, and we are not going to take that from them. Furthermore, I will not deny Barett Burleson his last will and testament that explicitly requested a funeral open to the public."

With this, Herman's eyes regained their steadfast resolve and his son understood implicitly the decision had been made.

"Now, people are starting to talk, and like it or not, it is our responsibility to see that the ship runs smoothly. Even if it is halfway sunk, the captain's gone mad, and the rudder's nowhere to be found."

"Yes Tatti," Adam replied dutifully. "I understand."

"Gut, gut. Now, you get over there, and remember to say what I told you now."

"Yes sir. When should I come join you at the gravesite?"

"Well," Herman said, wiping the sweat from his glasses, "When folks stop showing up, I guess."

As it turned out, Barett Burleson was a man of many enterprises. The son of Lithuanian refugees, he was brought up with the expectation that is thrust, wanted or not, upon so many American immigrants. To make one's own way. To shoulder the burden, no matter the weight. When Barett's father had arrived in this country alone as a young boy, he did not speak the language, nor did he know a single soul in this new land. He had no money, no connections, no prospects. But what he did have was far more valuable.

Grit and plenty of it.

And he'd need it too, because as he came to learn quite quickly, life was hard in Texas. Unforgiving. He became, in his later years neither a man of sympathy nor pride, and in Barett he had instilled the same ideals that he'd learned the hard way. From a very young age he had encouraged Barett to work for himself. To believe in himself, even when no one else did.

Through the years Barett had tried his hand working in many different fields. In his ascent to making Burleson a reputable name in Wheaton, he had held nearly every job in town, from ditch digger to city councilman. To many, he was many different things. Landlord, laborer, rancher, crafty farmer, failed politician, business owner, soldier, officer, but above all, a kind and gentle man. No matter the nature of the job or the company he worked alongside, Barett treated everyone he met with a great and earnest respect. In many ways, his greatest strength was not his work ethic, but rather his keen and genuine interest in people. In every person he met, Barett found something admirable. And as a result, most everyone admired him in return.

The turnout to his funeral was a testament to this fact. Rarely in Wheaton would the land-owning elite be found standing shoulder to shoulder with the dusty ranch hands who shoveled their show horses' shit. But in many ways, that was Barett. Inhabiting both worlds but belonging to none. To be capable of bringing together so many who lived in quiet ignorance of each other's existence was something of a feat in itself. Had he been alive to see it, the rather clumsy sight of all these different people packed together probably would have tickled him pink.

While the rich and the poor standing side by side would have typically been the talk of the town, it was wholly overshadowed by the presence of yet another divide. One far more insidious. A revelation that proved jaw dropping for many of the mourners in attendance.

Because standing just across the open grave from the town's typical cast of local characters was an even larger turnout from the rarely seen, rarely acknowledged, residents of Wheaton County's officially designated Negro Quarter.

Dozens upon dozens of families from the Quarter had arrived early to the service. Most had walked miles in their Sunday best just to be there. Assembled on the far side of the hollow grave they stood, patient and respectful, as a mass of whispering arrivals had slowly gathered opposite them for the last half hour.

In all that time, not a single person from the white community had crossed the threshold. Not a single handshake or hello.

The divide that so many chose to ignore day in and day out had been suddenly, inescapably thrust into the open. As real and tangible as the oppressive heat that bore down upon them. Eye to eye, yet completely separated by the gaping chasm between them, the two groups stood facing each other in the tenuous light of morning.

Just then, a voice called out once more across the countryside. "Ready! Aim! Fire!"

A second volley of gunshots rang out shattering the silence.

Outside the cemetery gates, Sheriff Hinkley paced back and forth with a cigarillo dangling from his lips. The Sheriff was a big man. Broad shoulders and barrel chested, though age had turned what was once hard, soft. His gut ballooned out over his belt, swallowing it whole. Only his muscular forearms remained, a relic of the bulldog of a man he once was. Beneath his beige uniform his sunbaked skin was cast bronze. Atop his bulbous head his sweat-stained cowboy hat wobbled as he feverishly patted over his pockets like a squirrel after a nut.

"Gat dammit," he mumbled as sweat brimmed upon his furrowed brow. "Where'd I put that thang?"

Finding no satisfaction, he moved to his pants, digging into his front and back pockets with hungry searching hands. At last, he felt the faint rattle. His tongue slid over his cracked lips. He grasped the cool steel of his flask and drew it out into the sun. Tossing it back, the old man drank deeply with great pleasure. Closing his eyes, he savored every burning swig until, in the distance, the sound of footsteps came fast approaching.

"Shouldn't we be getting back in there, sir?" a voice finally said. "Knowin Eudora, I don't think this funeral's gone last too long now."

Hinkley finished his long drink and smacked his lips with a satisfied delight.

"Well forgive me, Abbott," he belched, dragging his sleeve across his lips. "But I take moral offense to sharing too close a quarter with the coloreds. Makes my blood boil. Besides, a weaslin little Jew like Burleson receivin full military honors don't really sit right with me. Some damn immigrant treated like an American hero? I thought this country *won* the war. But if this what winnin looks like, well you can count me out."

With a sigh Deputy Clyde Abbott brought both hands to rest on his belt buckle. Beside his badge, the pistol at his hip rattled loosely in its holster. He was a young man. Dark haired and fresh faced, though he carried himself with a comfort beyond his years. His whole life he had been rather small and skinny -- the runt of the litter -- but it had given him a quiet resilience that needed no declaration. In his eyes there was a steadfast gaze.

Before him, the old Sheriff swayed a bit in his stance, as if a passing breeze could have done him in. Though it was now only mid-morning, the nip of the flask sure hadn't been his first drink of the day. Feeling a strange sense of shame, Abbott looked down at his dirty boots and considered his words carefully. Over the years he'd learned that to handle Hinkley when he was in this sort of state he required a delicate touch.

"C'mon now, boss," Clyde began. "Burleson fought that war same as me. And same as them other folks in there too. It made brothers of those boys. I tell ya what, don't matter what color you are, you're all American when you gettin shelled in some shithole in France. It ain't somethin I expect everyone to understand. Especially if you ain't…"

"If I ain't what?" snapped Hinkley, his eyes hot with warning. "You better watch your fuckin mouth boy. While you was off screwin hookers in Europe I was keepin this town safe. Y'know I been Sheriff since you was shittin your britches."

At this Abbott raised his hands, both reassuring Hinkley and keeping a cautious distance between them. Shuffling in his stance, the Sheriff brought the cigarillo to his lips and took a sharp, anxious drag. Clyde had seen him mad before, but for some reason today he was more riled up than a bull in the chute.

"Easy boss, y'know I didn't mean nothin by it," Abbott said softly. "Hey, you was the one wanted to come remember? I told you before you didn't have to come. Remember, I told you that, didn't I?"

"Bullshit, you know I got to show my face," Hinkley spat. "Where's your head at boy? Election's coming up, course I gotta show up. Just didn't think I'd have to suffer the humiliation of standing alongside coloreds in a damned Jew cemetery. You have any idea how that looks? My voters ain't never gone let me live this down."

Removing the cowboy hat atop his head, Abbott drew a handkerchief from his back pocket and dabbed the sweat steaming at his brow. A cruel smile crept across Hinkley's face.

"Somethin botherin you boy?" Hinkley prodded with a certain pleasure. "You got a problem with somethin I said? Did my language offend your delicate sensibilities?"

"C'mon, boss. These just honest people coming out to pay their respects. They ain't here to cause no trouble, you just let em go on now."

Suddenly Hinkley stepped forward suffocating the space between them. Unmoved, Abbott's eyes stayed locked on his boots.

"They ain't," Hinkley paused, his face twisting with agitation, "...*people*, Abbott. They're parasites. And if it were up to me, they wouldn't be allowed to breathe the same air, let alone stand on the same ground as me and mine. Y'Understand?"

At his side, Hinkley's hand writhed into a fist. Still staring down, Abbott felt the Sheriff's hot stinking breath wash over his face. It was sour and thick with whiskey. Calmly he placed the cowboy hat back atop his head before raising his gaze to meet Hinkley's.

But too late it seemed, for the Sheriff was already well into another deep guzzle from his flask. Just then a familiar voice boomed out once more over the cemetery walls.

"Ready! Aim! Fire!"

Close behind, the third and final rifle volley echoed across the county. A flock of black starlings rushed from the tree line.

Dropping the empty flask back into his pocket Hinkley raised his eyebrows with a sudden drunken glee.

"Suppose that's my cue," he chimed.

Seizing Abbott around the shoulder like an old friend, Hinkley strutted back towards the congregation of mourners as Napoleon marched triumphant into Paris.

"Where is Burleson's ol' bitch anyways?" Hinkley chuckled, slapping Abbott across the back, "I ain't even seen her yet."

"Speak of the devil," Abbott said beneath his breath, "and she shall appear."

Just ahead the black mass of onlookers shuffled about conversing quietly until one by one their whispers faded into silence. Taking their place amongst the crowd, Hinkley and Abbott stood watching.

Waiting.

Moments later, as if materializing from thin air, Eudora Burleson suddenly appeared. Looming over the flag draped coffin as it hung over the grave.

Cloaked in a black dress, her slight frame stood in stark contrast to the immensity of her aura. With black gloved hands clutched in silent reverence, her figure cut a sharp and striking silhouette. Colorless against the sun-scorched grass of the cemetery. Not a single inch of bare skin was exposed. Gazing out from beneath the impenetrable black veil draped over her face, the only visible sign of her humanity were the white locks of hair peeking out just so from under the latticed tulle. So indistinguishable was she in the all-black ensemble, that her haunting figure could have been anybody, were it not for the air of immovable defiance that surrounded her.

Beneath the searing eyes of those in attendance, she stood a stoic sentry.

Hidden deep in the assembly, Margie Watson watched with wide eyes. Her gaze fixed on Dora, she leaned over and tapped Rita on her shoulder.

"Do you know who the dressmaker is?" Margie whispered behind her hand.

"Couture," Rita replied. "Certainly not something you'd find in Wheaton. Houston, perhaps. But I doubt it."

"Well, I don't know who made it," Betty said, joining in. "But I believe that's what you call a 'revenge' dress."

"Ain't that what you wear to make your man jealous?"

"It's what you wear when you want to send a message."

"Well, who's it meant for?"

"The hell if I know, honey," Rita shrugged. "All I'm saying is, it's a statement. What that statement is, I haven't the faintest."

"How does she survive under that thing?" Betty groaned, shifting uncomfortably in her seat, "It's hotter than all hell out here, it's gotta be like a furnace under all that black. It's suicide."

"Yeah well, maybe that's the point," muttered Susan.

"Or, maybe," said Rita, fanning herself coolly. "She means to show us she ain't no stranger to suffering."

"Shush!" chided Margie. "I think somethin's happening."

As if instinctively sensing the commencement of some unspoken funerary rite, the gathered crowd huddled closer around the coffin. Across the grave, at the head of the Black congregation, Floyd Thomas stood with his head bowed. He was a tall, wiry man dressed in a pressed military uniform. Upon his chest hung the countless polished medals he had received during the war. Once a renowned boxer in the Army, his long sinewy frame still retained the easy grace of a tried and tested champion. Standing at attention with his hands clasped proudly behind his back, he felt the weight of every white eye crawling across him. Looking him up and down. He heard the sharpness of their whispers. Silently he bore the burden without complaint. It was not like the sensation was anything new.

Besides, he wasn't here for them.

He was here to lay his Captain to rest.

Suddenly, Floyd's concentration was broken as a tiny hand tugged at his sleeve. Looking down he saw his young daughter, Jo, summoning his attention with her finger. Her hair pulled back in braids, she swayed gently in her Sunday dress eager to relay what seemed to be a very important message. With a warm smile Floyd knelt to one knee to receive her quiet whisper.

"Daddy?" she squeaked.

"Yes, Jojo?"

"That scary man keep lookin at me," she said.

As Jo raised her tiny finger to point out the culprit, Floyd intercepted her hand and lowered it to her side.

"Just keep your head down, child," he whispered. "And don't be pointin at nobody, that's rude now. You just stand quiet, y'hear? Don't pay nobody no mind."

With a gentle smile, Floyd raised himself back to his full and towering height. Scanning among the rows across the grave, his eyes moved face by face before locking viselike with Sheriff Hinkley's sinister gaze. From across the grave the old Sheriff's face sneered with a cruel and drunken pleasure.

Floyd placed his weathered hands upon Jo's shoulders with a gentle touch. Looking up, the young girl smiled to see her father's loving eyes watching over her.

"There's my girl," he said. "We be outta here soon, jus' a little longer now."

She beamed back at him.

Once again, an unsteady stillness fell over the spectators of the strangely informal ceremony. Here and there hushed murmurs of inquisitive conversations began to crack through the awkward silence.

Finally, Eudora Burleson stepped forward towards the coffin. Drawing with her a complete and full attention.

Without a word, she kneeled.

The great black dress billowed around her like the mighty rolling storm clouds over the pastures in Spring. Placing a hand delicately atop the casket, her black clad form leaned in, as if to speak. In unison the huddled masses craned their heads like a murder of crows, starving to overhear just a morsel of the widow's final farewell.

Dora's black veil flickered with movement. Whether wind or woeful goodbye, none could discern from their vantage. Stretching out upon her toes for a better look, Margie Watson almost tumbled forward into the onlookers seated before her.

Then, without uttering a single distinguishable syllable, Eudora Burleson rose to her feet.

At this the undertaker took his cue. Nodding towards the men standing ready, they took their positions upon the ropes. Cracking and squealing into motion the pulleys began to give way as the casket sunk lower and lower into the depths of the earth.

Motionless as a shrouded effigy, Eudora bowed her head as a summer wind rattled through the trees.

Then, even before the first shovel of dirt was heaved upon the tomb, Dora turned an about-face and began marching towards the cemetery gates.

Spreading like brushfire across the assembly, silent expressions went wild. Suspicious looks were met with shrugs; inquisitive gestures returned baffled gesticulations. For a single moment the entire congregation -- rich and poor, Black and white -- stood truly equal, if only in their confusion.

Unmoved by the rumblings growing behind her, Eudora continued her steady march right through the gates to where the truck sat parked, the keys ready in the ignition.

Wasting no time Eudora bundled up the skirt of her dress and stuffed herself inside. The black mass billowed upwards, obscuring half the windshield and most of the steering wheel. She slammed the door behind her and revved up the rattling engine.

Shifting into drive, Dora slowly eased the car forward until it was framed perfectly between the two cemetery gates, eye-to-eye with the entire congregation of mourners.

Lost for words, they stared at the ghastly apparition leering back at them from beneath the black veil. Slowly, she leaned over towards the driver side window, as if to finally speak.

Only she screamed.

"THERE AIN'T GONE BE NO RECEPTION SO DON'T NONE A Y'ALL BE COMIN ROUND MY HOUSE!"

With wide eyes, the onlookers stood speechless.

Awestruck, Margie leaned over to Rita's ear.

"Good lord, the woman has lost her damn mind."

Her duty fulfilled; Dora slammed on the accelerator. As the truck gathered speed down the long gravel drive the engine squealed with effort until at last, disappearing behind a cloud of dust, she was gone.

That evening, back at home, Eudora Burleson opened the creaky doors of the mudroom chifforobe and reached into its shadowy depths. Behind the neglected winter coats draped in their plastic shrouds, her hand fumbled among the darkness before landing upon the unmistakable sensation of cold steel. Outside the sun had drawn long in the western sky, casting its golden glow across the pasture. But inside, behind the tightly drawn blinds, the house was cold, dark, and still. Though Dora briefly considered taking out the .22 or the 30.30, she reckoned that the kind of day she'd had called from something a bit stronger.

With her chosen rifle in hand, the immense weight of the Springfield 30.06 felt like just the ticket.

On the top shelf of the chifforobe, Barett's collection of cowboy hats sat arranged in a neat row, just as he'd left them. As that now familiar dread began to close in, Dora quickly lifted the hat on the far right. The one stained with copper-tinged bands of his sweat. The one hiding a box of rifle cartridges. Grabbing up a fistful, Dora turned and made her way out the back door as the screen slammed closed behind her. On the counter, the thin black lace of her funeral veil rose and fell, aloft on the passing air.

Outside, the glow of the evening sun was blinding. The heat was thick and dull, blunted but still coming down from the late afternoon's roiling intensity. Her hand held high to shield the light; Dora pushed on. Just out the back through the garage, was a wide and open side yard with a little windmill and past that, the untamed wilds of the ranchland beyond. A thousand acres of Burleson property stretched out before her.

But where Dora was headed, only about a hundred yards. Separated by a wood and barbed wire fence, Eudora stopped short at the old iron gate before the pasture.

Planting her boot heel upon the lowest fence beam, she watched for a moment as a small flock of starlings weaved impossible patterns beneath the deepening orange sky. Then, kicking the iron gate into reverberations, she stepped out into the pasture as brambles and dead grass followed close behind, trapped in the long trailing train of her funeral dress.

In the distance the cicadas roared in the trees.

Beyond the fence line rose a great gnarled oak tree. Sometimes, when they were both working outside, she and Barett would sit down for lunch beneath that tree. Not that it was their special tree or nothing, just they used to sit there sometimes, and Dora had always enjoyed doing so. The two of them, the cows, and nobody else. It was no secret that lots of folks in town found them a bit of an odd couple. Barett was a real people-person and Dora, quite the opposite. Suppose most people reckoned they were sort of like puzzle pieces that didn't quite fit. Course, their marriage had never been just sunshine and rainbows. That fiction you see on the television or read about in those damned ladies' magazines. Theirs was the real kind. The kind that didn't need any explanation or justification to nobody. It'd been thirty years of fussing and fighting and making up, but for all the right reasons. All things considered; Dora wouldn't have had it any other way. But that all seemed to be a passing dream now.

Like clouds rolling quick across an open range.

Arriving beneath the arms of that gnarled oak, Dora eased herself down upon a large mound of earth. Scrunching up her dress round her knees she drew the powerful weight of the rifle over her lap. It was Barett's rifle. He had taught her how to disassemble the thing from top to bottom. How to check the firing pin and adjust the sights. He had shown her how to clean it, how to carry it, and how to load it.

More importantly, he had shown her how to shoot it.

Dora unveiled the bullets as they tumbled gently in the palm of her hand. Laying them out atop her lap, she looked them over carefully before finally picking out a single chosen cartridge. Held between her thumb and forefinger, she admired the brass sheen in the light of the setting sun. Her eyes now acclimated; she gazed out upon the pasture.

Far across the prairie, a gentle breeze came sweeping over the bending bronze sea of switchgrass. Overhead, the wide-open sky burned red and incandescent, set off by towering constructions of pink and orange-tinted clouds stretching high into the heavens. In the afterglow, Dora's white hair, gone colorless long before its prime, shone golden and magnificent. Bathed in light, her face was suddenly smoothed from the weariness of its many years. She wasn't a beautiful woman in the conventional sense, but rather handsome in her own way. Gone was the proud grace of her forties, wasted on another world at war. Still, she had strong features, which served her well for she was quite a strong-willed woman, even in her youth. In those days there was a fire inside her. Or at least, that's what Barett used to say. He said that's what had drawn him to her in the first place. Her fire. Though now, it seemed that flame was all but extinguished. These days her eyes hung heavy. Too heavy. Burdened not with the weight of time, but rather the weight that only the brokenhearted can truly carry.

A weight that can only be carried for so long.

Her gaze drifting back towards the bullet in her hand, Dora took in a deep, tired breath. She just wanted the hurt to be over.

She chambered the single round into the rifle and racked the bolt shut.

Settling in against the trunk of the tree, she pressed the weapon firmly into her shoulder. Its weight was immense in her arms.

Calm and steady, her right hand crept into position, coiling around the handguard. Stretching out a thin finger, she laid it over the cold steel trigger. Taking her time, she tightened her hold, like a python squeezing the life from its prey.

Her mind made up, Dora drew in a long, steady breath, and held it deep in her chest.

With a smooth motion, she pulled the trigger.

Like some cataclysm from another world, a deafening shot tore across the pasture, followed by a deep pop of shimmering glass. In the ringing aftermath, Dora was left breathless. Downrange on a twisted log sat three empty whiskey bottles.

On the end, the remains of a fourth lay in ruin as a cloud of glassy dust drifted away in the breeze.

Licking her thumb, Eudora reached out to wipe a bit of dirt off the front sight. Satisfied with the adjustment, she quickly seized another round and chambered it into the rifle. Barett always said the Springfield kicked like a Jack mule. True to his word, the ache in Dora's shoulder pulsed hot with blood as a bruise began to form just beneath the skin. Downrange she lined up the next bottle between the iron sights. Quickly she drew a shallow breath. Exhaling, she squeezed the trigger until another crashing bolt rang out.

A rush of blackbirds fled shrieking from the treetops.

Faster this time she racked another round and sighted the third empty jug. Her heartbeat thumped through her shoulder. She timed the sensations, squeezed the trigger, obliterated the object of her wrath.

Another bullet.

Forcefully she racked the bolt forward and raised the cannon. The bottle in her sights, Dora levelled her aim before coming to rest just above the base of the glass.

But there, at the bottom of the bottle, a small pool of whiskey glowed amber in the sunlight.

As she stretched her finger towards the trigger, Dora paused and thought better of it.

No use in wasting good liquor.

Exhaling the low sort of groan that only age can muster, Dora rose to her feet and beat the dust from her dress. With the stock of the rifle settled against her hip, she ejected the live round, sending the brass cartridge spinning into the air.

Then, through the knee-high grass Dora marched.

As sweat rolled down her face she pulled a damp cigarette carton from her bosom. With a metallic flash from her lighter, the ember leapt to life as Dora filled her lungs with a cloud of the sweet perfume. At the targets, she picked through what was left of the shattered glass before seizing her spared prize in her hands. Holding it up to the light, she swirled the remnants of whiskey resting at its base.

From inside the house, a great hound bellowed out, haunting and deep.

"I know, ol' boy," Dora sighed. "I miss him too."

Raising the bottle, she tipped it towards nowhere in particular before draining the contents within. Then, shifting the cigarette back to her lips, she took another long pull and exhaled kerosene.

"Well," she muttered behind the drifting cloud of smoke. "S'pose now's as good a time as any."

Then, with an unfamiliar hesitation in her movements, Dora knelt beneath the makeshift shooting gallery. There, covered in a layer of shattered glass sat an old wooden box nestled in the dirt. With a heavy heart, she lifted it up into the fading light. Among the solitude of the pasture and the warm embrace of the setting sun, she cradled it briefly in her arms. But as she felt the tears making their unwelcome return, her fingers settled on the latch which sealed the box shut.

From the moment she cracked the lid, the ashen remains began to slip out, eager to take off on the gentle western wind.

"Well, g'on now," her voice trembled. "Knew you didn't want to be cooped up in no damn box."

As she unhinged the lid to its full breadth, Dora lowered it to her hip and without a single moment's pause for fear of changing her mind, she heaved it into the vast Texas sky.

Caught up instantly, the ashen dust danced out upon the breeze, like a great wild flock of mourning doves.

CHAPTER II

SMALL TALK

The next morning, Margie Watson had to stop herself from running as she rounded the final corner on her way to the Diamond Diner. Plastered up and down Main Street, the leftover decorations from last month's Fourth of July jubilee still hung with pride from the lampposts and shop doors. All down the block American flags lined the street. In the gentle morning light, with its hanging flower baskets and banners, the town square looked pretty as a postcard.

But Margie Watson paid that no mind because she had somewhere to be.

Nestled smack dab in the square, flanked on either side by the Starlight Theatre and Mo's General Store, the Diamond, as the townsfolk lovingly referred to it, was well known as the unofficial hub for every conversation worth having in the entire county.

And for the first time in a very long time, Margie Watson finally had herself something worth talking about.

Last night she'd hardly slept. Her alarm could not have come soon enough. Just earlier that morning, she'd sat dressed and ready at the kitchen table for well over an hour; her purse clutched tightly atop her knees. In agony, she'd watched as the hands of the clock ticked by. Her pomped red curls were tight and ready, her sagging cheekbones heavily rouged. With nothing left to do but wait, she reckoned it had been the longest, most torturous hour of her life.

And she'd birthed three kids, too.

But now, basking in the glow of the rising sun as her heels clicked sharp little echoes down the promenade, all was soon forgotten. At last, her moment had arrived. With hurried footsteps, Margie composed herself as she strutted by the front window of the Diamond. Catching her reflection, she righted her posture and adjusted the crisp starched collar of her brand-new dress. It was a regal little number in Royal blue. All of Audrey Hepburn's class and Elizabeth Taylor's curves. A real showstopper. Margie had been saving it for just the right occasion.

And in a town like Wheaton, occasions came few and far between.

At the door, she snapped a handkerchief from her purse and with quick, careful hands, dabbed the sweat from her face. Though the faint relief of night still hung upon the air, the square was dripping with a stifling humidity. For a moment, Margie wondered whether a few fake tears might do well to hide her rather obvious excitement or if perhaps crying in public might be considered a bit much.

Lost in the thought, she pushed through into the diner.

Overhead, an old copper bell jingled a sad tune announcing her arrival. Behind the counter, a rather swarthy looking man cracked a dish towel over his shoulder and turned round from the cooktop. His face, hardened with lines of a life hard lived, curled itself into a gentle smile.

"Mornin Margie," he offered with a sigh.

"Mornin Frank," she replied.

Inside, the usual suspects were seated somberly at the counter: a few lone ranch hands, some warehouse fellas fresh off the night shift, the odd elderly couple here and there eating their eggs and toast in silence. As was his custom, Frank grabbed a fresh pot of coffee and followed close behind as Margie marched her worn trail to the corner booth by the window. Going about their ritual, Frank turned over the mug upon her placemat as she sat down. Then, with a warm smile and steady hand, he poured out a steaming cup of his famously potent brew.

"Fresh coffee for ya there, Margie," he said with a lazy drawl.

Overhead, a puny air conditioner rattled weakly in the window. Straining with all its might the ancient machine trembled as sunlight flooded in through the windows. Outside, centered on an island in the square, the Wheaton County Courthouse towered over the shops behind, casting a long shadow backlit by the rising sun. At its peak, the great iron hands of the clock tower chimed the arrival of eight am in big booming tolls. Turning her attention back inside, Margie surveyed the diner with a disappointed scowl.

She'd thought there would be more people on a day like this.

"Oh Frank," Margie said wistfully as she returned her gaze out the window. "Ain't it just awful?"

"Certainly is Margie," Frank grunted, wiping his forehead with his apron. "I got no words for it. Just awful."

"What can you do? Lord, what can you do?" Margie continued, running a hand over her pomped red curls. "Seems if it's not one thing, it's the other, ain't it?"

"Sure is Mrs. Watson. Sure is."

"I simply cannot believe it," said Margie.

"Just awful," Frank muttered as his shuffling steps faded back behind the bar. "Awful."

Touching her handkerchief to her already dry cheek, Margie studied her sorrowful expression in the glass. As she practiced pouting her lips, the unmistakable sound of car tires came squealing around the corner. Across the square a red Chevy coupe skidded into view before screeching to a halt in a parking spot just in front of the Feed N' Seed. Then, just as soon as its doors flew open, three women piled out onto the asphalt. Slamming the doors behind them, they began their approach, fitfully adjusting their outfits as they scurried towards the Diamond.

"Oh, there they are!" Margie squealed, waving them on. "C'mon, ladies hurry up now!"

As the group of three stormed their way across the square, two frontrunners soon emerged. Like quarter horses coming into the home stretch, they charged forward neck and neck. On the right it was Betty Schneider, an enormous woman. On the left, the far more diminutive Susan Bertram. Coming to a head at the door, they grasped the handle at the same moment, exchanging thin-lipped smiles as their hands jockeyed for position. Shoulder to shoulder, they pushed through the entryway, battling for every inch. Though the exchange was fierce, it was over before it began. It was Betty, with the immovable girth of the famed Brangus bovine who came barreling through first. In the aftermath, Susan was left momentarily plastered into the door jamb like the dried corpses of so many lizards seeking shelter from the summer sun.

Once inside, Betty waddled quickly towards the table and squeezed herself into the booth securing the prime social real estate at Margie's left side.

Now most days, this type of pecking and fussing took place in petty little jabs or backhanded compliments hidden amongst pleasant conversation. In fact, it was in this regard that the ladies of Wheaton County had developed a very exceptional gift. Because most days, there was so little to talk about one had to really work hard to fill the gaps. And for the last twelve years whether the news was lacking or not, at precisely eight am on Mondays, Wednesdays, and Fridays, Margie Watson, Betty Schneider, Susan Bertram, and Rita VanBuren would sit down at this very same booth without a single damn thing worth talking about.

But today was not just any day.

Because just yesterday, the unexpected funeral of Barett Burleson had been one of the most bizarre events anyone in town had ever had the good fortune of attending. And after a whole sleepless night spent thinking about it, the ladies were positively buzzing to unfurl their far-flung theories regarding the who, the how, the why and perhaps most importantly, just what the hell was going on.

"Oh honey," Betty said, taking Margie's hand tenderly. "Oh sweet child, I'm sure you ain't sleepin much neither. I can't stop thinkin bout how sad it all is."

Halfway to the booth, a somewhat deflated Susan Bertram inserted herself in the conversation before even having sat down.

"That's what I was just sayin Marge, weren't it the saddest thing you ever seen? What in God's name is goin on in that woman's head? That's what I'd like to know."

Just then, Rita VanBuren came striding in with her effortless grace and mysteriously pale skin. Though they hated to admit it, the other ladies at the table secretly found her a rather enchanting woman. Perhaps because unlike themselves, Rita came from the city. In fact, she'd lived in not one, but *two* cities. She was cultured, as she'd once put it, and it was a point which she took great pride in.

"Oh, thank Christ for this air conditioner," Rita groaned as she settled into her seat. "It's hot as the devil's ass crack out there."

With all the ladies seated at last, a whirlwind of activity soon commenced. Purses were opened, makeup was retouched, hair was re-poofed, bangs were wrangled, and spectacles were both removed and applied.

Overeager in rummaging for her compact, Susan's purse strap snagged the silverware atop the table and sent it crashing to the floor.

"Sorry," she frowned.

"For God's sake, Suze," Rita exhaled, rolling her eyes. "Do you ever look at what you're doing?"

"Ladies!" snapped Margie. "Ladies, *please*. We are *all* on edge. This is…a very sensitive time for the town, us included. And I think before we get started, we should all just take a moment of silence and pay our respects to the deceased."

Around the table, the ladies nodded, save for Rita who was already rifling among the menus in search of a spirits list.

"Now, bow your heads," Margie commanded, shooting Rita a scornful look. "And let us pray for that poor, poor family and above all those poor, poor children."

In unison, the women of the table dropped their heads in reverent silence. Rita, meanwhile, flagged down Frank for a coffee. With her eyes closed, Susan reached across the table to clutch at Margie's hand, but the moment they touched, Margie swatted her away like a pestering fly.

Then, as the table sank into silent prayer, Frank approached with a pot of coffee and began flipping over each mug in its saucer. Her head still bowed; Margie snapped one eye open. Without pause in her heartfelt prayer, she focused her cycloptic gaze upon Frank, attempting with all her power to burn a hole clear through the man as punishment for his social ineptitude. Unphased, Frank continued whiling away at his task oblivious to the error of his ways. Finally, with all the cups filled, he smiled a warm smile.

"Y'all flag me down you need anythin else, ok ladies?" he said, snapping the towel over his shoulder before disappearing back behind the bar.

As he went, Margie counted the seconds until he was clear before finally raising her head.

"Ok ladies," she began, soon satisfied they were alone. "Now that the proper respects have been paid and the departed soul can be welcomed into the Kingdom of Heaven, y'all tell me everythin y'all know because I know y'all snoopin biddies been stickin your big ol' noses where they don't belong."

Itching to fire first, Susan kicked things off.

"Well, I heard the reason them little kids weren't at their Daddy's funeral was cause Dora sent em off to Barett's sister's place in Denver!"

A wave of gasps ripped around the table.

"Now what kind of mother would do somethin like that?" Margie fired back. "Those little boys need their momma now more than ever, and she's pawnin em off like... like... some old wash bucket?"

"I knew the woman was cold, but bereaved or not, I cannot vouch for such behavior. I simply can-not."

"Oh, I'd expect nothin less from a woman who came up in this world like Eudora Burleson," Rita said, lighting up a cigarette. "You remember her Daddy? Ol' man Burleson? My lord that man was prickly as a horn frog and twice as ugly. I don't think that woman knows the first thing about lovin her own. Maybe she was doing the only thing she knows how. Pushing em away, just like her daddy did."

"Well, I don't know about that," Betty murmured. "Sound to me like she's havin a hell of a time with it all and maybe she just couldn't deal with everything. The kids and all that. Might be easier to be on your own a bit. Get your mind sorted."

"Hooey, I say, that's a hell of an excuse. She needs to love those children," Margie declared, placing her hand on her heart. "It's her duty as a mother. To love! Not to send them off to some godforsaken remote wilderness. Out there with mountain lions and tigers and who knows what."

"Oh, they ain't livin in the wilderness," Betty hooted, waving the comment away. "Christ's sake. Them kids is just fine with their Auntie and it's only temporary I'm sure. Maybe Eudora just needs some time to be alone? To get herself together. How can you blame her for that?"

"Time to be alone," Susan scoffed, "Lord she's got the rest of her life for that!"

"Well, I can't imagine," Betty continued. "Think your husband's just headin out one morning, that he'll be back in time for supper. But supper comes around and he ain't there. And then you come to find out he ain't never gonna be there again."

"Wrong place, wrong time," said Margie behind her mug. "Y'know they said the buck Barett hit was bigger than anythin they seen in Wheaton County in 10 seasons. Can you believe it? Went in through the front window, straight out the back. Took his head right with it I heard"

"Hell of a way to go out," said Betty, her eyes lost out towards the square. "Just think, gettin sent over to fight the Germans, survivin all that hell, and you come home and think you're safe. You made it out. Gonna start that nice life with your family, then one wrong move. It's over."

"Well, I'm not sure I'd call Barett's life post-war much of a peaceful existence," Rita said, ashing her cigarette with a quick tap. "He may have always carried on with high spirits but all his rantin and ravin at them town halls put him on the outs with more than a few families round here. The wrong kinda families you ask me."

"Still didn't deserve what he got," muttered Betty.

"Course he didn't," Margie said, patting her hand.

"Any a y'all know where the crash happened exactly?" Susan added with a nonchalant air. "Not that I'm tryin to pry or nothing."

"Ha!" bellowed Betty. "You'll be snoopin around there later today, guaranteed! Tryin' to crack the case like one of them British Whodunnits you love so much."

"I will not," Susan deflected. "I was only askin cus yesterday, I heard Jessie talking on the phone with Greg Memphis. They was arguin about where the crash was, cus Greg Memphis was sayin that if it was on his land he might be entitled to some government reimbursement. Y'know for damages to his property or somethin?"

"Oh, c'mon Suze, it was out near old Burleson Road," Betty interrupted. "You know the turn off right there on Farm Road 261? Greg Memphis only wishes it was on his property, the greedy fool! Way I heard it, that big ol' buck deer jumped into the road right there at the turnoff. Bang! Just like that. Car went off the side of the road and flipped itself into the ravine at 60 miles an hour. Barett didn't stand a chance."

"Terrible," Margie said, shaking her head. "Could have been any one of us, y'know?"

As the table slipped into an eerie silence, the sounds of the diner filled the air. The thumping of the dishwasher, the sizzle of the cooktop, a chorus of rattling porcelain. As if engaged in some sacred ritual, Betty stirred a small spoon in her coffee, over and over and over again, though the sugar had long since dissolved.

"Who was it that found him?" asked Rita, tapping the filter of her cigarette.

A cold chill passed across the table as the air conditioner stuttered overhead.

"They said it was Clyde Abbott," Margie finally replied. "Hinkley's deputy. He's a good boy. Heard he's mighty torn up about it. The way he tells it, Clyde said somebody rang the station saying there was an accident or some odd thing off the road. But when he showed up there weren't no one else there."

Margie gazed out the window. The Wheaton County Sheriff's department operated on the second floor of the County Courthouse. Most mornings she waved to Hinkley as he made his way in for work. Sometimes she saw Abbott too.

"Thought it was gonna be a flat tire, or y'know... somebody overheated their engine or something," Margie continued. "Probably just thinkin anything other than what it was…"

As Margie trailed away, Susan picked up where she'd left off.

"Instead, he finds that car flipped on its head and Barett Burleson inside...dead as dirt."

"Oh, for heaven's sake, Susan!" exclaimed Betty, tossing up her hands. "Would you please, show some decency? A good man's dead and his wife, whatever you may think of her, is a widow. Show some empathy woulda ya?"

"Empathy?" chuckled Rita. "She doesn't know the meaning of the word."

"Well let me make it easy for you then," Betty said, waving her finger with every beat. "Do you understand that from now on, every time Eudora Burleson leaves her home, she has to pass right by that awful place and relive that day again and again? Can you imagine that?"

"Y'know, I think y'all givin her too much credit," Susan hissed. "I wouldn't put it past that woman that she's happy to be free of the burden. Never took her for much of a good Southern housewife. Never seen her at the grocery store, never done any entertainin at that big fancy house a' theirs. Never seen her runnin them kids around or nothin."

"Well, it ain't always used to be like that, y'know," Betty admitted with a sigh, running a finger around the rim of her mug. "I used to play softball in the ladies league with Dora when we was younger. Not that she weren't a bit prickly, even back then, but I got on with her swell."

Then, as Betty chuckled to herself, a smile stretched across her face, "She ain't so big but Dora sure could knock the shit out the ball."

"So?" Margie prodded. "What happened? What changed?"

"Don't know," Betty shrugged. "Like I said she always kept to herself. Then, last I heard she had some medical thing after having the kids. Be honest with ya I ain't seen her since."

"Well," Susan grunted. "All I'm saying is the woman hardly socializes at all. And that just ain't how you behave in polite society. She don't care about nobody in this town. All she cares about is herself and all her *fancy* clothes."

"Oh, don't be mad at the woman because she's got style," Rita tisked. "There are a lot of unsavory things I could voice my opinion on in regard to Eudora Burleson, but I certainly admit the woman knows her way around a Foley's catalog. Seasonally appropriate mind you. Lord knows I can't be the only one classing it up in this town."

"Class?" Susan snipped. "That woman ain't got no class. But I guess it ain't no surprise she don't know how to act. That's what you get when you grow up with the coloreds."

Taking a long drag of her cigarette, Rita shook her head, rubbing a forefinger across her brow.

"And does that bother you?" she jabbed, cocking her head towards Susan. "The 'coloreds' I mean, did they put you ill at ease at the funeral? Are you really so fragile? Did their presence make you feel undignified?"

"Oh c'mon now, Rita. Can't everybody be as progressive as you," Betty laughed.

"No, I'm serious," Rita said, tapping her cigarette into the ashtray. "Y'know them 'colored' boys you despise so much was takin bullets in the ass over there in Europe for us while you was sittin here spittin venom behind they backs."

"Let's put politics on the backburner shall we ladies?" Margie interjected.

Her face glowing bright red, Susan wasted no time as she saw an opportunity to shift the subject. Careful to avoid the fire in Rita's eyes, she leaned forward towards Margie and beckoned the ladies close.

"Y'know, this mornin Joe got a call from Luther Caruthers," she whispered. "Now Luther said he was drivin by old Burleson Road round four this morning, headin out to the construction site there at Denny Creek. Dark as the dead of night at that hour y'know."

Then, glancing around the diner to be certain no one was listening, she continued. "Well, listen to this, Luther goes on to tell Joe that he *seen* Eudora standin out by the road. In the middle of nowhere, in the dark! Standin there in her night dress, like somethin out of a scary story!"

Whether because of the caffeine or the sheer oddity of the claim, the table immediately perked up.

"Well did he stop?" prodded Betty.

"Hell, no he didn't stop! He said he was preoccupied with not pissin his pants at the sight of Dora out there like some damn ghost in the middle a' the night."

All at once the table fell into a pondering silence. Margie was lost out the window, Betty in her coffee. Across the table Rita stoked her cigarette as Susan gnawed upon her thumbnail.

"What would she be doin out there in the dark like that?" Margie wondered aloud.

"Maybe she was cryin," Betty offered. "Y'know like mournin the dead. Sayin goodbye?"

"Hell, I ain't never seen that woman cry," Margie scoffed into her mug. "And I'd be willin to wager no one else has neither."

In unanimous consent, nods went around the table.

"Well, I told Joe, to me, sounds like she losin her damn mind," proposed Susan. "I'd say her behavior at the funeral is proof of that point."

"C'mon, let's not be hasty now," said Betty. "I mean maybe she was lookin for somethin?"

"What the hell would you be lookin for that can't wait till daylight?" said Margie dismissively. "Don't make no sense. Be honest with ya, I'd bet either Caruthers was lying... as usual. Or drunk... as usual."

"Probably both," said Rita snuffing out her cigarette in the ashtray. "As usual."

The whole table nodded in agreement. Then, like a creeping morning fog, the quiet thoughtfulness returned, washing over each woman as they gazed long into their steaming cups. Somewhere a fly beat itself against the glass again and again in the silence. The air conditioner hummed a lazy tune.

"That funeral was the most plum crazy thing I ever saw," Betty finally said. "Honest to God."

"I'm just glad we were there," Margie replied. "I'd have never believed it had I not seen it myself. Not in a million years."

"And to think we almost missed the whole damn thing," Susan mused. "Biggest event in Wheaton history, and she just had to have it with hardly a day's notice. Strange thing ain't it, them being Israelites and what not?"

"Christ's sake, Suze, they're not *Israelites*," Rita seethed between clenched teeth. "They're Jews. Or at least Barett's father was. It's well known that in the Jewish faith the bodies of the dead are to be laid to rest as soon as possible. Y'know y'all oughta read a book every once in a while, it'll do ya good, swear to God."

"Well, call it what you want, but I'd say that's a damn bit inconvenient for the living," Susan muttered as her face flushed red once again. "I mean were we even officially invited?"

"Funerals aren't something you send invitations for darlin," Betty said, finishing her coffee. "Weddings have invitations...and open bars if you're lucky. You don't get to pick who comes to your funeral. And I ain't never seen an open bar at one neither."

"Y'know, I don't even think she took out an obituary in the paper," said Margie. "The only reason I even knew about the funeral is cause Regina Fulshear at the flower shop told me she got an order from Appelbaum to deliver arrangements to the cemetery. Nine am Sunday. I was the one who called everybody else."

"I bet Dora was prolly wishin nobody'd show up," Susan sneered. "So she could play poor lonely widow and have everybody in town feelin sorry bout her when she ain't never gave a damn about nobody but herself."

Just then, a modest blonde woman rose from the end of the breakfast counter nearby and made her way towards the table. As soon as she did, Rita was struck with an odd familiarity, but she couldn't place who it was.

Though it was Monday, the woman looked like she'd just come from church. And that's when it hit her. It was Pam Bradley, wife of Wheaton County Zoning Commissioner Jim Bradley. She must have entered the diner while they were lost in the gossip and judging from her proximity, she'd probably overheard every word they'd just said. Beneath the table, Rita poked Susan in the leg, who replied with a look as though they'd been caught passing notes in grade school.

"Oh lord, hope you ladies brought your bibles," Rita giggled beneath her breath. "Here comes Mrs. Prudence."

Her arms clasped tight before her, Pam greeted the table with a cold smile.

"Morning ladies," she began. "Y'know, I try not to eavesdrop, and I try not to judge others, but as a good Christian woman, I felt obliged to say something to you. Y'know we are a community here. Whether you like it or not. The Burleson's were a part of that community. Excuse me. *Are a part of that community.*"

Across the table, Rita rolled her eyes and reached for another cigarette as Pam Bradley continued her sermon.

"It is our responsibility to be there to commiserate and share this sorrow with everyone. Not to spread gossip or make snide remarks. This is a moment for unity. And, y'know what, for possibly the first time in her life, Eudora Burleson needs this town. Whether she believes that or not is up for discussion, but I am certain it's the truth. Now instead of kicking this woman while she is down, maybe we can lift her up. Get her out, get her active, get her involved with this community! Now, what do you say ladies?"

"Oh Pam," Margie muttered, shaking her head. "Honey, you try that with Dora Burleson and it'll be your funeral next, darlin."

A roar of laughter tore around the table. Susan cackled and Betty wheezed. The combined sound was so great and sudden the old rancher Shep Garrett, who hadn't once turned around from his seat at the bar in 73 years, craned his neck to see what all the ruckus was about.

"Quiet ladies, shush!" Margie stammered between the laughter. "Contain yourselves. Lord. Like a bunch of schoolgirls. We're sorry," she said, waving at the diners to carry on with their business.

Begrudgingly, Shep Garrett grumbled something to himself and returned to his meal.

"Composure ladies, composure now," Margie chuckled, wiping her tears. "But honestly, Pam, perhaps instead of trying to reintroduce Eudora Burleson to civilization…. Maybe you can just, oh I don't know, bring her a nice pie or a casserole. Tell her it's from all us girls."

"Well," Mrs. Bradley considered. "I suppose that might do. Maybe I will do that. Just to let her know, we're here for her and we're thinking about her, y'know? Laugh all you want but I think it's important. It's the Christian thing to do. And I'd expect y'all to do the same for me."

"Oh absolutely," Margie said reassuringly. "And y'know what? I'm sure she'll be just *thrilled* to see you."

Outside across the square, the morning rays of sunlight shone in full brilliance over the County Courthouse. Perched atop the great brick building, the heavy iron hands of the clock beckoned nine am as the shopkeepers went about their ceremonial sweeping of the front steps. Among the ancient towering pecan trees on the courthouse lawn, the squirrels chattered as the mockingbirds sang their lonesome melody, intermingling with the din of engines and crashing warehouse shutters. Rising to the call of another day, the square was alive once again. Already, the asphalt quivered with visible heat. Waves upon waves stacked one atop the other, disappearing out like some infinite river, slow and dreary.

At the table, Margie signaled for the check. Never one to miss a request for payment, Frank materialized suddenly from some back room, wiping the sweat from his brow with the bill in hand.

"Oh, hold on," Pam said, reaching for the check. "Frank, could you throw a pecan pie on there? It's for Eudora Burleson."

"Oh, bless your heart," Frank said with a sad smile. "You don't worry about that, Mrs. Bradley. Just grab it from the carousel on your way out."

"Thank ya, Frank," Pam said with a big toothy smile. "You're a sweetheart."

Collecting their paltry sum, Frank returned behind the bar, clicking and clacking the heavy keys of the cash register beneath his fat fingers. As the ladies sat finishing their coffee, Pam moseyed over to inspect the refrigerated carousel. Taking her time, she studied each pie as the shelves revolved slowly behind the hazy glass.

The moment Pam was out of earshot, Rita muttered from behind her compact.

"Pecan pie?" she scoffed, snapping the mirror closed, "A bit celebratory for a funeral if you ask me."

"I was thinkin the very same thing," echoed Susan raising her eyebrows. "Y'know her husband, Zoning Commissioner Jim Bradley? I heard he and Barett was really having it out at them town halls over that Fordham business. Pecan pie… or guilty conscience?"

"And what would you have her bring instead, hm?" huffed Margie. "Apple pie says summer fun and cherry pie is for lovers. What would a tuna casserole say?"

"Oh forget it," Rita muttered. "So long as I don't have to make the trip out to that house, she could bring a cow pie for all I care."

"I can't imagine livin way out there like they do," added Susan. "Practically next door to the negros. Not a neighbor for miles. Totally detached from civilized society."

Just then Pam Bradley returned, grinning a half-hearted smile with the fresh baked pecan pie held secure in both hands.

"Oh, it's beautiful," said Margie. "Just lovely, she'll be delighted."

Pam brimmed with pride.

"Tell her it's from all us girls," Rita gushed.

Their bill paid, the ladies rose and commenced the arduous task of repacking their purses. Soon, the bell of the Diamond Diner chimed to their exit as Frank sent them off with a friendly wave.

Outside, after exchanging the necessary pleasantries, Pam set off alone towards her car while the ladies lingered for a while by the windows. Once assured she was well gone Rita's smile turned quickly to a scowl. Then, as the ladies rounded the corner, Margie's voice could just be overheard beneath the air conditioner wheezing in the window.

"Y'know that Pam Bradley got some nerve preachin morals to us when everybody knows her husband's screwin half the schoolgirls in the county."

As Pam Bradley sat idling at a stoplight, she leered at the pie in the passenger seat.

"Oh," she mused to herself. "I hope she won't take offense to pecan."

Suddenly a horn blared behind her. Seeing the light had turned green before her she lurched forward making the final turn out of town towards Farm Road 261. Outside the evening breeze snapped through the opened windows as Pam looked in her rear-view mirror to ensure the driver behind was long gone.

"Asshole."

Down the two-lane blacktop, the Chevy thundered into third, devouring the miles of desolate backroad that lay before it. Her hand rising and falling through the passing air, Pam looked out upon the flat expanses of farmland until the horizon consumed what escaped the eye. Rows upon rows of knee-high starts fanned by, expanding and contracting like some never ending accordion. An endless sea of orderly green clipping by at fifty miles per hour in measured stride. Trapped in a sort of Goldilocks zone between the sun's infernal assault and the eternal, life-bringing Colorado River, things didn't just grow in Wheaton. Everything grew in Wheaton.

From one plot to another, just off a single stretch of farm road, one could see fields thick with maize, corn, wheat, cotton, and just about anything else that could stand the summer heat. Rolling past a neighboring plot, Pam watched the golden whiskers atop the maize bend and bow in the sweet, scented breeze.

But as a white barn came into view, Pam was soon startled back to her senses.

With a quick hand she downshifted, bringing the engine to a burbling crawl. She drew a deep and anxious breath. Then, she read the sign at the intersection ahead.

Burleson Road.

Unable to resist, Pam leaned over the passenger seat and surveyed what had been rumored as the site of the crash. Had a passerby not known of the grisly scene that had smoldered there only days earlier, they'd have driven right by this small stretch of road, just as Pam had passed over the miles that came before it.

But as she summoned the courage to look out the window, to her disappointment, there was no wreckage. No carnage. No car engulfed in flames.

No mangled body in sight.

She sank back into her seat, exhaling a heavy sigh. In her heart, she felt a strange blend of both relief and dissatisfaction. Then, remembering her commitment to delivering the gift, she turned the wheel and continued down the long single lane drive towards the house.

But as she did, in her driver side mirror, something on the asphalt caught her eye.

Thick streaks of rubber painted the road. A crisscrossed entanglement of chaos and doom. A permanent brand seared into the pavement during the last moments of Barett Burleson's life. Craning her neck, she tracked the tire marks. In wide erratic curves, they swept from side to side, side to side, until finally disappearing off the road and into the ravine. Where nothing had been only moments before, it was as though Pam could read the signs clearly now. The inconspicuously bent metal tubing in the ditch. The sheared grass of the slope. The oil-darkened vegetation stained slick and vile.

Pam's face flushed green and cold. She felt the presence of death. A thin film of sweat rose from her skin, chilling her in the breeze. The once peaceful silence of the countryside suddenly became unnerving. The screeching of the cicadas was too much to bear. Sure she would soon lose her nerve, Pam pressed into the accelerator and continued down the road.

That one lane drive seemed to stretch for miles. Paved, which was a pleasant surprise. A rare sign of wealth and stature around these parts. On the left, a field thick with bone dry maize marked the beginning of the Burleson acreage. On the right, long sprinklers on wagon wheels shot great arcing ribbons of water over the Calloway Grass Farm.

But just past the white Calloway Barn, it became all Burleson territory.

Lined down the lane stretched a seemingly infinite fence of barbed wire, crudely hammered into twisted mesquite stakes. Further up, a pair of black Brangus bulls languished in the shade of a great oak tree, chewing their cud with eyes closed. Slowly, they swung their heads after the sound of the engine, indifferent to the blackflies buzzing at their ears. At the end of the bull enclosure, the range burst open once again, unfurling into a great wide pasture dotted here and there with almighty oak trees older than the town itself. One in particular caught Mrs. Bradley's eye. A colossal monolith charred black and grey, split nearly in two by a single cleaving bolt of lightning long ago. So stark was the sight of the hollowed-out tree upon the hill that Pam hardly realized she was already crossing the small bridge over Brangus Creek.

Cutting through the great pasture, the man-made creek, now overgrown with trees and vegetation, was the only viable water source for the entire ranch. In an otherwise inhospitable landscape, the cattle often lingered during the hot afternoon hours in its cool shaded pools.

Passing over the water below, Pam shivered at the thought that it must be a haven for snakes, or gators, or worse. Like some sort of strange and savage moat, undoubtedly by design, to ward off unwelcome visitors.

Her mind drifting back to the road before her, Pam found herself gripping the wheel very tightly. Turning back was no longer an option. Fifty yards ahead, the twisted mesquite fence gave way to painted white beams. In the well-kept yard beyond, several great oak trees hung heavy and low, dripping thick with long ashen beards of Spanish moss. The entrance to the property was unmistakable. Two poured cement pillars served as gates, funneling all arrivals down a long and winding gravel drive. Standing guard atop each column were two carved statues of Great Danes striking heroic forms. To the right, a large stone slab stamped in bold bronze lettering read emphatically:

BURLESON

Continuing down the driveway, Pam's Chevy crept forward, parting through the oak trees like great curtains until the house appeared at last. It was a curious construction in such an environment. Something of a modernist experimentation, yet oddly, it coexisted in perfect harmony with the surrounding countryside. It was a flat one-story, set off in the middle with floor-to-ceiling windowpanes beneath great black beams in the adobe style. The pale orange brick seemed to exude the same warmth as the evening sunset, and though angular and stark in its design, the home felt as though it had existed in this place always. Old as time itself.

Killing the keys in the ignition, Mrs. Bradley gathered the pie in her hands while keeping a tentative eye on the windows at the center of the house. Though the shades were drawn, Pam probed instinctively for any sudden movement. In the absence of the engine's din, surrounded by the solitude of the pasture, she felt unnaturally exposed.

Summoning her courage, she forced back her fear, determined to complete her righteous quest. Front doors being the destination of solicitors and mail carriers, Pam instead opted to walk around to the back, and there she rapped gently upon the screen door.

Deep down, though she'd never admit it, she prayed that no one would answer.

"Dora, dear? It's Pam Bradley," she called out. "I just brought you a little something to eat."

In the silence, the ever-present symphony of cicadas shrieked from the trees.

Curiosity overcoming her fear, Pam cupped her hand over the screen door and peered into the darkness within. Veiled in the low light, she could only make out the familiar silhouettes of items scattered here and there. The dining room table, the rotary phone, a corner of the couch.

Throughout the entire home, not even a lamp was lit.

"Ok, honey. Well, I'm just gonna leave this right here for ya, alright? We're all thinking about you, and you need anything, you just give me a call, ok? Anything at all now."

Satisfied with her commitment, Mrs. Bradley placed the pie on an old wooden bench just outside the door before making her way back to the safety of her car with quick little steps.

As the key turned over in the ignition and the roar of the engine took hold, a wave of relief poured over her. With every passing inch of ground, the indefinable uneasiness that plagued her visit slowly faded into a distant memory. By the final turn off the property, happy to be rid of her duties, Pam's mind returned to her family and the pot roast she had left braising in the oven at home.

Meanwhile, from the depths of the house, shrouded in a thick haze of cigarette smoke, Eudora Burleson tracked Pam's car with a wary eye until the brake lights disappeared around the corner.

Then, with a steady finger, she lowered the cocked hammer on the Colt .45 gripped in her hand.

CHAPTER III

WOMAN'S WORK

The next day, as light filtered in through the dust laden blinds of Carl Stanwick's law office, Eudora sat eyeing a feeble looking rotary fan perched atop the side table. Though she'd been here a couple of times before, the drab wallpaper looked especially grim and lifeless today. Overhead, the grey paneled ceiling, stained a sickly yellow, filled the shabby little room with an oppressive and stifling presence.

Since Barett's death, Dora had spent an inordinate amount of time in rooms just like this one. The morgue, the bank, the insurance office. Sad little rooms you just couldn't wait to get out of.

Once, Barett had taken her to talk to the rabbi at the synagogue down the road. In his office, Dora was struck with the very same feeling as she had now. Just a sort of emptiness she couldn't quite explain. Years before the war Barett had been adamant about her conversion so that they could be married. So that they could be buried side by side on the family plot. But by the time he returned from deployment he just didn't seem to have the stomach for religion anymore.

Suppose he'd heard enough people screaming out for a God that never came.

After that, the subject of conversion never really came up again. Of course, that was just fine with Dora. She'd never really seen the point in all that nonsense anyhow. Religion seemed like one big racket that had managed to fool just about everybody, except her. To

Dora it was just a bunch of people dressed up in silly costumes, talking big circles about nothing, then asking for donations to boot. Like snake oil salesmen, but not half as slick.

No, religion wasn't for her.

The white man's religion anyway.

Years ago, she'd met an old Apache man, an antiques trader, who told her the gods of his people lived upon the wind and sang amongst the trees. He said you never had to go looking for his gods because you could feel them in the rain and in the dirt beneath your feet. Dora reckoned that sounded a hell of a lot closer, and if there was a god, he'd probably be outside, not cooped up in some musty room with grey old men. If there was a heaven, surely, it was in the freedom of the open sky.

On the other hand, if there was a hell, Dora was sure it was a room much like this one.

Leaning over in her seat, she stretched out towards the fan's switch and flipped it back and forth. Still, the machine remained motionless, stagnant as the air surrounding it.

"Figures," Dora muttered, sinking back into her chair.

Just then, the door to the office cracked open.

"Mrs. Burleson?" a soft voice called out. "Mr. Stanwick will be in to see you in just a moment. Can I get you anything in the meantime? Coffee perhaps?"

Without turning from her seat, the back of Eudora's head replied.

"Honey, it's one in the afternoon and a hundred fuckin degrees outside. No, I don't want any coffee. You tell Carl I'll see him now, this won't take long."

Without a word, the door closed with a gentle click.

Just outside the thin walls, frantic and hushed whispers filled the hallway as Eudora restlessly picked the lint from her trousers. The fine pin-striped Italian fabric, while incredibly chic, also came with the unfortunate consolation of clinging to lesser-made materials.

Moments later, overeager to get off to a good start, Carl Stanwick burst into the room. Exuding a trembling energy, he set about rifling through a stack of files balanced in his thin arms. He was an exceptionally plain little man, from his rather dull haircut straight down to his plain black penny loafers. In the low light of the drawn blinds, Dora could not distinguish whether his suit was grey, beige, or some other shade of lifeless neutrality. But one supposes that's what you ought to look for when you're in the market for an estate lawyer. Someone who'd have no use for your money, even if he had it.

"Good afternoon, Dora," Carl gushed, as the papers tumbled over onto his desk. "Terribly sorry for the wait, and uh, of course as I should have probably started, I am grievously sorry for your loss. Barett was a fine man and I think I speak for everyone when I say the whole town is worse for it."

Pausing for reply, Carl stood wringing his hands as he studied Dora's face for a sign of life. Silently, she stared back at him with a dissatisfied expression.

"Uh, well," he stammered, rifling through the files on his desk. "Anyways, as you well know, we have much to discuss regarding the will and the transfer of the land. The deeds and accounts must be rewritten in your name as laid out in the stipulations of the will of course…"

"I don't need to hear about the will, Carl," Dora interrupted with a wave of her hand. "I was sittin in this here seat the day it was written, and you was sittin right there, remember?"

"Yes ma'am, I remember," Carl conceded with a nervous chuckle. "Well then, perhaps first we should tackle the issue of the main stipulation of the will, which has, of course, named you as the sole beneficiary, as well as the executor of the estate and the properties at large…"

"Sell it," Dora said coldly.

Frozen by her words, Carl stopped his frantic searching among the paperwork. Slowly, his gaze rose up until it met Dora's across the table.

"But, Mrs. Burleson, uh the businesses, the properties, the farm?" he stammered, cocking his head with confusion. "I... I don't understand, this is your family's livelihood, it's Barett's life's work."

"Yeah well, he's dead now ain't he?" said Dora, rolling a piece of lint between her fingers before flicking it into the air. "Sides, the hell do I know about hockin real estate or runnin farmland?"

Perplexed, Carl shuffled among his files as if the answers were to be found somewhere within. Turning up no solution, he clasped his hands together beneath his chin and thought for a long while. Finally, he ventured to carry on.

"Dora," he began carefully. "As your lawyer, I'm obliged to ask you to reconsider. That farmland, your family... I know this is a trying time. And emotions can run high, which, on occasion, can cause us to make rash decisions."

"Do I look emotional to you, Carl?" Dora questioned, raising her brow.

As if presenting herself for inspection she turned her open palms towards the ceiling and invited Carl to take a look.

"Do I look rash?"

"Well," Carl stuttered adjusting his glasses. "Uh, no I can't say that you do."

"Y'know, I'll tell you somethin lotta folks don't know Carl. I haven't stepped foot in them godforsaken fields in 30 odd years and I sure as hell don't plan on startin up again now."

"So, you listen here, if I'm the executor as *you* say," Dora said jabbing a sharp finger towards him. "Well, I'm telling *you* what I'll do. Sell it. All of it. Save for the house, the pasture, and the east plot property."

"East plot," Carl repeated, turning back to his papers. "You mean that dusty lot of trailers out in Fordham? Eudora, I have to say this is ill-advised. You're essentially asking me to liquidate your most valuable holdings?"

"Very good, Carl," exclaimed Dora, flashing her first grin of the day. "Very good, I'm glad you're followin along. So, we're on the same page then?"

"Well, yes," Carl managed to reply. "I suppose."

Satisfied with his answer, Dora provided a hearty nod of approval and rapped her knuckles atop the desk. Then, as if suddenly preparing to take her leave, she began moving towards her bag.

"But, but, but," Carl tisked trying to corral her. "Dora, just hold on one minute there, it's not so easy as all that."

His mind already wandering to the mountain of work ahead, Carl began muttering, almost to himself. "We'll have to get each property valued and appraised. Inspections must be arranged. Uh, of course realtors must be acquired to sell the properties and so on…"

"Yes sir, I don't doubt it," Dora said, slinging her purse over her shoulder. "And since you got such a good handle on things, I'll just leave that all to you then. Just drop the checks in my safe deposit box when they're ready and pay yourself from the account."

"But Dora, please," Carl begged. "What you're asking me to do. It's a big decision. Just sleep on it and we can talk tomorrow."

"Oh, I'm not sleepin much these days, Carl," Dora said, drawing her sunglasses from her purse. "Haven't got the time, I'm a very busy woman, you know. Just drop those checks in the safe deposit box like I told you now."

Acknowledging the inevitable, Carl sank defeated into his chair as Dora slipped out the door without even saying goodbye. Left alone in the room, he looked towards the window in silent reflection.

What the hell had just happened?

He kept running over the conversation in his head, though it brought him no closer to any understanding. Some minutes later, Carl's assistant, Patricia, poked her head through the door. Seeing him slumped in his chair, she already knew the answer, but figured she ought to ask the question anyways.

"How'd it go?" she said with a sheepish smile.

"Well," Carl said, tossing his spectacles onto the table. "I don't know what I expected, but that certainly wasn't it."

Leaning against the open doorway, Patricia frowned warmly.

"She wants to sell," Carl grumbled. "Everything, pretty much."

"So, what'll she do now?"

"Of that, there is no telling," Carl sighed, sinking deeper into his chair. "But knowing what that woman's been through, I'm not about to be the one standin in her way."

Like so many who have survived hard times, Eudora's past was not one she cared to revisit. Fond reminiscing is a privilege reserved for the chosen few. If those born into a world of promise lead blessed lives, then by the same logic those brought into one of despair must be cursed. How many times she had lain at night thinking that very thought, she could not count.

For young Eudora, even life's most simple pleasures were wholly absent. Like the embrace of a loving mother or the recollection of a full belly. Her earliest memories of what could be misconstrued as a home consisted of a buckskin tarp pitched over a frame of branches bound in twine. Shambling around the makeshift tent was a man who may well have been a stranger had she not seen so much of herself in his feral green eyes.

He called himself her father. And though he was often looming near, Dora's days were spent quiet and lonely all the same. Course back then, she didn't think much of it. That's just the way it was.

The way it'd always been. In all those years she could hardly remember questioning much at all.

What she did remember was that no matter how many times they packed up and moved from one field to the next, at night the coyotes bayed miserably outside those thin leather walls.

Sometimes when the moon was high and bright, beneath the cracks where the tarp met the earth, she could see their hungry eyes flashing in the vast chasm of blackness that engulfed them. Peering into their silver gaze, she felt their hunger and wondered if they could feel hers as well.

For young Eudora there was no school, no church, no summer, no holidays, no weekends, no friends, nor family.

For her, there was only the fields and the labors that came with it.

Upon the desolate sunbaked plains where she slept, she worked. Along with the nearly twenty other families who had followed the same promise of meager pay in exchange for laboring the land. At the time, Dora never paid much mind to the fact that they were different from everybody else working the fields. Her father never mentioned it. But suppose on some level Dora had always sensed it. Despite the fact her skin was tanned from toiling in the sun, her hair was light and blonde. Everybody else was either Black or Brown. Sometimes, after setting up a new camp, a white man in fancy clothes and a shiny belt buckle might come out to tell them what needed doing but in all those years, she never saw another white person working the land.

In those fields there were lots of workers, yet they all carried the same sadness in their eyes. Though they'd traveled from different places they'd all arrived in this awful place just the same. From miles they came, like starving dogs on the trail of a sick and dying steer, shambling and shuffling along with all their worldly possessions strapped upon their backs. Baking like hollow corpses beneath the infernal summer sun. So desperate were they, that upon arriving to the infinite expanse of flattened field and seeing the impossibility of the endeavor before them, they still did not turn back. For where was there to turn back to? A thousand miles of dust and death? So rather than wasting energy cursing their luck, they quietly pitched camp and went to work. Where any rational person would have seen a stark dry pit of inhospitable soil, these downtrodden souls saw an opportunity to survive until next week.

Because if nothing else, in those times, the promise of some pay sure was better than the alternative.

Over the course of her life, Eudora lived in many different fields, though in hindsight, it may well have been the same one. Aside from the occasional tree or dried riverbed, they were all damn near the same.

Miserable.

Whether she was hunched over planting seeds, pulling weeds, tilling soil, setting rows, or digging trenches, the sun beat down, always. The summers dragged towards eternity. The nights were thick, heavy, endless. There was hardly enough food and even less water. On occasion, if ever it did rain, the earth, scarred and baked solid by the sun, would reject the moisture. Refusing to drink as if to commit suicide by protest. Soon after, the flooded fields would become stinking cesspools. Pits of hot steaming waste bobbing with the bloated corpses of drowned rats. The stench was unbearable.

But that was nothing compared to the mosquitos.

One could tell time by their arrival. Two days off the back of every rainfall they came like great dark clouds from the tree line. A droning plague. They invaded Dora's ears. Burrowed into her nostrils. Tormented her feverish sleep. Like smoke, they crept in and between the thin spaces of her clothing. Over time, whether willful decision or instinctual adaptation, Dora simply stopped slapping at them. What was the point? The more she killed, the more would come to take their place.

In those times, in those fields, life seemed based more on ritual than any true reality.

Rise before daybreak, work the fields, mind the chores, cook supper, prepare again to rise before daybreak. Even as a child Eudora's mind did not wander much. Not because she didn't want to escape. She simply did not know where she could escape to. This world of hardship was all she knew. So instead of making a fuss, she just looked down at her father's boots and followed in his shuffling footsteps.

All her life, Dora's father was very mysterious to her.

He spoke very few words and listened to far less. But beneath his savage green eyes, there did always seem to be something on his mind. Often in the late evenings as Dora prepared their meager supper, he would sit smoking his pipe, whittling away at a bit of wood, and staring deep into the fire. To Eudora, when he did speak, he spoke only in commands.

"Split that tinder."

"Carry this here."

"Get gone."

Communication was not a two-way street. And very quickly, Eudora accepted that she'd always know very little about the man who controlled her life. In fact, she could count on one hand the things she knew for certain.

For one, his name was Edgar.

Other than that, she knew he had a bum leg, stiff as a board straight through the knee, though she had no idea the cause. She had seen it only a few times naked and uncovered by any clothing or brace. The leg itself was thin and feeble, as if nothing but skin and bone. It made her sick to her stomach just looking at it. Perhaps because it was an image very much at odds with the man who walked upon it. Bound in a strange wooden frame, he often cursed the appendage out loud as if it were some separate entity. As though some parasite had attached itself to an unwilling host. Though she never dared to ask, Dora always thought he must have been very ashamed of it. On the contrary, Dora counted herself quite grateful for it.

She'd always sensed that had his leg been healthy, he might never have stuck around. Had he been able, she knew that he'd already be gone. Off into the bush that he was always gazing out into. Like some wild dog held prisoner by chains.

Another thing Dora knew was that he had been a soldier.

Aside from his disfigured leg, the man was a veritable canvas of human suffering. From head to toe, mangled masses of scars peppered his frame. Sheer holes could be traced through the front and right out the back of his body. Each one covered in twisted capped flesh. Of his few earthly possessions, he owned and meticulously maintained a Marlin 30.30 lever action repeater and a military issue Colt Navy. Always within arm's reach and always fully loaded. Every night, he slept with the pistol in his right hand. His left hand only had three fingers. The ring and pinky fingers had been missing ever since she could remember. Once, when Eudora had summoned the courage to speak, she asked what had happened to them.

"Talked too much," he replied.

She didn't ask again.

Working in the fields there wasn't much time for socializing. Like prisoners on a death march, it was a rather quiet affair. But most days around noon, having already been harvesting crop for some six blistering hours, the workers would often gather beneath the shade of the pecan trees for a quick lunch. The Black folks would gather under one tree. The Mexican families under another. Most of the time, Eudora just sat in silence with her father. But sometimes, his leg aching with pain, the old man would fall into a feverish sleep in lieu of a meal, leaving Eudora to fend for herself.

With cautious steps she would wander among the outskirts of the different groups, salivating at the smell of their paltry spreads.

Even then she was too proud to beg, though she never had to.

Out there, toiling beneath the vengeful sun, the workers stuck to an unspoken code. As long as you worked you were welcome. Pay was split equal because it took everybody to work the plot. That was the deal and there wasn't any squabbling because the money was always handed out fair. There was nobody trying to cheat or steal or cause any trouble with anybody else because when you work twelve hours a day, who's got the time?

In the fields there was a strange, sad camaraderie that cannot be explained to anyone who has not suffered through it themselves. Suppose when you suffer together, by definition, at the very least, you're *together*.

So, when this little girl came sniffing around their campfires, the families there did what families do. They fed her like she was their own. From their already meager supply of rice and beans. Sometimes even a little grits or ham or scraps of chitlins if they had it.

In return, the only thing they asked of her was if the old man snoring in her tent needed a plate too.

But she didn't speak a word. Doing the only thing she knew how, little Dora would squat there on the spot, voraciously devouring her food while the families talked and ate in the few minutes they were allowed the slightest moment of a human existence.

On the outskirts of one such group of workers, while Eudora was licking the remnants from her tin, a little girl about her age approached and knelt down beside her.

For some time, the two just sat there quietly enjoying the presence of one another's company though neither dared to speak. Then, finally, with curiosity outweighing her fear, the little girl gently tapped Dora on the shoulder.

"Where y'all come from?" she asked.

As she waited for a reply, the girl set about pulling blades of grass from the ground before letting the wind carry them away.

As Dora watched the little girl go about this, she wasn't sure what to say.

Normally questions were directed towards her father. But this time, someone was speaking directly to her. She scratched her head for a moment and looked down towards her bare feet. By now, they were so hard and callous, she didn't even feel the thorns stuck between her toes.

"I don't know," Dora managed. "Pa's from round these parts. Texas."

"Oh," the little girl said softly. "Mama says maybe you was from Mexico."

"Don't think so," said Dora.

"I ain't think so neither," the little girl said.

"Is that man over there your daddy?"

"Mhm," Dora grunted.

"What's wrong with em?"

Squinting over towards the tent, Dora could just see him lying there on the cot with his back turned. She thought about the question for a very long time before endeavoring to form an answer.

"His leg hurts."

"Oh," the little girl said. "You gotta momma?"

Across the desolate and arid cropland, a hot wind whipped over the earth. Soon, aloft on the whirlwind, the fine sandy soil stung Dora's face as she brought up a hand to cover her eyes.

"She's dead," Dora peeped.

"Oh," said the little girl.

As she pulled up another blade of grass from the ground, the little girl held it beneath the light of the sun and studied it for some time before throwing it into the wind.

"Why y'all out here?" the girl asked.

"I don't know," Dora replied.

And it was the truth.

"Daddy says ain't no white folk out here not runnin from something," the little girl recited. "Said ain't nobody *want* to be out here. Just people that *got* to be out here."

Her eyes pinned to the ground; Dora watched a line of fire ants as they scurried about their work. In a long formation they marched, one behind the other, off to fulfill some unknown task. Suddenly, Eudora found herself overcome with a strange uneasiness. She had often thought about such questions, but in searching her soul for an answer she always turned up nothing. No matter how hard she thought, no matter how many nights she tossed and turned, always nothing. It frustrated her to no end. Having all these questions inside and not a single answer. Raising her gaze to the horizon, Dora saw a man lurking near her father's tent. Her heart began to race. In that moment, something triggered inside her.

As fast as she could, she leapt to her feet and began to run with a savage and primal fear.

"Ain't you gone say bye?!" the little girl shouted after her.

But Dora could not hear. Her heart was pounding too heavy in her chest. Faster and faster, her tiny feet stamped across the endless dirt beneath her. Who was this man looming near their camp? What was it her father was hiding from?

Nearing the scene at last, a rush of relief washed over Dora as she realized it was only another laborer. He was a stout man she had seen around the fields. As she came up behind him, the man turned and nodded to greet her. His dark eyes smiled warm as the evening sun. He had a big bushy moustache that scrunched up like a caterpillar when he grinned. There was nothing unkind in his presence and Dora was thankful for it. Inside the tent, her father was already sat at the edge of his cot buttoning up his work shirt.

Suddenly, the man picked up where he had left off.

"Dos semanas más, pero no más dinero," he said, shaking his head. "Eso es todo lo que dijo."

Backing away from the opening of the tent, Dora braced herself for her father's response. Perhaps confused by the sun-drenched darkness of his skin, the man had mistaken her father as a fellow Mexican. It wouldn't have been the first time. But Eudora knew that her father was not a man who responded kindly to misguided visitors. Especially when they awoke him from one of his fitful afternoon dreams.

Yet to her utter surprise, her father calmly responded.

Though she could not understand a single thing he'd said, the foreign words rolled off his tongue in total and perfect control. She had never seen her father speak more than a few words at a time, let alone in another language.

As she listened to him, she realized it was just another reminder of the stranger with whom she lived.

That evening, overcome with curiosity, Dora dared to dig for more.

In the glow of the late setting sun, her mind was racing as she pinned laundry to the dry line. Many times already she had tried to speak, but the words remained lodged in her chest. Peeking out from behind the sheets, she watched her father from afar. As he sat by the fire, his eyes were calm and focused as he whittled away at the pommel of an axe with his penknife. He'd been at this project for days now. An intricate pattern that had yet to take shape. It was amazing how his hands worked in such easy, fluid motions, despite their crude and coarse appearance. They'd just eaten supper and Edgar seemed well enough at ease. It was the perfect opportunity, though that had never guaranteed a welcome reception in the past. As Dora willed herself to speak, she found herself surprised when the words finally came tumbling out.

"I didn't know you could talk Mexican," she blurted out as she clipped a shirt on the line.

Pausing in his work, Edgar's eyes lifted from the fire. Shifting the pipe to the opposite end of his mouth, he puffed gently as he considered his answer. Then, returning to his task, his hands resumed their easy rhythm.

"Ain't never asked," he replied.

"Well," Dora said, steadying her voice. "Where'd you learn it?"

"Mexico," he grunted.

Acknowledging the shortness of his reply, Dora pinned a set of stockings to the line before chancing for more. For a moment she studied him in the firelight. Above the dark tangle of beard that billowed from his chin, he had a sharp crooked nose that looked as though it had been chiseled from limestone. Every so often, he scrunched it up and wriggled it around as his fingers brushed away the wood scrapings from his work. Carrying on quietly, he shifted the pipe from one corner of his mouth to the other before exhaling a thick cloud of sweet-smelling smoke.

"What was you doin in Mexico?" Dora continued.

From beneath his heavy brow Edgar's eyes flashed a warning shot. Reflected in them, the pipe burned a fiery red. Dora received the message loud and clear.

"Just curious is all," she shrugged, returning to the laundry line.

The conversation stalled in silence; Edgar returned to his work. As the campfire hissed in the stillness of the evening, the muffled conversations of other families could be heard just off in the distance.

Even here, in this vacuum of life's pleasures, there was still laughter.

Though not in Eudora's tent.

As she finished with the laundry, Dora lingered at the line, gazing out into the fledgling light of dusk. Soon a symphony of grasshoppers would fill the night air with their chorus of rushing harmonies, bathing the fields in song. Soon a new day would dawn and the work would begin again. Across the way, Dora watched the tiny silhouette of the girl she spoke to that afternoon. In the warm lamplight of their camp, she sat beside her mother, singing soft lullabies over the prairie. The sound was sad and sweet, and though Dora did not know the words, it felt as though her heart followed the melody.

How she longed for a mother who would sing to her.

"Go to the barn and fetch another bundle," Edgar commanded from the fire. "Since you ain't got nothin better to do."

Her head bowed in unspoken obedience; Dora began the short trek towards the old rundown shack at the corner of the lot. Marching along a narrow-worn footpath through the grass, she kept her eyes fixed upon the earth. She hated looking at that shack about as much as she hated going in it. No matter the time of day, it was always a dark and musty den, riddled with spiders and all manner of things that creep and crawl. As she approached, the smell was enough to make her turn back. The damp rot of straw and mold.

In the eerie purple twilight, the structure seemed especially monstrous and frightening. Like a polished jawbone, sharp jagged beams of peeling white paint jutted up like gnarled teeth. Her palms were slick with sweat. Everything in her told her to run. But should she arrive back at camp without the firewood in hand, Dora knew she'd just have to return.

Only then, it would be even darker.

Standing the building down, she swallowed her fear and marched on. Before her, the open front door swung from its rusty hinges. A deep breath held tight in her chest; she pushed through the creaking frame as a dusky light crept out over the darkness within. With every guarded step came the sound of unimaginable creatures shuffling through the rafters of the tomb-like chamber. In the darkness, Dora's eyes moved from one distorted shape to the next as she journeyed on deeper into the barn where terror seemed to lurk behind every shadow.

As she rounded an old horse stall, her fumbling hands at last touched the dry stockpile of timber. Quick as she could, she began stacking branches in her arms. A feverish blood pulsed through her veins. The faster she stacked, the more she felt that familiar dread, clawing closer and closer in the darkness.

Sensing it upon her, as though it were breathing down her neck, she turned to run towards the door.

Suddenly a piercing shriek rang out through the decrepit shack. In horror, certain of her inevitable demise, Eudora flung the firewood from her arms and collapsed to the ground on her back. Adrenaline flooding her veins, she scanned the darkness in panic until finally she narrowed her focus upon her tormentor.

There, lazing in a bed of hay high in the rafters, a barn cat stared back at her, flicking its tail with an amused delight.

As the two studied each other, more tiny sets of eyes appeared from the darkness, mewing inquisitively from their perch. Overcome with a moment of childlike wonder, Eudora tore out of the barn sprinting back to her father. As her bare feet beat tracks along the footpath, she felt a strange sensation upon her face.

She was smiling.

Her entire being was alive with an indescribable energy.

Even before she had made it back to the tent, the words were already pouring out of her.

"Pa!" she shouted, grinning ear to ear. "Come quick, you gotta see, come on!"

"What?" the old man groaned turning around from the fire. "The hell you yellin for?"

"Come on, in the barn come look," she cried, waving him on as she ran. "Hurry! Hurry!"

For a man with a bum leg, Dora always found her father could move with an exceptional quickness when he wanted to. In no time he had nearly caught up to her, and with every glance over her shoulder, he was gaining ground. Sprinting madly, Dora reached the barn doors first and flung them open. But just as she stepped into the darkness within, a heavy hand seized her back.

"Godammit girl, tell me what the hell's goin on right now!" Edgar screamed.

The look on his face was grave and serious. His chest was heaving. In his right hand he held the pistol. The hammer was cocked and ready.

Her eyes wide with awe, Dora pointed toward the rafters. High above, the old barn cat was nowhere to be seen. But soon in the silence, just like before, a tiny set of eyes appeared gazing down at them with a curious attention.

"Look Pa," she said, tugging on her father's shirt sleeve.

But as she looked to his face, her excitement was quickly extinguished. His eyes did not reflect the same joy she felt in her heart. Instead, he just stood there, hands on hips, still struggling to catch his breath. Looking back towards the kittens, Dora was delighted to see more eyes appearing from the darkness. But when she turned back to her father, it was obvious his mind was elsewhere.

"Grab that feed sack, girl," he grumbled, wiping the sweat from his face.

Without a second thought, Dora scrambled over the musty stacked hay bales on her hands and knees. At the summit, against the wall were a few old burlap produce sacks. As she grabbed one, a cloud of frayed dust lofted high into the air, cutting powdery silver beams in the moonlight. Dora offered the bag to her father.

"No," he said waving her off. "You get em."

"But," Dora began.

"But, what?"

Uncertain of his intentions, but fully understanding the danger in ignoring the command, Dora turned reluctantly towards the loft. Just beside the rotted beams of the horse stall was a rickety old ladder leading up to the second level of the barn. With the bag in hand, she trudged over the hollow floorboards. Coming to the base of the ladder, she began climbing, rung by rung, as the steps creaked and bowed beneath her movements.

Reaching the upper loft at last, she crawled her way atop the platform. In the darkness the kittens were nowhere to be found, though Dora could still hear their awkward shuffling beneath the hay. The sound of uncertain steps just beginning to find their way. With soft cries, they called out for their mother. At last, a fuzzy orange head appeared from the straw. Dora's heart swooned as she stretched out her tender hand.

In the darkness, the kitten arched its back at the sensation of her touch.

"You get em in the bag?" Edgar's gruff voice bellowed out below.

"I am," Dora said.

"Get em all."

With great care, Dora picked up the first tiny creature. It was warm and soft in her calloused hands. Whispering loving affections in its ear, she placed it gingerly into the bag. Soon, the other kittens began stumbling out from their hiding places with clumsy little steps. Each was met with loving affections and Dora's warm embrace. So delicately she handled them.

Like some priceless jewel or pretty thing, though of these objects she had no understanding.

"Ok, hold on," she whispered, setting the last kitten into the sack. "Here we go."

Hoisting the bag softly, she laid it over her shoulder and began her careful descent back to the ground floor. Waiting for her, Edgar stood with his arms folded before him, his eyes already lost out the flapping barn door.

"Can we keep em?" Dora offered, suddenly terrified of the answer.

"Toss that bag in the creek."

In the aftermath of the command, an insurmountable silence stifled the air between them. Searching his face for any sign of humanity, Dora saw only stone. Then, without explanation or apology, he turned and hobbled towards the door.

In the darkness of the barn, Dora stood quivering as the kittens called softly from the bag.

"Why?" she said.

The old man stopped in his tracks.

"Who gone feed em? Hm?" he spat over his shoulder. "Want that food off your plate?"

"But I didn't…"

"Girl, I ain't askin you. I'm tellin you. Take that bag to the creek. Put a stone in n' toss it."

"I don't wanna," Dora whimpered, tears welling in her eyes.

In her hands she felt the kittens kneading at the bag. Their helpless wails echoed through the rafters, calling out for their mother. She wanted to cry out too. To cry for her mother. But who would listen? She had already gone too far. The kittens were rounded up, sealed in their death chamber. By her hands.

It was her fault.

How stupid could she be? She never should have told him. Never should have mentioned it. Never should have blindly obeyed his commands. Why did she think he would care in the first place? He didn't care about anything. He didn't love anything. All he saw were problems. Problems that needed hard solutions. In his eyes everything needed to be vanquished, killed, wiped off the face of the earth forever in a baptism of fire. She couldn't understand why he saw things this way. How anyone could see the world this way.

She couldn't.

"I can't," she said.

Trying with all her might to stifle the quivering in her lip, she could not stop the trembling of her hands. She could not bring herself to look at her father, until she opened her eyes and found herself face to face with him. Kneeling before her, his great hands held her firm by the shoulders as he spoke with unwavering words.

"There ain't nothin good in this world for them, y'understand? You seen that barn cat, starved to nothin but skin and bone. What she gonna feed them when she can't feed herself, hm?"

Dora shut her eyes tight yet tears still streamed down her face.

"Open ya eyes," Edgar scolded. "Ain't no hidin from this world. Cryin won't do no good. There ain't no mice to be had, cus there ain't no crops neither. Ain't nothin but dust out here. It ain't gettin' no better. Livin's hard, y'understand? That's just the way it is. If it ain't drownin it'd be starvin or the coyotes would eat em alive."

With one hand steadying his bum leg, Edgar struggled to his feet.

"You only a girl," he grunted. "You ain't seen nothin for what it is. Ain't no happiness to be had here, y'understand? That's it. Now do what I tell you, and don't think no more of it. Dyin's just part of livin. Ain't no difference 'tween the two."

Knowing she had no choice, Dora ran.

Clutching the bag tight against her chest, she didn't even make it to the door before Edgar snatched her by the hair and ripped her to the ground. Thundering his way across the hollow floorboards, he reached out to strip the bag from her.

"No!" she screamed, kicking and flailing. "No, get away from me!"

Unrelenting, he peeled her arms away from the sack. She tore at his arms with her fingernails like an animal striking out with all its might. Her rage engulfed her. She hated him. She hated this place. Most of all, she hated her own weakness. That she could be commanded so easily against her will made her seethe.

As the sack began slipping through her fingers, something inside her ignited. Seizing the meaty flesh of her father's forearm, she clamped her jaws ravenously. The taste of blood and sweat flowed across her tongue. A deafening pop. A dull, dizzy pain.

He'd struck her. The reverberations of his hand against her face echoed out through the old, jagged beams of the barn and into the trees beyond. Dora's world warped as she tried to gain her footing. With all her remaining strength, she fought to stay conscious. In urging her body to rise, it instead convulsively curled into a tight ball.

She despised her weakness.

In soft little fits, she began to cry.

Through the foggy haze, she faintly remembered watching her father's figure limping towards the light of the barn door. Seized in his hand, the burlap sack drug across the floorboards. In those final moments, Dora swore she saw the tiny paws within still struggling to break free.

Still fighting for life.

Once outside, just as she'd feared, her father's tall dark figure turned towards the creek.

"Don't," she tried to say. Though she could not be certain if the words had actually come out.

And it was there, alone and trembling in the dark, that Eudora Burleson swore to herself upon penalty of death that she'd never cry again so long as she lived.

CHAPTER IV

INTUITION

In the early hours of dawn, as Floyd Thomas lay snoring in his bed, a strange sound suddenly shook him from the warm comfort of his dreams. Just outside the bedroom window a rooster was busy clawing its way up onto the sill. Struggling to surmount the narrow ledge the bird beat its wings awkwardly against the glass until securing a suitable foothold atop the windowsill. Here, the cockerel proudly shook the dust from its feathers and puffed out its resplendent green chest. With great pride the bird stood tall upon his toes, drawing in a deep bellyful of morning air as he surveyed his domain. It was a modest little plot of dry earth, spread out upon a few acres of subprime farmland. Hardly worth the effort one had to put in to see any meager return. But better than nothing. Situated in the middle of the property was a worn old farmhouse with a wraparound porch that the Thomas family called home, though the property was technically leased.

But to the rooster, this was of no consequence. Looking out over his territory, he ruffled his feathers once more. Then like any good crooner, the bird warbled a gentle warmup, before shaking its comb with a self-satisfied delight.

Showtime.

"CRAWWWWWWK," the rooster began with a swelling intensity. "RAWWW CRAW DOOOODLE DOOOOOO-OOOO--OOO!"

Though the window was fastened shut the rooster's piercing rally rattled through Floyd's teeth. Clamping his pillow tight around his skull he rolled towards the far side of the empty bed.

"Jesus," he groaned. "Take this damn bird back to hell!"

"RAWWW RAWWW CRAAAAAAWK A ROOO DOOOOOOO!" the rooster roared defiantly.

"Alright," Floyd moaned, tossing the blankets aside. "Alright, shit! I'm up."

As Floyd sat silent upon the bedside, he rubbed his hands across his face. Lately it seemed like every day he woke up he was somehow even more tired than the day before. Outside, the young rooster pecked curiously at the glass before gearing up for another explosive volley. But this time, Floyd was ready. As the rooster stretched out upon its toes Floyd kicked his bare foot hard against the base of the window. Flailing from the ledge the rooster tumbled to the ground sending up a lofty cloud of feathers. Yawning wide and scratching at his underpants Floyd ambled over towards the dresser while his aching knees creaked in unison with the floorboards.

From the kitchen wafted the welcome aroma of fresh coffee and frying bacon. With eyes fastened shut, Floyd's bare feet began their plodding march over the worn and splintered floorboards. Soon, sensing the cold linoleum of the kitchen beneath his toes, Floyd's eyes snapped open to see his wife, Maybel, already dressed and busy preparing breakfast.

"Coffees in the pot," she said without turning from her work.

Standing in the doorway Floyd watched her working in the pale light breaking through the windows. It was hardly six am and already she had ten things going at once. On the stovetop pots bubbled and fry pans sizzled as she glided gracefully between them. A little stir here and a quick toss there then she was right back to the mixing bowl. Beneath a dusting of flour streaked across her forehead Maybel's eyes were fixed on the dough she was working. With swift movements she turned the mixture repeatedly seeking just the right consistency. At her ankles the flowing navy sundress she wore beneath her apron swayed with every powerful motion of her arm. Though she was consumed with her labors, she struck a lovely vision in the morning light. Glancing towards Floyd out of the corner of her eye her lips formed a sly smile as she noticed him watching her.

"Woman, you an angel," Floyd said with a yawn before making his way towards the kettle.

"Mhm, I know it," smirked Maybel. "JoJo, ain't you gone say mornin to your daddy?"

At the kitchen table Floyd's daughter Jo sat slumped in her school clothes. Nodding off over a bowl of untouched grits her eyes struggled to stay open. Patting her head warmly as he passed, Jo awoke from her stupor with a groggy smile. Unable to contain her childish energy she began to swing her legs like little pendulums as they dangled over the kitchen floor.

"Mornin Daddy!" she sang.

"Mornin JoJo," replied Floyd kneeling beside her. "You helpin your mama fo' you go to school?"

"Yes, daddy," she beamed. "I'm helpin."

"Tell ya, you can help me by eatin them grits, girl," Maybel huffed from her work at the stovetop.

"But mama," Jo whined. "I ain't hungry."

She crossed her arms and pouted her lips. Floyd couldn't help but laugh. She had her mother's fire, no doubt.

"Well give em to your Daddy then," Maybel finally conceded. "You know he make grits disappear real quick."

"You got that right," Floyd said, sneaking a spoonful as Jo giggled with delight. "But first I need me some of that famous Maybel made coffee."

As Floyd shuffled his way to the kettle a strange commotion outside the kitchen window caught his eye. Clamoring its way towards a new perch atop the hen house the rooster was once again in the midst of another perilous ascent. Upon conquering the summit, the bird unleashed another ripping cry beneath the early morning sun. Taking his mug from the cupboard Floyd winced as the shrill sound echoed sharply through the house.

"Y'know I only agreed to get that damn bird cus you tol me it was a hen," Floyd moaned running his hand across the grain of his cheek. "Hen my ass. So far it ain't lay a single damn egg! All that bird good for is peckin my legs and cryin all morning."

"I like him daddy," Jo smiled pushing the cold grits around her bowl. "He funny."

"Well, how bout you g'on out there and chase him round for a minute you like him so much."

"OK!" Jo cried with a great big grin.

Needing no more incentive, the little girl leapt off the chair and made a mad dash towards the door. Feeling a rush of wind pass behind her Maybel turned just in time to see Jo's dress disappearing through the screen.

"Hey, hey not in your school clothes now!" she shouted after her.

But it was too late. The door was already flapping in the wind. A moment later Jo's figure reappeared outside the window in hot pursuit of the fleeing rooster.

"Oh, she be alright," muttered Floyd, pouring himself a cup of coffee. "Ain't like she ever come home clean anyhow."

"Ok then Mr. Man," Maybel scoffed, taking up a plate in her hand. "Ain't been up five minutes you already fuckin up my day."

Fixing up a spread of bacon and bread Maybel untied her apron and hung it over a hook near the stove. Between the two of them the house was suddenly very quiet and for a while neither spoke in a collective appreciation of the fact. Pouring out a second cup of hot coffee Floyd handed it to Maybel and together they sat down at the kitchen table. Outside Jo's laughter and the sounds of the terrified rooster ran circles round the house.

"No biscuits?" Floyd begged.

"Those for Church," Maybel said, sneaking a piece of bacon off Floyd's plate. "Sides you got plenty in front of ya so just forget about them biscuits. What you got goin on today?"

"Oh, Mr. Rutherford wants me to come round and patch up a crack in his stone trough later this afternoon," Floyd said wearily. "Oughta be a few hours work. 'Fore that I was thinkin I may run out to the Burleson place see if there ain't nothin I can help with round the house."

"Hm," Maybel mused behind her coffee cup. Though she thought it quite subtle, it was a sound Floyd knew all too well. As he tucked into his bread he watched as Maybel's mind began to turn.

"Well," Floyd pried with his mouth full. "Ain't you gone tell me what you cookin' up in that head a' yours?"

"Oh no, it's just…y'know," Maybel shrugged. "Suppose I was just wonderin if you got any idea what Dora gonna be doin with them Fordham plans?"

"I knew it," said Floyd with a satisfied chuckle. "Gotdamn, I knew the second I woke up. I said to myself 'Floyd, that woman only cook bacon when she got bad news or a favor she need doin swear to God!'"

"Oh c'mon Floyd. It's just a simple question. I don't see no harm in it."

"I tell ya the harm in it, Barett ain't been dead but a few days! Now I just told you I'm goin over there to make sure she doin alright, not to be troublin her bout no business. She got enough goin on. If you ain't notice at the funeral, I don't think she's takin it too good."

"Well," Maybel scoffed, bobbing her head defiantly. "She oughta be happy somebody offerin to take that mess off her hands then. Just one less thing she got to be worryin about."

"Maybel," Floyd said with a grave turn in his voice. "It ain't yours to take. It's their land. *Her* land now. Don't you think she oughta be the one that decide what do with it?"

"It was promised to us."

"Barett promised it." Floyd replied with a wag of his finger. "But she ain't Barett. I'm tellin you right now, I ain't fixin ta go over there and ask for no fifty-acre handout a coupla days after the man's funeral."

"I ain't askin for no handout, Floyd. I'm only askin if she's gone take them development plans to the board for a vote. And if not, I'm only askin that she let me take it forward for her. Because, I tell you right now, that's exactly what I'm gone do if she ain't mean to do it herself."

"Oh no you're not," Floyd laughed hotly.

"Oh, yes I am Floyd. Any citizen of Wheaton County can bring forward business before the board. I checked. Barett already signed off on everythin before he died, somebody just got to be there to see it through."

Chewing on a piece of fatty bacon Floyd gazed with narrow eyes down his nose at Maybel. With her arms folded immovably before her he knew outright that this was no bluff. She meant to follow through and frankly it didn't matter what he had to say about it one way or the other. Her mind was already made up.

"Since when you know so much bout all this anyhow?" Floyd huffed.

"Since them county board fellas cut city water supply to our Quarter," Maybel replied unflinchingly. "Since we had to start goin back to the well my grandmama used to use. I swore then and there, next time these county folks tried to pull some shit like that again, I'd be ready. And I am."

Taking a long sip of coffee Floyd mulled this over in his mind. Looking out the kitchen window he watched Jo as she squatted outside the chicken coop tossing handfuls of feed to the hens. She seemed so happy, but how long would that happiness last he wondered? How long until she knew what life was really like for Black folks in Wheaton?

"Y'know," Maybel continued. "If we keep rollin over every time they take somethin from us, they gone keep right on takin. It's what they do. It's what they always done."

There was a very earnest sadness in her voice. The kind that can only be acquired through hard earned experience. And upon hearing it, Floyd realized that perhaps she was right.

"Darlin," he muttered behind his mug. "You picked yourself a real dangerous time to go pokin the hornet's nest."

"I know the timin ain't ideal Floyd. Ain't nothin about this ideal. But we ain't gonna get this kinda opportunity again. Barett hardly managed to scrape together the votes to get this thing through in the first place."

"Well, you ain't wrong there," Floyd grumbled. "That county board was on him like stink on shit."

"That's right and now he ain't around to fight for us, is he?" Maybel pleaded. "They made sure a' that."

"Oh, c'mon," Floyd grunted dismissively. "What are you sayin' now?"

"I'm sayin there are a lot of people in this town who want these new zonin plans to go away. Same folks trying keep us stuck out here in the Quarter. Same ones who shut off our water. Same ones who wanted Barett out the way. Men like that Hinkley fella and all his crooked buddies."

Upon the very mention of that name an unwelcome shudder ran down Floyd's spine. There was something truly sick in the way the Sherriff had looked at him during Barett's funeral. There was murder in his eyes.

"Don't y'see Floyd," Maybel continued. "That's exactly why we gotta bring this to the floor. To show em we ain't gonna bend so easy. To show em we ain't afraid. Because if we gone let em get away this, doin us like they done, then we may well just up and leave 'cus it ain't ever gonna get no better round here. From here on, it's only gone get worse."

Studying her from across the table Floyd listened to her words. But during his time in the war Floyd had learned very quickly that what's right and what is rarely seemed to go hand in hand. Righteousness won't save you when your backs against the ropes, no matter how much you wish it would. Hope don't count for shit in foxholes. Belief never stopped a bullet. The world doesn't work in favor of good or evil. In combat, Floyd had watched plenty of good men die. Rewarded with gruesome deaths for all their heroic deeds. Now he was home and he'd just seen one of the best men he'd ever met buried for all his efforts. And now his wife wanted to jump into the very same arena. She just didn't understand. You could have all the faith in the world, but sometimes keeping your head down works just as well.

"I ain't tellin you to roll over for nobody," Floyd began gently. "I'm just sayin we got to pick our battles. You take this plan up there, they just gone vote it down easy as that. Then you'll have a target on your back, and for what? You gotta know when to cut your losses and fall back. Or else you'll be stickin your neck out for nothin."

"It's the principle, Floyd," Maybel declared. "The principle! Fordham is what we deserve, it's what we've worked for, and it's here now. Right in front of us. Imagine, a place for Black families that ain't 10 miles outside town. Imagine a place with water and electricity. Now this as close as we ever been. Barett showed us the way. He brought us to the door. I thank him for it, but now we gotta fight for it, Floyd. They ain't just gone give it away."

"But you'd ask Eudora to give her land away?"

"I'm askin her to do the right thing," Maybel said with sad eyes. "If nothing else, ain't we allowed to ask for that?"

"Right... wrong," Floyd began waving his hand wistfully in the air. "Fact is they gone vote it straight to hell, anyhow. We got to think about ourselves now. You think they came for Barett, well just think what they'd do to us then? Think what they done to Black folk for a hell of a lot less round here. Now, I don't see no point in stirrin this shit up any more than it already is. Our heads already on the choppin block. I'm tellin ya just leave it Maybel. Ain't no use dyin on that hill."

Though Maybel knew that Floyd was only looking out for their safety, his words left her heartbroken. Turning her gaze out the window she watched as JoJo ran giggling among the chickens as they trailed close behind her. What future did she have here? When would she realize that nothing was as it seemed? That nothing would ever change. That in this place, it was better to quietly take what was given to you, rather than stand to fight for something better.

Looking back at Floyd, Maybel wanted to scream, but instead she couldn't help but feel a great and overwhelming pity. It was a damn shame to see a brave man reduced to such a timid state. It was as though all the fight had been sucked right out of him. Leached from his spirit by the slow, gnawing defeats that compound quietly one atop the other until you find yourself hardly able to breathe beneath their weight.

"I expect better a' you Floyd," she finally said softly. "I really do. I know you seen terrible things, darlin. And I know you don't want to bring none of them things on your family, but we gonna be part of this fight whether you want it or not."

Across the table Floyd stared into his empty coffee cup. He could not bring himself to look at Maybel because he knew that she spoke the truth. He knew this because it sounded exactly like what Barett would have said. During the war, when they were broken and hurting the most, he always knew what to say to get them over that next hill. He always knew how to remind them what was worth fighting for.

"Don't y'see there ain't no stayin out of this 'cus it's happenin all around us," Maybel continued. "Always has been. All we can do is keep movin forward. Let em vote it down if that's what they gone do. That ain't the point. Point is we gone keep comin, from here on out. We ain't gone let em treat us like this no more."

Reaching out across the table, Maybel took Floyd's hand in hers.

"I know y'all boys thought goin to war would change things for Black folks everywhere. I bet them boys who fought the Civil War thought the same damn thing too. That maybe once we show em who we are, this country would finally treat us a little better. See us for who we are. What we've always been. A people who's fought, built, and bled for this country. But after all this time and all we've given, in their mind ain't nothin changed, Floyd. Only thing changed was us."

Later that morning as his truck sat idling in the driveway, Floyd Thomas savored the last few moments of his cigarette before snuffing it out in the ashtray. With his eyes fixed upon the strange house before him, he couldn't help but feel a stark and unsettling departure from his last visit to the Burleson property. Though the same great oak trees towered mightily in the yard and the same cows lazed half sleeping by the fence, something was terribly amiss that he couldn't quite put his finger on. The only difference he recalled for certain was an old swing made of tires which the Burleson children used to play on. It used to be tied up in one of the oaks there just off the driveway. But not anymore. Only a couple of weeks ago he had stopped by for a visit. The children had come running out towards the fence drawn by the sound of the truck's rattling engine. Together they'd chased him down the drive just like the cows come trotting out in pursuit of trucks loaded down with hay.

"Uncle Floyd's here," they'd yelled waving him on. "Hey Dad! Uncle Floyd's comin!"

The very first time he had met the children, Barett had told them just that.

"Go on and say 'Hi' to your Uncle Floyd."

There was something immediate and unshakable in the simplicity of the sentence. The implication of family. Something completely foreign yet strikingly familiar. Such a small gesture, yet it had stayed with him always and he'd never forgotten it. But now, sitting in the Burleson's driveway, Floyd was more inclined to believe that maybe the whole scene had been a figment of his imagination. Maybe there never were any children or happiness in this place at all. The sun was shining today as it did then, but the light of the place was wholly burnt out. Though it was standing just the same, it was a ruin. And Floyd had marched through enough bombed out villages during the war to know that only ghosts live amongst ruin.

"Here goes," he grumbled as he killed the engine.

Upon opening the driver side door Floyd winced at the intense heat that had gathered since dawn. Sweat stinging his eyes he searched the bed of the truck for his work gloves. Once in hand, he slapped the dust from the tanned leather and stuffed them deep into his back pocket. Then, hoisting up his worn steel toolbox in hand, he set off making his way around towards the back as he had so many times before.

The weight of his worn boots clicked over the flagstone walkway. Hearing his approach, two enormous heads popped up from the front porch. The Great Danes. Rising to their feet the two gargantuan hounds lumbered their way down the front steps licking their noses and laying back their ears.

"Well, there y'all are," Floyd smiled, as they rubbed their heads against his hip. "Good dogs."

They were magnificent creatures. Dappled in black and white like dairy cows, but with piercing blue eyes. Barett had bought them as pups for Dora a short while before he'd left for his military service. Knowing there was a very real possibility that he'd never return he'd gone out and found the biggest dogs money could buy to protect the family in his absence. In those long years apart, Dora had trained them well and they were devoted to her absolutely. From room to room, they'd follow her around the house all day and night. By now they were symbols of the property. Stoic guardians and watchful sentries. Though these days, getting on in their age, they often slunk off to snooze in the quiet shade of the porch or beneath the oak trees in the yard. Despite their intended purpose and fearsome size, they were rather docile creatures at heart.

As Floyd made his way past their insistent noses they soon settled back into their spots and returned to their slumber. Guardians as they were, they knew well enough the difference between friend and foe.

As he passed through the garage, the echo of Floyd's steps doubled back on him as he strolled by Barett's old work truck. Realizing it was parked in the spot usually reserved for the family's prized Cadillac, the thought of the fateful crash returned in Floyd's mind. During the war that Cadillac was nearly all Barett had talked about. He'd go on and on about how it was going to be his first order of business upon his triumphant return. His very own Cadillac Coupe Deville. Something to look forward to. A reward for surviving the war. Before he'd returned, he'd already picked out the color from a catalog – Triumph Blue.

Wondering if he'd ever see that car again Floyd quietly made his way around the truck and soon found himself face to face with the backdoor. With dragging steps, he scrubbed his boots on the mat before knocking hard against the wood frame. Then, drawing a deep breath, he called out into the darkness beyond.

"Howdy there, Mrs. Dora? It's me, Floyd...Floyd Thomas? Was just comin by to see if there's anythin round the house that needs doin."

For a moment after he spoke there was a silence so great, that it could only have been intentional. Like the sudden freeze of a deer as it cocks its head towards the sound of a snapping twig. In the stillness Floyd leaned closer towards the door. Then, indistinctly at first, in the cavernous distance came the sound of shuffling footsteps. House slippers across the stone floor.

At last, the steps fell quiet just beyond the entryway. From the darkness a form appeared. The deadbolt snapped unlocked. With a soft click the screen door drifted open as a rush of cold air wafted over Floyd's face.

"How bout you cut the 'missus' there Floyd," the shadowy form before him grumbled. "Never known you as one to stand on ceremony and I've always appreciated you mightily for it. Don't make me change my mind now."

Without another word or welcome, the figure lurched back towards the interior of the house.

"Alright then," chuckled Floyd following behind. "You got it, Dora."

Stepping inside, Floyd closed the door behind him before gazing out into the chilling abyss within. The air conditioner was cranked to full bore. The blinds drawn over every window. Everything was cold, damp, and dark. With each passing second Floyd's eyes began adjusting to the light. In the gloom he first caught sight of documents piled high on every tabletop. Everywhere haphazard stacks of papers flowed like whitewater. Shifting tides crashing off countertops and spilling over onto the floor. A thin buzz hung unsteady upon the air. The phone was hanging off the hook. The trash was full to the brim. The smell of stale liquor, cigarette smoke, and refuse was overwhelming.

As she waddled along in front of him Floyd surveyed Dora's figure for any signs of immediate concern. She was draped in a long dirty house robe which she clutched together at the front with one hand. Gripped in the other, Dora's thin fingers clung to a near empty whiskey glass. The white mat of frazzled hair upon her head jutted out in a million different ways. None of which were correct. As her house slippers drug over the flagstone floor of the hallway, Dora began to mutter something to herself. But Floyd did not hear, for his attention was turned to the cigarette butts strewn upon the floor like a thousand dead house flies entombed upon a windowsill. As they marched on towards the living room, they passed dozens of hollow and spent whiskey bottles collecting dust on the mantle. It had only been a few days since the funeral. Yet Floyd reckoned he had never seen so many empty bottles in one place. And that was saying something considering Floyd had worked a few years as a local barkeep before the war.

And he thought those boys could drink.

"Good god almighty," Floyd stammered, taking in the state of the home. "Looks like a damn twister tore up this place."

"Yeah, well," Dora grunted with a careless shrug. "Ain't no one here to be givin me no guff about it so I been doin as I please."

"I can see that."

As they approached the living room the frail ice at the bottom of Dora's whiskey glass tinkled softly. As if suddenly reminded of her manners Dora shot a sharp gesture, pointing Floyd towards the bar cart.

"You want a drink?"

Atop the messy counter the usually impressive assortment of liquor had been cut to a mere trickle. All that remained were the flavors Dora had no taste for. Vodka, gin, absinthe, port. Weighing his options Floyd noted it was hardly eleven in the morning. A little early, even for him.

"Got any iced tea?" he said.

"You know I do," Dora grumbled. "G'on and make yourself a glass, it's there in the fridge."

Carefully stepping his way over empty bottles and paperwork, Floyd maneuvered himself around the kitchen counter and made his way to the fridge. As he pulled the door open, he recoiled momentarily as his fingers made contact with a viscous and sticky substance coating the handle. Raising his hand towards the flickering fridge light, he rubbed the dark goo between his fingers and smelled it apprehensively. The tarry scent of machine oil. Wiping the mysterious substance on his trousers Floyd grabbed the tea pitcher and began searching for the least filthy cup among the open and ramshackle cabinets.

"Sooooo," he called out over the kitchen counter. "What you been getting' up to round here? Sides the bottle I mean."

"Oh, y'know," Dora's hollow voice called back. "This n' that."

With drink in hand, Floyd made his way back to the dim lit living room where finally he bore witness to the full extent of Dora's drunken labors.

Before him, every piece of furniture in the room had been cleared to make way. Chairs, couches, and coffee tables were set flush against the walls. Arranged atop the once open floor was a vast sea of bolts, metal tubes, springs, and levers all laid out in various stages of deconstruction and reconstruction. Beneath this odd assembly were great black oil stains, strange schematics and overflowing ashtrays scattered about carelessly. And nestled right at the epicenter of this indefinable network, sat its creator.

"What the hell is all this?" Floyd managed, his face twisting with genuine concern.

Scanning over the parts laid out before her, Dora crawled out on her hands and knees to grasp a piece in her hands.

"Oh, c'mon Floyd," she said, holding up a peculiar object in the dusky light. "I think you know exactly what this is."

As she ran a dishcloth over the hunk of metal, Dora paused for a moment to admire the weathered sheen it reflected.

"Tell me what's this look like to you?"

As Dora tossed the contraption in his direction, Floyd snatched it out of the air with a lightning-fast hand.

"Still got the hands champ," Dora chuckled.

But Floyd was not smiling. Setting down his glass, he held the cold metal in his hands thumbing over it carefully. Though his mind was still struggling to catch up with what was laid out before him, Dora's words rang true. The piece felt oddly familiar in his fingers. An artifact from another life.

"This is," he began, turning the piece in his hand. "This is a receiver. A shotgun receiver.... looks like a Winchester. M97?"

"Mhm," Dora nodded, returning to her work.

Flipping it over Floyd ran his eyes over the serial number stamped into the casting.

"But that can't be," he said trailing off.

"G'on," Dora prodded.

"This is government issue," said Floyd. "US Army."

"Mhm."

"This the most illegal shit I ever seen," Floyd barked. "How you get this here? Y'know you ain't supposed to have nothin like this."

"Oh, I'm well aware Floyd. Well aware," Dora grumbled dismissively. "Remember when y'all was deployed, how Barett was always shippin them packages all the time."

"Well," began Floyd searching his memory. "Well, I reckon I do...the fellas liked to give him a hard time bout it. But he said they's gifts… for you and the boys."

"Yeah well... they wasn't exactly gifts for me," Dora scoffed. "Certainly never had a British Enfield on my wish list."

"God almighty," Floyd mumbled, baffled at the arsenal pieced out before him. In long steady strokes he rubbed his hand over his bald head as the wheels began to turn in his mind. "How y'all manage this? Thought they'd be checkin all GI shipments back home."

Feeling a touch unsteady Floyd sat against the edge of the couch. Slowly he ran his eyes over the disassembled M97. "Think they'd a seen a fuckin trench gun going out in the mail."

"Yeah, well they wasn't necessarily checkin officers' post," Dora grumbled. "Especially no white officer. Besides, Barett was too smart to be shippin nothing conspicuous. He was a troublemaker, but he wasn't no dummy. He broke em' all down to the bolts just like this," Dora said holding up a small piece in her hand. "Shipped a single gun in, oh about fifteen, twenty packages or so dependi' on size. They'd arrive piece by piece over the course of a few months. Then I'd build em here, that was my job."

As she set a slide atop the exposed frame of a 1903 Colt hammerless Dora chuckled to herself. "Y'know I'll give it to him he was some fox that one. He'd ship em out in things you'd never expect. Envelopes, tiny little boxes, what have you. Sent me a couple 30 round magazines in candy wrappers once. Valentine's Day, I believe it was."

"Holy shit," Floyd whispered, taking in the full scope of the weaponry laid out before him.

"Yep," Dora continued. "After four long years of deployment we ended up with quite a collection of military firepower. Courtesy of the United States government. They even paid for the post," Dora said, draining the remains of her glass. "Fuckin least they could do in my opinion."

"Don't be showin this shit to nobody," Floyd muttered as his eyes landed upon the distinct contours of an M3 submachine gun. "Dora, they put you in jail for this."

"Oh, I won't tell if you won't," Dora said tapping her finger to her nose. "Besides, this is peanuts compared to what I got in the back office."

Raising her eyes from her work, Dora's gaze met Floyd's as he took a long hesitant swig of iced tea. Gathering his thoughts, Floyd paused for a moment and considered the consequence of his reply.

"Y'know my wife told me not to be gettin involved in no crazy shit over here," said Floyd.

"Well, I know you a military man but I never took you for one to do everything you told."

Unable to help himself Floyd cracked a smile.

"Ha. Shiiit. Y'know Barett would get a kick outta this, draggin me into some bullshit. You two like peas in a pod."

"Come on," Dora grinned, rising to her feet. "Follow me."

Still clutching the empty glass in her hands, Dora waved Floyd on as they left the living room behind. Ambling down the long hall, away from the stifled light of the main room, the two descended further into the darkness. Past the old family photos of happier times lining the corridor, they moved in reverent silence as mourners move through a tomb. Without a word they slipped past the empty children's room and though Floyd tried not to look at the bright yellow walls they called out to him through the darkness. As they passed, he wondered if the room would ever know the sounds of their laughter again. He wanted to ask about the kids, to hear that they were doing fine with their aunt in Colorado. Suppose he just wanted to know they were ok. But somehow, he felt that bringing it up might do more harm than good. Despite the rumors he knew Dora loved those children, in her own strange way of course, and if she'd shipped them off, she probably had a damn good reason.

Before him Dora shambled onwards, clutching her robe until at last her slippers fell quiet upon the carpet of the bedroom. From this entryway, the tight confines of the hallway stretched out behind in a straight line some 25 yards ending directly at the back door where Floyd had come in. For the very first time Floyd suddenly noticed this rather peculiar alignment. Softly he smiled to himself. Leave it to Barett to ensure his home came laid out with a defensive choke point. It wasn't a hallway at all. It was a god damn shooting gallery.

"Just here," said Dora.

Once through the door of the bedroom, the space sprawled out wide. Though the blinds were drawn down, Floyd could just make out a mess of sheets tangled atop the mattress. Overall, the bedchamber was far tidier than the rest of the house. If anything, Floyd thought, a sign of Dora's preoccupations elsewhere.

But it was not the bedroom to which Dora was leading, but the backroom. Again, directly in line with the back door and the threshold to the bedroom door was an oddly recessed brick wall. At first glance perhaps, one might not have even noticed its existence save for a painting hanging there in a gold gilded frame. Housed within, standing regal and saintly, was an oil painting of Sir Galahad. The purest of the knights. With hands folded at his front in dignified contemplation the young knight stood gazing out towards some great and predestined endeavor, accompanied by his noble mare. The artwork was flanked on either side by two military sabres. On the left corner of the frame, was a cavalry sabre which Floyd recognized immediately. The engraved sheath in silver and black shone earnestly, even here, in the absence of all light. It was Barett's sword. Awarded upon graduating the officer's training course at the top of his class from the Texas Military Institute. Like some general of wars long forgotten, Barett had carried the sabre all through his deployment, maintaining its cleanliness religiously.

On the contrary, the sabre that hung upon the other corner of the frame retained no such luster. Unsheathed and unadorned with any ceremonial embellishment, the black stained blade was haggard and scarred with the markings of battle. All down the ashen steel, notches were cleaved into the edge. Although battered from years of use, the wooden handle still proudly bore the scorched initials branded long ago, "E.B."

Stepping into the shadowy recess before the painting, Dora turned on her heels and pulled upon a ball chain dangling overhead. Suddenly the cavernous hollow was illuminated in the buzzing warmth of the lightbulb.

"After you," she said, gesturing to her left.

Standing there, Floyd was perplexed. It seemed the wall was nothing but a dead end. But upon stepping deeper into the recess, from the corner of his eye he spied a narrow passage. Only a few feet wide, the white brick walls funneled into a corridor that snaked its way into a dark void beyond. His eyes questioning, he glanced towards Dora, who nodded him forward.

Taking a deep breath, Floyd pressed on, feeling his way along the cold painted walls. As his fingers traced blindly over the damp brick and coarse grout he slipped further into the crevice.

Looking back Floyd could still see Dora's silhouette outlined in the dim light of the bedroom.

Pushing on he continued into the unknown.

Just then a switch snapped and a soft hum filled the air as the bulbs warmed into full illumination. There before him lay another hard turn, but just around the corner he could make out the promising glow of light. Flattening his thin frame, he squeezed through the jaws of brick and popped out into the space beyond.

The first thing that struck him was the smell. At once so distant yet so intimately familiar, like the comfort of family long since seen. It was the same moist, leather worn, military grade footlocker scent that permeated the halls of Fort Shaw. The smell of barracks, cement, and sweat.

The smell of brothers in arms.

All along the walls, resting on shelves were the recollections of a life so many had tried to forget. Call them history, souvenirs, or the spoils of war it was all here on display. Like the heads of animals in the trophy room of a hunter. The bullet riddled helmet of a Nazi sergeant. An SS patch pinned against the wall, dangling lifeless beneath the blade of a Ka-Bar knife. A spent assembly of an M72 LAW's rocket. The very same weapon Floyd had hauled halfway across Europe, before unloading it into the sheer side of a German Panzer. Floyd couldn't believe his eyes. As he ran his fingers along the aluminum frame of the rocket assembly, a figure standing to his left suddenly jostled him from memory. His heart skipping a beat, Floyd leapt away with a startle before realizing it was not a body, but the torso of a mannequin wearing a World War I era gas mask. Leaning in closer, Floyd studied his reflection in the hollow and haunting glass eyes. Mirrored back he saw Dora come drifting in behind him, running her hand atop an old mahogany desk covered in the paperwork of Barett's final labors.

Flipping on a desk lamp, she turned the warm light of the bulb against the wall. There, pinned sheets deep into a cork board was a collection of clippings that could have filled the halls of the Smithsonian ten times over. Newspaper headlines calling out everything from the advance of Hitler into Poland to the attack on Pearl Harbor and the undertaking of D-Day. Placing his enormous hands over the back of the worn desk chair, Floyd leaned forward to survey the documents more closely. As he poured over the assortment, the metallic sheen of dog tags caught his eye. Reaching out, he turned the thin stamped steel in his hand.

"Burleson, Barett," he read aloud under his breath.

Running his fingers over the rough raised lettering, Floyd's eye was drawn to yet another pair of tags. But unlike standard dog tags these were strangely circular in shape. Bound together by only a thin frayed string. His curiosity peaked, Floyd turned them over in his hands and read the name aloud.

"Marijus Steniwitz 90th Infantry."

"Barett's father," chimed Eudora. "From the first war to end all wars, y'know. Deployed to the Argonne. Unit out of San Antonio. Texas and Oklahoma boys the lot of em. The 'Tough Hombres' they were called. By god, they lived up to the name."

"Marijus Steniwitz," Floyd repeated. The name sounded strange on his tongue.

"Lithuanian," Dora grumbled. "Even back then Jews weren't too welcome in East Europe. Whole Steniwitz family got wiped out. Except for one. I knew him as Mo. He was a hell of a man. I liked him very much. Y'know when I married Barett it was Mo who insisted he take my last name. Said he'd seen enough people killed for havin a name like 'Steniwitz' to last a thousand lifetimes."

"What is this place?" said Floyd.

"Ain't it obvious?" Dora said, raising her hands. "It's Barett's office. Or hideaway, I suppose. Figures how you look at it. 'Every officer needs an office.' he'd say. Course, Barett figured he'd put his in a fuckin fallout bunker. That's why the entryway there got all them narrow twists and turns."

"Radiation can't cut no corners," said Floyd, recalling the nuclear fallout training he'd received in boot camp.

"Yessir. So long as we ain't ground zero for the next A-Bomb these four walls will still be standing while the world's burnin," Dora said, slapping the brick. "Though I never really saw the point. If all that's left is a wasteland, I say just drop that thing right on my head and get it over with. Holed up in here eatin canned beans ain't sound like much of a livin to me."

On the wall, a photo caught Floyd's eye. It was the company photo of the Fighting 151st. There weren't many all Black units during the war. Even fewer led by an officer who volunteered for the assignment. For most it was a form of punishment. For Barett it was the honor of a lifetime. When all was said and done, Barett had written to the press secretary praising his company for their courage and fortitude in battle. In the letter, he requested full honors for each and every man and stated the 151st was the greatest group of soldiers that any officer ever had the privilege of commanding in combat.

And by God, he believed it too.

As Floyd's eyes moved among the familiar faces, he found himself, smiling and looking 40 years younger. Course it hadn't been so long ago. But war has a funny way of aging those who survive. The photo was grouped alongside hand drawn battle maps from the field and aerial photographs outlining the family farm plots. On the desk, set apart from the rest of the ephemera, a photo of Dora from a lifetime ago. Young and beautiful, her sun-soaked skin glowed upon some sandy beach. Her face covered with big movie star sunglasses. She smiled at the man behind the camera.

"Forget all that," Dora suddenly grunted, waving Floyd away from the photo. "This here is what I come to show ya."

Turning away from the desk, Floyd noticed an old workbench positioned against the wall. Set atop the table was a large crude object, shrouded beneath an oil-stained sheet. Pinching an unlit cigarette between her lips Dora stood next to the mysterious item with a wily grin. For a moment she let Floyd's anticipation build, until she could see his heartbeat pulsing in his forehead.

"Hold on to your panties," Dora grinned, as she ripped away the shroud.

As the sheet fell to the floor, there on the table was a sight Floyd thought he would never see again. An exquisitely maintained Browning M1917 A1 Fully Automatic Machine Gun. The hammering right hand of the Fighting 151st.

"You gotta be fuckin kiddin me," Floyd stammered, his eyes wide and beaming.

"This one took a year or two," said Dora, proudly patting the gun.

Reaching his hand out, Floyd ran his fingertips along the great cylindrical barrel which he himself had hauled halfway across Europe. Weighing in at over 110 pounds fully assembled, the tripod mounted .30 caliber water cooled machine gun was capable of dealing death at 500 rounds per minute. It devoured lead hot off a belt fed munitions box strapped like a cinder block to its side. Broken down for travel, it required 3 men to carry. A worthy tradeoff for the equivalent firepower of an entire battalion. By any standard this wasn't a gun, it was a buzz saw. A mountain cutter. A meticulously engineered mower of men. A striking scythe designed to reap human souls. And here it was, in all its sinister glory, in Wheaton County of all places.

Floyd was awestruck.

Mounted to the side of the work bench another sight soon caught his eye. The ammunition belt loading mechanism. Nearby a loose bin of .30 caliber rounds sat alongside two boxes of freshly loaded ammo belts. In civilian terms, Floyd was standing in front of 2000 rounds of canned thunder ready to rock at a moment's notice.

Dora, it seemed, had been very busy indeed.

"Alright," Floyd began with a slight hesitation in his words. "Y'know I come over here just to see if there was anythin need doin. Take out some trash or help you clean up or somethin. Now you showin me all this, and to be honest with ya, I ain't sure what to make of it."

"Oh g'on now," Dora said, leaning up against Barett's desk. "Bet you can take a guess."

"Well," said Floyd, running his hand over his head. "I tell ya, last time I saw this many guns...we was goin to war."

"Mhm," Dora nodded, lighting her cigarette with a quick flash of her lighter. "So, what does that tell ya?"

"Are you goin to war Dora?"

"Very good," Dora replied with a wicked grin.

"With who?"

The cigarette still smoldering between her fingers Dora slowly raised her hand like a pistol and aimed down the sights towards the wall behind the Browning. As Floyd traced her line of sight, his eyes fell upon a strange display. There, pinned against the wall, were hundreds of letters tacked pages deep.

"Better question is who ain't we fightin," Dora grumbled behind a thick haze of smoke.

Running his eyes over the letters the words began to jump out at Floyd like lashes of lightning, stinging and cold. Words of hate, fury, and fear filled each and every page. Words that can only be conjured at the basest levels of human depravity and decency. Words that carry the same hopeless desperation as the hearts, hardly human, in which they reside. Though he wished it were not so, Floyd knew these words better than he cared to admit. He had heard them his entire life.

But in the midst of their rambling chaos, one letter in particular hung as a sinister centerpiece among the rest. Written in large frantic script, as if scrawled by some rabid beast frothing at the mouth, the madness of its message rang clear.

"BLOOD AND SOIL"

The old Nazi slogan.

"Dora," Floyd began, backing further away to survey the nightmarish collection in its entirety. "The hell is all this?"

"That," said Dora, "is just a samplin of the true thoughts and feelings of the fine people of Wheaton, County Texas. Started showin up in the post the same week Barett began takin an interest in those Town Halls."

"My god, Dora," Floyd muttered, stroking the stubble of his chin. "They must be hundreds here."

"Reckon so," Dora snorted, "y'know at first I wasn't much bothered by Barett goin to them things. Then one day I get this letter in the mail. Somebody threatenin to burn the damn house down, so I says to him 'Barett, the hell you say at that meetin get someone riled up enough to send us a letter like this.' But Barett he didn't think twice y'know and he says to me, 'I thought we buried the Nazis back in Berlin but by God they been right here in Wheaton all along."

"Sounds bout right," Floyd chuckled.

"Yeah," Dora continued, running a hand over Barett's old desk chair. "But by god, he was right, wasn't he? Maybe they not walkin round with swastikas on they arm no more but they the same kinda sick. And they sure came crawlin out the woodwork the day Barett walked into that first town hall meetin."

On a shelf across the room Dora caught sight of a framed photograph of Barett smiling towards her. Like some recurring nightmare the stark realization that she'd never see that smile again seemed to suck the air from her lungs.

Though the photo was from only a few years ago, he had the same look on his face that he did the first time they'd met.

As the story goes Dora was living with some roommates at the time and in their attempt to rid themselves of her they'd tried to pawn her off on some local fellas to get her out of the house. Despite her objections, they'd give out Dora's phone number to anyone who'd take it. Course she was such a bulldog that most boys couldn't make it five minutes on the telephone with her. Eventually, as it was in small towns like Wheaton, one of the boys they called up was Barett and he leapt at the chance. While Dora didn't know it at the time, Barett had seen her once before at a softball game and thought her to be a magnificent sort of woman. At one point in the eighth inning Dora charged the mound and socked the opposing pitcher with a solid left hook, dropping her where she stood. Barett said he'd made his mind up then and there. On the evening he called, Dora was ready to give him the runaround, but Barett told her he was already headed over and she could wait to make up her mind until he got to the door. In fact, his specific instructions were to look out the window and if she liked what she saw, he'd take her out. She reckoned that took more guts than most people can muster in a lifetime. Ten minutes later when he was standing outside her window, with that handsome halfcocked grin of his, she too had made up her mind.

Shaking herself from the thought, Dora rose from the desk and stepped closer towards the letters.

"All the money in the world and you couldn't buy the guts that man had," Dora continued. "Just imagine the look on the faces of the county board when the son of a Jewish immigrant, the proud commander of Black soldiers in the Great War…come walkin up to that podium in front of all those people."

Though her eyes were sullen, Dora's was voice brimming with pride. "Imagine their faces when he told em maybe if a Black man was good enough to fight and die for his country, he ought to come home to a country that treats him with the respect he deserves. Maybe, all that talk about separate but equal wasn't never equal at all."

"Shoo," exclaimed Floyd shaking his head, "bet that went over real good."

"Oh they laid into him, alright," Dora said with a halfhearted smile. "Only a few of em had the stones to threaten him to his face. Most of em just sent letters. Ain't even got courage enough to sign they names. Letters were all different, but the themes stay the same. Talkin bout how Blacks and Jews are in cahoots, cheating the white man outta his land and country. They go into great detail about how they'd like to 'hang us in the front yard,' or 'burn us at the stake.' This one here says they gonna 'crucify the kids.' No tellin where they got the inspiration, hm? Shit's biblical ain't it?"

"Somethin like that," Floyd sighed.

"Y'see, Barett put them letters up to remind us we was behind enemy lines, surrounded by these motherfuckers, and we best not forget it. They either hate ya cus you a Jew or a gypsy, a woman, a colored, a homo, or they hate you cus you're brown and you got more of a claim to this land than they do. But all they do is hate cus they hate themselves and they sad fuckin lives and they ain't got the mental faculty required to deal with it. It's easier to blame someone, something…anything."

As Dora stood staring at the letters a foul sneer began to form upon her face. Sensing her blood boiling inside her she turned away with a quick step and took a sharp drag from her cigarette.

"Yep," she sighed, settling back atop Barett's desk, "this town been sendin us this shit for years now. Only with renewed vigor since Barett bought the Fordham property. Just a dusty old trailer park, nobody never paid it no mind. But say you gonna build a community owned neighborhood in Wheaton where Black folks can raise they families and suddenly the world's up in arms."

"Look Dora," Floyd said, turning away from the wall, "you ain't gotta convince me that Wheaton is full of some racist motherfuckas. That ain't news to me. But right now ya livin room looks like a munitions locker, and you back here loadin up a machine gun. So I'm gonna ask ya now," he said, pausing to draw a deep breath, "what exactly you plannin on doin here?"

"Y'know, that's an interestin question Floyd. I been thinkin about that a lot lately. See I got more'n a year's worth of death threats round here and cops got nothin to say about that. Now my husband's dead. They got nothin to say bout that either. It don't take no Sherlock Holmes to piece this one together. Now they tellin me, 'the death just wasn't suspicious. It was an accident, Eudora. Just ain't suspicious.' But you know what? I find it very fuckin suspicious. Cus not more than three days before I was identifyin his body down at the morgue, Barett was in the clerk's office signin in his bid to run for County Commissioner. And his first campaign promise? A Black owned community in Fordham, walking distance into town square. Right smack dab in the middle of Wheaton."

Taking an uncertain step back Floyd sank heavily into a stool beside the workbench. With long strokes he ran his hand across his head as his eyes chased his thoughts around the room.

In silence Dora studied the red glow of her cigarette's ember and allowed her words to sink in.

"And you think," Floyd began with a grave pause. "You think they killed him for it?"

"Y'know what I think?" Dora replied without hesitation. "I think if it looks like shit, and it smells like shit…and it tastes like shit? Partner you probably eatin shit, and you should do somethin about that. And that's exactly what I'm gonna do. Tell me, how is that everybody in this town knows every-fuckin-body, but no one know nothin bout these here letters? This town and every slimy two-faced snake livin in it knows who behind this, but they don't wanna say. Because it's them. It's their mothers and fathers, friends, and neighbors. They spit their venom in secret and smile at us in the Diamond on Sunday. Snakes, every fuckin one."

As Dora went for another pull from her cigarette she found her hand trembling with fury.

"You're godamn right I think they killed him," she spat, pointing to the letters on the wall. "Done in by the same bastards who showed up to his funeral! The same sons of bitches that wanted to offer me they condolences?! Well, escuse me, I don't want no fuckin condolences! Not from them or nobody! I want someone to look at this shit! But the Wheaton Police about as crooked as they come, ain't they? Hell that draft dodger Hinkley is the man in charge and he hated Barett more than anyone! So where am I supposed to go, hm? The capitol? Tell em we got big trouble out here in little Wheaton County? 'Help, we got racists and bigots in small town Texas', imagine that! They'd laugh us out the room. I bet those city slickers couldn't find Wheaton on a goddamn map."

Her chest heaving, Dora raised the cigarette to her lips, desperate for a draw. Taking a long pull, she exhaled an unsteady cloud of smoke.

"Forget the wild west, we may as well be on the fuckin moon out here," she grumbled.

As Dora stroked her fingers across her brow, she took a moment to collect herself.

"Ain't no one coming to help us, Floyd," she said after a long while. "So I guess we gotta help ourselves."

Absorbing the weight of her words Floyd rubbed his face with his enormous hands.

"I could produce a smoking gun and they wouldn't so much as look at it," Dora continued. "I mean here's your smokin gun, it's right here," she said pointing again to the wall. "Motive! Probable cause. Intent. All you got to do is look. And since ain't no one wanna look at it, well goddamn, I'm lookin at it! And it stinks to high heaven. Now I ain't bout to sit twiddlin my thumbs waitin for the slow hand of justice that won't never come. I'm gonna raise some hell! This town's always wanted a reason to see me burn, well godamm I'm gonna give it to em."

Rising from the desk Dora's feet set into motion. Across the cement floor she paced back and forth before Barett's desk with her hands clasped behind her back.

"Them guns out there is just an insurance policy. By god, I'm ready to meet fire with fire," she declared. "I bear no reservations regardin the depravity of *my* enemy. I have seen their depths! And I do not expect them to go quietly or listen to reason. Way I see it, ain't no reasonin to be had! That General Sherman, I think he had the right idea, you know. Scorched earth! Hell, maybe if they'da let him have his way we wouldn't still be dealin with this sorta shit. Half this country still think the South gone rise again! Well, if they want war they got it. I don't care if I have to burn this whole town down to the brick along with every person it! I got a thousand acres of pasture out there, plenty of room to bury a few bodies. From where I stand if they didn't do it, they was complicit in the act, and there ain't no difference to me no more."

His arms folded in quiet contemplation; Floyd gazed cold at the wall of letters before him. In the written rantings and ravings, he saw the same hatred that had permeated his life, and the lives of everyone he had ever loved. He saw the dashed dreams of a young soldier, eager to fight for his country, only to return home to face an enemy all the more cruel.

"So that's it," Dora said with a heavy sigh, "that's what I'm doin and I ain't changin my mind. Tell ya, only you, me, and the cows know bout this. And I'm only tellin you cus to Barett y'all was good as brothers. I know I ain't got to tell you that."

Across the room Floyd's heavy head sunk even lower into his chest. Though he tried to hide it, Dora watched as he snuck a quick hand to his eyes.

"But look here Floyd," she continued, "this ain't your fight one way or the other y'understand? Now I don't know what's gonna happen, but I reckon there's gonna be some dyin goin on. You done your fightin, I won't be askin you to do none of that. But I tell ya, I haven't got much for allies these days. I'll take em where I can."

Before Floyd could consider his answer, it had already escaped his lips.

"You know you never got to ask Dora. Me and Barett, we bled just the same and that was always good nuff for us. Y'all ain't never been nothin but family to me, and in my family you come for one, you come for all."

"Well, you may come to regret that, but I'm glad to hear it."

Considering his reply Floyd laughed a nervous laugh, though Eudora found it reassuring nonetheless.

"But uh, since you offerin n' all," Dora began, "there is somethin I could use your help with."

Instantly their eyes met through the haze of cigarette smoke lingering in the dim light between them.

"I gotta pick up the Cadillac."

CHAPTER V

POKIN ROUND

A short while later, beneath the full fury of the afternoon sun, Floyd Thomas pulled his truck around to the front of the house.

There, waiting coolly beneath the awning, Eudora Burleson sat upon an old teak bench nursing the last few puffs of her cigarette. Never one to be caught underdressed on an excursion into town, she had cleaned up miraculously since Floyd had left her only a short time ago. Seated there in her crisp white blouse and fine olive-green slacks one would never have assumed the squalor from whence she'd come. Draped over her shoulder was a woven shawl of Mexican design. Her eyes remained shrouded behind the black veil of her thick rimmed sunglasses. As Floyd racked the truck into park Dora rose from the bench with a weary groan. Stepping out from the awning and into the sunlight she took one final puff from the cigarette before pitching it back against the house.

Leaning over the passenger seat Floyd popped the door open and watched with a certain delight as she stomped on down towards the truck.

"Lil hot for that poncho ain't it?" he grinned as she climbed into the cab.

"Yeah, well if you dressin for the weather round here you'd never be able to wear no clothes at all," Dora muttered, slamming the door behind her. "Sides I ain't dressed for comfort, Corporal. I'm dressed for war."

Though he laughed on the outside, Floyd couldn't help but wonder what he'd gotten himself into. With that thought rattling around his mind, he shifted the gear stick into first as the truck began its slow crawl down the long gravel drive.

As the miles came and went silently between them Floyd found his mind consumed with the thought that just a few hours earlier Eudora had been a wretched sight indeed. Fueled by whiskey and cigarettes she'd been wandering around the dark squalor of the house day and night, assembling an arsenal of weaponry all the while looking as though she hadn't bathed in weeks. During their entire exchange back in Barett's office, Floyd reckoned she had probably polished off at least an eighth of whiskey in front of him and who knows how much more in the hours and days prior to his arrival. But somehow, even beneath the drowsy haze of drink, the fire of her spirit was evident. Smoldering fierce, just beneath the surface. Floyd knew that she had meant every word that she'd said back at the house. And in the coming days he was certain her actions would surely prove it.

As the two of them rode along to the steady clip of the truck, past the sprawling farmlands stretched out to the horizon, Floyd was struck with the sudden realization that Eudora was not at all out of place amongst the harshness of the landscape. On the contrary, the tenacity of her spirit reflected the hostility of her environment. Though she carried herself with an air of refinement, underneath she was jagged and coarse.

Like the bloom of the prickly pear, she was something to behold, but rather sharp to be handled.

At last, they began to approach the outskirts of town. Just a minute further and they'd be entering the Quarter. An area reserved at the far fringe of society for those exiled and cast from it. With each passing mile the derelict shacks began to appear here and there. Hollow and uninhabitable looking structures, like crumbling tombstones upon a dusty plain. But these were not vacant vestiges of a civilization long since abandoned. Simply old constructions built from what could be spared at the time - repurposed wood and rusty nails ripped from old barn doors and fence beams. Once as a child working in a field not far from where they were now, Dora had once wandered into one of these strange structures to see what it was like. She recalled being curious to the idea of a house that could not be packed up and moved. Branded into her memory was the foreign sound of the floorboards creaking beneath her weight. In her naivety she recalled questioning the purpose of laying boards along the floor, when the exposed dirt beneath her tent at home was so much quieter.

Here on the fringe of town, in the rotting and ramshackle homes handed down from the poor to the poorer, lived the Black citizens of Wheaton County.

A stark departure from the bustling energy of the town square just a few miles down the road, life here was a daily struggle. Among these homes, hungry bellies rationed rice and beans and drank warm water boiled from the river. No electricity, no plumbing, no nothing. In these homes babies were born and the dead were buried in the backyard. Here hardship was as reliable as the rising sun. And all the while, though you'd never think it, just a few miles down the road white families beat the heat in the air-conditioned comfort of the Starlight Theatre. Sipping ice cold Cokes and crunching on big bags of popcorn.

Before long, the Quarter came and went in the rearview mirror.

Floyd sat up a bit in his seat. A few short miles and they'd be on the main road into town. And town was a very different world altogether. A hostile world where neither Floyd nor Dora ever felt particularly welcome. In quick glances Floyd's head began to move on a swivel. Like the hunted, his eyes grew wide and searching.

Sitting beside him, Dora watched his hands grow stiff and rigid against the wheel.

"Won't be but a minute," Dora said, sensing his tension, "you can just drop me off and be on your way."

"Nah, I ain't leavin ya alone until you in the car and headin out," Floyd replied, shifting in his seat.

"I think I can manage," said Dora with a reassuring confidence.

"No doubt about that," Floyd smiled, "but I'll stick around a minute just in case."

As Floyd's truck rattled around the final corner the sign they'd been searching for appeared before them. There, high above the street rotating in slow orbit, the great swooping neon bulbs read out emphatically, "Raymond's Service Station". And squeezed in just below that, the rather repetitive slogan "Service with a Smile!" Quite ironically, for all the grand promise encapsulated in the glow of those futuristic neon bulbs, the shop itself was a stunning disappointment. A paltry and dilapidated two pump one car garage, owned and operated by Raymond Fisk Jr. who had inherited the place from his late father Raymond Fisk Sr. Once renowned as a symbol of Wheaton's promising future, the paint was now worn and peeling from the formerly modern façade. Perhaps, at this point, a better representation of the town's true nature.

Aside from the occasional necessity of a full tank, the only redeeming quality of the entire place was that a few years ago Raymond Jr. had installed a Coke machine outside the shop office. A half-hearted attempt to boost his establishment's flagging revenue.

As the truck squealed to a stop just outside the garage Floyd racked the engine into neutral. Dora peered into the darkness beyond the open shutters of the shop. Inside the cluttered workspace, spare parts and junk teetered to the rafters. Rusted out chassis littered the exterior. Like any good rat, Raymond lived in a rat nest. That was no surprise. But there amongst the rubbish, shone the unmistakable paint of Barett's prized Cadillac. Triumph Blue.

Without a word Dora opened the passenger door and stepped out of the truck as Floyd kept the engine running. Making her measured approach she flipped the shawl over her shoulder, giving Floyd a brief glimpse of what she'd brought with her.

"Oh shit," he muttered.

Stepping into the shaded recesses of the shop, Dora's heart began to hammer as she moved closer towards the car. Setting her sunglasses atop her head, she knelt down at the back bumper. Much to her surprise, it was exactly as she had remembered it. Not a screw out of place despite the police report stating the car had been flipped on its head no more than a few days ago. Though he wasn't particularly known for it, Raymond sure made quick work of this one. As Dora reached out to touch the gleaming steel, a door suddenly opened from the side office as a sniveling voice called out in the gloom.

"Uh, scuse me," the voice offered warily, "can I help you, sir?"

"Well that all depends, Raymond," Dora said, rising to her feet.

"Oh, Mrs. Burleson," the man recoiled, "I didn't know it was you... you uh...you musta got my message then."

A rather squat man, Raymond Fisk Jr. was exactly the kind of character one would expect to encounter in the dark confined spaces of the cluttered shop floor. In fact, Dora had always found his resemblance to the common mole to be quite striking. His beady eyes, magnified behind near telescopic prescription lenses, were fitting for a subterranean creature. Additionally, every time they crossed paths he always seemed to be covered in grease and filth, as though he had been out all-night rooting around flower beds for grubs. But despite his rather uncouth appearance, Dora knew that above all Raymond fancied himself to be a creature of cunning. Fortunately for her, not one that thrived under the pressures of direct confrontation.

"Y'know, what Ray?" Dora began, setting her sunglasses back over her eyes. "When I heard the the car was in here for repair, I tell ya, I was mighty pleased…"

"Oh, well, I'm glad to hear it," Raymond replied with a sigh of relief.

"Well, now," Dora said, brandishing a reproachful finger, "you didn't let me finish there, Raymond. I was sayin I was mighty pleased to hear it, not cus you a great mechanic... but cus you a terrible liar."

In the silence that hung between them Raymond slowly cocked his head at the remark, like a chicken registering a passing fly.

"See I got some questions Raymond and I'd like to think you got some answers for me."

"Well, I'll certainly help where I can," said Ray, flattening his portly frame as he squeezed around the car.

"Uh, now, what's on your mind?"

"The police normally tow cars to your shop?" Dora hooted, taking a step closer towards him. "Is that what you'd call standard procedure in your line of business?"

"Uh, well...sometimes...if they's a crash that's blocking the road, or a... well, a how you say a f-fatality," Ray stammered. "Mean, they gots to take it somewhere, either the impound or sometimes if it's an accident y'know, yeah they'll bring it here."

"Hm," Dora replied, folding her arms indignantly. "And who told you to just go about your business fixin up this here Cadillac? Cus I sure as hell didn't."

"Well...this here is a *repair* garage," said Raymond puffing out his chest. "Dora, I'll have you know this vehicle arrived to me in a terrible state. Sitting out there in my lot, all busted up, glass everywhere, a real mess of a thing. Safety hazard, you know? And uh... Well, I know who's it was. Y'know Barett's and all. And I just got to thinking he wouldn't want it lookin like that and so I just..."

"Who told you to fix the car Raymond."

"Now, Dora," Ray jabbed, "c'mon now, just hold it right there. I won't be taking no grief for doin my job."

"I didn't ask you to do no job," Dora balked, waving him away. "Now who you expect gone pay for this?"

"Oh, this here's a matter for insurance Dora. Won't be nothin out of your pocket if that's what's got you riled up," Ray said, smiling a weaseling smile. "I guarantee it."

"Well, ain't that clever of you, Raymond," Dora hissed. "Got all your bases covered. Bet you're real pleased with this lil' racket you got goin on here."

"Scuse me?" Raymond scoffed.

His face was sweating profusely though he refused to acknowledge it. Beneath his eye a little twinge contracted in rhythmic spasm. He was treading water but just managing to stay afloat. As Dora took another step closer towards him, he backed away instinctively before bumping into a shelf.

With his back against the wall Dora closed in tighter.

"See Raymond, I been out lookin at where the crash was," Dora mused, mere inches from his face. "And since we bein honest today I tell ya, I been out there a lot Raymond. I really have. See there's just somethin bout it that strikes me as very peculiar. It's these tire marks all over the road, just the way they went from side to side. Felt like I had seen somethin like it before but, by god, I just couldn't place it."

As if awaiting a response Dora fell silent as her gaze burned into Raymond's soul. His lip aquiver, Ray struggled to find his voice. But then, just as he was about to speak, Dora cut him off.

"But then I *did* remember, Raymond," she exclaimed suddenly. "See when I was a little girl, we never had much money for goin to no ballgames or picture shows. But sometimes them moonshiners who used to work them stills out in Bear Bottom, well they'd race they cars up and down them ol' farm roads. Practice makes perfect I suppose, specially when part of your job is tryin to outrun the police with a car full o' shine. Why it was good ol' fashion fun for the whole family, I tell ya. All the workers would come out for a little Saturday night entertainment and bootleg liquor. We'd pick our cars at the startin block and cheer them boys on while they tore it up racin through the corn fields."

"Ok," said Raymond.

"Those drivers was somethin else I tell ya," Dora sighed as the memory unfolded before her. "They had this little maneuver called the bump n' run. Maybe you heard of it? They just give the car in front a little tap from behind, but when you pushin 40 miles an hour, the wheels give out. The car starts buckin like a cart on cobblestones."

"Ok," Raymond muttered, "and what's this got to do with anything?"

"Tell me Raymond," Dora said with a sudden coldness, "you notice any damage on the back bumper of this here Cadillac?"

"Well," Ray began, scratching at his nose. "Now, y'see the car rolled itself when it hit the ditch. There was damage all over. As you'd expect."

"Right, but see, that ain't what I asked," Dora replied undeterred. "What I asked ya was... was there any damage to the back bumper?"

"Well," Ray paused lost in thought, "yes, I reckon there was...but like I was sayin..."

"See that's fascinatin to me. Cus the police say, this buck killed Barett on impact. So, I guess my question is if he's dead on impact, then how is he swervin all over the road like he was on the receivin end of a bump n' run?"

"I don't know what to tell ya."

"Well, ain't that convenient," Dora sneered. "And course, I guess we'll never know now cus you fixed that bumper right up, didn't ya Raymond? Bet they was *all kinda* interestin things you fixed up without so much as askin me."

"Look, I'm just a mechanic," Ray said as he attempted to sidle past Dora. "They brought me a car needed fixin so I fixed it."

With a quick sidestep Dora positioned herself before him and jabbed a finger into his chest.

"*Who* brought the car here Raymond?"

"Tow truck brought it," Raymond fired back.

"And who called the tow truck?" Dora returned quickly. "I didn't call no tow truck. I was down at the morgue identifyin the body. Next thing I know the Cadillac ain't nowhere to be found. A couple days later, I get a call. 'Cadillac's all fixed up.' Sittin in Raymond's shop. Imagine that. Just enough time to buff out the evidence...wipe the whole thing clean."

At this, Dora ran the tip of her finger across the trunk of the Cadillac and showed the result to Raymond. Even surrounded by all this filth and clutter, it was spotless.

"There weren't no *evidence*," Ray declared, folding his arms, "cus there weren't no crime."

"And who told you that Raymond?"

"Look here, this vehicle was brought here by the police. And I did my job under their authority and that's all there is to it."

"So... what?" Dora mused, "They bring you they dirty laundry you clean it up and collect the insurance money is that it?"

"What?" Raymond balked, as sweat streamed down his face. "What the hell are you on about Dora?"

Just then, without warning, a pounding din suddenly reverberated through the air.

"William!" Raymond called out. "What's all that racket?"

But again, the unmistakable sound came crashing through the air. Only faster this time. BOOM BOOM BOOM.

"Hey!" a voice howled just outside. "I'm talkin to you boy!"

Eager to seize his chance for escape, Raymond began edging his way out of the garage to see what all the noise was about. But as he wriggled past, Dora placed a heavy hand on his shoulder, stopping him dead in his tracks. Carefully she removed her sunglasses and waited for his unsteady eyes to meet hers.

"Understand we ain't done here," she whispered gravely. "I'll be seein you again real soon."

Dodging the daggers in her eyes, Raymond slid his spectacles up the bridge of his sweaty nose and continued outside into the sunlight. As he went Dora snorted deep then spat onto the floor where he had stood.

"What the hell's all the racket!" Raymond repeated, shielding his eyes from the sun.

Beneath the blazing light of the service station parking lot, a young man in oil-stained coveralls was hovering just outside Floyd's driver side window. Seeing Raymond fast approaching from the garage the young man shouted towards him.

"I got it under control, Boss. I's just askin this colored what the fuck he thinks he's doin on this here property! This here service station is for whites only! Fellas just sittin here with the engine runnin. He probably means to rob us blind."

Before Raymond could muster a reply, Dora emerged from the darkness of the garage.

"Y'know, I thought that voice sounded familiar."

Dragging his hands from the hood of the car, the young man's face turned with thought as he gazed towards the strange woman approaching him. Beneath the scorching sun he drew back his shoulders and rose to his full height. Towering well over six feet tall and filling out every inch he struck an intimidating sight. But puff himself up as he liked, in the light of day his features were soft and meek. He was still just a boy, covered in acne and fledgling scruff.

"Well, well, well," Dora said, sizing him up. "If it ain't little Willy LeClaire. You done grown up ain't ya boy?"

As the young man took her in a look of realization finally crawled across his face.

"It's William now," the boy said.

"What's that?" replied Dora, placing a finger behind her ear. "Say it with your chest son, I can't hardly hear ya."

"I said it's William now!" the boy shouted.

From beneath her sunglasses Dora raised her eyebrows in feigned interest.

"Well, ain't that somethin," she shrugged taking a few slow steps forward as Will's wary eyes tracked her every movement.

"Easy there big boy," she taunted, sliding a pack of cigarettes from her pocket. "Ain't nothin to fret…That is, less you know somethin I don't?"

"Shoulda figured this colored's with you," the boy spat, "cus that's just your business ain't it, Burleson? Puttin negros where they don't belong."

Dora slid a cigarette from the pack with her lips and drew her lighter.

"Hey, you can't light that thing here!" hollered Raymond. "This a service station!"

Without pause Dora sparked the lighter and brought the flame to her cigarette. Back inside the truck Floyd cranked the window down and leaned out the driver's side.

"Dora, we gettin out of here or what?" he called.

"Just one minute, I'm havin words with lil Willy here," Dora said, pocketing the lighter. "See, this just the kinda boy I was tellin you about. Ain't even been out the house an hour yet, and we found ourselves just what we was lookin for, imagine that."

"No shit," Floyd snorted.

"You got somethin you wanna say?" William jeered.

"Y'know Willy," Dora said, stoking the ember with a deep drag on her cigarette. "I know your Daddy."

"Oh's that right?" the boy laughed incredulously.

"Yeah," Dora replied with a defiant air, "He's a real piece a shit."

Across the lot, Will's wry smile stuttered to a halt as the slight slowly registered in his mind. Shifting his attention from Floyd's truck he now locked Dora in his sights. His eyes seething, he stepped forward from the curb, but like a flash Raymond was in front of him. Wedging his stocky frame in place, Ray set himself like a doorstop against the boy's chest and pushed with all his might.

"Whatcha think you doin boy, get your ass back in the office and shut your mouth," Raymond roared, "I said get, boy!"

"Yeah, that's right," Eudora taunted, "You just a chip off the ol' block ain't ya junior? All bark and no bite."

"You best mind your tongue," Will fired back as Raymond shoved him into the office.

"Or what?" Dora chuckled.

"Leave it!" commanded Raymond.

"Ray, how bout you make yourself useful and pull round the Cadillac?" Dora said. "This has been fun and all, but I got bigger fish to fry. And I got you to thank for it, Willy boy."

Needing no more incentive to get her off the property Ray went to work rummaging through the cluttered office in search of the keys to the Cadillac. For a while William lingered in the office. But soon he drifted back into the doorway. There he leered at Dora until finally he found himself unable to contain his words.

"Y'know your husband got what's comin to him, far as I'm concerned," the boy began, "everybody round here think so."

"Oh lord, here we go," Floyd groaned as he began rolling up his window.

Taking a final drag from her cigarette, Dora dropped it to the pavement and ground it out mercilessly beneath her boot. In the radiant glow of the early evening sun, the two stood facing one another.

"Y'know Willy," Dora began with a wicked smile, "you big in the mouth but I bet just like your Daddy you ain't too big in the britches. Now if you lookin for trouble...I'll give ya some. You ain't gotta keep yappin just c'mon over here and step up to the plate, son. I ain't goin nowhere."

Incensed, the boy began stalking towards her. But Dora stood steadfast. In a quick motion she shrugged off the shawl draped over her shoulder. A cloud of dust rose from the asphalt. In the evening sun the sinister black steel of the Colt .45 holstered at Dora's hip commanded full attention. In a flash she flipped open the clasp restraining the pistol, leaving only a fragile distance between her steady right hand and the draw.

Instinctually, the boy shuddered at the sound. Like the death rattle of a Diamondback lying in wait. Struck with a moment of clarity, William found himself exposed. His pulse pounding, he took a measured step back into the safety of the office. But just as he set foot into the room, an ear-splitting boom rang out. In a moment of hot panic, William seized the blinds and fell crashing to the floor.

As the backfire from the exhaust still rang in distant echoes the Cadillac came growling out into the lot.

Her hand still hanging over the pistol, Dora smiled a big toothy grin as she watched William collect himself behind the office glass. Pulling the car alongside Dora, Raymond went to work cranking down the window before noticing the gun strapped to her hip.

"Hey, hey!" he shouted pointing at the weapon, "gatdam don't even be thinkin bout that! We sittin on a thousand gallons a' gasoline, woman! You'll blow us all to hell!"

"All the same to me," Dora grumbled, turning her attention back towards William. "So...how bout it boy? You wanna show me what kinda man you is?"

As the driver's side door swung open Raymond tumbled out onto the asphalt. Keeping low, he scampered on hands and knees towards the safety of the office.

"Just g'on now Eudora!" Ray hollered once inside. "Just take your car and git!"

"I said how bout it, Willy?!" Dora offered once more.

"You'll get yours soon enough Burleson."

"Oh?" Dora replied. "But you not interested in settlin up now? Cus I got the time."

"Fuck you."

"Yeah, that's what I thought!" Dora spat, dragging her sleeve across her lips. "Willy!"

Her business settled, Dora snatched up the shawl from the ground and tossed it into the open door of the running Cadillac.

"Well ladies," she muttered with a scowl, "a real fuckin pleasure as always."

Easing into the driver seat she slammed the door behind her. With a quick hand she racked the car into gear, pulling forward until she sat face to face with Floyd at the wheel of his truck.

"All set there Floyd?" she asked, with a casual ease.

"Yes m'am," he nodded.

"Alright then, follow me."

Pulling out of the lot Dora revved the engine for the sheer pleasure of raising a little hell. The crackling roar of its power buzzed in her seat and tingled through her fingertips. With delight she stomped on the accelerator as the great wide beast lurched out onto Main Street beneath a cloud of singed rubber and dust. In the rearview mirror Will and Raymond argued in muted tones, gesturing wildly to one another as Floyd soon fell into view just behind.

As the miles rolled by, Dora shifted smoothly through the familiar gears. The wind howled through the open windows. With the long evening light drifting across the dash, the upholstery glowed in strange and golden hues. In the empty passenger side, the gleaming steel of the belt buckles rattled to the hearty aspiration of the engine. Barett had wanted this car more than anything. And though Dora always thought it a bit excessive she had to admit, she always loved riding along with him. Never seemed to matter where they were headed.

Just so long as they were together.

Once back across the tracks on the Black side of town, Dora pulled off onto the first side road she saw. Winding through the desolate flats of tilled cropland she continued until finally rolling to a stop in the midst of a sea of great corn hedges.

Soon after, Floyd's truck came to a stuttering halt close behind. As the old engine hissed and popped from the long journey, Floyd stepped out from the cab and approached Dora. Already leaned up against the Cadillac, she was busy lighting a cigarette.

"Shit, I thought you was gone have it out right then and there."

"Yeah, well," Dora said, snapping her lighter closed. "I ain't even have to pull on em. That Willy LeClaire nearly shit himself when the ol' Caddy came back to life."

"I think he shit hisself the second he saw you comin out the garage," Floyd said with a tired smile. "Boy, looked like he seen a damn ghost."

In the still evening light, the two chuckled softly together, if only for a moment. Though the humidity of the day had not yet broken, something in the way the wind danced across the corn made the world feel a bit lighter around them. Beneath the clear blue sky and the lush green stalks, it felt like one could breathe again. Far away from everyone and everything in town.

Funny how getting away from people can make you feel more human.

Offering her pack of Marlboros, Floyd drew a cigarette as Dora sparked a light. Then, settling against the hood of the Cadillac, the two of them stood enjoying one another's quiet company.

"So," said Floyd, breaking the silence, "let's hear it. Cus you clearly on to somethin that I ain't followin."

"Willy LeClaire," Dora grumbled, shaking her head in disbelief. "You recognize that name?"

"Ain't never seen that Willy boy before, but I sure know the name LeClaire."

"Damn right you do," Dora nodded, "that's cus his father, Lawrence LeClaire, is the head honcho for the Wheaton County Ku Klux Klan."

"And?" Floyd said with a shrug.

"And I think it's mighty interestin that the police brought they dirty work to a shop with blood ties to the KKK," Dora scoffed. "Hell, ain't nobody in town dumb enough take their car to Raymond! That place look like it ain't seen a profit in a thousand years. He's desperate and that's exactly the kinda man the Klan use to cover their tracks."

Pinching the cigarette between her lips, Dora took a sharp drag.

"Y'know only two of them death letters up on Barett's wall is signed," Dora spat. "Both by Lawrence LeClaire. You wanted me to identify the enemy. I say we found em."

"Shit Dora," said Floyd running his hand over his head. "Don't go bitin off more than you can chew here. Cus if you tellin me that the police and the Klan is in cahoots. That's like stickin dynamite to a hand grenade. You keep askin questions, you ain't gone have to find nobody, they gone find you. LeClaire the only name you got...who knows how many more they are."

"I don't give a damn," Dora muttered.

"Well, you should give a damn! That Lawrence he's a real piece of work. Every year in the Fourth of July parade he out there marchin in front of the whole Klan handing out applications. He the only one who don't wear the hood. Thinks he doin God's work. Wants to rid the country of anybody ain't part of his divine white race and he damn proud of it."

"I know," Dora said, staring at her boots, "He'd told Barret that they'd be out to the house payin us a visit if he kept on."

"The Klan got people all over this town. You never know when they eyes is on ya. They want ya to live with that fear."

"Yeah, well," Dora muttered, ashing her cigarette in the breeze. "At the end o' the day it's just a buncha men playing clubhouse. And lucky for me these men bout as bright as a pack of dead lightbulbs. You just got to get your hands on the dumbest one you can find and make em squeal."

As she pushed off from the car Dora began to pace the gravel in thoughtful swaying steps.

"Which brings me to my next point," she began, her arms clasped behind her back. "Y'know who I always see pallin around with that Willy LeClaire boy? Donnie Schneider."

"That dunce that works for the septic company?"

"That's the one."

"Y'know he ain't all there Dora."

"I ain't gonna hurt him," Dora scoffed, "we just gonna have a nice talk is all."

"Well, I just seen your last nice talk," Floyd chuckled. "Didn't go so good."

"Oh, that weren't nothin," Dora said, pitching her cigarette to the ground. "Look, I gotta get back. I'm expectin company. You do me a favor though Floyd, keep your head about ya. I tell ya, these fellas don't know it now, but they gone know somethin ain't right real soon."

"Alright then, Dora," Floyd nodded.

"Alright then, Floyd," Dora said with an easy salute.

Turning to make the short march back to the truck Floyd nursed the last precious puffs of his cigarette before pitching it against the ground. Then, just as reached for his keys a voice called out behind him.

"I appreciate what you done for me today, Floyd," Dora said. "I really do."

Stopping in his tracks, Floyd turned and looked back. Still standing there beside the Cadillac, Dora was staring up into the wide-open sky. Above them, streaks of pink and orange were just beginning to lick out across the horizon as the sun dipped behind a great mass of rolling cotton clouds.

That evening, as the sun yawned long beyond the towering oak trees in the yard, Dora lounged in her old wicker rocking chair on the front porch. At her feet, the Great Danes dozed in quiet little whimpers. In this way, idling away the hours since she'd returned, Dora had watched the shadows cast by the fence as they stretched out further and further beneath the clouds painted in the shifting palettes of dusk. In the trees the Spanish moss swayed aloft in the passing breeze as night made its slow approach like some great creature, old and ancient. Flitting here and there, the mockingbirds filled the final stages of light flashing their white under-feathers and singing sweet and lonesome songs.

Setting her glass down on the side table Dora adjusted the shawl draped over her lap. Between her legs was a fully loaded .38 Special. A snub nose revolver, perfect for getting up close and personal. Quickly, she double checked that the safety was off, then covered it over again.

Just then, off in the distance, Dora swore she heard the unmistakable sound of car tires shambling down the road. With a sudden start, the dogs' heads popped up from the flagstone. Their eyes wide and alert they gazed fixed towards the street beyond the fence.

"Well, I'll be godamned," Dora muttered as a Sheriff's cruiser pulled into view.

For a moment at the stone entryway, the car sat idle. Though she could not make out the person in the driver's seat, Dora could feel their gaze upon her. After a short while, the car began creeping down the drive towards the front porch. Rising to their feet, the Danes yawned and began drifting out into the yard beneath the dying light of day.

"Ay, easy now," Dora said firmly, "come." With tails wagging the Danes soon turned back and sat obediently beside their master. The car still approaching, they nuzzled at her hand, hungry for a treat.

"Down," she commanded.

With a deep groan the dogs settled back at her feet facing out towards the yard. Finally, the car came to a dusty stop in front of the porch. The driver side door swung open. Sheriff Hinkley emerged. Adjusting his gun belt around his ballooning gut he took in a deep snort of air before slamming the door behind him. The polished spurs affixed to his boots rattled with every step. Without a word he slowly moseyed up the walkway. His presence was one of power and intimidation. But Dora was having none of it.

Beneath her sunglasses she remained etched in stone.

"Howdy Ms. Dora," Hinkley finally said, tipping his hat. "Fine evenin ain't it."

"Certainly was."

Unflinching, Hinkley smiled wide revealing a gold framed tooth glinting out from the dark recesses of his mouth. Then, placing both thumbs behind his belt, he raised his boot and brought it down with a hefty stamp on the porch.

    Without reply Dora continued rocking steadily in her chair, squeezing the revolver tight between her legs.

"Well ok then Dora, if that's how it's gone be," Hinkley grumbled, looking out over the pasture. "I's just comin by to…"

"Sure came out your way," Dora interjected.

Removing his old Stetson with a scoff, Hinkley slicked back the thin hair clinging to his skull and fanned himself for a moment before placing it back atop his head.

"Scuse me?" he retorted.

"I said you sure came out your way," Dora repeated, louder this time. "Little late in the day for police business. Or is this business… more personal? Off the record."

"I wish it was, wish it was," Hinkley began, with a modest chuckle. "But, no unfortunately. Y'see, I got a call today, Dora. Said a white-haired woman and her colored accomplice were down round Main Street flashin pistols, threatenin citizens, and generally causin one hell of a scene."

"The police got a call or *you* got a call?" Dora said.

Again, the sly grin flashed the golden tooth.

"Well…in case you forgot," Hinkley said, tapping the badge pinned to his chest, "I am the police, Dora."

"Had me fooled," Dora snapped back. "When Barett died you was a mighty hard man to find. I was callin and callin but they tell me 'Hinkley he ain't got the time.' Murder in cold blood in a little town like Wheaton. But you ain't got the time? You'd think a Sheriff up for reelection be chompin at the bit to get his hands on a case like that. Guess you had better things to do. Course now some dummy pay you a prank call and here you are. Come runnin like a good dog. Guess all I had to do was whistle."

"Dora, you best mind yourself now," warned Hinkley, narrowing his eyes upon her. "Remember who you talkin to. Now I apologize if you disagree with the facts. But darlin that don't change the facts of what happened. Sometimes they ain't no rhyme or reason. Your husband was in the wrong place at the wrong time. Hit the biggest buck outta Wheaton County in ten seasons."

"Yeah and where's that buck now?" Dora prodded.

"It's roadkill Dora," Hinkley pleaded, with an air of offense at the question, "it was disposed of. Now, I looked at all the evidence personally and ain't nothin led me to believe there was no foul play involved. That's just the way it is, you can take it or leave it for all I care."

"Mhm," Dora grunted incredulously. "I guess I'll leave it then."

"Now I understand you upset, Eudora. Hell, I don't blame ya for it. But I can't have nobody, no matter how upset they are, thinkin they can come into my town pullin pistols on everyday folk."

In the yard a gentle wind shifted through the treetops as the Danes lifted their great heads to taste the scent of evening. Standing just before them, Hinkley reached out his hand but instinctively the dogs recoiled from his touch.

"Well, I don't know nothin bout that," Dora grumbled. "I was sat right here with the dogs all damn day."

"Is that right?" Hinkley said resting his great forearms atop his knee. "Now choose your words real careful Dora, wouldn't wanna be lyin to me now."

"I was sat right here all damn day," Dora repeated. "Boy... somebody sure made a fool outta you. Got the Sheriff himself come out here chasin goose with all his *precious* time."

"You sure bout that?" Hinkley fired back. "Cus I got eyewitness says you sped off from Ray's place in Barett's old Cadillac. Matter fact, I think I'll take a gander in your garage to see if I ain't mistaken."

With challenge in his eyes Hinkley drug his bootheel off the porch and began to move around back. Triggered to action the Danes rose to their feet in a flash. Standing like sentinels before him the gentle warmth in their eyes was suddenly gone, replaced by a testy readiness.

"Not before I get a look at a warrant you don't," Dora muttered coolly. "Less... you ain't got one that is?"

Frozen before the Danes, Hinkley snapped his eyes back towards Dora.

"Y'know, I was hopin we could be civil bout this Dora," he seethed between pursed lips. "I really was. Wishful thinkin I suppose."

"Well, if we ain't bein civil what you wanna be instead?"

At this, Hinkley snorted with a genuine amusement. She truly was as feral as they claimed.

"You got me all wrong, Dora. Now I know your husband and I had our," Hinkley paused, searching the air for the right word, "our *disagreements*. But that's because we just two men of principle. Different principles of course, but two sides of the same coin y'understand? Now I didn't come all the way out here to convince you one way or the other. Don't matter none to me. I came here to tell ya I won't be standin for no more trouble from you. That's the bottom line. Not in my town. I catch you walkin my streets with a pistol again, there's gonna be hell to pay. Now that's for your own good, believe me."

"Oh, I don't need nobody lookin out for me," Dora said with a knowing smile. "I can handle mine myself."

"I beg to differ Burleson," Hinkley chuckled, "lonely ol' widow like you, way out here, all by yourself? Boy, I bet the nights are mighty dark out here."

"Dark don't bother me none."

"Well," Hinkley said, his smile fading. "I know you fancy yourself bout as tough as a ten-cent steak, but ain't nothin can survive out here all alone."

At this Hinkley turned his head up towards the sky. Far off in the clouds a pair of vultures soared big arcing circles above them.

"Not even the buzzards," he continued, "I reckon you must be bout two hours from the nearest hospital out here, ain't that right?"

"More or less," Dora grumbled.

"Mhm, more or less. Well suppose somethin happened to ya way out here. Who'd come to help you, Dora? Nobody. Save for the coyotes that is. Course they'd pick your bones clean by sunup."

If Dora was frightened, she hid it well. Hinkley felt as if he was talking to a brick wall. Sensing that an impasse had been reached, he stood tall sliding the leather gun belt back into position below his ballooning gut.

"You just think bout what I tol ya now," he said with a tip of his hat. "And don't be startin no trouble in my town."

As Hinkley walked back towards the car he heard a deep throat clearing rasp followed by a great wad of phlegm splattering against the flagstone behind him. Ignoring the vile display, he moved to the driver side door and opened it. With one boot in the vehicle, he admired the final gasps of sunset before turning towards Dora to deliver a final word.

"Y'know you ain't got a friend in all the world," he said with a wicked grin, "I suggest you don't go addin no more enemies to ya list y'hear?"

"Oh, they's always room for one more," Dora grumbled from her chair.

Hinkley couldn't help but laugh to himself. The audacity.

"Woman, you ornery as hell I'll give you that," he said with a certain glee. "Just like your old man. It's that Burleson blood, I tell ya. Say, how many bullets it take to finally kill your daddy? Somethin like seventeen, if I recall."

"Eighteen," Dora snapped, "and not one in the back, neither. Now get the hell off my property.

CHAPTER VI

BURLESON BLOOD

For all the myth surrounding the man, the only agreed-upon account of Edgar Burleson's character was that he was a profoundly gifted "Knife Man". Though, what exactly the moniker implied seemed to vary based on who was spinning the yarn. Over the years Dora must have heard them all. Each one retold in hushed whispers with the occasional glance over the shoulder, as if the simple act of speaking his name would summon the devil himself.

The stories were never quite the same. And in those twisted retellings who could discern what was fact and what was fiction?

The infamous blade at least, Dora knew to be very real.

Edgar kept it with him always; dangling close and heavy from his belt. In reality it was more akin to a small sabre than a knife. He called it an "Arkansas Toothpick", though Dora couldn't imagine the size of a man who could use it as such, no matter where he was from. Forged from crude hammered steel and a bison bone handle it weighed more than a brick of iron. As a little girl Dora could hardly pick it up with both hands. The rather savage looking spear point blade ran the length of a grown man's elbow to his fingertips, well over a foot long.

As one witness had described it, it was about long enough to be stuck in your front while also sticking out your back.

But while the knife itself was real, Eudora knew that most of the things she'd heard about her father were just stories. Or at least, stories from drunk old men who always seemed to have more teeth than sense. Though, she had to admit, it seemed like everywhere she went her father's name followed right behind like a long dark shadow. The stories may have been far flung but the weight the Burleson name carried in these parts was evident. Over the years, the more Dora thought about it, the more she realized that the tales had to have come from somewhere.

Yet, headstrong as she was, Dora trusted only what she knew for certain. What she had seen with her own two eyes.

And what she saw in the man she called "Pa" didn't seem to fit a single one of the fantastic characters from those stories. The man she knew had a withered leg and had never stood up to anybody in his whole damn life. She'd seen him get chewed out without so much as a scowl on his face. She'd never really seen any of this fire and fury everyone talked about. She'd never seen him hit anyone, except for her. Maybe he was broken. Like a lame horse the owner couldn't bring himself to kill. Just laying out in the pasture waiting around to die. Of course, she told herself this, but try as she might, Dora never could shake one recurring thought from her mind.

All those stories about her father had to come from somewhere. Just like the scars and bullet holes that covered his body.

They had to have come from somewhere.

1886

SHOTGUN WOMAN

Somewhere South of Hidalgo County, Texas.

In the blue dawn of morning, as the solitude of night crept slowly back into its crypt, the eyes of a traveler creaked open from another restless slumber. Shuffling beneath his blanket atop the rocky earth, he was soon struck by a terror known only by the hunted. His body still and motionless, his eyes grew wide. Hot blood flooded his veins. Slithering beneath the blanket, his hand coiled firmly around the handle of a great knife. Flipping open the clasp, he listened and waited. Each muscle in his emaciated body tensed and tightened.

Then, as he surveyed the silence of dawn, when even the birds have not yet begun their chatter, the rustling of some unknown adversary triggered his primal fury.

Drawing the knife with a wild slash he severed the misty morning air. The great knife pointed outwards; he stamped and snorted in circles like a wild mustang. His only desire was to face the enemy. To see the whites of their eyes. To defy them one final time.

"C'mon," he snarled, "c'mon then!"

Behind a thicket of thorny brush, his painted pony watched curiously with ears cocked forward at full attention.

Realizing the sound had only been his horse, the man collapsed to the ground. His head hanging heavy, he ran his swollen tongue over the cracked valleys of split skin peeling from his lips.

For weeks he had been moving at a suicide pace. No time for hunting game or locating water. No fire for cooking or comfort. As a scout in the army, he had learned the hard way that in the blackness of night, light only serves as a beacon for the enemy. And his enemy was closing quickly. For days he had seen no sight of them, but everywhere he smelled their stink in the air. He heard them in the unnatural silence of the wild and the reticence of the birds. A band of shadows hot on his tracks, roughly eight or so, but no more for they moved quick enough to keep up. His flight was one of survival.

A struggle between life and death. Though now the extremes of his escape were beginning to manifest in the gnawing hunger in his belly and the desert laid bare upon his lips.

Looking up, the man gauged his surroundings. Situated atop a slight rise in the flat expanse of wilderness the wily traveler saw a small canyon taking shape just ahead. It was an arroyo. A sun scorched spit of earth covered in dry creeping veins. The dusty remains of where a river had once flowed. Here and there scraggly brush clung to the edges of the arroyo as it trailed down into the canyon. In these badlands even the vegetation was tough. Whether covered in thorns or solid as steel, every bramble and tree and swaying patch of razor grass seemed to stand as a warning. To survive here, one had to be strong. But strength alone is not enough.

He needed water and he needed it yesterday.

If any were to be had it'd be at the bottom of the barrel, the lowest part of the canyon. But in these parts, the traveler knew he wouldn't be the only one seeking a watering hole. And therein lied the problem. He could either die of thirst or die trying to quench it. Of course, such situations were nothing new in this inhospitable land. The trick was weighing the odds. The man reckoned in one, maybe two more days, he'd probably lie down and never get back up. On the other hand, he could make a break for water and run into the very people he'd been running from.

One was certain death…the other, a roll of the dice.

He reckoned that made the decision easy.

As he set about packing up his spartan camp the traveler surveyed the tools at his disposal. One Colt Navy, five bullets, and an enormous blade which some called an Arkansas Toothpick. The measly arsenal wouldn't amount to much in a fight. Aside from his weapons, the remainder of his worldly possessions amounted to a blanket, an empty canteen, the worn boots on his feet, and the dusty cowboy hat he placed atop his head. Packing his equipment into the saddlebags he took the pony by the reins and together they began walking down the bone-dry riverbed as the sun unfurled its first beams of silky light across the desert valley.

In that magic hour, as night relinquishes its hold upon the day, the stars in the sky still shine, even as the brilliant and shifting shades of morning ascend over the horizon. Taking the stage first, pink flourishes drifted across the clouds before washing away into warm hues of orange and gold. In these lands the performance was a daily ritual. The heavens awakening in all their glory. But just as one had enough time to take it in, the colors would slip and bleed into a thousand fiery shades of red. Like Indian paintbrushes upon the first taste of spring. Beneath the symphony of this ethereal display, the traveler walked on, taking constant account of the features of the land in his mind. Close behind the horse limped along, treading wary steps over the jagged rock that paved their way. Watching over them above the brush line, the enormous arms of the saguaro cacti basked happily in the sun, welcoming the light of another sizzling day.

As the riverbed wound its way down the slope, the traveler noted that at one point the side of the fledgling canyon reached a height of nearly twelve feet where the once mighty river had cleaved its way through the stone. Though that had been many years ago now. Just how many he shuddered to think. Soon a great expanse devoid of any shrubs finally shook the man from his meditative steps.

Slinking low he crept forward to get a better look.

Down the slope a piercing light glinted into his eyes so that he had to raise a hand to shield himself. But then, just as a great cloud rolled before the sun, the blinding reflection faded away revealing a paltry pool of stagnant water glistening in the morning light.

At the base of the reservoir, streaked bands cut like scars across the earth where the water line once stood. One could trace the drought month by month as the line inched downwards, descending at last into a dark, fly-infested pool at its base. A thin buzz cut sharply through the air as their silhouettes zipped frantic circles over the water. Rotting varmint carcasses surrounded the putrid pit. Like the weary traveler, they had come from miles in search of life. Only to be dealt the cruel hand of death.

Gathering himself, the traveler considered his next move. If he had found this place, so could others. As the old saying goes, where there is one snake, there is sure to be another. Behind a thicket of brush, the feral man surveyed the area one final time.

His mind made up, he tied off the pony at the base of a mesquite tree, cinched his gun belt round his emaciated waist and fixed the great knife in its sheath behind his back. With a silent swiftness, he rummaged through his pack and removed the old canteen as his tongue ran over his bleeding lips. Crouched low, he looked out one final time.

All was silent and still.

Scurrying out from the brush he made his break. As he reached the edge of the pool the cloud of blackflies scattered as he submerged the canteen into the murky abyss.

Bubbles slowly belched to the surface. He dunked his head, swallowing great gulps of the foul fluid. But as he rose for air, his eyes were drawn to a man suddenly standing just opposite him on the far bank.

He was clad in faded riding chaps and a great wide brimmed sombrero. His dark weathered skin told the tale of his journeys as a sly smile crept over his face. Strapped across his chest was an ammunition belt. He shouldered his rifle and took aim.

Trapped in his sights, the traveler leapt back like a startled armadillo. Gathering his feet beneath him he began to run for the pony, until a voice called out, just beyond the shrubs.

"End a' tha line, Burleson."

Dropping the canteen, Edgar went for his pistol, only to hear in return a sinister chorus of cocking weapons. As his eyes searched the brush, he could just make out the presence of their spectral movements. Black clad forms crouched behind cover. Rifles fixed and ready. How many he could not be certain. Too many.

Alone and exposed in the clearing with only five shots to his name, Edgar knew beyond all hope that he'd been had.

"Now g'on and drop that shooter," the voice called out again.

Looking at the revolver in his hand he considered drawing in one final blaze of glory. One final firefight to deliver himself to the devil upon a storm of hellfire and hot lead. But looking out into the bush Edgar could hardly tell the difference between tree and target. Besides, by the time he drew he reckoned he'd already be dead. Looking to the pistol once more, he thought of turning it to his head. Blowing his brains all over the basin.

But perhaps that was too easy of an out for a life so hard lived.

"Drop it or we gone drop it for you," the voice said, interrupting his thoughts.

In the warm morning air, Edgar Burleson drew a long deep breath. The pistol clattered to the ground.

"Now put your hands high," the voice boomed, "and if you so much as think about movin you'll be dead before you do."

As Edgar raised his hands, the shadows began drifting out from their positions. Behind him the footsteps of the rifle-toting rider began moving cautiously around the reservoir. Closer came the crunching steps until they fell silent just behind him. Without warning he felt the walloping thump of the rifle butt in the small of his back. Dropped to his knees Edgar's frail body folded. His face slammed against the ground. From his cracked dry lips, he drew in and out his final breaths in swirling, stinking, clouds of dust. With bleary eyes caked in filth, he counted the mirage-like forms of five more men moving towards him from the bush. Six in total.

"Strip him," the voice commanded.

At this a hailstorm of blows reigned down upon him. Boot heels, rifle butts, and fists pummeled his withered frame. Claws and knives ripped and slashed the clothing from his body. Driven by instinct alone Edgar clutched at his gun belt. His limp carcass was dragged across the rocks. A fist slammed bluntly into the back of his skull. Fighting for consciousness, he forced his eyes open only to see a man with wild hair pulling the worn boots from his bare feet. With searching hands, he went to draw his blade but found nothing but the bare skin of his naked body.

"Lookin for this?" a voice sneered as the blows finally fell silent.

Opening his eyes Edgar found himself stark naked, lying in the dirt surrounded by the men who'd hunted him for weeks. Towering over him, a man with a scarred face ran his fingers along the length of the blade with a grim satisfaction. Edgar struggled to raise himself to face his executioners but was struck unconscious before he could stand.

By the time he came to, he was not sure if days or minutes had passed.

Lying naked, he looked down and saw the strange sight of his toes half buried in the pale dirt. The vision in his left eye was blurry and obscured casting warped and disfigured shadows upon the ground around him. In his skull a throbbing pain grew more intense with every passing heartbeat. The blood pumped slow and painful through his veins. Everything inside him cried out to lie still. To die in this broken state. But Edgar Burleson refused. He searched the horizon for his hunters but found no trace of them save for the miserable state of his shattered body.

Had they left him? Or was this hell? To wander these great desolate expanses for eternity, naked, starving, and dying of thirst.

Surely, the devil could do better.

"Mornin sunshine."

Turning around, Edgar saw them just before the watering hole. Mounted atop their horses, gazing down upon their prey, the six riders waited in silence. The man who spoke was the same voice who had commanded him to lower his weapon. A surly looking desperado with disheveled hair and yellow rotting teeth. Sucking on a thick pinch of tobacco he spit onto the ground as he shifted in his saddle.

"Almost had ya out in Durango," he continued, "but yer a slippery bastard ain't ya?"

Beneath the roaring afternoon sun Edgar rose as a wake of hungry vultures circled high overhead. In the shaky silence the riders' horses snorted and tossed their heads.

"Y'know there's quite a bounty on your head," their leader grumbled, "but I ain't come all this way for money."

All the while the scar faced rider loaded his pistol with a casual indifference.

"I come to make ya pay for ya sins," the leader continued with a sadistic grin.

Just then a howling wind snapped over the cracked earth.

"You led 50 men into the heart of Comanche country and left em to die."

Stirring in their saddles the men narrowed their gaze upon Edgar. As he opened his mouth to attempt a reply, no words came out. Only a hacking cough of dry blood and dusty air. Upon the horses the men howled with laughter at the pathetic sight before them, until finally a raspy utterance escaped their captive's bleeding lips.

"They dug they own grave," Edgar croaked as his captors fell silent, "I just left em' to lay in it."

In a flash the lead rider drew his pistol and levelled it towards Edgar's heart.

"That were my brother and kin you left to die," the lead rider bellowed, "Way I hear, you ran like a yella coward. So fast not even the braves could run ya down, ain't that right?

Staring down the barrel of the pistol Edgar prepared himself for what was to come.

"Y'see, I didn't come all this way for no bounty," the leader continued, "I come to see if it's true…"

At this, he drew back the pistol's hammer with a mighty metal clack. The other riders unsheathed their weapons with an expectant revelry.

"Well… g'on then, rabbit," the man sneered, "let's see if you can outrun me."

Edgar's body sprung into motion, shedding its trail-weary fatigue for primal adrenaline. Breaking for the brush line his bare feet beat madly over the sunbaked earth. As he dashed across the exposed tract of dry lakebed the crack of bullets exploded around him. A chorus of mad laughter reverberated through the air.

Into the thicket Edgar bolted headlong. Hands outstretched he weaved through the brambles. The brush slashing his bare skin with every stride. He did not know where he was going. It did not matter. In this moment, movement was life. Hesitation was death. The body was in control.

Just behind, the gunfire ceased only to be replaced by the sound of thundering hooves storming across the riverbed. Whooping with glee the riders howled out like coyotes, haunting and shrill. Soon Edgar felt their speed consuming the ground he had covered. Closing in great strides their thunder drew nearer and nearer until he felt their power rattling through his bones.

As he ran, he did not dare look back, for only death awaited. Looking towards the horizon he saw a rise in the plain. A sheer verticality that would be too high for any horse to summit.

He charged on as shots rang out behind him. Whizzing viciously through the brush the bullets cut through the brambles and shattered against the trees.

Edgar's legs burned caustic and bitter. His lungs screamed with pain. He seized the cliff and climbed over the bluff like a man possessed. Once over, he collapsed, gasping for air. But again, Edgar willed himself forward. To stop here was certain death. He surveyed his surroundings. All around the desolate plains stretched on for miles, but there in the distance he saw a miracle.

A weathered old chapel, hardly standing beneath the weight of the sun.

Drawn instinctively to the cover, Edgar broke off into a trot as the sound of the horses in the canyon thundered off in search of an alternate path.

Alone on the open plain Edgar's raving and emaciated frame ran wild. His bare feet, flayed and impaled with all manner of thorns and shrapnel grew numb as his bloody steps painted the ground crimson behind him. His lungs screamed with every stride. Soon a torrent of blood flowed from his nose and mouth. Edgar had experienced this reaction before in horses run past their breaking point. The lungs, strained to their fullest extent, had hemorrhaged and torn. With every gasping breath he spewed clouds of bloody vapor as the gore poured down his chest.

Nearing the decrepit chapel Edgar dared for the first time to look over his shoulder. In the distance, only one rider had closed the gap, charging at breakneck speed across the plains.

The scar faced rider.

Whipping his horse madly he came tearing across the plateau leaving a storm of dust barreling up behind him. Held high in his right hand like a cavalry sabre he brandished Edgar's knife as it glinted savagely in the sun.

The race was on.

Summoning his strength, Edgar charged with everything he had left as the hooves closed in behind him. The rotting shack was so close now. He could see the door, hardly attached to its hinges. The stone chimney. The slumping roof. Behind he felt the carnal heat of the horse drawing nearer. The rolling doom of its hooves signaling his own.

In a matter of moments his severed head would be lopped off in one fell swoop, rolling across the ground. Still blinking back at his lifeless corpse.

Exhausted and at his end, Edgar's stride slowed with loose flopping steps. Coming to a standstill, he drew one final breath as the horse barreled towards him. In that final moment, just as the rider was about to overtake him, he turned to face his fate.

One last act of defiance.

Standing his ground, drenched in his own blood, Edgar stretched his arms wide and roared with all his fury.

Startled by the hideous display, the horse reared in terror as the rider struggled to control the reins. In just a few bucks the scar faced rider was launched into the air until his body smashed against the ground with a bone crunching thud. The horse galloped off towards the horizon.

Delirious, the dazed rider made a hollow move to draw his weapon only to find his hand pinned beneath a bare and bloody foot. Gazing up from the dirt, he saw the crimson stained figure towering over him - a great rock gripped between his blood-soaked hands.

In the silence of the expanse, they stared coldly at one another in a moment that seemed to stretch towards eternity. Then, Edgar hoisted the stone high and caved in his skull.

In the distance the remaining riders dotted the horizon, rapidly approaching on horseback. Edgar fell upon the body, tearing at the gun belt pinned beneath the rider's corpse. The dead weight was limp and immovable. Soon the crack of bullets began kicking up the earth around him. Edgar felt their heat on his skin.

There was no time left.

But there, glinting beneath the dirt, he saw the sheen of his knife. Snatching it up in his hands Edgar tore off towards the chapel as bullets slammed against the outer walls of the rotting timber facade. As the riders closed in behind, they watched their prey's naked and bloodstained body disappear into the shadows within.

Galloping past the corpse of their comrade another volley of shots rang out over the open plains.

"Hold your fire godammit," the lead rider roared. "Christ, he ain't even got a fuckin gun! Spread out! McAllen, get yer ass on that door! He's just one man for godsake!"

Dismounting from their horses, the riders drew their weapons and fanned out around the old chapel. Speaking only with their eyes they signaled to one another in silence as their boots crunched over the ground. Spitting into the palm of his hands McAllen pulled a sawed-off Winchester repeater from its scabbard and cocked the lever.

Flanked by another gunman at his back, McAllen took point and began stalking forward towards the lone entrance.

Creaking upon rusty hinges the door teetered open in the breeze.

Within the pitch-black interior all was quiet save for the drifting particulate passing peacefully through the slivers of light. Drawing a steady breath and levelling his rifle McAllen kicked the door off its hinges and dashed inside. In the absence of sunlight, his eyes struggled to adjust. Suddenly the sound of unseen footsteps came charging across the floor. A cleaving force jostled his arm followed closely by a second, chilling blow.

The sickening pop of sinew and flesh.

The crash of the rifle against the floorboards.

McAllen's breath came quick and shallow. He clutched his arm in the darkness. But there was no arm left to clutch.

In shock McAllen staggered back into his companion who threw him aside mercilessly. A booming shot rang out. In the space where his companion had been, McAllen saw only a crimson cloud hanging heavy in the air. Inside the shack, a rifle lever racked back and forth in succession.

Moments later a second shot rang out; silencing McAllen's screams with a grisly splatter.

In response, a thundering volley of shotgun shelling tore through the chapel. As light poured in behind every blast, Edgar dropped to the floor.

Hanging thick in the air, that old familiar stench.

Gunsmoke and carnage. Iron and fear.

On bare and bloody feet Edgar crept across the floorboards in the darkness. His eyes remained fixed to the door. But in the cracks of light fanning across the room he caught the shadowy silhouette of a rider inching his way around the perimeter of the building. His eyes growing wider, Edgar licked his lips.

Raising the rifle to his shoulder, he centered the target in his sights, and pulled the trigger. In an explosion of wood pulp and red mist another lifeless body dropped.

Just then a figure burst through the doorway with guns blazing. Aimlessly the attacker emptied his bullets into the darkness. A stray bullet buried deep into Edgar's gut. Another bored through his chest. As the smoke settled in the room, his bloodstained figure laid motionless in the corner.

The rider pulled the trigger to finish him, but the pistol clicked empty. Dropping it, he unsheathed a small dagger hanging at his belt. The blade trembled in his hands. With wary steps he approached Edgar's slumped body. As the rider stepped into the light, Edgar saw he was only just a boy, eyes wide with fear.

"I got em," the boy shrieked out the door, "sonuvabitch, I gottem!"

Bathed in black blood Edgar sat with bated breath. Even as the boy stood in front of him, his eyes were hardly open. Traversing the boundary between life and death, he let the boy inch ever closer. Even as the kid was on top of him, Edgar did not move. Not until the boy was so close that he could feel his breath upon his skin.

Like a viper, Edgar struck out in the darkness. With all his strength he plunged his great blade through the boy's knee with a splintering crack. Instantly he was on him. Suffocating his cries. In the blackness Edgar gored at the squirming body beneath him. The blade scraped against bone. The boy's flailing hands slapped helplessly against Edgar's face. A wellspring of blood bubbled from his lips.

Soon the life drained cold and quiet from the kid's eyes. In the aftermath, the chapel fell silent. Feebly, Edgar tried to plug the torrent of blood pouring from his belly. But how much blood could he possibly have left? He scanned the air, listening for the last rider as the singed scent of gunpowder drifted like a fog through the room.

Outside the walls the pop of a match ignited, soon followed by the shattering of a half empty glass bottle.

Flames began creeping across the rotted wood beams of the roof. Another bottle came singing through the entryway splattering liquid flames across the floor. As smoke filled the room, Edgar searched over the boy's body and drew a small pistol from his boot. Snapping open the chamber, six rounds gleamed back at him as the fire rose higher all around. Setting the cylinder into position Edgar took up his mighty knife in hand and gripped the pistol in the other. Impossibly, he rose to his feet and stumbled towards the door. His blood painted the floorboards.

The end was near.

Standing before the blaze, the final rider waited with his guns at the ready.

From the rising inferno strode Edgar's naked body, bathed in blood.

"Die you devil," the lead rider roared, as he steadied Edgar in his sights.

Cracking out across the canyon gunfire peppered the air as the birds scattered from the brush. In the barrage both men bore down on each other without mercy. Bullets tore through both their bodies and in the open, the exchange was short lived. But as the dust cleared and the crackle of gunfire echoed off in the distance the lead rider dropped to a shaky knee clutching the holes in his chest.

In the brief silence of shock, bare, bloody feet stumbled across the ground.

Gathering the strength to look up, the rider saw the ghastly apparition standing over him. Staring into those feral green eyes, the rider watched in disbelief as Edgar drew back the enormous blade before bringing it down like a hammer with a final cleaving thud.

Standing on teetering legs, the burning chapel roared at Edgar's back, sending breathless flames across the open sky.

The knife still clutched in hand; Edgar plodded a few more aimless steps before collapsing to the ground. Gazing up into the clear blue, he watched the buzzards soaring motionless upon the wind.

He welcomed Death with arms outstretched.

But Death would not come.

Time held no meaning as he drifted feverishly between this world and the next. Blinking beneath the sun one instant, the cold moon the next. Time passed. Or did not pass. The world was a mirage soaked in ether.

Only the buzzards were absolute. Hovering hauntingly overhead.

Drifting towards death, Edgar counted their shapes outlined black against the sky.

His breath became shallow and short. He felt cold beneath the blistering sun.

But again, from the blackness, Edgar's eyes cracked open. Roused from death by a strange sensation. It was a scraggly headed buzzard feasting upon a kill. Ravenous, its bald head burrowed deep into a gory chasm, pulling taut a long strand of mangled tissue.

Edgar's leg twitched in convulsions.

Hobbling awkwardly just out of reach the wily scavenger ruffled its dusty feathers and settled, waiting in the distance.

Still, its beady eyes leered hungrily at its meal. Soon it would have its fill.

Passing into unconsciousness, Edgar suddenly snapped awake again.

Gathering his final ounce of strength, he clutched haplessly at his knife. In his final act he'd behead the foul bird when it came for him. Soon enough, a figure shuffled into view.

But this was no buzzard. Rather a peculiar form draped in vivid green and blue.

"¿Qué es esto?" a faraway voice called.

"¿Estás vivo?' the figure whispered.

The light was fading now.

A frail stick poked at Edgar's ribs.

"¿Qué es esto?" the faraway voice repeated.

Footsteps treading softly across sun scorched earth.

"Creó qué es el diablo!"

The blackness was closing in.

A mass of robes, leading a mule.

"No diablo. Es solo un hombre," the voice said, "ayúdame."

CHAPTER VII

THE WALLOWS

In the quiet light of dawn, Eudora shuffled her slippers along the flagstone towards the kitchen. A cigarette dangled unlit from her lips. Close behind, the Great Danes trod with lazy plodding steps as their enormous mouths yawned wide. Pulling a kettle from the cabinet, Dora placed it beneath the faucet and turned the cracked porcelain handles to full bore. From the depths of the sink the sharp scent of chlorine wafted up, curling her nostrils as the water made its gradual shift from cloudy to clear. From the drawer she took a jar of coffee grounds and placed it atop the counter. The heavy glass echoed through the lonely halls of the house.

With a mighty sigh Eudora tossed a few heaping spoons of coffee into the kettle and set it atop the burner. Turning the knob, a gasp of gas creaked from the pipes as a blue flame suddenly snapped to life.

Wrangling back the mess of white hair upon her head, Dora leaned over and lit her cigarette upon the stove.

At her hips, all the while, the Danes wailed soft little cries. Insistently, they poked at the back of her knees with their wet noses. Their long faces sagged expectantly. Their hungry eyes darted from their empty bowls to Dora and back again. A daily morning ritual.

"Alright, it's comin," Dora grumbled as she shuffled across the room.

Trailing her towards the cabinet the Dane's tails beat against the wall in unspoken unison. With all her strength Eudora heaved a giant bag of kibble from the closet. Gathering up their bowls she dipped each one into the bag. Thick bands of saliva dripped from the dogs' drooping lips. Puffing their cheeks with tiny whimpers they sat patiently with eyes fixed on Dora.

Setting a heaping bowl in front of each hound, Eudora leaned back against the counter with her arms crossed. The Danes trembled with anticipation. Still Dora waited. Just like everybody else in this world they had to work for their meals. On the stovetop, the kettle puffed curling clouds of steam as the two parties exchanged wary glances between the cigarette smoke.

"Alright then," said Dora, ashing her cigarette over the sink.

Without a moment's pause the Danes dug into their feed bowls with voracious intent. Watching them with a quiet fondness Dora admired their appetites. In the last few days, she'd lost hers entirely. Coffee, whiskey, and cigarettes seemed to be all she could stomach. And though she hadn't thought about it much since Barett's passing, this was quite unusual for her. Up until a few days ago she'd had what one might call a mortal fear of hunger. The second she felt it coming on a genuine terror would seize her body and soul. Sometimes, just the thought of her belly rumbling could make her ill. For the longest time she'd always carried crackers, or beef jerky, or maybe even a ham sandwich in her bag, everywhere she went, just in case she got caught out too far from supper. Course being who she was she never talked about it. This strange phobia she hardly understood herself.

It was Barett of course, who'd told her a story upon returning from the war that finally put it all in perspective. He always had a way of doing that, understanding her better than she did herself.

Now, the way he told it, his unit has been out on operations around Northern Germany when the men stumbled across an internment camp out in the woods. He recalled the prisoners there were lined up like cattle at the fences. Nothing but skin and bone. More dead than they were alive. In fact, they'd been starved for so long that even when they were liberated the medics only allowed them to eat a little at a time. In their emaciated state, consuming too much too fast ran the risk of rupturing their shriveled stomachs. Barett said those boys hollering for more food from the infirmary was something he'd never forget. Like the screams of the damned.

Barett said even after they'd recovered, that hunger never left their eyes. They could eat an entire Sunday roast but still, that haunted look remained just the same.

It was a look of fear.

The fear of starving to death.

When Dora was a little girl out in the fields, her belly howling and her lips dry, Edgar would sometimes give her a river stone to suck on. An old trick he'd learned to stave off the suffering. But as that smooth stone rattled between her teeth Dora couldn't help but think that perhaps death would be preferable to a life spent wearing rags and sucking stones.

Just then, the kettle began to screech as Dora pulled it from the flame. Grabbing a mug, she swirled the steaming kettle a bit before pouring herself a cup. Coffee grounds and all, right to the brim. She always filled it right to the brim. Not that she was particularly trying to. It just always seemed to happen that way. Barett sure loved to give her guff for it. Each morning he'd be in stitches as she tried to walk that five-foot tight rope from the counter to the kitchen table. With every step the steaming black brew would lap at the edges as Barett watched the comedy unfold with an expectant twinkle in his eye. She'd hardly made it but once without spilling. But she just kept right on because it made him smile. Besides, Barett would always clean it up. Laughing that goofy laugh of his.

Those were good times.

But that was all over. His seat at the table was empty and this time there was no laughter to be had.

As Dora grabbed the scalding mug and stepped around the dogs a great splatter of coffee slapped across the floor. Leaving a trail in her wake, Dora shuffled past the hall just across the kitchen, where a lonely old rotary phone sat beneath a film of dust. In the dim light Dora turned on a lamp and opened a little black notebook atop the counter. Between sipping her coffee, she flipped through the pages and mumbled through the names. In the distance the sound of the dogs licking their bowls clattered like a thunderstorm round the kitchen floor. Her long thin fingers searching over the rows, she finally stopped near the bottom of the page.

J.R. ANDERSON - SEPTIC SYSTEMS INC.

Glancing up from the book Eudora eyed the clock in the kitchen. Nine am on the dot. Snatching the phone off the hook she pinned the receiver between her shoulder and began to dial. With a steady hand she slid the numbers in sequence as the rotary assembly lurched back into position following each entry. As the call was being connected, she grabbed the base of the phone in hand and dangled it gently as the line finally clicked over and began to ring.

After a short while, a gravelly voice answered from the other side.

"Joseph Anderson, Septic Services Incorporated," the voice chimed, "How can I help you today?"

"Mornin Joseph, Dora Burleson here."

"Well howdy, Dora. What seems to be the problem?"

"Well I tell ya, it ain't pretty," Dora said taking a sharp sip of coffee, "suppose a critter or some odd thing musta crawled up into the septic pipe again cus there's shit floodin the field and ain't a single toilet in the whole damn house seems to be working."

"Good lord," Joseph said aghast. "Y'all still runnin the line out to that septic pit in the pasture?"

"That's right," said Dora.

"Y'know that set up ain't ideal. Or, y'know, legal for that matter."

"Well, I didn't install the damn thing, did I?" Dora snapped. "That was your job so don't go straight on me now."

"No, you right. I'm just sayin is all," Joseph stammered, "it's just… y'all so far out there, it ain't no easy job to run all that pipe. Barett insisted I just get it done and sorted. God rest em. He's been in our prayers y'know."

"Yeah, well that's nice and all but how bout some sympathy for the livin? Now, I'm out here all alone and ain't even got a workin toilet. You want me to start diggin holes in the yard or you gonna get somebody out here, today?"

"Dora that's gonna be a hell of a job to get that thing sorted right. We gone have to run pipe all the way out to the interstate," Joseph said with a heavy sigh. "And uh, well I hate to do this to ya but I'm booked up right through August."

Staring out the window, Dora paused for a moment. Across the line she felt Joseph squirming in his seat. Leaving him to stew in the silence a bit longer, Dora finally continued.

"Well, how bout you send that boy you got workin for ya? Just send him round, see if he can straighten out this mess."

"Oh, Dora that boy ain't good for diddly squat. He got less brains than a june bug. Look I'll…I'll try and free up some time next week and maybe I…"

"Mm, mm," Dora chided, shaking her head vigorously. "I ain't gonna make it to next week. Just send that boy round! I need this done today. You mean to tell me he ain't got enough sense to fish a dead possum out a sewer pipe? Even a hog knows how to wallow in shit."

Weighing his options, Joseph paused on the line.

"C'mon Joe," Dora prodded gently, "I need some help out here, please. Just send the damn boy round…"

"Gah, well," Joseph began, stroking his brow with a heavy hand, "well, alright, Dora. Have it your way. I'll send him round first thing. Lord, I shouldn't even let that boy drive the truck, but I reckon you must be in dire straits out there to be callin. Just remember now, you the one asked for this, I can't guarantee…"

"Say no more," Dora declared, "I'm sure the boy will do a fine job. It's mighty appreciated."

"Well alright then, you can expect him round within the hour. And you just let me know if there's any problems, ya'hear?"

"It's mighty appreciated, Joe. I knew you'd come through."

"Alright Dora, buh bye now."

As she hung up the phone, Dora turned to the dogs sitting by the backdoor.

"You hear that boys?" she cooed as their ears perked up, "we got company comin."

Meanwhile, across town at the police station, Clyde Abbott sat at his desk gnawing at his thumbnail. It was a long-standing habit his mother had deemed a 'compulsion of the nerves. But try as he might he never could help himself when thoughts weighed heavy upon his mind. Beneath the table his knee bounced in time as he stared towards Sheriff Hinkley's office. Around the modest police department, a few clerks and bookkeepers worked quietly as the occasional deputy drifted in and out of the backrooms. It was a small operation, none of the fancy doodads of the city departments. Just a bunch of regular folks going about their business. It was the kind of place where everybody knew everybody, for better or worse. Outside the office windows the swaying green leaves of the pecan trees bowed in the breeze. Through the blinds fine slivers of morning light streaked parallel beams across the walls. The day had begun slow, as it did most every day, but on the inside Clyde's blood was all aflutter.

Sat there with both his thumbnails whittled down to stubs he reckoned it was now or never.

Bracing himself with an uneasy breath Clyde rose from his chair and made his way towards the name plastered across the frosted window of the door.

SHERIFF JOHN J. HINKLEY

Inside, obscured by the frosted glass, a large form loomed hauntingly behind the desk. Rapping his knuckles against the door, Abbott turned the knob in hand.

"Hey, Boss?" he said, as he pushed through into the office.

In a hot flurry of activity, Hinkley threw his hands beneath the table as a look of sheer terror fell over his face. But as he realized it was only Abbott standing there in the doorway the panic soon turned to a flush of childish embarrassment.

"Chrissake Abbott," he grumbled irritably, "what's the point of knockin if you ain't gonna wait for no answer? Just get in here, close that door behind ya."

Shutting the door behind him, Clyde watched as Hinkley's hands returned above the desk. Setting down his empty mug he went back to fumbling over the cap to his flask.

"Lord, I was drinkin with the skeletons last night," the old Sheriff muttered, as sweat dribbled down his forehead. "Just a little Texas medicine to get me movin in the right direction."

Overhead a ceiling fan beat slow revolutions as Hinkley wiped his hand against his shirt before finally unscrewing the cap. His eyes hungry, he poured a heavy dose of whiskey into his mug. Still standing by the door Clyde looked out the window sheepishly. He'd seen the old man in this state before, but the last week or so had been particularly excessive, even by Hinkley's standards. As he took a quick swig from the mug, the Sherriff moaned with a satisfied delight as the hot vapors wafted out from his mouth.

"Well," Hinkley grunted, turning his attention towards Abbott, "you come in here to shoot the shit or you got somethin for me? Sit down son, what's on your mind?"

As Clyde moved to take a seat Hinkley cleared the flask from the table with a trembling hand. Tossing it into the drawer a chorus of empty glass bottles rattled in return. With an expectant shrug the Sherriff raised his eyebrows as Clyde eased into the seat across from him.

"Well sir," Clyde began, removing his hat, "suppose I'll get right to it. I've been lookin at the Burleson incident again."

Absorbing these words Hinkley sunk deeper into his chair with a bothered grimace. The folds of his neck fat ballooned out like a toad as he propped his hand beneath the massive weight of his head. Taking in a big breath he scanned his deputy with dubious eyes.

"And why pray tell are you doin that Clyde?" he muttered with an exasperated tone.

"Well, sir. To be honest with you I've been getting calls from Mrs. Burleson."

At this Hinkley's eyes rolled back like a tumbleweed.

"Sometimes she's callin as late as three or four in the mornin," Abbott continued, "most times I'm hardly able to get a word in she's talkin so fast. Tellin me all manner of things. Most of em bout as crazy as you'd expect, but y'know...every once in a while, she'll say somethin that makes a whole lotta sense and uh, well... I just want to make sure we doin our due diligence."

"Due diligence, huh?" Hinkley scoffed.

"Well, yessir," Abbott nodded.

"The case is closed, Abbott," Hinkley said with a careless tone. "Closed. Ain't that due diligence for ya? Hell, there weren't never a time when the case was open! It was a traffic accident, clear as day. Shit, if we launched a godamn investigation every time some dumb bastard crashed his car off the side of the road, we'd be workin till the cows come home."

"I guess what I mean to say is, maybe we missed something," Abbott offered. "That's all."

"Well, you was the one who found the car, Clyde. Maybe you mean *you* missed somethin?"

At this Hinkley chuckled, brandishing a knowing finger. "Ohh, now I see…See she got *you* thinkin *you* missed somethin out there. That it? Is that what's got you all hot and bothered? Don't give it another thought, son. That woman's in your head."

Happy to have settled the matter Hinkley tucked into another slow swig from his mug as Abbott sat before him.

"I ain't questionin what I saw," the deputy declared, "or what I put down in the report."

Smacking his lips Hinkley narrowed his gaze. As he set the mug atop the desk the Sheriff clasped his hands together and leaned forwards onto his elbows. In the silence between them the swooping revolutions of the ceiling fan struck a steady rhythm.

"Then, what are we talkin about here, Clyde?"

Shifting in his seat, Abbott cleared his throat and looked Hinkley square in the eye.

"I feel like my report may not have been thoroughly reviewed, sir."

"Oh Clyde," Hinkley chuckled, "son, that woman has got you turned all upside down."

"But what about the tire marks, Boss? I made notes that it looked like Barett had at least made attempts to regain control of the vehicle. Now that ain't consistent with death on impact. And…and what about the damage to the rear bumper? I collected pieces of broken taillights that matched the Cadillac and delivered them to evidence myself. Now Dora keeps saying over and over, why the damage to the bumper if the collision took place in front of the car?"

"Why!?" Hinkley exclaimed with wide eyes. "I'll tell you why! Cus a gatdamn two-hundred-pound buck smashed through the car Clyde! Christ, you think a deer like that hittin a car at sixty miles an hour ain't gonna cause some collateral damage?"

"But the glass from the taillights was all over the road, boss. Well before the tire marks swerved outta control. Now how could a brake light be busted out before any impact?"

"Ok, Clyde, Ok," Hinkley cajoled, "I guess we'll just have to agree to disagree then. Cus I'm hearin ya and I know all about that glass you collected but it don't scream foul play to me. Now, anything else from you and your crack partner Mrs. Burleson you think I oughta hear?"

"Well," Abbott continued bashfully, "she also claims to have some letters."

"Letters?" Hinkley scoffed slouching back in his chair. Gazing up towards the ceiling, he waved Abbott on, "Ok, let's hear it, Clyde. Can't wait for this one."

"Dora says they've been gettin death threats ever since Barett brought his plans for the Fordham property to that public hearin. Now evidently there were people making serious threats. Folks who wanted Barett dead. And now he's dead. And I'm sayin, from my observations, Dora's theory that maybe somebody run him off the road ain't too far-fetched."

"And where the deer come from Clyde? Did the devil put that there too? Just to fool us?"

"Well as a matter of fact, that's another thing I wanted to talk to you about."

Sitting up a bit in his chair, a newfound curiosity suddenly crept over Hinkey's face.

"Do tell," he prodded.

"Well, I was talkin to my brother the other day and y'know he's quite a hunter hisself. Now he told me the boys down at the lodge was all in a sweat about that buck. Said ain't no way in hell a big boy like that woulda been caught out here at this time of year. But then Earl Callahan says to my brother that none other than Lawrence LeClaire was braggin not a couple days before, that he'd gone up round San Marcos and bagged himself a ten-point buck."

"My god Abbott," Hinkley groaned. "You wastin my time with *this*?! Lawrence LeClaire once told me he caught an alligator gar out the Brazos the size of a fuckin double wide trailer! With his bare hands! That drunk bastard can't tell the difference between the truth and his damn shoestrings. Now tell me, did anybody else get a look at this monster buck?"

"No," Clyde confessed. "But! It matches the description. And Leclaire told the fellas at the lodge he drove that buck right back here to Wheaton County to get the thing butchered over at Prosek's smokehouse."

"So what? He got hisself some venison, that ain't no crime."

"Except I went over to Ol' Prosek's place and he said LeClaire never showed up. So, what'd he do with the deer?"

"Ok, Abbott," Hinkley said, taking a moment to suspend his disbelief, "so...what you tellin me is...in your professional opinion... I should go round up Lawrence LeClaire with no godamm evidence because a buck he prolly never even shot was used to frame up a murder that was really just a car accident. All because Eudora Burleson says she got some letters. Is that about right? That what you tellin me?"

"I'm tellin you, that I think there needs to be further investigation to find what really happened on that road, Sheriff. That's all I'm saying."

"Well, I disagree Abbott," Hinkley spat. "That's what *I'm* sayin. End of story. Now unless you've got any more fuckin conspiracy theories bout flyin saucers or little green men I suggest you get the fuck out my office. Y'know, I got halfa mind to suspend you for this.

Snoopin round behind my back. Lucky for you I ain't got the energy to deal with it today."

Realizing his race was run, Abbott solemnly placed his hat back atop his head.

"Ok then, Boss," he muttered. "If that's the way it is."

'Yep," Hinkley sneered, "that's the way it is."

As he stood from the chair Abbott tipped his hat and made for the door. Behind him Hinkley's drunken ranting filled the room as that familiar top drawer rattled open once again. Closing the door behind him, Abbott felt the eyes of the entire department though none dared to look up from their work. Given the thin walls of the office, he was sure they'd heard the entire exchange. But perhaps it was for the best. The way Clyde figured, it was high time folks started getting a taste of the truth anyhow. Though he'd hardly expected a warm reception, he'd played it right by the book and brought his concerns through the proper chain of command. So why did he still feel so rotten inside?

With these thoughts weighing upon his mind Clyde Abbott walked right past his desk and straight out the front door.

Back at the Burleson residence, Eudora lingered by the great windows in the living room.

Pushing aside the blinds she gazed out towards the road beyond the fence. Aside from the quivering heat waves breaking across the ground, nothing stirred beneath the incendiary sun. Just as the last time she'd looked. And the time before that, only a few seconds earlier.

Idly she paced circular steps around the blue shag carpet with her hands clenched tight behind her back. Here and there she stopped her dawdling to stare at a wall and rehearse her rather rusty pleasantries.

"Oh, really?" she said behind a forced smile, catching her reflection in the glass. "How interesting! Tell me more about that."

Her flexed cheeks felt strange and foreign. The whole act was overblown. Like the ladies in the pictures at the Starlight Theatre. But fools had fallen for less. With a tired groan she buried her head into her hands. She reckoned it'd been two or three hours now she'd been waiting. Her patience dwindling, she rubbed her weary eyes. Suddenly the dogs were standing at attention by the window. Their wet noses nudging inquisitively at the blinds.

Rushing over, Dora threw back the curtains. There in the distance a van puttered up near the fenceline. Inside the cab a rotund figure shuffled in his seat, rifling through paperwork and craning his head out the window. He must have been roaming these backcountry roads for hours.

"The names right there," Eudora grumbled, holding the blinds open between her fingers, "right there, clear as day on the wall you dummy."

After another minute of careful observation, the van moved along down the road, past the entrance, before disappearing behind a line of trees.

"Idiot," she muttered to the dogs, "Joe wasn't kidding. This boy's dumber than a box of rocks."

In a huff Dora set off towards the back door as the dogs followed close behind. Outside the sweltering heat raged as the cicadas roared with delight in the trees. Then, just as Dora set foot on the front porch, the van came backing up along the road. Descending the porch steps, Dora stood in the full light of day waving a red bandana from her pocket.

"Here, you moron," she shouted. "Right here!"

From the window of the van, a boyish face popped out and waved back graciously. Then cranking the wheels down the drive, the vehicle lurched forward in fits until rolling to a stop just before the porch. As she dabbed the sweat from her neck Dora waited beneath the shade of the awning as the dogs laid down upon the flagstone at her feet. In her mind she had acted out this scenario a hundred different ways, but still, she had no idea how this would play out. Would he be hostile, defensive, or just downright rude? Whatever road this visitor was about to take Dora had to be ready to roll with the punches.

But soon as the van door opened, Donnie Schneider was already talking before his feet had even hit the ground.

"Whoo lord, sure glad I seen ya comin down," he hollered. "Boy I was more turned round than a screw in a twister, I tell you what! Ain't never been out round these parts. Didn't know no white folk lived out here. Funny lookin house y'all got. All square like a block or somethin! Ain't never seen me a funny house like this. Say lady, where are my manners, I ain't even introduce myself yet, is you a Miss uh…"

Lost in thought, Donnie tugged on the wiry hairs below his chin. He was quite a big boy. Not particularly strong or anything, just kind of big and soft with chubby cheeks like a baby. At his feet, both his shoes were untied. Atop his head a messy mop of blonde hair exploded out every which way beneath the ill-fitting paperboy cap which bore the J.R. Anderson logo.

A disembodied plunger flying into a toilet.

Licking his lips as his brain ground gears the boy rooted through the pockets of his overalls until he pulled out a wad of crumpled paper. Beneath his furrowed brow he struggled to read the words.

"Miss Barrelin? I mean, Barrelsin?" he mused, "well, anyhow my name's Donnie Schneider, I'm here to fix the lines!"

"The name's Burleson," Dora scoffed, hardly able to believe her luck. "And I know who you are Donnie. I know your momma, son. We played softball together. Betty was the meanest catcher this side o' the Mississippi."

"Oh y'done say? Well, that'd make us good as family then, huh Miss Burson? I'm gonna get you right fixed up, you got my word on that."

"Oh, of that, I have no doubt." Dora sighed, taking in the sad sight before her.

"Good lord," the boy gasped with a start, "would ya look at the size of them dogs! Them's the biggest dogs I ever seen."

"Oh, you like dogs do ya, Donnie?" Dora said.

"Sure do miss," the boy replied with a great big grin.

Somehow sensing the conversation had shifted towards them, the Danes rose to their feet and sniffed the air curiously. The boy smelled of fried ham and buttermilk biscuits. The dogs began to drool.

"They bout as big as them cows out there!" Donnie gushed. "Look like cows too! All black n' white. What you call them dogs?"

"Why these here are Great Danes," Dora said, scratching one behind the ears. "This here's Crockett. That one there's Scout. They may look big but they just big softies."

Then turning to the dogs, Dora asked cordially, "Y'all wanna go say hello to our new friend Donnie here?"

Swaying from side to side the two dogs loped over towards the boy. With heads held low, they licked their chops, sniffing and snorting the ground around him. Kneeling down, Donnie put himself face to face with the Danes and extended a tender hand. Sniffing him all over, their wet noses tickled at his ears and back round his neck. Donnie giggled like a schoolboy. Nuzzling him softly, Crockett's prying snout tipped the hat off the boy's head setting loose the springing mass of wild blonde hair underneath.

"This the best day of work I ever had," Donnie chuckled, picking up his hat from the ground.

Happily, he slapped the dust from the cap and placed it back atop his head.

"Well, you ain't done no work yet," Dora replied, "septic pit's out this way."

"Yes mam!" the boy said eagerly.

Hustling over to the van, Donnie flung the doors open and grabbed a utility belt and a few other strange looking contraptions from the cab. Then, with his tools clutched against his chest he smiled proudly at Dora.

"Lead the way, Miss!"

Stepping out into the sun Dora swiftly pulled a pair of sunglasses from her shirt pocket and put them on. As the two walked along the side of the house Dora could hear Donnie's fumbling footsteps trampling over the scorched grass behind her. Just past the house was a small brick fortification for burning trash, and just further, a long fence dividing the house's mowed lawn from the sprawling grasslands of the pasture. Together they arrived at a little iron gate between the fence boards as Dora unhooked the chains and pushed through. About fifty yards on, they came upon a wide hole in the ground surrounded by a crude barbwire fence.

"This here's to keep the cow's out," said Dora, "just pull it back at the post here."

Confined within the barbed wire perimeter, a stinking sludgy pit of sewage sat stagnant and festering. Were it not for the curious blue pipe protruding from the ground, one might have assumed it to be a bog or some foul watering hole. Over time the pit had grown its own kind of ecosystem. Strange green algaes rose like spires beneath the abyss as the occasional flitting water beetle traipsed gracefully across the surface. But take a step too close and the pit revealed its true nature in the sun roasted stench of festering excrement and urine.

"Alrighty miss," the boy said snapping on a pair of rubber gloves. "You just tell Big Don what's your trouble now?"

"The hell if I know, son," Dora grunted, "That's why I called you. Figured this here problem called for a professional opinion. A man of your caliber. Now, Randy tells me you the best in the business. I say just roll up your sleeves, wade on in, see what you can find."

"Yes m'am," the boy replied with gusto. "You just leave me to it."

"Well, that's what I like to hear," Dora said with a certain amusement. "Tell you what… it's hotter than all hell out here, how bout I go inside and get ya a nice pitcher of iced tea?"

"Why that'd be mighty fine, Miss!" the boy said with glee. "Said it before and I'll say it again, best day of work I ever had."

"Well alright then," Dora shrugged, "If you say so."

As Eudora made her way back to the house, she heard behind her the distinct splash of the boy jumping feet first into a pit full of crap. Looking back over her shoulder, she saw Donnie already waist deep in the crater, ramming his hand up the length of the pipe searching for the obstruction.

"Happy as a pig in shit," she mumbled, shaking her head in disbelief.

At the backdoor the Danes were already pawing at the screen eager to feel the cool relief of the air conditioner. With sad eyes they wailed softly, pushing past her the moment she opened the door. At the refrigerator, Dora stood for a moment relishing the rush of cold air as it washed over her damp and sticky skin. Rifling past the spoiled contents within, Dora brought out a large pitcher of iced tea and set it on the counter. Making up a tray she organized the arrangement on the kitchen table. Momentarily she thought of adding a little jar of sugar, in case Donnie preferred his tea sweet, but remembering her mission she quickly thought better of it.

Perhaps his cherub like disposition had summoned some last vestige of maternal tenderness within her. Though she'd given birth twice, Dora reckoned she'd never been much of a mother. Barett was the one who'd wanted a family. It wasn't so much something Dora desired but rather something that just happened. As a matter of fact, when the kids were born, Dora could hardly bring herself to look at them for quite some time. Odd as it sounds those were some of the darkest days of her life. For years she felt nothing when she held them. Most women love babies more than life itself. To Dora they seemed to be nothing but shrieking, shitting little monsters. But as time passed and the children grew, they became more like Barett with each passing day. They were courteous and polite. Innocent and happy in a way Dora had never been. With all that had happened, she wondered if they could ever be that way again.

Shaking the thought off with a grimace Dora recalled herself to the task at hand. Strange as it seemed, this boy, of all people, had thrown her a bit.

Suppose she had just expected something different. Someone more like LeClaire. A boisterous hothead itching for a fight. Or at the very least a kid with a heavy chip on his shoulder. But Donnie was something else entirely. He was like the three stooges all rolled up into one. A half-wit true, but really just a big harmless kid. In truth, she had planned to make this friend of LeClaire wallow around all afternoon through that septic pit. Let him roast in the summer sun. Sifting through shit on and endless search for an obstruction that didn't even exist. All the toilets were working just fine. Dora had just needed a reason to get him out here, alone. Regardless, she thought the punishment a fine penance for the crime of association. Like something out of a Greek myth.

But at this point, it just didn't seem right.

Donnie was just a dunce. Through and through. And somehow, despite the Burleson's being the talk of the town over the last week, the boy didn't even seem to realize who she was. Of course, that suited Eudora just fine. The less he knew the better. Far as that boy was concerned, he was just out on a house-call to some nice old lady.

And what harm could possibly come of that?

Content with the organization of the serving tray, Dora took it between her hands and pushed through the screen door back out towards the pasture.

In the short journey out to the septic pit, the ice had already melted. But as Dora came upon the barbwire surrounding the pit, she saw no sight of the boy. Perhaps she had underestimated him. Maybe he had a lick of sense after all and made a run for it the moment she'd left. But turning back towards the house she saw the van still parked idle in the driveway.

Confounded as to where he'd gone Dora stood motionless with the tray in hand.

Then suddenly, the boy breached the surface of the stinking cesspool blowing a misty cloud of sewage from his mouth. Stunned, Dora watched with her mouth agape as the boy came crawling out of the pit.

"Christ almighty," Dora scowled as he squirmed onto dry land.

"I ain't find nothin yet, Miss! Boy, you can't see a lick down there, but I'll get to the bottom of it. Say that tea looks mighty fine, thankya Miss Burson!"

Setting the tray on the ground Dora backed away a bit to give the boy some room to air out.

"Go on and serve yourself there, junior," she managed, choking back a gag. "I think maybe I'll just have a cigarette instead."

As she pulled the pack from her pocket Dora slid a cigarette from the box and placed it between her lips. Drawing her lighter she paused for a moment to watch the boy slithering over the grass towards the pitcher like some horrible primeval amphibian. As if it would help, Donnie wiped his hands over his shirt before pouring himself a tall glass. Then, with long gulping swigs he drained the tea in seconds.

"Mmm Mmm!" he exclaimed, running his sleeve across his face.

Shaking her head in silent objection, Dora lit the cigarette, rejoicing in the smooth aroma of the toasted tobacco. As she exhaled a thick cloud of smoke through her nostrils Dora knelt and studied the boy from afar.

"So, tell me Donnie," she began, placing the cigarette between her lips, "what's a boy like you doin pallin around with Willy LeClaire?"

"You know Will?" Donnie said, slapping his knee. "Well, ain't that somethin! That's my best buddy right there. Me and Will been together since we was just a couple small fry. His momma used to drop him round our place and we'd go to school together. But all that schoolin ain't for us though, no mam. Schoolin don't pay! That's why I'm a workin man now."

"You got that right Donnie, and you doin a fine job out here," Dora nodded, "but I bet workin men like y'all gotta blow off some steam every now and again, am I right? Bet y'all some real ladykillers."

Beneath the filth dripping from his cheeks Donnie blushed. "Aw, you know. We just good ol' country boys. Go round the Dairy Freeze, shoot snakes down by the creek. Sometimes Will let me drive his truck out round the dirt lots behind the Drive-In. Y'know we just like to fly by the seat of our pants. Pissin in the wind!"

"Mhm, mhm," Dora nodded following along. "Say, you must know Will's Daddy. Lawrence?"

"Oh sure, sure," Donnie agreed, "Mr. LeClaire. He's alright. Throws me an odd job every now'n'then. Mighty nice of em. Hell, sometime he even let us tag along for brews and barbecue with a bunch of his fellas out east of El Campo."

"Is that right," Dora said, taking a slow draw from her cigarette.

"Oh sure, just a bunch of good ol' boys drinkin and carryin on. Have a big ol' bonfire, get good and drunk."

"Well, now we're talkin," Dora said, "I do love me a good bonfire."

"Yeah, but…it's kinda for the fellas only. A men's club, y'know. Me and Will, we ain't even supposed to be there but Mr. LeClaire said it's alright cus we kin and we hard workers. Says they can always use a few hardworkin boys to fill the ranks."

Pausing for a moment, Donnie looked down at the ground. As if struck by a rare thought, Dora could tell he was thinking mighty hard.

"Say," he continued, "don't go tellin nobody none of this alright? I forgot it's supposed to be secret."

"Oh, course Donnie," Dora said, bringing her finger to her lips. "Men gotta have they secrets. Can't have no ladies around chewin your ear off when you trying to have a good time with the fellas, ain't that right?"

"You said it!" Donnie chuckled, draining his glass. "See you alright, Miss Burson, you alright."

"Well, I think you alright too Donnie," Dora grinned. "Say, I was wonderin who else you see out round these parties? Sounds like they sure get hoppin."

"Oh some nights feels like the whole town's out there!" Donnie said, pouring himself another drink. "Mr. LeClaire he kinda runs things you know. But oh let's see uh Shep Garrett, Dan Harvey, John Morgan, Jeb Stuart, The Heckler Boys, Gerald Ruthers…"

"And what about Sheriff Hinkley?" Dora interrupted sharply. "You ever seen him round one of these parties?"

"Uh," Donnie hesitated, searching his memory, "Well…I reckon he don't come round every time, but y'know I seen him out there once or twice, sure. He usually off on his own with Mr. LeClaire but he don't stay out too late or nothin."

"Well, he's a busy man bein Sheriff and all," Dora said, passing the cigarette to her lips. "What about Clyde Abbott, you ever seen him out at one of these parties?"

"Mmm," Donnie thought, tugging at the whiskers on his chin. "No. Don't reckon I have. Hinkley, he don't think much of that Abbott fella. I know that sure nuff. He thinks he's a dandy or somethin."

"So, what else y'all get up to way out there?" Dora pressed. "Besides the booze I mean. Don't suppose a bunch a rugged men like y'all just out there playin party games?"

"Oh, no, it ain't that kind of party," Donnie laughed, "I don't know, sometime Mr. LeClaire do some kinda preachin or somethin. Gives speeches. Like Sunday school or one o' them tent preachers. Be honest, I can't really follow a damn thing he say he talkin so fast and angry like, but it sure gets them fellas riled up. Between you me and them dogs over there, I ain't hardly listenin. I'm too busy tryin get my hands on a coupla beers before they kick me out."

As the boy guzzled down another glass of tea Dora thought about this comment for a good long while. Lost off in the distance she ran her thumb over her chin in quiet contemplation.

"Why would they kick you out Donnie?"

"Oh, them fellas get all up in a fit and say the youngins gotta get on home. Say they takin the party on the road, and it ain't no business for boys. Shit, I don't ask questions. Just stuff my pockets full a' free beers and get on my way," Donnie chuckled mischievously.

"Mhm mhm," Dora mumbled as she snuffed out her cigarette into the side of an ant mound. "And what do you reckon they get up to when you gone?"

"Beats me," Donnie said casually, "but if I was a gamblin man, I'd say they go round spookin people or somethin."

At this Dora perked up a bit.

"What makes you say that?" she asked, gazing intently at the boy from behind her sunglasses.

"Well," Donnie began, "this one time I was fixin to head out. But 'fore I left I went out in the trees just takin a leak or whatever…suppose they musta thought I was long gone cus soon enough I seen them fellas comin out the house. Musta been oh, two or three in the morning. Pitch black, y'know. Couldn't even see my own damn feet in front my face. But out they came from that house, one after the other, like a long snake or somethin. But listen here, cus this the part it gets scary now," Donnie said, glancing over his shoulder. "So, like I says they comin out the house, right? But every single one of em was all dressed up like *ghosts*. White sheets head to toe, no shit. And they had these big ol' torches in they hands like they was goin' to raise the devil or some odd thang. I tell ya I nearly jumped out my damn skin. Mean, I ain't no yellow belly… but tell ya what that's a hell of a sight to see in the middle of the night. All them white sheets, floatin round in the dark."

Beside them a blackfly droned incessantly. Suddenly, Dora realized her mouth was open. Her mind reeling, she took off her sunglasses and folded them neatly before placing them in her shirt pocket.

"Donnie," Dora said gravely, "You hold that thought right there. I'll be back in a jiffy, you dont go running off now."

"Well, I ain't goin nowhere, Miss," the boy replied scratching his head in confusion. "I just got here."

Quick as she could Dora made her way back to the house. Trampling across the pasture she swung open the fence as her mind raced circles around what she'd just heard. Hinkley and Lawrence LeClaire. Klan meetings at the fringe of town.

As soon as she was out of sight from the boy she broke into a trot.

Back round the house, up the porch, through the backdoor she went. Inside, the dogs stirred from their naps, cocking their ears at the ruckus as Dora tore open a drawer and rooted around inside before tossing out a notebook and a pen. Taking them up against her chest she was halfway out the door before stopping dead in her tracks and turning on her heels. Running down the long hallway towards the bedroom she burst into the bathroom and flushed the toilet three times. Her task complete she sprinted out the back door and made her way back under the garage, over the porch, and down into the front yard. Near the trash barrels she slowed her pace, gathered herself, and collected her breath before strutting out cool as you like into the pasture. As she approached the pit, Donnie was lying by the edge of the putrid pool as bubbles belched to the surface.

"Miss Burson, Miss Burson!" the boy shouted with genuine excitement. "Pipes are flowin! Beats me what I done to fix it, but I reckon I done saved the day!"

"Well would you look at that! My lord Donnie, what can't you do son? I'm gonna have to put in a call to your boss cus I am one satisfied customer."

As the stinking pit produced more bubbles from its depths, Donnie crawled back from the edge and sat with his legs crossed like a child.

"Say Donnie, you already done so much this morning, but could I ask you just one more favor?"

"Name it miss," the boy said triumphantly.

"How bout you run me through them names just one more time."

Over the course of the next hour, Donnie talked and Dora listened.

As fast as her hand could move, she noted everything he had to say about the people he saw, the things he heard, and the monthly meetings that happened like clockwork. The boy, riding so high off his unexpected victory over the septic pit, answered every question with the glee, offering up details that Dora hadn't even considered. As he packed up his tools, he talked. As he walked back towards the van he was still talking. Despite the heinous scent that now clung to his clothes, Dora followed close behind, hanging on his every word while making her studious notes.

As the boy finally loaded up the last bit of gear into the dusty old van, he slammed the door and ripped off a receipt from his clipboard. His soiled hand outstretched towards Dora, he smiled warmly, pleased that he had been able to help.

"You can settle up with Randy whenever you ready," Donnie said, "he says you an important customer, though he says that bout everybody. But y'know I think he really mean it this time! Sure was nice talkin to you Miss Burson."

Taking the receipt in her hand, Dora felt that strange feeling wash over her again. Some faint and foreign remnant of a mother's instinct, perhaps. It passed as quickly as it came.

As she watched the boy climb into the driver's seat and start the car, Dora turned back towards the house. But before setting foot on the porch, she stopped for a moment, and walked back.

Inside the cab, Donnie was busy consulting an old torn road map with a perplexed look on his face. He'd already forgotten the direction from which he'd came. As Dora rapped her knuckles against the glass, the boy rolled down the window.

"Just take a right out the property, a left on the farm road, drive till you hit the interstate," Dora said.

The boy nodded graciously.

"Oh and Donnie," Dora added, "do me a favor alright?"

"Yes miss?"

Looking out across the pasture, Dora watched the cows staring back at her and considered her words with great care. Though it wasn't much her nature she felt it was something she owed the boy.

Flashing a look of warning from her eyes, Dora spoke firmly. "Don't be goin to no more of them parties. You just leave them fellas alone, y'hear? Ain't no good come of what they get up to. You understand what I'm tellin you now?"

"Yes mam," Donnie said with a blank expression.

"Well, ok then," Dora nodded, patting her hand on the hood of the van. "Alright, that's all."

Although the boy smiled back at her she couldn't tell if her words had actually registered inside that hollow mind of his.

Stepping away from the vehicle Dora began walking back towards the porch. In the van Donnie strained the clutch before jamming his foot on the gas sending the vehicle lurching forward. As the engine nearly stalled, a second surge of the accelerator revived it back to life. Puttering up to the entrance, Dora watched as the van wheels slowly turned left.

"I said right, you moron," Dora muttered.

Correcting himself at the last moment with a jerky turn, the boy turned right, disappearing behind the tree line and waving all the while.

CHAPTER VIII

A COLD CALL

As Maybel Thomas stood before the dingy service station telephone booth, she found herself suddenly questioning her own methods. Typically, she wasn't one to second guess herself. But Floyd had been so adamant in his opposition to the whole idea that it'd thrown her off her usual self-assured nature. Even more than she cared to admit. Of course, if Floyd had simply done as he'd been asked, like he said he would, she wouldn't have been in this situation in the first place. Funny how men always fancy themselves such grand leaders but when it comes time to shoulder the yoke, they always act like they got something better to do.

Course, they've got no problem going to war and killing one another but ask a man to have a frank conversation with a woman and suddenly they're shaking in their boots.

All Maybel's life she'd been told that a woman's place was right by her man. And after all this time she reckoned that was probably true. Who else was going to be cleaning up the messes they're always leaving behind? Maybel liked to think that men were sort of like dogs. Creatures with too much strength but not enough sense. One minute they're rooting through the trash, then they're digging up the flower beds, but soon as you give them a well-deserved dressing down you feel downright guilty inside. Though they mean well, they're rather helpless and simple when it comes down to it.

It's just their nature.

That said, every once in a while, you've got to pop the leash to let them know who's boss.

Now it was true that Floyd had told her to leave this business well enough alone. But, on the other hand, Maybel figured *she'd* told *him* to handle it in the first place. So, if he wasn't going to listen, then she wasn't going to listen either. That made things even-stevens in her mind. Besides, what he didn't know wasn't going to hurt him anyhow. This wasn't his battle; he'd made that very clear. Reckon that meant it was hers. And so long as this little phone call didn't touch off World War III in Wheaton, Maybel figured it was well worth a roll of the dice.

Outside the vacant old filling station, a stinging wind whipped across the fields in the distance. Raising her hand to shield her eyes Maybel squinted as the sand fell sharply across her face. Her left hand buried deep in her pocket she busied her nerves fiddling with a folded scrap of paper. Over and over, she turned it between her fingers, unable to determine whether the feeling in the pit of her stomach was that of fear or fury.

At this point probably a cocktail of both.

"Christ, May, it's just a phone call," she mumbled to herself, "ain't like you gettin in the ring with the woman."

Last Sunday at Church the pastor had made it seem so damn easy. As Maybel had sat there with little Jo and Floyd, it was as though the word of God were speaking directly to her. Lecturing the congregation from on high the pastor preached the importance of reaching out to one's neighbor. Lending a hand in the darkest of times. He had said that the act of coming together for a common purpose was the holiest act of all. That there was no deed on earth more natural and beneficial to all of humanity. He had said that was the key to His holy kingdom. Helping your fellow man and allowing them to help you in return. At the time, Maybel had thought that those were very nice words indeed. Sitting there among the pews that morning, surrounded by her friends and family, she had felt something beautiful swelling inside her soul and even called out a mighty Hallelujah.

But now, standing outside the phone booth, beside this dusty little gas station, the magic of those words seemed a distant memory. Behind the pulpit the pastor had seemed so righteous and powerful in his beliefs. As though in all his life he had never encountered an obstacle that the healing words of God could not overcome.

Clearly, he had never met Eudora Burleson.

Pulling out the scrap of paper from her pocket Maybel unfolded it in her hands. On it, scrawled in her own rushed writing was the number to the Burleson home telephone. She had copied it down as quickly as she could from Floyd's papers while he was in the bathroom. Then, she had lied that she was going out to the market with Miss Dubois, and instead had walked a clear six miles in the other direction to this service station on the outskirts of town. It was one of only two working phones in the entirety of the Quarter, and at long last it was sitting right in front of her.

Only now, she didn't much feel like making the call.

Maybe it wouldn't be so bad she tried to convince herself. Maybe Dora would be happy to have someone give her a call. She must be mighty lonely in that house. All alone, with no one to talk to. Maybe she'd even take an interest in the community's plans at Fordham. Anything to take her mind off the grief. For all her fretting it was possible that Dora was sitting right by the phone, just waiting on a ring. Waiting to hear any kind word in this trying time.

The thought gave Maybel a welcome chuckle.

"Yeah," she laughed finally stepping into the booth, "And I'm the Queen a' England."

Once inside, Maybel closed the shutter door behind her though there wasn't another soul in sight. In the hollow calm of the booth, she set down her bag and took a moment to study the telephone instructions. It wasn't that she had never made a call before, but it certainly wasn't something she did very often. And no wonder. Locals calls cost ten cents to connect. Who the hell's got ten cents just to talk to somebody? Back in Maybel's day, conversations used to be free. But fortunately, she had a little trick for just this kind of situation.

When she was a little girl Maybel used to sit with her sisters out in the back alley behind the corner store. Together they'd take pennies and grind them down on the asphalt until it was the size of a dime. There was a real art to it and you had to practice a whole lot to get any good. If you were lucky somebody already had a dime and using that as a guide you'd grind and measure, grind and measure, until you can't tell the difference with your eyes closed. Then when nobody's looking just pop that ground penny in the slot of a vending machine and scamper off with your Coke, or candy bar, cigarettes or what have you. Then, with the grand heist complete, Maybel would sit out in the pasture with her sisters. Drinking their sodas, they'd always laugh thinking about the man who came and cleaned out the coin slots. Poor bastard was probably expecting a small fortune and ended up getting only a handful of useless ground down pennies. Course, Floyd would probably call that stealing. But add that to the list of things he didn't need to know. That's why Maybel had let Jo grind down the penny for her.

After all, it's important to pass knowledge on to the next generation of self-sufficient women.

Now, taking the worn penny from her pocket she slid it into the slot. It was a perfect fit. Jo had done good. Releasing it into the machine the coin clattered down through the maze of metal innards until it rattled to rest with a heavy clink at the bottom of the bin. With her ear pressed firmly into the receiver Maybel listened with anxious intent. For a moment there was nothing on the line and she feared the trick didn't take, but at last a thin hum buzzed to life.

Pinching the scrap of paper between the rotary and the base of the telephone, Maybel began to dial the number with a careful hand.

She quite literally could not afford to make a mistake. After selecting each digit, she waited patiently for the dial assembly to grind back into place before entering the next. The whole process was painstakingly slow. In the fields beyond the service station a dust devil snapped savagely across the empty lot. On the line a phone began to ring. Taking a deep breath Maybel chewed the inside of her lip as the line rang again and again and again for what seemed like an eternity.

Then, just as she had almost given up hope, a clattering sounded in the receiver. A stark and unsettling stillness. Listening on, Maybel's eyes searched from side to side as if lost in the dark.

"Hello?" she offered out into the emptiness.

"What?" a gruff voice croaked back.

"Hello, Missus Burleson? This is Maybel Thomas callin. Floyd's wife?"

There was no response. Maybel couldn't tell if the line was cutting out or if this was how most calls went with Eudora. Regardless, she was determined to press on. She would not be shaken so easily as Floyd had been. This was business, and this business had to be done.

"Hello?" Maybel repeated. "Missus Burleson, you there?"

"I'm listenin," the raspy voice answered back, "ain't no need to yell."

"Oh, ok... well, I'll get to it then," Maybel said standing tall in the booth. "I's just calling because... y'know I done told Floyd to ask you bout this in person. But, course he ain't do it. So, well here we are, and anyways I's callin because I was wonderin if you was plannin on bringin forward them plans for the re-zonin of the Fordham property at the next Town Hall? Y'see they scheduled to put it up to a vote but somebody got to be present or they…"

"Yeah, I know how it works," Dora interrupted.

"Oh," Maybel stammered, "Oh ok... so I s'pose you already on it then?"

On the line Maybel swore she caught the muffled sound of a scoff. Already it seemed the conversation had not gotten off to a cordial start. But at the very least she had Dora's attention. Patiently she bore the silence and waited for her reply.

"I didn't say that," Dora finally offered.

"Oh, well... what are you sayin then?"

"I'm sayin, I know how it works," Dora returned. "Look I been busy alright. I got other things goin on."

"Oh, I bet you have. Floyd tells me you been mighty busy in that house. But see, that's why I'm callin. Cus if you too occupied with all your business to be mindin them Fordham plans...well then I'd be more'n happy to take it off your hands. That way you ain't got to worry bout showin up for no town hall or nothin. Cus I'll take it up there for ya and see that it's handled right. I give you my word."

"Is that so?" Dora pried. "You think it's just easy as that, huh?"

"Well, I don't see any reason why not."

"Hell, I can think of a few," Dora snapped. "Y'know most colored folks steer clear of town. For good reason too. Especially that courthouse, especially with a man like Hinkley runnin things."

"Well, if any white folk want to take my place, they can be my guest. All I'm sayin is if you ain't gone do it, and they ain't fixin to do it, well shit I think somebody oughta do it, don't you? You and I both know if Barett were alive today that he'd be up there leadin the charge."

"Yeah and he'd have got the same result too. They gone laugh you out the building, Maybel. And that's if you lucky."

"Dora, I don't give a goddamn what they do. That's outta my control. But you know what I can control? Makin sure that that measure gets up there in front of everybody, like it's supposed to. I don't care if it ruffles a few feathers. Cus frankly, I'm tired of livin in a town that treats me and my family like we're some kinda animals. After everything we done for this country."

For a moment Maybel considered whether this admission had been too much but the silence on the other end of the line spurred her on.

"I'm gone get up there because it's the only way we can fight back. If you ain't notice there's families out here in the Quarter with no water, no electricity, no nothin who need that land so that they can have a better life. I'm gone get up there because somebody got to. Because it's the right thing to do. Don't you think Barett woulda done the same?"

"First off, it ain't your land," Dora's voice snapped in the receiver, "it's my land last time I checked and I'll do what I damn well please with it. Second, I don't need no lecture on what my husband woulda done by some woman I hardly know. If he'd have kept his nose out of this town's dirty laundry and watched out for his own instead'a everybody else, then maybe he'd still be here right now."

On the line, it was as if a great wind had gone out of Dora's voice as it trailed away to silence. Still, Maybel could hear the rising and falling of her breath, hot with a passion which she had never heard before.

"But, y'know what," Dora's voice began again, "he ain't here. And he ain't comin back to save nobody. I tell ya, ain't nothin good gonna come of draggin that damn proposal up there. They'll never pass it anyhow. I told Barett the same and just look what come of it. It'll kill everythin it touches. It's a godamm curse is what it is."

"Well," Maybel began cautiously, "if it ain't gone pass the floor you ain't got to worry about it do ya, Dora?"

"Look, I ain't got time to tell ya how the world works, ok? You the one who called me. And for what, my blessin? Save yourself some heartache. This ain't worth dyin for."

"Well, alright then," Maybel sighed in the booth. "If that's how you feel about it, then fine. But y'know what, Dora? Before I go I'mma tell you somethin you prolly don't wanna hear. But frankly I couldn't give a shit cus I think you oughta hear it. And if nobody else gone say it then I guess I'll be the one. I'm done bein told where my place is in this town. By them, by you, by anybody. Now I know you think you got dealt a real bad hand in life. And y'know what? You ain't wrong Dora."

Maybel was shocked that she had gotten this far without rebuttal. Briefly she considered pulling back but the words were coming easily to her now and if she didn't unload them at this moment, she knew she may never have the opportunity again.

"But just how many colored folks you think livin out here got dealt hard lives too? Do y'all ever think about that? How many generations of sufferin out here? Only difference between us and you is your hand in life was a stroke of bad luck. Ours was guaranteed. You grew up workin the fields? Well, how many Black folks out here been workin the fields since the day they could walk? Just like you. Hell, longer than you. Barett's death made the papers. Out here, death ain't news. I promise ya ain't no police ever come knockin on our door offerin no help. They too busy roundin up our boys on trumped-up charges and sendin em off to the chain gang in Sugar Land. Y'know most them boys don't ever come back? Worked to death or worse. Buried in the same damn fields they was murdered in without so much as a headstone. Now, you ain't gotta convince me your husband was killed. I'm with you on that. We *all* with you on that. Ain't nobody need to tell *us* how this town works and who's pullin the strings. But I tell ya, Barett weren't the first and he sure as hell ain't gone be the last if we let em slink off like they always do."

"That ain't gonna happen," Dora said hotly.

"It sure will if you drop that measure like they want you to! They killed Barett because they wanted to stop Fordham. To stop Black families from livin too close to their good life. You see that Dora, I know it."

At this point, Maybel expected no reply. Perhaps this too was a losing battle. But much like Fordham, it was one that deserved to be fought.

"Now us bickerin among ourselves is exactly what they want," she continued, easing her tone. "They want us seperated, y'understand? Lookin at our neighbors hopin they just as tore down as us. Peckin like hens bout who got it worse instead of giving it right back to the bastards who put us here in the first place. I mean that's the rub ain't it? Segregated. Just a fancy word for separated. That's exactly what they want! Cus they know so long we stay divided, we weak. We can't fight back and they know it. But together, we can be strong, y'understand? But it's gone take all of us puttin aside this petty shit and comin after em on all fronts. In the places it hurt em most. In public. In front the whole town. Where they got to play by the rules that they invented. And, yes we gone lose some battles. A lot more'n likely. But that ain't nothin new! No matter how many times they beat us down and slam the door in our face we gotta keep comin."

Breathless, Maybel waited for a reply.

"Well, if it's a hero you lookin for he's buried in the Wheaton County Jewish cemetery," Dora muttered. "Cus that's where they're puttin em these days. But you g'on and knock yourself out if that's what you wanna do. It's your funeral. Wonder how you gone do all your do-goodin from six feet underground but I'm sure you'll find a way."

"And what are you gonna do, Dora?"

"I prefer to spend my time on plans that will actually create the desired effect. For what it's worth, go ahead and do whatever it is you wanna do. Just do me a favor and leave me the hell out of it."

"Y'know," Maybel said with a sigh, "it'd break Barett's heart to hear you talkin like that."

"Yeah, well he broke mine so I guess that makes us square."

Slamming the telephone into the hook Dora found herself flush with rage. Against the tiles her feet shuffled with stumbling and heavy steps. Her eyes welled with tears. From the floor the Danes watched her with long faces.

"I need a fuckin drink."

Reaching for the bottle her hand trembled. But it wasn't Maybel's call that remained on her mind.

It was the image of Hinkley, reigning on high from his throne. With his knowing smile and his forked tongue. Dora's stomach turned at the thought of his grand plans coming to a nice, quiet, little end. A perfect victory. All wrapped up in a bow and placed upon his lap. Barett dead with all his work alongside him. The smug look on Hinkley's face when he'd stood there at the funeral. The snake.

But then, an altogether different image arose in Dora mind. The look upon Hinkley's face as Maybel Thomas raises her voice in that courtroom. Oh, the horror that would follow. The outrage. Hinkley would shrivel in his chair like the little worm he was.

In the end, they'd kill the proposal, without a doubt. Without Barett, the dream of Fordham didn't stand a chance. But perhaps, that was half the humiliation. One final act of defiance. Spitting in the face of the conqueror. A great stain upon their victory.

That is, only if Maybel were truly willing to bear the burden. To step forward in front of the entire town and carry that weight for herself required an uncommon fortitude. But Dora knew she could do it.

Because she had just spoken to a woman who would not be denied. And that, Dora could respect.

At that moment, she stopped her pacing. Cocking their heads with curiosity the Danes flopped their tails happily against the flagstone. Slipping a cigarette from the pocket of her house robe Dora snapped open her lighter. Taking a quick draw, she pinned the receiver against her shoulder and dialed a number from memory.

After the second ring an attentive voice answered on the other end of the line.

"Hello, Carl Stanwick Law Office, how may I direct your call?"

"Put Carl on," Dora muttered, ashing her cigarette atop the side table.

"May I ask who's calling?" the voice replied.

"I said put him on," Dora commanded, "now."

"Just one moment."

As the line clicked over, Eudora gazed out the window at the sunset just settling in above the treetops. All through the pasture the grass swayed in shifting shades of red and gold, whipping as the wind played freely across the range. Just atop the ridge leading down towards the creek a small herd of white tail deer rushed along the brush line before breaking towards the water. One by one they disappeared down the narrow cattle trail until finally only one small doe remained. Calmly it surveyed the pasture, craning its neck in all directions as Dora watched its every move from behind a thin haze of smoke. On the line a voice finally answered.

"Carl Stanwick speaking."

"Carl, it's Eudora."

"Well, good evening Mrs. Burleson, how can I be of service today."

"I need to make a change to the will."

"Oh?"

"In the event of my death, the Fordham property goes to Maybel Thomas."

CHAPTER IX

LONESOME TEXAS BLUES

Off a singularly lonely stretch of interstate on the outskirts of the Quarter, there is an unmarked turnoff onto a single lane gravel drive.

The lane looks just like any other, a pale dusty road trailing off into the distance towards nowhere in particular. But if one were to momentarily suspend their disbelief and follow that trail until it disappeared behind the mighty columns of pecan trees, past the rolling farmlands and the derelict old shacks long since abandoned, there'd be a sign waiting in the crossroads that told you all you needed to know.

Suspended from a skinny stake of rusty rebar, clinging on by a dogged chain, an old porcelain sign bore the faded image of a fish with whiskers and a simple arrow directing you to make a left.

Take that left turn down yet another nondescript gravel drive and continue round the bend until the gentle sounds of the mighty Colorado River come just within ear shot. Then, and only then, off to the right in a little thicket you'd catch your first sight of a sad little shack. Assembled with a crude mixture of materials, the building had been thrown together from a mind-boggling assortment of sheet metal, salvaged timber, and the occasional advertisement billboard hammered into place. Beneath the shoddy tin roof, the whole structure slumped to the side, like an old work horse bowed at the back. In the daylight, any sensible person would have kept their distance, for the simple fact that the construction seemed moments from mere collapse.

But in the evenings, when the bullfrogs were just beginning to croak up the air, you'd find a very different place altogether.

Because contrary to the silent heat of the afternoon, the nighttime was filled with conversations. Crickets and all manner of critters chirped and howled, but they weren't the only animals who found solace beneath the moonlight. Like moths to the flame, people came from far and wide to that glowing little shack amongst the darkness. There, silhouetted against the warm light from the windows, their figures stood on the rickety porch smoking their hand rolled cigarillos if they had them, or bumming a puff if they had not. Surrounded by the wilderness, in the sweet relief of dusk, the shabby little construction felt oddly welcoming. The moonlight smoothing out all the rough edges of the day. From inside, the muffled sounds of music thumped steady against the walls, interrupted only by the crashing rattle of beer bottles being hocked from ice buckets. Hung over the front door, an old green locomotive lantern burned bright as moths fluttered close, captivated by its allure.

During the day the building was nothing but a hovel. But come sundown, this was Catfish Charlie's. The only colored bar in all of Wheaton County.

Inside, a regular sight in this old place, Floyd Thomas was busy racking up a set of pool balls on the table. In the corner a dusty radio glowed its amber aura as the receiver crackled and popped before jumping back into the rhythmic and steady thumping of an out of tune guitar. Hanging round the bar, a few working men straight from the fields sipped from big brown bottles, their faces set hard as stone. At the end of the counter a pair of grey old-timers sat close together, holding each other round the shoulders. One of the drunk old men was whispering something to the other who listened intently for a very long time until finally a sly smile crept across his sullen face. From the radio a raspy voice began to sing, backed by the jangling strings of his guitar. The wailing voice was rough as gravel and sweet as syrup. All through the bar it hung in the air thick as smoke. Low and dreary.

Propping his pool cue against the wall, Floyd rolled up his shirt sleeves and ran his arm across his sweaty forehead. Across the table, leaned up against a stool, a big fella with shifty eyes muttered something to himself, cursing his luck. With a sour look on his face he watched Floyd's every move with his arms folded tightly across his broad chest.

"You done fucked up now, Book," Floyd chuckled, taking up his cue. "This table's mine son."

Lining up his shot, Floyd picked out the 9 ball in his sights and with a quick smooth motion rested the pool stick in the split of his fingers. Then, with a mighty crack the ball rattled into the corner pocket as Booker watched with a sick look on his face. His defeat assured; his big shoulders slumped heavily.

"What'd I tell you?" Floyd shrugged, stifling a laugh. "Boy, I tol you didn't I?"

Defeated, Booker rummaged around in his pocket before pulling out a few bits of loose change into the palm of his hand. Picking the lint from between the coins, he focused with an intent brow as his lips lagged just behind his fingers in counting out the sum.

"Ay," interrupted Floyd, laughing from across the table. "You get the next round of beers, and we'll call it even."

With a gracious smile Booker nodded and made his way over towards the bar. Behind the wide wooden slab a few bottles of liquor lined the walls. Some in glass with proper labels, but most in unmarked ceramic whiskey jugs topped with a cork stopper. Call it bootleg liquor, hooch, or shine, here at Catfish Charlie's it was called the house special. Running the show, beneath the warm red glow of neon bulbs, a weathered old man stood wiping down a glass with a dish rag. With fast hands he worked in great sweeping strokes. Pausing for a moment, he held it up beneath the light. Studying the polish with a marksman's eye, he examined it as if nothing else in the world existed, save for that one glass.

Then, finding sudden contentment with his handiwork, the old man slid the glass beneath the bar and snapped his suspenders against his chest with a crack.

"What'll ya have? What'll ya have?" he beckoned with a gruff voice.

"Two beers here, Lou," Booker said, sliding his change onto the counter.

"You gettin cooked over there!" the old man hooted, "I can tell. Don't look good! No suh!"

"You blind as a bat old man," Booker said with a scowl, "you can't see shit."

"I tell ya, I wish I was blind - watchin your sorry ass! Hah!" His laugh was like a slap. Impactful as a wet towel hurled in your direction. Hah! The sound shot out from his mouth with staggering accuracy. It'd hit you clear across the room as though the man was an inch from your ear.

"Hey!" Floyd chuckled, approaching the bar. "Take it easy on em Lou! Pick on someone your own size."

At this, the old man smiled. The only thing he loved more than running his bar was verbally sparring with the customers.

"Big Book about three a' me, but he got the brain of a peanut!" Lou fired back. "What I need round here is a cat with a wit sharp as mine."

Snatching a couple cold beers from the ice bucket Lou popped the tops with a skilled hand and slammed them down on the bar.

"But I ain't gone hold my breath fo' that, no suh! Hah!"

Wincing at the impact of the old man's laugh, Floyd cocked his head to the side. But as the piercing sound faded away and Floyd's eyes dared to creak open, he saw what he'd been waiting for. There, just past the old men at the bar, a familiar figure stood on the porch outlined in the green glow of the locomotive lantern.

"Careful what you wish for ol' man," Floyd warned, grabbing his beer and gesturing towards the door.

Squinting towards the sound of the screen rattling shut, Lou narrowed his gaze on the blurry figure approaching. But before his hazy vision could make out the face, the perfume told him all he needed to know. Like wildflowers in the spring.

"Ho-Lee-Shit," he stammered, as the lines went soft upon his face. "What's the word, little bird?"

"Good to see you too, Lou," Dora replied warmly.

Sliding the stool aside Eudora leaned up against the bar brushing away the cracked peanut shells littered over the tabletop. Taking her in, Lou smiled, though his eyes were filled with a genuine sadness. She looked lovely as always. Wearing one of Barett's old work shirts, a pair of cuffed blue jeans and duster boots. A bandana tied up round her white hair. The only white person in the place. Only woman too. But right at home, nonetheless.

"Yes m'am, good to see you too, sure is," said Lou.

Taking up Dora's hand in his he patted it with an honest tenderness.

"Y'know I was damn sorry to hear it. How you holdin up there Miss Dora?"

"Well, you know me. I got more sympathy than I can stomach, but godamm could I use a stiff drink from one of them magic jugs you got."

"Yes mam," the old man beamed with pride. "I got some of that good Bourbon right here," he said, turning to the bottles behind him. "Got just the thing. Sure to cure what ails. Just a sip a' this here medicine and you'll be feelin right as rain."

From behind the bar Lou took up one of the big whiskey jugs and laid it sideways across his arm. Popping the cork stopper, the aromatic liquor guzzled out from within as the glass filled to a double.

"Howdy Mrs. Dora," Booker said, his sheepish eyes cast down.

Taking up the glass in her hand, Dora tipped it towards Lou who winked back in silent reply. Then, turning round, Dora leaned against the bar and took in the big fella.

"Howdy there, Book. Hope you ain't lettin Floyd collect your paycheck again," she said, taking a quick sip from the glass.

"I almost had em' this time."

"Yeah, I bet."

"Well," Floyd said, taking a seat at the bar, "is he gone show, Dora?"

"Said he was," Dora replied with an uncertain sigh, "but we'll see if he's got the stones."

"Is who gone show?" asked Lou.

Leaving Dora to her drink, Floyd took Booker round the shoulders and gave him a big pat across his back.

"C'mon, Book let's rack em up again. No bets this time, ok?"

As they walked back over towards the pool table, Dora turned to face Lou. She was sure he wasn't going to like the answer, but it was his place after all, and she reckoned he ought to know.

"Who's comin?" the old man repeated.

"Clyde Abbott," Dora said frankly. "*Deputy* Clyde Abbott."

"The law!?" Lou wheezed, throwing up his hands. "Dora, c'mon now! Shit!"

"Oh, he alright. Don't get yourself up in a huff. Course I ain't fixin to call him no ally, but he sure as hell ain't the enemy neither. I got a feelin he knows somethin ain't right with Hinkley."

"Gad-dammit, Dora. I ain't fixin to have no lawman sniffin round this place! I don't give a got damn who he is."

"Look, do it for Barett alright," Dora said, locking eyes with Lou. "Just like he'd a done for you."

Just hearing that name seemed to calm the angry wrinkles tightening upon the old man's face. Settling back behind the bar he chewed it over for a few moments as Dora took another slow sip from her glass. Then, wedging his thumbs into his suspenders he cleared his throat and nodded, without a word.

"Couldn't have met him nowhere in town now, could I?" Dora said with a sly grin. "Surrounded by every rat snake in Wheaton. That's why I wanted to meet here. It had to be here. Outside their reach. C'mon, don't tell me you lost your nerve in your old age, Lou."

"Hey, now," Lou snapped, "gator don't sweat."

"Goddamn right," Dora smiled.

"Shit," Lou grumbled, running his creased hands across his face, "Well, maybe I oughta have myself a little somethin too then."

Pouring himself a short glass from the jug, Lou held it up towards Dora in the warm light of the bar.

"To the man, then," he said.

"To the man," Dora replied.

Together they clinked their glasses as the ancient radio filled the stale air with the dissonant plucking of another sad old country song. Tossing his head back with a snap Lou drained his shot and set the glass bottom upon the bar.

"Lord, I remember the first time that man come in here," Lou said, drifting off towards some daydream. "Barett come walkin in through them doors right over there. That big ol' cowboy hat on his head. Hah! I seen that and I says to myself, 'Shit he must be the law!' White man with a big ol' cowboy hat comin in a colored bar. Figure he mean to bust us up for some thing or another."

Behind the bar Lou's weary eyes gazed long towards the door, watching the scene unfold before him, clear as day.

"But he come right on up. Yessuh, plop that hat right here on the bar. Lord I was ready for trouble, I tell ya. One hand reachin for my shooter, no shit! But he look me right in my eye and says to me, 'Howdy, friend!' Hah! 'Howdy!' he says to me. Big ol' grin on his face. He put his paw out there to shake my hand and I says to myself right then, 'Oh shit the law tryin to pull one over on ol' Lou.'"

At this Lou laughed a great hacking wheeze of laughter. The old death rattle of a man baptized in cigarettes and drink. He laughed so hard even Eudora couldn't help herself from modestly joining in, if only for a moment.

"But no," said Lou, wiping a tear from the corner of his eye, "he weren't no lawman at all was he? I'd never believed it but he was the ringleader of them boys from the Fighting 151st. Floyd, Mac, Tops, Book's old man. Quite the company. Went everywhere together once they got back. I'da never thought. But by god, they got on better than brothers. Like toads on a log, they got right on. I reckon I never seen a white man carry on like that with colored folk. They'd be here into all hours of the night, shootin pool, dealin cards. Havin themselves a good ol' time."

"Bullshit, you call getting stumblin drunk a good ol' time," Dora muttered behind her glass.

"Hee hee, you not wrong there. No mam, not wrong there. But I tell ya, he was A-OK around here though. Just treated ya like a man, y'know? Just looked you right in the eye," as he said this Lou drew up his open hand like a blade, pointing his focus directly into Dora's eyes. "No shit. Just like that. Black, white, brown, no shit. Didn't see nobody for nothin they weren't that man. In here we was just people. Just people and nothin else."

"Yeah well," Dora grunted draining her glass, "sons of bitches come in all colors."

Lou chuckled warmly, taking up the jug of Bourbon "They, sho do. The good ones too, no shit."

Hoisting the bottle Lou poured another generous helping of liquor into Dora's glass.

Just then, a cold silence crept across the room like the chill of death. In the staggering silence only the radio against the wall carried on still spinning that same sad tune. Following the shifting eyes, Dora turned towards the front door. There, smoothing a hesitant hand over his hair, Clyde Abbott stood with hat in hand, his face pale as a ghost. Beneath the weight of their gaze, he cleared his throat and pressed on, nodding a modest smile to the stunned reception.

Without a word of welcome or reassurance Dora watched him come towards her. Pulling out a stool from beneath the bar he set it down and eased into the seat. Across the bar he nodded towards Lou, who reluctantly resumed his task of polishing glass.

"Quite a place you chose to meet, Dora," Clyde said. "Suits you though, I'll give ya that. Man's gotta have some stones to walk past them fellas on the porch out there. Them looks alone was sharp enough to cut."

"Yeah well," Dora grunted. "Guess now you know how they feel."

Pausing to consider the comment, Clyde nodded agreeably.

"Reckon, I do. Still...don't think they much appreciate my kind comin round this place."

"Can ya blame em?" Dora asked, rotating her glass on the bar.

"Well," Clyde said with a heavy sigh, "I'm here ain't I? Came all this way cus you said you got somethin for me. Let's hear it."

Shifting in her seat Dora dug deep into her back pocket and pulled out a folded piece of frayed paper. Turning it over in her hand beneath the light she tossed it on the bar in front of Clyde. For a moment he just stared at it with a blank expression. Already he felt that sinking feeling one gets upon realizing they've been duped. He'd already had it out with Hinkley on her behalf. He'd just driven clear across town for a matter Dora had described as 'of the utmost urgency.' Instead, he was looking at a crumpled piece of paper she had stuffed into her back pocket.

As the radio played Clyde scratched his head with a pained look on his face. Then, with a tired sigh he took the paper in hand and began to unfold it. He reckoned he'd come all this way so at this point he'd might as well see for himself what all the fuss was about.

On the sheet was a list written out by Dora's frantic hand.

At the top, in double underlined emphasis, was the name John. J. Hinkley. But as Clyde's eyes ran down the page from there, his mind began to wander as the list rambled on.

"This is just a buncha names," he said, stroking the scruff of his stubbled cheek.

"That's right," Dora nodded, "the names of the Wheaton County Ku Klux Klan."

She'd said the name so loud that at a booth in the back of the bar an old man choked a bit on his drink. As Dora shot a glance over her shoulder, everyone's attention suddenly snapped back to their tables. Nobody wanted a piece of that conversation. Not even Lou. Behind the counter, cleaning with a newfound fury, he grumbled curses to himself.

"Fuckin shit," he stewed, polishing the glare off a glass.

As Dora returned to her drink somewhere in the bar the old man still struggled to stifle his coughing.

"The klan, huh?" Clyde continued. "Says who?"

Swirling the remaining liquor around the bottom of her glass Dora watched the light as it bent and shifted against the bar.

"A witness," she said calmly. "A witness who seen em with his own eyes. Look here," she continued, tapping on the paper, "that's your boss right up there at the top of the list. Course, he only associates with the Klan's shot callers. Y'know, don't want to get his hands muddy with no common folk."

As he passed his eyes down the list again a sharp focus hardened across Abbott's face. He had to admit, if only to himself, each name did fit the bill. Whether by outspoken affiliation or relative association, there wasn't a single name on the entire list that stood out as particularly surprising. Save for Hinkley, but then again, maybe that wasn't a surprise after all. It was an election year, and these were some of Hinkley's most devoted followers, and more importantly, his biggest donors.

"Who gave you this here list?" Clyde pressed.

Setting her empty glass on the bar Dora scoffed.

"You gotta work with me, Dora," Clyde continued, "I can't help you if you gone fight me every step of the way now."

"You want a drink?" Dora asked, placing a cigarette between her lips.

"I'm workin."

Sparking her lighter Dora drew a deep drag and motioned towards Lou to come over.

"Maybe you should have a drink," she said pointing to Clyde.

"What'll ya have?" rasped Lou.

"I don't want a drink," Abbott said firmly, "I want to know who gave you the list Dora?"

Running a gentle finger across her brow Dora cleared her throat. Then, she exhaled a name so softly that Abbott almost missed it.

"Donnie Schneider."

"Oh my god," Clyde said, breaking into a hopeless laugh. "Of course! You got your big break from a boy who can't hardly spell his *own* damn name. You think this'd hold up in court? Five minutes on the stand and they'd crack that boy like humpty dumpty."

"Well fuck you then," Dora fired back, snatching the list from Clyde's hands, "if you so smart what the hell you turn up, Sherlock?"

"I ain't got shit! But least I know it," Clyde laughed. "Oh, c'mon now don't get yourself ruffled, let me see that list again."

Eyeing him dubiously from behind her cigarette, Dora watched Clyde extend his open palm. Behind a thick cloud of smoke hanging in the air she slapped the list into his outstretched hand.

"By god that boy sang like a canary," Dora said, ashing the ember as Clyde looked over the list. "But y'know what? I reckon these here names and everything else he told me ain't nothin you don't already know. You know where they have them rallies. At the very least you know they havin em."

"It ain't illegal to congregate Dora."

"Don't you dare get smart with me, Abbot," Dora spat behind a sharp look. "The rally is just assembling the troops. It's what they get up to after that I'm talkin bout. How many people you think they've killed, huh? Ain't that illegal? How many colored folk get found dead round here without so much as a fuckin investigation?"

"You gat-damn right," Lou interjected from behind the bar.

"And that goes for everybody in this goddamn town," Dora continued, "all these fine small-town folk. They know exactly what's goin on round here and way I see it you either part of it, you support it, or... you're too chickenshit to do somethin bout it."

"Dora, I am doing somethin about it," Clyde said, "but that's my job, no one else's. Now I appreciate that you been workin on this, honest to God I do, but I'm tellin you this ain't gone hold up in court. You wanna connect Hinkley to the Klan? We gonna need firepower. And by that, I mean hard, iron-clad, evidence. And a secondhand account from a kid who flunked outta junior high ain't gonna cut it in front of a Wheaton County jury. Especially when you tryin to convict the actin Sheriff."

"You missin the point, Abbott," Dora grumbled, shaking her head in frustration. "You got a good heart, but my god, you naive."

As she searched for a better explanation Dora began to get a strange sick feeling she'd heard this all before. Like a scene replayed from a life lived long ago, the characters were different but the story just the same. Empty promises delivered with despondent eyes. The assurances that said all the right words but still left you feeling downright empty inside. It's how people talk to you when they know you haven't got a hope in hell. The first step in the long march towards surrender.

Barett always said, in the heat of battle, most people were quick to give up when darkness outweighs the light. He said the measure of a person isn't how they react when they're up, but how they fight when they're down. Because no matter how hopeless it seems there's always something you can do to turn the tide. More often than not, victory comes with a heavy price. The outcome is decided by those who are willing to pay.

"You tell me we need evidence," Dora began, her words steady and certain. "Well, I'm tellin you, evidence or not, somethin has to be done. You know Hinkley ain't right. I can see it in your eyes, son. Now the Klan got they hand in every corner of this town. Business owners, the county board, the Sheriff's in their pocket. Goddamn, they're killin folks Clyde, just look around ya."

Taking a long sip from her glass Dora welcomed the pain as it burned down in her belly. Around the bar uneasy eyes avoided their conversation as Lou's sad face nodded along to Dora's every word. Beneath the music drifting through the air, there was a heaviness that even the saddest songs could not begin to describe. And though he wanted too, Abbott could not seem to muster a reply.

"So, if you ain't gone stop em now," Dora continued, "then when you think you gone get started? Cus they gettin stronger by the day. Bolder too. They been stackin the rules in their favor for years. Killin their critics. Takin pages right out of Adolf's playbook. Don't you see, they dug in? And if you don't move now it's only gone get harder to root em out. I say we at the point of no return. There ain't gone be another chance."

Lost in her thoughts Dora gazed into the last sip of whiskey remaining in her glass. Bringing it to her lips, she paused, savoring the scent as it singed her nostrils.

"They're a cancer and they need to be cut out."

"Dora, listen to me alright?" Clyde said, shaking her from her thoughts. "If I can't prove in a court of law that Hinkley is doin what you think he's doin, then he's gonna stay right where he is. He's made sure of that. Now I am lookin into it, I give you my word Dora. And look, I weren't gone tell you this… but tomorrow, I'm headin to Austin. The state capitol, straight to the top. And I'm bringin all the evidence I can muster and I'm gone show it to anyone who'll listen and I'm gonna get us some help. Now I will follow this wherever it leads. But you gotta give me time. We gotta play by the rules here."

There they were again. The false promises. Defaulting to procedure and protocols in a hopeless attempt at delaying the inevitable. But for Dora, defeat was no longer an option. She'd already lost more than she could bear.

Suppose every human being on earth has a limit, and Eudora Burleson reckoned she'd had just about enough.

"Oh, to hell with rules. You kiddin me? That's all just a crock of shit made up centuries ago by the same wife-beatin, Black-hatin, land grabbin, tax evadin, evil sons of bitches we dealin with now. They made the rules to give themselves the power. So, they could stay in power! Didn't bother thinkin a nobody else. Ain't nobody gone help you in Austin. You gone get there and get the same runaround you get here. You think they want equality? Ain't we talkin bout the same rule of law that said a woman ain't worth a vote? Same law that said a Black man ain't no man? Well y'know what, I'm sick of what they got to say, and I ain't hearin it no more."

"So, what then?" Abbott snapped. "You think you just gonna take matters into your own hands?"

"Look around Clyde!" Dora said, gesturing around the bar. "Ain't no law in this town! They killed my husband and left his body on the roadside like yesterday's trash. Ain't that against the law? Is that part of your rules? How is it we gotta play fair while they fight dirty? Y'know what, last I checked nobody consulted me on any of this shit. And I sure as hell don't remember agreein to no fuckin rules. Hey Lou! You remember agreein to the white man's rules?"

"Fuck no," Lou fired back.

"You remember agreein to be a second-class citizen in your own god damn country?"

"Hell no," Lou spat.

"Well, there you have it, Abbott," Dora said, snuffing out her cigarette in the ashtray. "Them's the breaks and that's all there is to it."

"So, what then, you just gonna get up in arms and go settle it like Lone Ranger? I'm telling you right now to leave it be. You break the law and I can't do nothin for ya. This is a matter for the police."

"That's where you wrong, Clyde. This ain't a police matter no more. This is war, son. Time for soldiers. Line in the sand just like ol' William Travis said. This ain't the time for sittin on the fence. When it matters, I hope you remember that."

Snatching up the list of names in her hand Dora folded it carefully before tucking it back into her jeans. From the chest pocket of her shirt, she pulled a few bills and placed them down on the bar.

"Mighty good seein you, Lou. That drink was just the ticket. Keep the change."

"Thank ya Miss Dora. You come back soon now, y'hear?"

"Yes sir, I will. You take care."

Easing herself down from the stool Dora hit the ground with a wobble in her legs. As the floorboards bowed beneath her weight the whole room seemed to shift. Lou's magic concoction packed one hell of a punch. Bracing herself with one hand on the bar Dora gathered her legs beneath her and exhaled the burning vapors from her lips.

"C'mon Abbott, walk with me," Dora said, waving him on. "Less you plannin on stickin round for a few while I'm gone."

Readily, Clyde placed his hat atop his head with a disgruntled sigh and tipped it towards Lou.

"Apologies for the disturbance, sir."

Behind the bar, Lou nodded back in silent acceptance as he took up the empty glasses in his hands. Between songs, the radio in the corner hummed a thin static as Dora looked out over the patrons of the bar. The men at the lonely corner booth turned back round towards their warm beers just as her eyes fell upon them. At the pool table, Floyd smiled gently as Booker licked his lips lining up his shot. Just then the dark melody of a jangly 12 string guitar drifted out seeping into the cracks of the floorboards and the absence in conversation.

Halfway to the door, Dora stopped and turned around.

"Who sing this one, Floyd?" she called out. He always seemed to know these things.

"Why, that'd be the man himself," Floyd said chalking up his cue, "Mr. Huddie Ledbetter. The legendary Lead Belly."

Pausing to listen to the haunting voice on the airwaves, Dora felt the words sink deep in her heart. She wasn't much for music but somehow the blues had always spoken to her in a quiet way she'd never truly understood. It sounded like those songs from the field, sung by those families whose hearts were filled with the same kind of hurt she carried in hers.

Strange how some musician you've never met can understand you more than people you've known your entire life. Funny how a few notes plucked along on an old guitar can say everything words cannot.

"Ain't that somethin," Dora whispered.

Then, rousing herself from thought, Dora shot an easy salute across the room towards Floyd before making her way to the exit. Pushing through the screen door she stood for a moment and took in a deep breath of the cool late-night air. Behind her, rocking in their chairs on the porch, silhouetted figures bobbed like buoys puffing on their cigarillos.

"Evenin Miss Dora," they chimed together like a chorus.

"Howdy, there fellas. Nice night for it, huh?"

"Sho is," a gruff old voice replied.

Pressing through the screen door Clyde stepped out onto the porch beneath the glowing green lantern on the wall. As he sidled up beside Dora, he tipped his hat to the gallery just behind, greeting their presence with a quiet, "Gentlemen."

Silently they stared back behind burning embers.

"Can I give you a ride home?" Abbott asked.

"Think I'll walk," Dora replied.

"It's a long way."

"Yeah, well I like walkin."

"Alright, suit yourself."

For just a moment, the two stood together looking out onto the sweeping countryside before them. Hanging high in the sky, the full moon shone brilliantly against the curtains of cloudy haze, illuminating the landscape with its soft pale light. Around them the sounds of nocturnal creatures hummed their haphazard serenade as their songs mingled against the gentle movements of the mighty Colorado River just beyond the trees. Behind them, the chairs continued to rock steady rhythms, in time to the sounds of all things.

Stepping off the porch first, Eudora walked out past Abbott's police car. Following just behind Clyde stopped at the vehicle, watching Dora's figure as it paused to light another cigarette beneath the moonlight.

"You sure you alright to walk?" he called out.

"Oh, don't worry bout me, Clyde. I know these fields like the back o' my hand," she said, holding her fingers up beneath the moonlight, "You just think bout what I told you now."

"Don't go doin nothin you gone regret, Dora," Clyde replied.

Taking a deep drag Dora looked up at the halo around the moon hanging high overhead. Studying it intensely for a moment, she blew a thick cloud of smoke into the air, then returned her gaze towards Clyde.

"Of that you have my word."

Then with the cigarette held firmly between her lips, Dora stuffed her hands deep into her pockets and turned off down the road. As Clyde's rumbling engine turned out of the lot, the beaming headlamps cut a long cast shadow of Dora's figure across the trees. As he passed her by, he tipped his hat and continued on, until his glowing red taillights disappeared round the corner. Walking on to the end of the road, Dora marched straight across the drainage ditch and climbed up the ravine to the fence line. Placing a heavy boot against the lowest beam, she hoisted herself up, careful to avoid the barbwire between the panels. Straddling the top beam, she swung her leg over and hopped down into the sprawling pasture beyond. Gazing up into the night sky, behind the glowing ember of her cigarette, she aimed down her arm towards the heavens until she found the North Star. Orienting herself beneath it, she turned to face home.

South by southwest.

Then, into the darkness, she walked.

Meanwhile, deep in the backwoods of Eastern Wheaton County, beneath the very same moon, an altogether different sort of gathering was well underway.

Before the weathered facade of a crumbling farmhouse a congregation of trucks sat bathed in the light of a towering bonfire. On the lawn the burning beams of timber crackled sinister and cruel as a sweeping wind from the east aspirated the infernal structure. Flames lashed out into the starry night sky. Just outside the intensity of the blaze, a great gathering of men lingered round the light like some primordial ritual. In the reflection of the inferno their savage eyes shone bright as they spat and cursed and drank and drank and drank. Out here, far from the reaches of civilization they ranted and hollered, rejoicing in their freedom with a carnal delight. Shrouded in the darkness their features became indistinguishable, twisted, and obscure. Greeting one another with thunderous slaps across the back they raised their hands and smashed their beer cans together. They howled into the night sky like coyotes. Though the sound was somehow all the more miserable.

Beyond the teeming mass of men gathered in the yard the ragged farmhouse glowed from every window as busy silhouettes passed between rooms. The two-story structure had once been a fine work of craftsmanship, though left only to the hands of time, nature had begun its inevitable reclamation. Vines crept in through the windows. The old rotting beams buckled, pained by a crudely fashioned second story expansion. Teetering upon stilts just off the western facade the haphazard addition remained coarse and unfinished, just as the ramshackle wooden staircase that led the treacherous path towards the door. And though elsewhere revelry raged, this one room remained silent and still. Because everyone knew that when those lights were on, that meant there was business being had.

And when Lawrence LeClaire was handling business, he was not to be disturbed.

Back on the lawn, to the whooping delight of those looking on, young William LeClaire strutted out into the yard with a gasoline canister hoisted upon his shoulder. A lit cigarette dangling from his lips, he basked in the roar of the congregation.

As he stopped short of the blaze, he paused to offer himself before his audience as a deafening confirmation rumbled in return. Then, off-loading the fuel canister to the ground, William spun the lid off and pitched his cigarette. Somewhere among the crowd a barbaric chant began, low and steady.

"Will-yum, Will-yum, Will-yum"

Taking the canister in his hands the boy felt the chorus fueling his strength.

"Will-yum! Will-yum!"

With a mighty heave he slung the gasoline into the inferno as a thunderous boom erupted into the sky.

In the aftermath, as the fireball faded into the night, cheers once again filled the air, echoing out across the miles of untamed wilderness surrounding them. From somewhere amongst the rabble, a pistol shot rang out. William raised his hands towards the heavens. A volley of gunshots peppered the sky. Beneath the moonlight the seething mass squealed with glee. Like a pack of wild dogs, they moved and breathed and thought as one. Their hearts beat proud in their chests, stoked by the flames of the pyre. Like the rising blaze before them, they felt their spirits soar.

Inside the second story office, Hinkley peered out into the yard from behind the curtains.

"Think that boy of yours got a death wish," he muttered.

Across the room behind an old officer's desk, Lawrence LeClaire busied himself over a file bearing the seal of the County Commissioner. Despite his reputation, in the dingy light of the office he wasn't much to look at. In fact, Hinkley had thought him an accountant the first time they'd met. But the moment they shook hands he knew, beneath Lawrence's unremarkable features lurked an altogether different animal. He had a savage cunning about him, as if your safety in the same room with him was never quite assured. He was a man who was always thinking, and that sort of thing has a way of making people mighty uncomfortable, especially in a town like Wheaton. As Sheriff, Hinkley had come face to face with more than a few killers, but still, there was a cold calculation behind LeClaire's pale blue eyes the likes of which he'd never seen before.

"Oh, he just testin his strength," Lawrence grunted, peering down the glasses perched atop the tip of his crooked nose. "Hungry to prove himself. Wants in on our next ride, y'know?"

"Yeah well," Hinkley began, stepping away from the window, "now ain't the time for that. We got enough heat on us as it is. Got my own damn deputy breathin down my neck. I'm startin to think all this Burleson business been more trouble than it's worth."

"That old bitch ain't got a leg to stand on, just like her old man," LeClaire grumbled dismissively, his eyes fixed on his work. "Sides, she sure as shit ain't followin through with Fordham. Town Hall's tomorrow and nobody's filed the paperwork yet. I say let her rot in that house. She'll drink herself dead before the year's up, no doubt in my mind."

As Hinkley eased his weight into an old lounge chair he uncorked a mighty groan. He hadn't been sleeping too good as of late. Though everything seemed to be going well enough along, he had a funny feeling nagging at him he couldn't quite set his sights on.

It was something in the way Dora had looked at him on the evening he paid her a visit.

Hinkley hadn't been able to get their conversation out of his mind. He'd meant to send her a message. A word of warning. But the whole time she looked at him like he wasn't even there. Like she could see right through him.

"Ain't no predictin crazy, Lawrence," Hinkley groaned, running a tired hand over his face. "It's always the snake you ain't see that gets ya in the end. I don't know what she up to but she stirrin the pot round this place. I can feel it in my bones."

"Good, let her stoke the fire then," Lawrence said, closing the file. "Let her get everybody whipped up in a panic. The streets ain't safe! White men bein murdered in cold blood. The Black man's runnin wild! Hell, we'll shout it from the rooftops. But fear not, cus we got just the man for the job!"

Perking up at the mention of his eminence, Hinkley's eyes widened.

"The right hand of God, the fire and the fury. Judge, jury, and executioner. Sheriff Hinkley, four more years!"

"You a real clever bastard you know that?" Hinkley said with a wink.

"Just be glad we on the same side."

"Hell, I'll drink to that," Hinkley croaked reaching for his flask.

Their partnership was one that neither of them had ever really anticipated.

Less of a calculated merger, but rather a merging of paths headed in roughly the same direction. Like minds you could say. The arrangement started simply enough. Hinkley would bail out one of LeClaire's boys for drunken disorderly, or for putting a whooping on some woman or colored, and a few days later Hinkley would get a check in the mail. Small stuff at first, but what folks forget is that over time the small stuff adds up. You go from doing favors to owing favors. Then pretty soon you're the one under the gun. And at that point what option do you really have? In Wheaton, it's said you either work the fields or you work the people. When it comes down to brass tacks, those were really the only two options a man had. From a very young age Hinkley had always wanted to be Sheriff because they call the shots. He'd never really given too much thought to whether he wanted to be a good Sheriff or a bad one, just that he wanted to be one. Truth be told, Hinkley held no regard for service or righteousness, because frankly that wasn't how the real world worked. He'd been around long enough to see that firsthand. It wasn't about justice or oaths or equality or none of that. It was about power. Because that is how the real-world works. Ask anybody. Black, white, rich, poor - everybody knows.

There's only one man you aren't allowed to fuck with and that's the man who wears the badge.

Back downstairs young William LeClaire was busy slithering his way through a crowd of men packed into the kitchen. High off his victory over the bonfire he snatched himself a couple beers from the ice bucket and made his way back outside. As he shuffled past, some of the fellas tousled his hair and slapped him on the shoulders. He was the youngest one there, but still, he hated being treated like a damn kid all the time.

At last, he stumbled outside onto the back porch and settled himself upon the steps. The night air was a welcome relief. In the treetops the Eastern wind was howling, which in these parts meant one hell of a heat wave was on its way. It was nearly midnight now, but the night was young. Before him, in the backyard two bare chested men were wrestling in a ring of dirt as a circle of onlookers cheered them on, cash in hand. As the two drunks battled, their audience watched with frantic and hungry eyes. They wanted victory, yes, but more than that, they yearned for the scent of blood.

Cracking open a bottle against the deck, Will took a long swig of the cold and bitter brew before rooting around through his pants to see if he could scrape together any betting money. He turned out the empty fabric of his pockets. He spat at his luck and returned to nursing his beer. This night was turning out to be a real bust. But at least the beer was cold. Just then, a big fat hand slapped down upon his shoulder. God, he was sick of these fellas pushing him around like their kid brother. Turning back ready for a fight, his fury faded in an instant as he saw Donnie Schneider towering over him.

"Donnie!" he exclaimed. "Where the hell you been, boy! I been waitin for you all night"

"Ah hell, just out making this cash," Donnie grinned, flashing a folded wad of bills, "ain't no big deal."

Dressed in his typical outfit of filthy overalls and untied boots Will found that Donnie struck a rather strange sight holding any money at all. As he jumped to his feet, Will leaned in closer to inspect the cash as Donnie waved it in front of his face.

"Holy shit," Will whispered mesmerized by the bills, "where the hell you get that money! You rob your mama's pocketbook again?"

Unable to contain himself, Will swiped a striking hand towards the cash. But, snatching it out of range at the last moment, Donnie tucked it into his shirt pocket with a big shit eating grin on his face.

"Hell no, I ain't steal it," he fired back. "Ol' man Anderson sent me on a job today. Shit, I done so good he took me for burgers and beers after. Got that ol' man so piss drunk he gave me this here bonus for a job well done."

"Shiiiiit! That's what I'm talkin bout! Musta' been hell of a job to get you a roll like that!"

Stuffing the bills into the center pocket just below his chest Donnie patted his treasure securely.

"I tell ya it weren't even no sweat. I's in and out in an hour flat," Donnie gloated. "Think that old lady had the hots for me too, ooo-wee! Maybe I go back round there and get me some action off the clock!"

"Bullshit," Will laughed, waving him off, "now, I know you lyin you horse's ass."

"I ain't lyin boy! She was all over me! Wanted herself a lil' Schneider sandwich. Served me up some iced tea too. Shit, she wanted to come out tonight to get in my britches, but I told her this here was men only. You know, I tol her 'we handlin men's business out here, lady.' You damn right, that's what I tol her."

"Oh, you fuckin liar," Will chided, shoving Donnie back, "Who was it then?"

"Miss Burson. Or Buren or some shit, hell if I know."

Taking a moment to process, Will stood with his hands on his hips squinting dubiously at Donnie. A sly smile sat upon his lips.

"VanBuren? Rita VanBuren?" Will laughed. "Now I know you lyin that woman tighter than a nun."

"Nah, that ain't the one," Donnie said waving him off, "shit I'd take her for a ride too if she want it though!"

Together the two boys howled with laughter. As Donnie motioned towards one of the beers, Will cracked it open against the railing and placed it in his hand. After a quick clink of the bottles, Donnie took a long guzzle and smacked his lips before uncorking a powerful belch.

"Nah, it was some ol' white-haired lady," Donnie continued, stifling another burp. "Real funny house way the hell out there off the Interstate. Fuck me, took all mornin just to find the damn place."

At this comment, Will's laughter began to fade away as a strange and stern look took its place. Deep in thought, he stared at Donnie as he took another hesitant sip of his beer.

"Say you ain't talkin about... Burleson, now are ya? Eudora Burleson?"

"Hell, I don't know, maybe that's the one," Donnie replied with a careless shrug. "Hey, those fellas takin bets over there or what? My moneys on the big fucker."

But as Donnie began to make his way down the steps Will moved to block his path.

"Hold on a minute," Will said, half laughing, though his gaze was grim and cold. "Are you fuckin kiddin me right now? You was out at Eudora Burleson's place? She's the old bitch that pulled a pistol on me at the service station!"

"Uh," Donnie laughed nervously, "I don't think we talkin bout the same lady."

"White hair, always got sunglasses on, dressed up all fancy," Will exclaimed, gesturing emphatically with every word, "Eudora – Fuckin - Burleson!"

"Well shit," Donnie said, scratching his head. "Guess that's the one. Reckon I ain't never seen her before but she said she knew my mama. She mentioned you too now that I think about it."

In that moment a look of shock ran rampant across Will's face.

"Wait just one godamm minute," Will said, seizing Donnie by the overalls, "weren't you just sayin she wanted to come out tonight?"

"Did I?" Donnie said helplessly.

"You said 'she wanted to come out tonight.' Why would she know about tonight? Y'ain't supposed to tell nobody bout my Daddy's business Donnie!"

"Oh, I didn't say nothin," Donnie mumbled, "we was just talkin…"

"Talkin about what!"

"Well, lotta things I guess."

"Got-dammit," Will seethed, "come on Donnie. Think! Use that fuckin pea brain for once."

As a blank look washed over Donnie's face something triggered inside William. Seizing him by the suspenders the two marched around the corner of the house out of sight from the rest of the gathering. In the dark shadow of the house Will took Donnie in both hands and backed him up against the wall, pinning him against the boards.

"Donnie," he said sternly, pointing a sharp finger, "I ain't messin round now. What the fuck did y'all talk about?"

"I uh…I don't know," the boy stammered. "She was askin bout, uh, what we get up to… y'know? Who come out and stuff. I don't know, just talkin."

"Jesus Christ, Donnie," Will said, releasing his grip. "What the fuck are you sayin right now, Donnie? Why were you talkin to her anyhow!"

"What's got you all worked up?" Donnie grumbled, "Who cares? I said she ain't comin."

"Come on, we gotta talk to Dad."

As Will shoved Donnie towards the office, he found his friend suddenly immovable. Frozen against the wall in the darkness Donnie's shifting eyes searched for an escape.

"Uh...uh, y'know what," he stammered, "maybe, maybe I oughta just get on home."

Grabbing the boy's face by his cheeks Will gazed deep into Donnie's eyes.

"I ain't askin Donnie, this shit is serious. We gotta tell Dad right now. He won't get mad if we tell em but if he find out about this and it ain't from our fuckin lips we are both dead do you understand me?"

"Dead?" Donnie's voice trembled.

"Yes, Donnie! That name not ringing any bells to you? Burleson? As in Barett Burleson? As in public enemy number one as far as the Klan's concerned. Remember the dead guy they pulled out the ditch few days ago?"

"Oh god..."

"Yes, Donnie," Will said shoving the boy. "Use your fuckin brain!"

"Oh my god," Donnie whimpered, searching his recollection. "She tol me not to come."

"What's that?"

"Will?" Donnie mumbled, as tears began to well in his eyes, "I think I fucked up."

"It's gone be alright Donnie, just…trust me. C'mon now…we gotta go see the boss."

Upstairs in the office, Sheriff Hinkley and Lawrence were just wrapping up the business of the evening when they heard the tentative footsteps approaching up the stairwell. Behind his desk, LeClaire swiftly closed the file he had been reviewing and with a steady hand slid it carefully into the back of the drawer.

Expecting a knock at any moment, the two sat completely still as an unsteady silence filled the room.

Just beyond the door, a quiet conversation of anxious whispers could be faintly overheard. Casting a peculiar glance towards Hinkley, LeClaire slipped his hand below his desk, wrapping his palm round the cold grip of a pistol sheathed to the interior. Hoisting himself out of his recliner, Hinkley too unfastened the clasp of his holstered sidearm and made his way to the side of the door. Outside the hurried voices picked up again before falling silent.

With their eyes locked upon one another, LeClaire nodded towards Hinkley who flung the door open. Outside, frozen beneath the hazy glow of the porchlight, William and Donnie stood cowering just beyond the threshold. Rolling his eyes with a heavy sigh Lawrence released his grip on the pistol as Hinkley laughed at the pathetic sight that had given them such a startle. Bringing down a slapping hand behind Donnie's neck Hinkley pulled him into the room as Will followed sheepishly behind, his gaze cast downwards to the ground.

"Ain't nothin but tweedle-dee and tweedle-dum," bellowed Hinkley, smacking Donnie upside the back of his head. "By god boy you smell like shit!"

As he collapsed back into the easy chair Hinkley kicked up his boots up on the coffee table and busied himself spinning his great emerald ring round his pinky. Studying the boys faces Hinkley sucked his teeth as he tried to determine the nature of their visit. As he looked them up and down, something in their mannerisms piqued his interest. Donnie for one, could not seem to control the quivering of his bottom lip. The boy looked like he was about to wet himself. Behind the desk Lawrence sensed something was awry as well. His son's eyes were still glued to the ground.

"The hell y'all doin creepin up the backstairs like that?" LeClaire barked. "You got business for me you bring it to my office like a man. And you best have somethin for me, cus I know y'all ain't eavesdroppin again."

In lieu of a reply, the hum of the bulbs filled the room. Though neither Donnie nor Will could hear it over the blood pounding through their veins. For how long the two stood before this tribunal none could say, but for everyone in the room the moment seemed an endless purgatory. Behind the desk LeClaire shot Hinkley a what-to-do look while Hinkley just chuckled silently at the folly unfolding before him.

Then, unable to endure the silence any longer, William was the first to break.

"Donnie got to tell you somethin."

Suddenly a flush of heat shot through Donnie's face. His pulse was beating so fast he thought he was having a heart attack. He began to break out in a sweat.

"Tell em' Donnie," Will prodded behind pursed lips, "tell em what you tol me."

Shutting his eyes in some desperate attempt to make the scene disappear before him Donnie felt tears trickling in little rivers down his cheeks.

"I tell ya I had about enough'a this already," Lawrence roared from across the room. "Just spit it out boy!"

"He talked, ok!" Will cried, as if the confession would extinguish his fear. "To Burleson! He tol her about our meetins."

His eyes filled with tears Donnie looked at his best friend as though he were looking up from the grave. But William's eyes remained fixed on his feet. As Donnie tried to defend himself, he found his words choked in his throat, held back by some impassable barrier. The walls were closing in.

"She got me all turned round," he finally exploded, "It was all a trick! I ain't know what I was sayin, she's just talkin and talkin, I was just talkin back. I didn't say nothin bad, honest. I swear! Please, I swear."

Gasping for breath, Donnie's shoulder heaved with every blubbering exhalation as Lawrence slowly rose up from his seat. Without a word he made his way out from behind the desk. His pale blue eyes locked on the whimpering boy before him. Though his movements were calm and steady, something insidious burned just beneath his gaze. Unable to look upon him any longer, Donnie's eyes feel to the floor in shame.

Soon, he felt LeClaire's heavy hand as it fell upon his shoulder.

"What did you talk about, son?" Lawrence asked with restraint. "Tell me. It's ok."

"Please, I ain't tell her nothin," Donnie mumbled, sucking for air, "honest."

Sitting up in his chair, Hinkley slowly leaned forward. Deep in thought, he spun the ring around his pinky as his mind began to make the connections.

Burleson.

That woman was like a dog on a scent. But what was she after? Any way you sliced it, it wasn't good. As he too stood up Hinkley's eyes caught a sharp glance from Lawrence. Understanding the command implicitly the Sheriff made his way towards William who gazed petrified at the ground. Taking the boy by the shoulders, Hinkley gave him a hearty pat on the back and walked him towards the exit.

"You done the right thing, son," he said, opening the door and guiding Will towards the flickering light of the stairs. "Now you g'on and let us handle things from here."

In stark contrast to the suffocating mood of the office, outside the revelry of the Klan roared with careless abandon. High in the sky the pale moon cast a haunting glow over the countryside as the bonfire raged upon the lawn. Though he had been here many times before, for the first time William felt utterly and entirely alone. Standing there at the top of the stairs, he may well have been a castaway on some forgotten desert island. Just then a sick feeling rumbled in his belly. But as he turned back towards the office it was already too late. He could only watch as Hinkley closed the door before him.

And though he only glimpsed it for a moment, what he saw would remain forever branded into his memory.

Inside, held in his father's crooked embrace, Donnie's helpless eyes looked towards him as the door snapped firmly shut.

CHAPTER X

BOILING POINT

By sunrise the next morning, a stifling heat wave had fallen over great swaths of the state's Southwestern counties. But in Wheaton in particular, it felt as though hell itself had come to town. Up and down the sun-soaked streets every window with a latch had been flung to the shutters. Like hallow desperate mouths they yawned wide, gasping for the slightest taste of a passing breeze. Even in the shade the pavement sizzled, sweltering and inhospitable. The air bore an oppressive weight. Unseen perhaps but felt undeniably by all. High in the trees and down among the brambles not a leaf dared move. Not a branch bowed. Not even the birds designed to stir for fear of bursting into flames. The sun's incendiary ascent had triggered that instinctual urge hardwired into all living things to curl up into the deepest, darkest cavern one could find to ride out the storm.

The square was a ghost town. The shops sat empty and still. Motionless, save for the quivering heatwaves radiating up from the asphalt.

Inside the Diamond Diner, Frank alone languished miserably behind the counter. He'd never seen the place so desolate. The mere thought of coffee and hot eggs must have made all his regulars sick to their stomach. But still, there he sat, slumped over on a stool like an old hound dog. His head hanging low over a newspaper, he basked in the feeble relief of a rotary fan. A droplet of sweat dangled ever larger upon the tip of his nose. His eyes stumbled over the headlines on the paper, backtracking occasionally as he mumbled along.

Turning the page, sweat splattered across the text, melting the words in front of him into an inky swirling pool.

Just then, the bell above the front door chimed to life. Looking up from his musings Frank was surprised to see Margie Watson standing in the doorway. Turning to check the clock on the wall, he noted the time.

8 am on the dot.

"Boy, I weren't expectin nobody be movin round in this heat," Frank said, peeling himself off the stool. "Not even you Miss Margie!"

Without a word, Margie's feet stumbled along towards the corner booth by the window.

In the deserted diner, each and every footfall echoed against the glass looking out towards the square. Collapsing into the booth, Margie slid over the searing leather bench seat and situated herself beneath the air conditioner as it wheezed in agony.

As she settled in with a blank expression, Frank watched her with a puzzled look. It wasn't like Margie to not even say hello. Yet there she sat. Staring out the window towards the courthouse. From behind the bar Frank cocked his head to catch what she was looking at, but squint as he might everything became a blur out past the parking lot. In the reflection of the glass, he studied her face. It looked sickly and pale. Hollow even.

Behind him on the burner, gentle curls of steam drifted up from a fresh pot of coffee. Taking it up in his hands, Frank snapped a towel over his shoulder and made his way towards the corner booth.

"I say G'mornin there Marge," he said as his footsteps resounded after him.

At the table, Margie remained lost out the window with a trembling hand hovering just over her lips. Baffled, Frank shrugged and began to overturn her mug in its saucer.

But just as the porcelain rattled in place, Margie jumped with a startled shock.

"Ohmigod," she cried, clutching at her chest, her eyes hot with terror. "Oh my god, Frank! You scared the bejeezus outta me!"

As she said this, it was as if a light had come on in a dark room and she realized where she was for the first time. The steaming coffee pot still clutched in his hands; Frank stood frozen in confusion. Her heart still racing, Margie pulled a handkerchief from her blouse and swatted it admonishingly at him.

"Sneaking-up-on-a-lady!" she said, accompanying each word with a stinging swat. "Get-outta-here-with-that! C'mon Frank, I got a bad heart you know that!"

"You the one gone give me a heart attack woman," Frank returned, snatching the handkerchief mid swipe. "You actin squirrely as a hen in a foxhole. I was talkin to ya the minute ya walked in the door! Ain't ya hear? Been starin out there like you waitin on Jesus come walkin cross that square. Now how bout you tell me what the hell goin on now?"

"Oh, I'm sorry Frank," Margie blubbered as her voice faded away with a tremble. "I'm so sorry."

Her gaze drifting out towards the square, she drew in an unsteady breath.

"It's just… I was over at the hospital this mornin…it's Betty's boy. Donnie."

Her hand held over her quivering lips she looked at Frank as tears welled in her eyes.

"He all busted up," she stammered at last, shaking her head in disbelief. "They got him hooked up on all kinds a' machines and he got...pins and needles all up and down his legs, my god Frank it's awful. Said he weren't hardly alive when they got him."

At this Frank set the pot down on the table and eased into the seat across from Margie. Taking the stained towel from his shoulder he offered it to her, but she waved him off with a sweet smile.

"Thank you, honey, I'll be ok," she said, taking in another breath and blowing it out between her pursed lips.

"It's just...Y'know I can't do hospitals no more, not after Wayne," she continued, clutching at the cross around her neck. "God rest em. But I had to be there for Betty. My god she so tore up. Breaks my heart. She won't leave him. That poor boy. She just holdin onto him and cryin. Just can't stop cryin. And Donnie... he all bandaged up. What you can see of em's all black and blue. He got some kinda machine doin his breathin...cus they say one of his lungs ain't workin right."

Choking on the words Margie pressed her hand to her heart and coaxed herself on.

"Said he may not make it. I can't believe it, but that's what they said. We got to give it to God now. It's all we can ever do. Give it to the Lord."

Bringing her hands together in front of her, Margie locked her fingers and murmured soft prayers into the spaces between.

"My lord," Frank said sinking lower into his seat, "what happened Margie?"

"They said he fell," Margie mumbled; her eyes still fastened shut.

"Who said?" Frank asked.

"Well," Margie began, breaking her prayers with a sharp sniffle, "it was Will LeClaire they say brought em in. Round two or three in the mornin. Now the way he tells it they was out boozin and Donnie took a hard fall down a set of concrete stairs. Said he smashed his head somethin fierce against a rail. Then his body just went on tumblin down."

As Margie's lips began to quiver, Frank closed his eyes and buried his chin into his hands. He'd always known Donnie to be a fine boy. A doofus, yes, but sort of like a big puppy dog. And Betty, well she'd been coming into the Diamond for going on thirty years and he just couldn't imagine the hurt that woman was feeling. She loved that boy more than anything on earth. Sat there, Frank just shook his head back and forth unable to find a comforting word.

From beneath her hand Margie's voice continued, "Betty says he come home yesterday evenin before headin out. Says he was all excited cus ol' man Anderson gave em a bonus at work. And he was just so excited, y'know, and he wanted to go out and celebrate. She tol him not to be out too late or go gettin in no trouble. Then fore you know it's past four in the mornin and he ain't turn up home. Now you know Betty. She was up all night worried sick pacin round the house until the phone started up. It's the call every mother fears. The hospital on the line. Told her she need to get over there quick cus they might not be much time."

"God almighty."

"Then Betty called me, I called the girls, and we been over there ever since."

"That's terrible," Frank grunted. "Just terrible."

Outside in the square a black car passed by and the two watched it quietly, grateful for the momentary distraction. But as soon as it came it was gone again and the square was once more still as the tomb. Overhead, the droning rattle of the air conditioner became too much to bear, just as the thoughts weighing upon Margie's mind broke forth from her shuddering lips.

"Oh, he looked awful Frank. Just awful. I can't hardly explain. He just a mess. Look like he got run over by a freight train," Margie said, shielding her face and looking out the window. "Y'know, we talked to the doctor outside," she sniffled, "Me and the girls, while Betty weren't round."

Then, taking a quick glance around the empty diner Margie leaned in, drawing a curious Frank forward as well.

"And between you and me, that Doctor....well, he told us that he don't think no injuries like that could come from fallin down no stairs. He said it look like that boy been through all kinds a hell and he lucky to be alive. Now, I ain't no doctor but to tell you the truth... I agree with him."

"Well, what you think happen then?" Frank whispered.

"I haven't the slightest idea Frank," Margie admitted, blowing her nose. "I really don't. But there ain't a building in all of Wheaton County with stairs that could bust up a boy like that. He'd a had to fall down the damn Empire State building. I can't explain it. But all we know for certain is he went out to one of Lawrence LeClaire's little ranch parties high on the hog and he came back hardly breathin. So, what's that tell ya?"

Leaning back into his seat, Frank folded his arms and thought deeply.

"Well, what's that supposed to mean?" he huffed. "Let's not go accusin one another now."

"Oh Frank," Margie chided, "Don't act like you ain't seen how LeClaire treat that boy of his. Them bruises on his face. We all seen it, just like we all ain't said nothin bout it. And that's his own flesh and blood. Sides it ain't no secret what that man capable of. Everybody in this town know the Klan march to his drum. And that's just what we seen with our own eyes. Now if that's what he do in public, just imagine what that man keeps hid."

"Oh, c'mon Betty, how Lawrence discipline his boy ain't got nothin to do with Donnie Schneider," Frank grumbled defensively.

Across the table Margie's eyes burned.

"Well, you go see that broken boy and his broken momma and tell me if that's what discipline looks like to you," she cried.

With a great sigh Frank folded his hands together and dropped his head in humble acknowledgement. As he thought of Betty in that hospital, crying over her dying son, he felt a great shame at what he'd just said. He didn't even know why he'd said it. Just a gut reaction to hearing something so unusual. Avoiding the fire in Margie's eyes he searched the table before him as if some solution were somewhere to be found amongst the salt and pepper shakers.

"Ah, I'm sorry Margie," he confessed. "Just things been so strange round here lately, I just don't know what to think no more. Reckon I ain't never thought so low of nobody in this town to be hurtin nobody else and now that's all that seems to be happenin round here."

"I know, honey," Margie said with a frail smile. "It's like we seein for the first time."

"You think this got anythin to do with Burleson?" Frank pondered aloud. "Seems like that's where all this craziness got started."

"I don't see how," Margie sighed, sinking back into the seat. "Not yet anyways. But I tell ya if it does, we gone find out soon enough. Somethin vile's bubblin up to the surface round here, Frank. And with this foul heat and the way things been goin I think this a sign that the good lord means to test us."

As she spoke Margie ran her finger around the base of the overturned mug before her. Then, lifting it from the saucer she peeked beneath.

"Be honest with you, if God almighty is fixin to take a hard look at this town, I'm worried what He might find."

In the long silence that followed, a storage truck rolled through the square and backed into the loading ramp beside the courthouse.

As men began to haul in tables and chairs, Margie wondered what lay in store for the evening ahead.

"Say, you going to the town hall tonight?"

"Reckon I might," Frank nodded.

"Good, cus we goin," Margie declared. "All the girls. For Betty. Cus I don't know about you but I'm scared, Frank. Scared of what this town is turnin into. I really am. And so are a lot of folks these days."

"You ain't wrong there Ms. Margie," muttered Frank as he glanced over his shoulder at the silent assembly of tables behind him.

"You think Burleson will be there?" Margie asked, watching the men outside. "Tonight, I mean? They supposed to vote on Barett's Fordham plan, you know. I bet she got somethin to say bout all this. And I for one feel like maybe it's time we oughta hear it."

"Uh," Frank chuckled, dabbing the sweat from his forehead, "I think you givin her a lil too much credit there Miss Marge."

"Oh?" Margie chimed curiously. "How do you mean?"

"Let's just say, from what I been hearin about Eudora Burleson... roundabout 5 o'clock these days she hardly able to stand... let alone stand up at no Town Hall."

"Yeah, well," Margie lamented with a wave of her hand, "I guess we'll just have to see about that."

Like most days spent suffering through the summer heat, the hours passed at a dreadful pace.

But pass they did, until the withered clouds of morning burned away revealing a bare blue sky blanched stark and pale. All through the creeping hours of the afternoon, the pastures, just as the square in town, lay roiling and desolate save for the cicadas screaming from the trees. In their ancestral wisdom, the cattle lingered like statues beneath the shaded embrace of the towering oaks. Still and motionless they let the day pass them by, only breaking from their trancelike state to swat the blackflies droning in their ears.

And just as Frank had predicted early that morning, as the hour of five came and went, Dora too lay motionless in the dark confines of the house.

Throughout the vacant corridors her snores reverberated off the glass and rattled down from the vaulted beams. Like a stone skipping across a lake, the rhythmic din of her breath droned through the halls. Sprawled out in Barett's old easy chair in the living room, Eudora mumbled in fits. In her hand she clutched the remains of a half empty whiskey bottle to her bosom like a child.

Deep in the feverish dreams of drink, Dora began to drift back towards an unwelcome awakening. In her stupor she felt cold sweat upon her skin and hot whiskey burning in her belly. Her mouth was brambles and cotton.

"Barett," she cried out, hoarse and pitiful into the darkness, "Barett!"

Startled by her cries, Crockett scrambled to his feet. From the floor Scout's head shot up and looked towards the door. Hearing that name, his tail began to wag, eager to greet the man who'd never return.

"Barett gatdammit!" Dora hollered out towards the ceiling.

As she rolled over onto her side the early evening light fell across her troubled face through the blinds. Somehow, its warm embrace against her slick and icy skin pained her even more. She was hot and cold all at the same time. Her belly both starving and nauseous. Then, as the dull sound of the whiskey bottle bounced off the carpet, Dora's eyes shuddered open.

And there it was again.

The excruciating realization. Dora buried her face into the cushion and groaned miserably into the chair. The woeful sound was so haunting, that even the dogs understood the meaning. Somewhere between whisper and weeping, she clutched the arm of the recliner and mumbled into it all the burdens that weighed upon her soul.

For some time, she carried on like this. As long as the words would come.

Minutes or hours, she did not care to count the time. But as the well of words at last ran dry and she could think of no more curses, she slowly sat upright in the chair. For a while she just sat there, motionless in the void. Then, shaking her head in fits she roused herself enough to realize where she was. And also perhaps, when she was. As for what she was, that was simple.

Dead drunk.

Leaning over the arm of the chair, she took up the whiskey bottle and clutched it close. With heavy hands she cinched her filthy house robe. Then, without anywhere in particular to go, she set off. Like a newborn calf finding its legs she stumbled with every step. First, she collided against the couch sending her ricocheting into the bookshelf. There, clutching at the shelving she collected her balance beneath an avalanche of tumbling papers as the room tilted and pitched around her.

"Barett!?" she howled as picture frames fell and shattered behind her. "Oh! Look what they done to us Barett!"

Bringing the bottle to her lips she suffered the fire of another stinging swig.

"Look what they done," she screamed, as the whiskey dribbled out from the sides of her mouth. With every step she waded deeper into that sea of anguish as wave after wave broke over her. She took another drink. She spat to the floor. The ground shifted beneath her.

Another picture frame crashed to the ground shattering against the flagstone. Dora paused for a moment but couldn't bring herself to look. She knew the frame. She knew the photo. The family in front of the old barn. Onwards she fumbled, drunk on misery and heartache. Near the children's bedroom she lingered, but again, she couldn't bring herself to venture inside.

"I'm prisoner," she slurred, swinging the bottle through the air, "in my own damn house! Those bastards. Those fuckin yella bastards they've ruined us, Barett!"

Faintness began to wash over her. Supporting herself against the wall, Dora's feet stomped down the long hallway. Crashing through the bathroom door, she collapsed against the sink.

"God won't nobody help me?" she bawled as she clamored up, hoisting herself over the tile countertop. "Ain't nobody got the guts?!"

Her breath shuddered against the cold steel of the tap. Her eyes searched for an answer to her prayers.

There on the counter as she had left it days ago, the black steel of the .38 special called to her.

In the clinical bathroom light, it glowed like a beacon. Like an answer. Six brass shells gleamed out from the chamber, offset against the bone white tile. Clutching the sink Dora set down the whiskey bottle atop the counter. Her head hanging low she stared down the black abyss of the drain. The nausea came in great waves now. Deep from the pit of her stomach.

Saliva dripping from her lips, she spat into the basin. Raising her gaze to meet her reflection she found a hollow and unrecognizable creature staring back at her. A demon, fueled by both spirits of the bottle and those buried deep in her past.

She'd seen this monster before. But where? The nausea returned but she couldn't look away. Perhaps there truly was no escaping one's own fate. No matter how cruel the curse had been set.

"Yeah," she sneered, "yeah? You just gone let em whip you like that, then? Huh! That it then!?"

With each admonishment her voice grew louder until she found herself screaming at her own reflection. "You gone let any man whip you like that!" she spat against the mirror. "Gonna fold like that, I'll show you!"

Seizing the bottle in her hand she threw it back as the whiskey drained into her open mouth. Emptying the contents, she spiked the bottle into the bathtub as the glass shattered into a thousand shards against the porcelain. Seizing the revolver in hand, she jammed the barrel against her temple, pressing it hard into her skin.

"You gone let em run you round your whole fuckin life, then just do it!" she roared with tears in her eyes, "Why can't you do it!"

Her finger twitching against the trigger she tested its tension. It felt as though it were an immovable weight. It felt as though it were held only by a thread. The heat of her breath fogged the glass. Bearing down upon the trigger, she suddenly found herself unable to stand the weight of her own gaze.

At the final moment, she looked away.

What would her father have to say about such a sight?

What would Barett make of such a pitiful surrender?

Tears dripped from her nose.

She spat into the sink.

Raising to meet her reflection once more, Dora suddenly found her eyes filled with a different kind of fire. In that moment, she decided. Their victory, if they were to have it, would not be so easily won. If her fate was to suffer, then she would show them what it was to truly suffer. On her way to hell, she would destroy them all. By any means necessary. This wasn't about law & order. It wasn't a question of right and wrong. It never was, she saw that now.

This was life and death.

Just as it always has been in these savage lands.

Lowering the pistol, Dora let it slip from her limp fingers. In that moment, she knew what had to be done. On shaky legs she steadied herself against the sink, closed her eyes, and drew in a great breath.

Then, without hesitation, she forced two fingers deep into her throat unleashing a floodgate of whiskey and bile.

Meanwhile at the county courthouse, the Town Hall had already begun. In his chair at the head of the bench, Sherriff Hinkley droned through the recitation of the evening's agenda.

Viewed from the gallery below, the pulpit towered over the lowly citizens of Wheaton County. Beneath the lights, the finely lacquered sheen of the lectern shone in its full glory. At its centerpiece hung a plaque emblazoned with the seal of the State of Texas, carrying with it all its grand and terrible weight. The stately bench, like all things designed by those in power, was designed with purpose. In this case, to separate. To declare superiority, demand reverence, and command subservience. To clearly demarcate the border between the powerful and the powerless. Flanked on both sides by six indistinguishable white haired old men, Hinkley mumbled his vapid words into the microphone and gazed upon his dominion. The disinterested lull of his voice drifted out over the gallery, reaching high into the rafters, and resounding off the paneled walls. But beneath Hinkley's intentionally subdued delivery his nerves withered under the gravity of the moment.

In the pit before him was the largest turnout for a Town Hall that Wheaton County had ever seen.

Hours before the doors had even opened the crowd had assembled early and eager. Huddled beneath the shade of the pecan trees, they waited with homemade sandwiches. Between mouthfuls of gossip, they sipped on iced tea and sucked down lukewarm beer. Something was happening, though nobody really knew what. Soon as the great wooden doors were opened, they came pouring in. A river of faces. Their identities lost among the crowd. Jockeying for position like cattle through the stockades, they ate up every seat within the tight confines of the courthouse until even the spaces between were filled with standing spectators. Backed up against the wall, townsfolk stood shoulder to shoulder like a living tapestry.

There was an electric energy in the air. Like the breathless moments before a world heavyweight bout, an anxious anticipation coursed through the crowd. Whether drawn to the square by fear, or outrage, or the simple call of curiosity the gathered masses all waited expectantly.

Earlier, gathered in Hinkley's chambers before taking their seats, all six members of the board had listened as the stampeding masses thundered into the courtroom just outside the door. And though they tried to downplay the circus that awaited them, what they could not ignore were the tiny particles of dust raining down from the vibrations in the ceiling tiles.

The building was alive with energy.

As the mob had poured into the gallery, Margie Watson was one of the first through the doors followed closely behind by Rita and Susan. Taking up position in the front row ahead of the others, Margie clutched to a sign she had brought along for the occasion.

At home she had spent hours devising the slogan and painting out the lines. In the largest letters she could, written in red for the color of revolution, the banner read, "Justice for Donnie." Of course, Rita had suggested something a bit more original, but Margie reckoned it was the clarity of message that mattered most.

Outside the courthouse, the sign had already worked a charm. At the request of every curious passerby, she'd retold the story again and again. To anyone who'd listen she laid out the timeline, the peculiarities, and her side of the case. To each person she read the full list of Donnie's extensive injuries. Each time her performance ended the same. Pleading for help in convincing Hinkley to launch an investigation into the assault. To Margie's surprise, most hadn't even heard the news about Donnie. They'd come to see if Eudora Burleson was going to make an appearance.

They'd come to see if she had the guts.

Now, sitting before this tumultuous sea of faces Hinkley cursed himself for not being more drunk. His nerves were shot and everyone could see it. Or at least, it felt like everyone could see it. He didn't really know for certain because normally he wasn't this sober. Between a late night out at LeClaire's place and a drunken slumber that lasted well into the afternoon he hadn't the time to refill his flask or pop into the liquor store. Even the reserve bottles in his desk had already been drained dry.

As Hinkley paused in his speech, the thin paper he held trembled in his hands. The room had just been called to order, but he was already sweating like a summer hog. The more he tried to control the tremors, the more violently they returned. His body was in revolt. His mouth was a desert that no amount of water could quench. His soul cried out for the warm comfort of whiskey.

A few minutes earlier back in the safety of Hinkley's chambers, as the fervor was assembling just outside, Zoning Commissioner Jim Bradley had issued him a stark warning.

"John, that madhouse out there only want one thing," he'd said, poking a stern finger into Hinkley's chest. "They want a leader, you understand? They need a man who will lead them through the shadow of doubt. Now I know that you are that man. I just hope you know you are that man."

Though he wasn't one to take kindly to this type of lecturing, Hinkley bore the admonishment with a thin smile. Bradley was one of his biggest campaign contributors and at this point he couldn't afford to lose any confidence.

"You just got to show them that you got what it takes," Bradley had continued, jabbing his finger. "I'm countin on you to maintain order, no matter what. White blood has been shed on *our* soil. The people are rattled. The rats will come soon enough, tryin to get what they can. We can't afford to show no weakness, understand?"

"Of course," Hinkley had grinned with confidence, "of course, Jim. It's all under control."

But inside his guts were bubbling. Fomented by a singular fixation that hung over him like a storm cloud. Over and over, he repeated a halfhearted prayer.

He prayed that Eudora Burleson would not have the courage to show her face.

Snapping back to the moment at hand, Hinkley managed to steady the quivering paper before him as he concluded his opening remarks. A few lines down he saw the words on the page fast approaching.

Hesitating, Hinkley cleared his throat.

"On the docket today, we have votes on the Agricultural proposal for zoning. Trade Union Proposal - 2B. And also, the Chamber of Commerce Expansion, Initiative 3A. Now, once the day's voting is concluded the board will hear any new business, and then we'll open the floor to public comment."

Glancing down into the gallery, Hinkley surveyed the silent congregation seated before him. Like cattle the townsfolk stared back at him with empty eyes. His trick had worked a treat. With his lengthy introduction he'd bored them into a trance. Leaning down the line of his fellow board members Hinkley caught a knowing look from Jim Bradley as he thumbed his nose. At last, a smile crept across Hinkley's hot face as his shoulders eased their tension.

Perhaps it wouldn't be so bad after all.

"Alright now," Hinkley continued with renewed confidence, "since we got so many newcomers with us tonight, fore we get started anybody got any questions about the evenin's agenda?"

Suddenly a soft voice cut through the silence.

"I have a question."

"Alright then ma'am, go ahead," Hinkley replied, squinting over the gallery as he searched for the source of the voice.

After a brief pause, the faceless voice called out again. Only louder this time.

"What about the vote on Measure 5A? Residential Zoning Permissions for Fordham."

A twinge in Hinkley's neck began to pulse in spasms. Searching for a response he tugged at his collar and wiped away the acrid sweat quickly percolating upon his brow.

"Uh, ma'am? Could you step up here in front the podium?" Hinkley grumbled. "I can't hardly see who I'm speakin to."

At this request the gallery began shifting uneasily in their seats. All through the courtroom heads craned up and around in every direction, swiveling from side to side. In the quiet murmur, whispers called out to one another, accusing, and searching for the objector in their midst. Soon their energy reached a volume so great that Hinkley began to make a move for his gavel. But just as he took the hammer in his hands the commotion was swiftly cut silent.

Looking up amongst a chorus of appalled gasps, Hinkley's heart sunk into his belly as he saw Maybel Thomas come shuffling her way through the crowd. Close behind her, wearing his perfectly pressed military uniform, a stone-faced Floyd Thomas trailed with his hands clasped behind his back. Beneath the weight of scornful glances around the room the two humbly made their way to the podium. Stepping into the arena, Maybel arranged a small stack of papers before her as Floyd stood at stoic attention with his chin held high and his eyes locked steadfast on Hinkley.

Standing before the stunned assembly, they were the only Black folks in the entire room.

"Um, scuse me miss," Hinkley started softly into the microphone, "I think y'all must be confused. This here the *Wheaton County* Town Hall. Ain't you coloreds got your own meetins? In some shanty on your side of the tracks?"

From the gallery the sounds of muffled laughter drifted through the assembly. Emboldened by Hinkley's remarks, they hissed from amongst the anonymity of the crowd.

Unmoved, Maybel spoke defiantly into the microphone.

"Mr. Commissioner, the last time I checked, this the United States of America. Land of the free. We got as much right to be here as anybody. Now my name is Maybel Thomas, and this here is my husband Floyd Thomas. For six years he served this country with honor, can you say the same?"

At this, gasps began to ripple through the congregation. From the gallery a man stood upon his seat and roared, "America don't want you! Go back to where you come from!"

Seated in the front row Rita VanBuren stood and fired back, "This is where she come from you stupid asshole!"

The room erupted. From the upper level someone hurled an empty beer bottle that shattered against the floor.

"Oh, let her speak you cowards!" Rita spat towards the mob, "Let her speak!"

In the commotion her demands were drowned out. Washed away with the churning tide. Margie tried to sit Rita down but was rebuffed on contact. She'd never seen Rita so livid in all her life. The woman was positively incensed. At any moment Margie half expected her to burst into flames.

Maybel turned to Floyd who still stood proudly behind her. His eyes meeting hers, he nodded her onwards.

"Now, as I was sayin," Maybel continued into the microphone, raising her voice over the rabble, "as a citizen of Wheaton County, I am here to bring forward Fordham Residential Zoning Initiative 5A, which has been filed through due process with this board."

A second surge of commotion ripped through the gallery. From somewhere amongst the teeming mass, somebody spat as a thick band of yellow saliva splattered across Floyd's shoes.

High upon the pulpit Hinkley gazed upon the disorder of the courtroom with a certain glee.

In their hatred and fear, he felt his strength grow.

Taking his time, the old Sheriff adjusted his microphone with a cool hand as the gold tooth glinted out from the depths of his mouth. With a sick grin he raised his eyebrows. Like a lizard in the sun, he basked in the chaos.

"Quiet down y'all," he called out, reassuring the mob. "Hush, I say. Y'all, let me handle this now."

Gradually the crowd settled back into their seats. Pausing for dramatic effect, Hinkley waited for a total and commanding silence before proceeding. Looking out over the gallery he studied the red and flustered faces as they gazed spitefully upon Maybel and Floyd. Savoring the moment at hand, Hinkley licked his lips.

"Tell you what," he began, clasping his fingers together, "now, I see you two got all gussied up in your finest duds, tonight. I mean look at you, Floyd. Very impressive. Got all your shiny medals on just to come out here and get these good folk all riled up. Well, ok then, I'll play ball. Now this woman here call herself an American citizen. Let's just agree to disagree on that."

Here and there a few groups began to applaud. From the pulpit Hinkley reveled in the theatre, glowing with confidence.

"But since y'all so eager to participate in civilized society this evenin, how bout I give you a little lesson in civility? You want a vote on your little de-segregation measure? Well, you got it, darlin. Let's put it to a vote! Distinguished members of the board…" Hinkley boomed, turning to his peers. "All in favor of havin these white-hatin, negros infestin Fordham and livin next door to you and your kin say aye."

In that moment a cold quiet descended upon the board. Six long faces stared down indignantly upon Maybel and Floyd. Feigning an astonished intrigue, Hinkley leaned all down the line to allow the silence of the committee to sink in. To cut deep into Maybel's heart. To strangle out every ounce of hope she had left. Then, raising his eyebrows high, Hinkley shrugged his shoulders before returning to the microphone.

"All opposed?" he offered.

Without hesitation a chorus of six "nays" sealed the proposal's fate.

"Well, there you have it," Hinkley grinned, tapping the gavel lightly against the block. "Measure 5A - *Killed*. See that? That right there is what we call American democracy. Now get the fuck out of my courthouse."

Unable to suppress the cocktail of emotions roiling inside her, Rita VanBuren leapt up from her seat.

"How dare you," she cried, tears welling in her eyes. "You draft dodgin piss ant. Think your some kinda big man up there talkin to a woman like that? You ain't no man, you ain't nobody!"

Exploding up from their seats an avalanche of opinions rang out all at the same time so that not a single thought was clearly conveyed. Everywhere people were bumping into one another, arguing, and hollering. The courtroom roared but no one was heard. From the bench Hinkley shouted into the microphone but only his lips seemed to move. Through the crowd a hand seized Rita by the hair and dragged her back into the pews. Seeing this, Margie's face ignited with a savage heat. Furious, she turned round and took a swing at the unknown assailant with her sign.

"Get your damn hands off her!" she howled, flailing the sign like a battle ax.

"Remove Mrs. Watson & Ms. VanBuren from the room!" Hinkley roared into the microphone. From the wings three enormous bailiffs were already closing in through the crowd. Casting a wary glance down the line of disgruntled board members Hinkley caught the frustrated eyes of Jim Bradley searing into him.

He was losing control.

"Get em out!" Hinkley commanded.

In the end, it took all three bailiffs to restrain Margie Watson. She was kicking and squirming with such ferocity she lost her shoes as they carried her off to the holding cell. Grateful for an exit, Rita shuffled closely behind, clutching to the bailiff's backside. As they disappeared through the side door, the room was left buzzing with a frantic and nervous energy.

Taking up the gavel Hinkley slammed three heavy hammers on the block.

"Order!" he commanded, "I said order!"

Still standing behind Maybel at the podium, Floyd sensed the point of no return fast approaching. With a calm hand, he placed his arm around his wife's shoulder and whispered softly into her ear.

"You did good, darlin. All you coulda' done. But we got to go. Right now."

Defeated, but standing tall, the two turned away from the pulpit and walked together through the storm surrounding them on all sides. But with each step, the path to the exit constricted tighter and tighter before them. Onward they waded through the rising sea until suddenly, the presence of the horde was suffocating. The heat of the room seemed to suck the air from their lungs.

During the war, as most soldiers do, Floyd had developed a strange knack for sensing the moment before battle.

It could be quiet or loud, in a busy street or an empty countryside. The location didn't seem to matter so much as the feeling. It was a swelling of the atmosphere that served as the harbinger of bloodshed. It was an instinct ingrained since the dawn of time that warned a man when the presence of violence was close at hand.

And this was it.

But just then, as Floyd's hands began clenching into fists, a percussive boom slammed against the great wooden doors to the courtroom. Stopping in his tracks, Floyd positioned himself before Maybel, ready to face whatever awaited. In unison the confused assembly cast their uncertain eyes towards the door. As dull murmurs began, another booming echo rang out through the room. Maybel's heart leapt in her chest as the door rattled in its hinges.

"Open this goddamn door!" a hoarse voice shouted.

Behind the bench a cold shudder bristled down Hinkley's spine.

From the frozen assembly it was Floyd who stepped forward. He alone knew what awaited on the other side. All he had left to do was unleash it. Pushing against the bumper the door cracked open.

Like a freight train, Eudora Burleson came barreling into the gallery with a head full of steam.

Blowing right past Floyd and Maybel's stunned faces she stormed straight to the podium as mouths around the courtroom dropped to the floor. Here and there gasps of disbelief began wafting up through the air. Her hair was disheveled and wild. Her face bare and weary. Though she'd dressed herself well enough her usual easy grace was lost. Her eyes saw only one thing.

Hinkley, seated high upon his pulpit.

In terror he watched her approach. But as she stepped to the podium, he noticed something peculiar in her gait. A familiar movement he himself had experienced many a time. As she reached for the microphone, her hand missed by a country mile. Then, drifting back she snatched at it with hapless movements, as a kitten bats at a fly.

The sly old smile slithered across Hinkley's face.

"Eudora Burleson," he hooted, "you're drunk!"

Clutching the edges of the podium Dora steadied herself against its solid foundation.

"You shoulda seen me earlier," she slurred into the microphone.

Her entire presence reeked of liquor. Her whole frame wobbled with an uncertain air. The gallery leered at her with disgust. From the safety of the pulpit, Hinkley observed her with amusement.

"Give me one good reason not to arrest you right now for public intoxication and indecency?" Hinkley challenged.

"I'll do you one better cus I got about forty good reasons right here," Dora blurted out, patting her shirt pocket. "Somewhere, here I... I think I got it."

Searching with heavy hands Dora checked each pocket before moving down to her hips. As she felt among the empty fabric her face shriveled with confusion as she turned out nothing but lint.

"Shit," she muttered under her breath, "well... Hell, I don't need no damn list. Cus I can name the Nazi bastards off the top a' my head."

Behind her a clamor of dissent began to rise up from the assembly. With nervous eyes Hinkley searched the room for the bailiffs, but they were occupied battling Margie in the back holding cells.

"I don't give a damn if you don't like it!" Dora spat at the mob over her shoulder, "Y'all gone hear it today! My husband was murdered! In cold blood! Over a spit a land nobody in this town never gave two shits about! Why? Cus law don't run this town. The Klan run this town! And they'll kill anybody who get in their way. And now, I know who they are, the yella murderin bastards. Lawrence LeClaire, John J. Hinkley, Nathan Evans, Shep Garret!"

As Dora ran through the names the room began to fall hush behind her. If not for curiosity at the spectacle unfolding before them, then perhaps for fear of hearing their name announced next.

"Bill Barksdale, Henry Benning, the list goes on, but I got em. Oh, I got em. Every single one," Dora scowled, "And y'all know how I know? Donnie Schneider! That's right little Donnie Schneider all busted up in the hospital."

From somewhere in the back-rooms Margie screamed out in agony.

"That's right, he the one gave me this here list, not a day ago. And just look what happened to him! Guess y'all figure he can't do much talkin if his jaws wired shut, ain't that right Hinkley? And I tell all y'all in here, the second any a y'all step outta line they'll come for you too! The second you won't bow down to lick the mud from their boots they will come for you. And who gone save you then? The law? Shit, ain't no law out here! So go on, keep tellin yourselves 'it ain't me they after.' It ain't me. It ain't me. Y'all make me sick! What y'all oughta be sayin is IT AIN'T RIGHT WITH ME... AND BY GOD I AIN'T GONE STAND FOR IT NO MORE!"

"Chairman Hinkley!" Bradley barked down the pulpit, "Get her outta here now! Call this room to order!"

"Why if it ain't Jim Bradley, nice a you to speak up!" Dora grinned. "Y'know you on my list too."

Bringing down the gavel, Hinkley called for order as a low murmur began creeping out among the gallery. Looking out upon the crowd, Hinkley sensed a strange shift in the air. Folks were looking at him differently. Feeling the flush rising through his face he clutched his hand into a trembling fist. Though he tried he couldn't swallow the lump lodged in his throat. His eyes were fixed upon the door to the holding cells. Finally, a bailiff reappeared.

"Bailiff!" Hinkley commanded standing up from the bench, "Remove this woman to my chambers immediately! I call this meeting of the Town Hall to recess."

The gavel slammed down.

Without delay Hinkley tore off down the back corridor towards his chambers tugging at the tie around his neck. His body shivered with rage. As he quickly descended the steps from the pulpit Jim Bradley's forceful hand fell upon his shoulder. Whirling around with astonishing speed Hinkley broke Bradley's grip and shoved him against the wall. Witnessing this confrontation from afar, the trailing members of the board held up beneath the shadow of the stairs and watched the struggle unfold.

"Careful Bradley," Hinkley bristled, flashing his teeth. "Don't forget who you're dealin with. I am handlin it."

Shoving him aside, Hinkley stormed off down the long dark hall as Bradley stared daggers into his back.

"Well fuckin handle it then!" he shouted after him.

After a short trip upon the bailiff's shoulder Dora was thrown into Hinkley's chambers. As she gathered herself, she heard the deadbolt lock behind her. The windowless room was cold and clinical. Her breath came quick and shallow. She cursed herself for forgetting the list. Cursed herself for not bringing a gun. In her drunken state she'd played right into Hinkley's hands. This was his turf. His domain. She began to pace back and forth like a caged animal.

She was trapped behind enemy lines.

Outside, the two bailiffs' standing guard snapped to attention as Hinkley's brooding figure came storming down the hallway.

"You two," he said pointing towards them, "beat it."

Obediently the guards marched off down the hall. Outside his chambers Hinkley watched until they rounded the corner. Then he waited until the echo of their boots fell silent. Finally, assured of his privacy, he unlocked the door to his chambers and slipped inside.

Setting the lock behind him, his eyes instantly met with hers. Alone with Hinkley, Dora became suddenly aware of the enormity of his size. As he slowly stalked towards her, he tugged at the gunbelt strapped round his gut. Everything inside Dora told her to retreat. But she refused to give him the satisfaction of a single inch.

"You meddlin bitch," Hinkley spat with a sneer. "I don't know who you think you're dealin with but I promise you I am much, much, worse."

Defiant, Dora stepped forward. With only inches between them the two sized each other up. Hinkley could hardly believe his eyes.

"Ain't nothin worse than a cockroach like you," Dora snarled.

Hidden from the judgement of prying eyes, something inside Hinkley snapped. In a flash, he seized her by the throat, sweeping her off the ground. He pinned her against the wall. Kicking and squirming beneath his grip Dora's feet fluttered high above the ground. Hinkley buried his fingers into her skin, clamping down like a mad dog. His lips curled back around his teeth. As the light began to fade from her eyes Dora clutched her hands round Hinkley's forearms and thrust up her knee with all her fury.

The Sherriff's face flooded white with shock. His mouth gasped for air, like a fish upon dry land.

Unleashing another vicious kick into Hinkley's crotch Dora felt his fingers weaken and peel away. The moment her feet hit the floor, Dora stumbled into the desk, catching herself on its edge. In short, labored breaths the air began to fill her gasping lungs. All the while her eyes stayed fixed on Hinkley as he writhed, cursing in agony upon the floor.

Quick as she could Dora shuffled towards the door. Unlocking it, she peeked outside. The bailiffs were nowhere to be found. Down the dark hallway an exit sign glowed in the blackness. Pausing in the doorway, Dora turned back.

"Y'know, John," she wheezed, rubbing at her throat, "I believe we have reached an impasse from which there is no return. If you wanna settle this like the man you claim to be, just come round my place 9 tonight and I will give you satisfaction. Just you and me. And let that be the end of it."

CHAPTER XI

MOONLIGHT MILE

Later that evening, as the long light of day shed its weary skin, a stark and unsettling twilight crept across every inch of the Burleson property. In the front yard the towering oak trees, once welcoming in their shade, now clawed out like skeletal hands stretching desperately towards the pale light of the full moon. At their feet, the overgrown grass shifted in eerie tides like a sinister sea. This was no still and peaceful darkness, but rather the peculiar sort of dusky gloom that sets the mind on edge. And though the sun now slept far beyond the horizon, its heat remained, steady and immovable. Like a kettle with the lid clamped tightly shut. The atmosphere was slick with moisture. Viscous and pressurized.

Inside the house, the Danes' long bodies lay sprawled across the cool tile of the kitchen floor. Listlessly, Scout yawned wide. Cocking his head, he stared at the wheezing air conditioner as it dripped a pitter patter of condensation onto the floor. Through the home, darkness filled the halls, save for one lamp burning bright upon the bedside table.

But beneath the unmade sheets Eudora Burleson was nowhere to be found.

Upon leaving the courthouse earlier that evening, she had driven straight home as her plans unfolded in her mind. When she'd arrived, everything was soon set into motion. Packing up a few beers, a box of ammunition, and a bag of beef jerky in her pack she unsheathed

Barett's Springfield 30.06 rifle from its case before strapping it across her back.

It was a whale of a gun.

A portable cannon, capable of knocking a fist sized hole clear through a sheet of metal. If Hinkley had the audacity to show himself tonight, she'd be waiting. Not in the yard, or on the front porch like some proud fool. But in ambush.

This was war after all.

The declaration had been sealed the moment he put his hands on her.

There was no going back, not anymore.

Her plan was simple enough. She'd wait hidden on the roof with one steady eye cast down the scope of the Springfield. If he showed, the moment he turned his tires down that long and winding driveway she'd set him in her sights. Then, soon as she had a clear shot, before he even had time to open the driver door, she'd put a round right through his chest. He'd be in hell before the engine cooled down. Afterwards, Dora figured she'd pull Hinkley's pistol from his belt and press his fingerprints into the grip. Using his cold dead hands, she'd pop off a few rounds towards the house and claim she'd shot him in self-defense. Granted, she wasn't too sure how it would play out in the courts. And yes, she'd probably have to swallow her pride and play the role of the frail and weeping widow before the jury.

But then again, even if she was confined to a jail cell for the rest of her life, with this deed done maybe she'd finally be able to get a good night's sleep.

Now, lying prone atop the roof of the house, draped in government issue camouflage netting, she checked the time on her watch.

11:42 p.m. Hinkley was late.

"Chicken shit," Dora grumbled.

She'd been sweltering beneath the thick cargo netting for hours. In her boots, her feet were drenched in sweat. The scent of the rifle's freshly oiled receiver filled her nostrils. The stock pressed achingly into her cheek. Shrugging off her discomfort, Dora wiped the sweat from her brow and grabbed another piece of jerky from the bag.

"The marksman's favorite meal," she mumbled to herself.

That's what Barett had always said. He was the one who had taught her how to hunt. Feral hogs mostly. But so far, hunting men wasn't all that different. Just a whole lot of waiting around doing nothing. The only difference was the bait. The hogs had a penchant for getting out into the corn fields when they got hungry. They'd move from one plot to the next like a plague of locusts. They could root up and devour an entire season's worth of work in a single night. After filling their bellies they'd hollow out enormous wallows and bathe themselves in mud. It'd look like someone dropped a bomb right in the middle of the crop lines.

Once, after losing a few acres to this sort of thing, Barett had recruited Eudora for a special operation.

On a cool autumn day, they trekked about a mile into the tree line out near Bear Bottom. There they spent the afternoon setting a trap. First, they built a lure to draw the enemy into position. In this case, a hastily dug hole filled with a few gallons of milk and a sack of dry corn. After a day or two the mixture would begin to ferment and rot. Soon, the putrid stench reeked out from the earth. The hogs couldn't resist. The next night, with rifles at the ready, Barett waited in one tree while Dora sat high in another. Soon, the swine assembled beneath them to gorge on the foul brew.

And this was how the killing was done.

In the crossfire, there was nowhere for the hogs to escape. They dropped like flies beneath the bullets. The hunt was all just a matter of patience. Like the pit viper, lying in wait, motionless beneath the leaves. Sometimes it could take days, sometimes weeks. But one must always be ready to strike.

Tearing another strip of smoked jerky with her teeth, Dora chewed the tacky beef and returned her steady eye down the sights.

As the hours passed so too did the beers. Soon, with a pile of empties at her side a drowsy stupor began to take its hold upon Eudora. The day had been long as lifetime and the hangover she had awoken with that evening was now returning with an insufferable vengeance. In the vast expanse before her, a chorus of bullfrogs roared with content in the murky gloom. Checking her watch again, she marked the time.

1:07 am.

Exhausted, Dora rested her head upon the wooden stock of the rifle. Closing her eyes, she listened to the soothing sounds of the countryside. That curious harmony of staggering silence and the shrill cries of creatures unseen. It was the most comforting sound Dora could imagine. Drifting off once again, she finally forced herself up from the ground with a weary moan. Peeling back the netting she stretched her aching bones and basked in the relief of the damp night air upon her skin. She had laid motionless beneath the stifling cover for over five hours. Her mark had been too afraid to show. That's just how the hunt goes sometimes. Taking in a deep breath Dora spat and flicked the safety into place on the rifle. Then, lying it down beside her, she quietly set about rolling up the netting and stuffing it back into her pack. Taking special precaution to remain hidden from sight she belly crawled across the roof towards the back of the house. With wary eyes, she surveyed the dark pasture before her. Then, upon confirming that the coast was clear, she shimmied her way down a thin service ladder until her feet met the ground. Stalking around the perimeter of the house, she made her way under cover of darkness towards the sliding doors and unlocked the deadbolt with a key.

Inside, the sharp rattle of the Danes collars jangled in the distance.

"Psst," she whispered sharply, "c'mon dogs, let's go."

Soon their massive bodies came trotting out into the yard. Happily, they greeted her with wiggling butts and cold noses, sniffing and snorting at her jerky scented breath.

"Shh," she commanded, taking a knee beside them. "Eyes."

On command the dogs sat, fixing their eyes upon her. Resetting the deadbolt on the door, Eudora adjusted the pack on her shoulders and took her rifle in hand.

"Heel."

Setting out towards the fence line she moved low and swift as the Danes loped quickly behind her. Tight on her bootheels they followed in her tracks until Eudora's searching hands found the chained lock of the gate. In silent understanding, the Danes laid prone on the ground as Dora unhooked the clasp and pushed through into the infinite plains of the pasture.

As they walked on beneath the light of the moon, further and further from the house, Dora felt a certain comfort swelling inside her with every measured step. She had walked these lands all her life. Day and night. As a little girl only candlelight and moonlight lit her way. Her only map lie in the stars above. Even still, somewhere deep inside, all the lamps, light bulbs, and electric gizmos of the house were always a strange and foreign thing to her. Unsettling in some odd way she could never, and had never, tried to articulate. All she knew was everything was simple in the moonlight. Beneath the trees and among the stars. The feeling of the earth beneath one's feet.

Looking back towards the house, now tiny and far-off, the lamp in the bedroom still burned bright as a beacon.

Sensing herself far removed from its light, Dora stood a little taller.

Turning back to the footpath before her, carved out by generations of cattle marching in order towards the creek, her boots resumed their steady progress. Somewhere along the way her tired mind went blank. She knew the path by heart. Before long she came to the great oak tree split down the center by that fated lightning strike and here, she turned right, up a slight rise in the plain. The incline was gradual but steady and soon Dora found herself at the highest point in the entire thousand acres of pastureland.

Barett's Keep.

From this point in the property, the surrounding miles were laid out like a map before the beholder. The line of sight stretched clear out to Farm Road 260 and the start of Burleson Road, even on a dusky night like tonight. Just down the bluff, Brangus Creek meandered beneath the bridge and out towards the next property beyond the horizon.

As Barett had called it, the position was a scout's delight.

And it was here beneath a mighty lone pecan tree that a modest camp was already made. Really nothing more than a mat in the dirt situated next to a tiny ash-stained fire pit and a stack of dried kindling. But it was this primitive campsite that had served as Dora's sleeping quarters every night since Barett had died.

It was a strange experience, returning to their bed when he was no longer there to fill it.

One of those things you don't pay much mind to until it happens to you. The night after Dora had identified his body, when it was time to for bed, she just stood near the edge of the mattress and found herself oddly unable to touch it. Somehow it was no longer hers. The thought of lying in it alone made her stomach turn towards the ceiling. And so, ever since that fateful day, when Dora's bleary eyes could no longer stay open, she'd call up the dogs and venture out into the wild darkness of her childhood home. Where she had been alone for so long before. Where, perhaps, she could be alone once again. Only in an occasional drunken stupor had she awoken within the confines of the house since Barett's passing.

In those moments, it was the cruel revelation that it wasn't all some terrible nightmare that cut her the deepest.

So, it was only here, beneath the pecan tree, that she found any rest at all. Her head in the dirt. A loaded pistol tucked securely in her pants. The Danes at least, seemed to approve. Content to be together they curled up next to her and served as a sort of alarm system in the night. Though out here the only real threat of invasion came in the form of the occasional blind and shambling armadillo, searching among the grass for beetles.

More than comfort, Dora saw the camp as necessity. If anyone were to come looking for her, they'd go to the house, which was exactly why she wasn't there.

As she set the rifle against the tree, Dora dropped her pack to the ground and set about removing the rolled cargo netting inside. Lying down upon her mat she unfurled the cover over her body like a sheet and disappeared beneath its shroud. At this, the dogs collapsed in their places with exhausted, heavy groans. Soon, their eyelids fluttered shut to the sound of insects humming in the night.

In her dreams, it was always Barett.

Always.

Often doing the most mundane things. Like buying groceries from the store or clipping linens on the line. He'd hand her a sheet from the basket, and she'd pin it up. The sun was always shining and the air was unnaturally cool and crisp. In these dreams she always seemed to have something to tell him but could never quite remember what it was. In the absence of conversation, they would go about their work quietly, side by side. Each with a smile upon their face. But then, inevitably, Dora would feel the scene slipping through her fingers. As suddenly as water finds its way through the cracks of your hands. Triggered by some noise or convulsion, the backdrop would begin to burn away like morning mist beneath a fiery sun. No matter how quickly she ran towards him, Barett's smiling face drifted further and further until her eyes snapped open and she found herself alone in the dark.

But this time, she was not alone.

The dogs were standing over her.

Their eyes and ears focused sharply at attention off towards the road.

Drawing back the netting Dora sat up against the tree. In the distance, the far-off glow of yellow headlights cut through the night. The dogs had heard the engine far before they'd seen it. They smelled the burning motor oil upon the air. Her eyes wide in the darkness, Dora watched as the vehicle crawled just past the white barn before the turnoff to Burleson Road. There the vehicle came to a creeping stop. Killing its lights, the truck then shifted into reverse and backed into the lot beside the barn.

Taking up the rifle in her hands, Dora placed her eye down the scope and watched with steady breath.

The driver side door opened first. Beneath the pale light of the moon a shadowy figure stepped out. Then the passenger door opened. Two more anonymous silhouettes. Like black ants they communed together for a moment before setting off in line through the corn rows.

Studying the swaying stalks, she tracked them in her sights as their path cut through the field towards Burleson Road.

Situated upon the bluff, Dora pondered her next move as the scene played out before her. In the remote darkness of the pasture, she was utterly invisible. Like a barn owl high in the trees. From the safety of her perch, the moment felt strangely surreal, as if she was watching a movie on the screen. Below her, the figures popped out from the corn and scampered across the road towards her side of the property. Staying low they helped each other over the barbed wire fence. Together they set out across the pasture towards the house. In just a few short minutes, they had already passed right over Barett's Keep. Without moving an inch from her bed, Dora had secured the flank behind them. It was almost comical, watching these men as they skulked and commando crawled from one cover to the next. All the while, unknowingly trapped in the reticle of her scope. As they approached the fence surrounding the front lawn, they huddled together, gesturing sharply to one another before breaking off to take their positions around the house.

As two of the men crept around the side, only the driver remained in position. Like a moth drawn to a flame Dora watched as he gazed towards the single yellow light glowing from the bedroom window.

After a few minutes of observation, he made his move. Flattening himself against the ground he slithered beneath the barbed wire and crawled towards the house. On cue, the others did the same, and soon the three of them formed a triangulation around the building. They'd done this kind of thing before, that much was certain. As Dora watched, one silhouetted figure finally reached the outer walls of the house. Pressing himself against the brick, he rose to his feet and stalked around the perimeter.

Meanwhile, Dora situated her pack in front of her and covered herself with the cargo netting leaving only the rifle exposed. She rested the weight of the weapon upon the bag. She gazed down the scope and placed the crosshairs over the silhouetted figure as it peered into her bedroom window.

Her pulse rising, she flicked the safety off and let her finger rest comfortably against the cold steel trigger. Taking a deep breath, she steadied her heartbeat and focused her gaze downrange. Her target in the crosshairs, she centered the reticle in the thick of his back.

The wind was absent.

The range, roughly two hundred and fifty yards.

Dora adjusted her sights just so to account for the bullet drop.

Barett would have been mighty proud.

Slow and smooth, her finger curled round the trigger. She drew in a breath and held it firm in her lungs. Then, careful not to pull the shot, she squeezed.

There is a myth, prevalent in the hearts of untested men, that under fire they will react with a steely valor. That when suddenly faced with overwhelming odds, an innate strength will surge forth and carry them towards victory. But it is not so. It is said that in the heat of battle both the best and worst of mankind is laid bare upon the table. All our courage and cowardice. Though what most fail to understand is, unlike the heroism depicted on the silver screen, it is the opposite that truly defines bravery. It is not the lack of fear, but the acceptance of it. It is not a brazen disregard for death, but an understanding and appreciation of one's own mortality. Bravery is knowing that even though your death is damn near guaranteed, sometimes the deed must be done, regardless. This is what goes through the mind of truly courageous men. Men like Floyd and Barett. The soldiers of the fighting 151st.

These were the kind of men who won the war.

And the moment Dora fired that first shot, she knew.

They were not these men.

A spattering of blood sprayed against the bricks. As the echo rang out across the pasture, the others scattered like cockroaches beneath the sudden illumination of a lightbulb. The two remaining silhouettes tore off towards the road without a second thought for their fallen comrade. Racking the bolt back a hollow shell ejected from the chamber. The smell of singed gunpowder hung heavy in the air. Dora's ears rang with a deafening din. Chambering another round, Dora led her targets in the crosshair. Squeezing off another shot she heard the zipping echo of the bullet ricocheting off the road. Like startled deer the figures bolted in one direction, then another as Dora rained shots upon them. Finally, the silhouettes made a break for the tree line. At this distance, the chaos of their erratic movements made them impossible targets in the night. Nevertheless, Dora pumped a few more rounds in their general direction until their panicked forms disappeared into the darkness of the woods.

Cracking off a final round into the trees, Dora ejected the spent cartridge and triple checked the firing chamber in rapid succession.

All clear.

In the stillness that remained, Dora felt a hot adrenaline coursing through her veins. She had killed. Now there truly was no going back.

"Good."

Dropping the spent magazine from the Springfield Dora slammed in a freshly loaded clip. With a smooth motion she racked the bolt back and forth, chambering a new round. She searched through her shirt pocket for her carton of smokes. Pulling out the crumpled box, she slid a bent cigarette from the pack with her lips and lit the tip with a trembling hand. Then, after a long deep drag, she exhaled a curtain of smoke into the sky.

"Alright dogs," she said, clamping the cigarette between her lips, "let's go see what we got."

With the Danes at her heels, Dora made her way back towards the house. All the while she kept a keen eye on the tree line across the road but at the speed those boys were moving, she reckoned they were probably into the next county by now.

Dora knew full well they weren't coming back. They were running to their masters. The cowards that sent them.

Shifting her focus back to the business at hand Dora pushed through the iron gate into the property surrounding the house. Still crumpled in a heap against the wall she saw the limp body of a man as it lay motionless beneath the yellow framed light of the bedroom window. Taking cover behind the brick divider of the trash incinerator, Dora peeked around the corner and studied the body for any signs of life.

The man's face was smushed up against the wall. The shirt on his back bathed in blood. She couldn't tell if he was breathing but it certainly didn't look like it. Through his torn shirt, the entry wound just above the shoulder blade oozed black. Above the stagnant body a great splatter of gore dripped thick like syrup from the bricks. Quickly, Dora slung the strap of the Springfield across her back and drew Barett's .45 from its holster.

"Stay," she whispered to the dogs.

Flicking off the safety, Dora moved out from cover with her weapon at the ready. With steady steps she made her approach with her finger tight on the trigger. Closer and closer she marched until she could smell the iron of blood in the air. Then, reaching out, she grabbed the man by his crimson stained shirt and rolled him over onto his back.

As the weight of his body shifted, a feeble moan escaped the man's lips.

Beneath the glowing light from the window, Dora watched as his woozy eyes rolled around in his head.

He was alive.

Without delay Dora set to work searching him. At his hip, a small pistol was seated in its holster which she removed and stuffed into the back of her waistband. In his limp hands, a buck knife gleamed in the moonlight. Stomping her boot heel into the meat of his wrist she pinned it to the ground before kicking the blade away into the darkness. At this sudden jolt, the man's eyes drifted back into place.

Blinking himself back into consciousness he looked bewildered at the lone woman standing over him.

"You," he sputtered, "You... shot me."

"Damn right I did," Dora said coldly, staring down the sights of her pistol, "and I got half a mind to do it again. If my aim was any better you'd be dead by now. But I tell ya, from this range... I'm lethal."

"Ughhh," the man moaned, "god damn... it hurts like a sonuvabitch."

"Good," Dora snapped, "now listen here. You bleedin like a stuck pig, and frankly I couldn't give a shit one way or the other. But if you want to live to see sunrise you gone tell me everything I wanna know and you gone tell it to me right now. Understand?"

On the ground the man's face began to grow pale. He tried to speak. Then, like a snake going belly up, his eyes rolled back into his head.

Standing over him, Dora lowered the pistol to her side. With a heavy sigh, she collected herself for a moment beneath the moonlight. Lost in thought her eyes drifted to the tool shed off the side of the house. There, a rusty old wheelbarrow was propped up against the wall. Peering out from behind the brick facade of the trash pit, the Danes whined softly.

"Heel," Dora commanded, as she holstered the pistol at her hip.

When the man finally came to, he found himself seated upright against a pole. Behind him he felt a strange sensation. A tightly wound pressure upon his swollen wrists. Craning his head for a better look, a fierce pain radiated out across his chest. He winced in agony. Scrunching up his neck, he gazed down at the blackened carnage seared shut over his mangled shoulder. He heaved weakly at the scent of his own singed skin, but nothing came out. His breath came fast and shallow as he realized he was in the only situation worse than death. Captivity. His eyes searched overhead. The shutter door above him was filthy and overrun with cobwebs. With groggy fingers he felt over the restraints that bound his hands. An impossible knot of wire and cord.

Exhausted, he sunk back against the pole.

And that's when he saw her.

An apparition seated before a glowing fire. Just beyond, framed in the entrance of the open garage, the great expanse of pasture was still awash in a sea of darkness save for the haunting glow of the full moon behind the clouds. He watched as the ghastly figure before him poked at the flames. In its aura, her white hair was alight with a fiery brilliance.

Shuffling his feet in a pathetic attempt to stand, the man kicked out weakly.

"Please," he whimpered, "Please, let me go."

Peeking over her shoulder, Dora studied the man for a moment. Then, without sympathy, she returned to her task. After a while, she spoke into the flames.

"Well, well, you finally awake." she grumbled, prodding at the crackling coals. "I took the liberty of burnin them holes in ya shut. Guess that means I done saved your life. Though by sunrise you prolly gone wish I hadn't."

A great lump lodged itself high inside the man's throat. As he forced it down, the sharp sting of his cauterized flesh began to throb.

"I'll admit," Dora continued, her eyes lost in the fire, "you had me scratchin my head for a minute there. See, I was half expectin a familiar face when I rolled your carcass over. But I ain't never seen you before. Though... more I get to thinkin I figure they got Klans all over these parts. Maybe things was gettin a little too close for comfort, so Hinkley called in some outside help to clean up his mess. That about right?"

"Please," the man wept, "Just let me go."

Amused, Eudora snorted and spat a wad of phlegm into the flames. Buried deep within, two long irons jutted out from the glowing embers.

As she put on a pair of rough leather gloves, Dora gazed deep into the inferno. For a while she loomed there, motionless.

Then, at last, she spoke.

"I'm sure you heard all kinds a' terrible things about me. Bout how I'm the devil and I do the devil's work. And how the white man's life ain't worth dog shit to me. And y'know what? They ain't wrong."

Firmly, Dora wrapped her gloved hand around the iron buried deepest in the fire.

"They ain't wrong," she muttered again, "I am the devil... to men like you."

With a searing hiss she withdrew the Burleson brand from the depths of the glowing embers. At the end of the long iron, two B's with a strike through the center radiated with a luminous brilliance.

Even from this distance, the stranger felt the heat stinging upon his skin.

In the cavernous garage, Dora's boot heels clicked across the concrete. The brand screamed with a sinister heat. As tears began to well in his eyes the stranger squirmed in despair.

"Now," Dora said, centering herself before him, "I asked you a question, son. And I ain't gone ask again."

Steadily she raised the scalding brand towards his face. Eye to eye with the screeching iron, his long lashes curled back towards his skin in a scorched mass of stinking tar.

"Tell me what I already know," Dora commanded.

CHAPTER XII

DEATH RIDES A PALE HORSE

"Dead?!" Hinkley snarled into the receiver. "What the hell you talkin bout dead, who's dead?!"

Inside the confines of LeClaire's office, the Sheriff's heavy steps tread the length of the floor. The coiled telephone line trailed behind. Across the room, Lawrence LeClaire sat silent in his chair stroking the coarse grey stubble of his cheek. This was not how he'd hoped the night would go. Leaning back, he gazed out the window towards the hallow moon glowing just beyond the clouds. It was now just past 3 am. The most silent and still hour of all. But contrary to the slumbering country roads outside, the office was a hive of manic energy. Like blackflies Hinkley's eyes zipped side to side as he awaited a response on the line. His white knuckles clung hard as ivory against the receiver.

He could not afford another failure.

"Cockrell! Ain't you listenin!?" the voice on the line hollered back, "Cockrell's dead! Christ, Hinkley, they blew his brains out!"

At this, Hinkley stopped his pacing. Beneath his pale, sweaty brow an eyelid began to convulse in tiny rhythmic spasms. Lawrence stared motionless out the window. Somehow Hinkley found his lack of reaction to be all the more terrifying.

"Who killed em gatdammit?!!?" Hinkley returned, barking into the phone, "Burleson!?"

Deep in his gut a sickening tidal wave of shifting organs grumbled uneasily. Though he waited for a reply, he already knew the answer. His unsteady legs were all the confirmation he needed.

Burleson.

Hinkley wiped his sweaty palms down the side of his pant leg. The more he tried to keep it together the more he was falling apart. His head was pounding. With every nervous movement he radiated heat like a furnace.

"I don't fuckin know who it was," the voice on the line fired back, "We weren't there more'n ten minutes fore all hell broke loose. You sent us into an ambush, John. They was waitin! Had us surrounded the minute we got there!"

With every exclamation the frantic voice grew louder and faster as Hinkley listened on.

"Bullets was flyin every which way. Musta been ten or twelve men out there along the tree line takin shots! Christ, we ain't had no choice but to run for it! We was outnumbered ten to one!"

Behind the desk LeClaire buried his head into his hands. Though he considered himself a man who planned for the worst, this had exceeded all expectation.

Hinkley beat the receiver against the wall like a madman. In the aftermath three gaping holes were left crumbling in the drywall.

Taking a moment to collect himself, Hinkley licked his lips before bringing the receiver back to his mouth. As he searched for the words, his wild eyes burned hot as the whiskey upon his breath.

"Tell me you brung him with ya, right?"

"Who?" the voice cried back.

"Oh my god," Hinkley groaned, dropping the receiver in his hand, "don't do this to me! Tell me you got Cockrell's body? I know y'all didn't just leave him there. Tell me you idiots got his fuckin body!"

In the absence of reply an eerie silence filled the room. Behind the desk, LeClaire shook his head deep in trance.

"No, we ain't got his fuckin body," the voice snapped back, "We got the fuck outta there is what we got! We barely saved our own skin, there musta been a dozen men out in them woods! Ain't you listenin? You want his body you go get it yourself you fuckin asshole!"

"You left him!?" Hinkley bellowed, "You morons, he might still be alive!"

"HE'S DEAD, HINKLEY!" the voice screamed back. "Dead! Y'understand? I was there! I seen it with my own eyes his brains was drippin off the walls! That good enough for ya? Cockrell's brains was outside his fuckin skull! Is that dead enough for you? If we ain't get the hell outta there there'd a been three dead bodies to collect insteada one! You wouldn't a done no different!"

"Gatdamn you good for nothin little shits!" Hinkley hissed as saliva spewed from his lips. "You've ruined me. Y'all realize that? Couldn't even snuff out some withered old woman! You've ruined me!"

"Yeah, well, that ain't my fuckin problem!" the voice roared through the receiver, "Y'know our High Wizard only agreed to this as a favor for LeClaire. And guess what partner, that favor just run out. We done cleanin up your mess. Done, y'hear?! We already halfway back to Hebron. You lucky we even stopped to call. You made your bed pig, now you fuckin lay in it."

After a clatter on the receiver, the line clicked over. The frantic voice was gone. In its place only a frail buzz hummed through the stagnant air. Clutching the dead telephone in his hands, Hinkley stared at the wall for a long while until his arms dropped lifeless to his side. The heat of embarrassment burning in his face was unbearable. But his humiliation had only just begun.

Behind him, LeClaire's silence became more insufferable by the second.

"Alright," Hinkley began, unsure of where his words were leading. "Ok, that's it then. I made a mistake and... now... I'mma...I'm gonna take care of it."

Across the room LeClaire leaned back into his chair as it creaked beneath his weight. Taking off his hat, Hinkley wiped the sweat from his forehead before continuing his aimless thoughts. "I'm goin out there. Yessir, that's what I'll do... get a couple squad cars and we gone go out there, say we got reports of gunfire and..."

"You ain't doin nothin John." LeClaire interrupted, turning round in his chair.

"C'mon now Lawrence," Hinkley begged with a quiver in his voice, "c'mon, let me handle this."

"No, John," LeClaire replied firmly, holding up a defiant hand. "You had your chance. This Klan business now."

Klan business.

The last time Hinkley heard those words he had found himself dragging a couple dead bodies into the morgue's incinerator after hours. Course, that was business as usual as far as the Klan was concerned. But this didn't feel anything like business as usual. This felt different. Like some kind of turf war that had gotten way out of hand. LeClaire was growing reckless. Why just last night Hinkley had stood watch as Lawrence beat the living tar out of young Donnie Schneider for about an hour straight. During that time, he'd considered saying something, maybe stepping in to spare the kid, but LeClaire was on him like a man possessed. He'd laid into that boy so hard and for so long that Hinkley thought he was dead for sure. It happened in this very room, right there in that corner. The boy's blood still stained the carpet. Hinkley could almost hear his strained breathing begging for mercy beneath the pummeling. Begging for his momma through his broken jaw.

But Lawrence never let up.

As he sat there now behind his desk, Leclaire's bruised and swollen knuckles were clasped beneath his chin. Though he was as far across the room as he could get, Hinkley felt those pale blue eyes boring into him like a hot bullet through butter.

Beneath the weight of that gaze, Hinkley's figure shriveled to that of a child.

"You was the one who came to me, remember?" LeClaire began with a sharp tongue. "You wanted Barett out the picture. We was more than happy to oblige. But you was supposed to keep us out the spotlight, John. Sweep it under the rug like you done so many times before. But you have failed us, at every turn."

Pausing, Lawrence allowed his words to sink in.

"This time you run into a little problem you weren't expectin didn't ya? You thought you was gonna start a hare from the brush but fore you know it you found yourself knockin on the devil's door. And I told ya, didn't I? I told ya she wouldn't take this lyin down. I shoulda run this shitshow from the start, took em both out. Then we wouldn't be in this mess to begin with."

"C'mon, Lawrence," Hinkley sniveled, "I was only tryin to keep our distance from this whole mess. Keep our names out the mouths of this town. You know how they talk. Now, ok, it was a mistake callin in them out of towners, my mistake, I see that now. I shoulda handled it myself. Just give me one more chance."

"No, John. We past that now," LeClaire commanded. "That's my final word. Now, I'll be the first to admit that bitch more than any of us bargained for. She's a real pistol, I'll give her that. But now, thanks to Burleson's little stunt at the courthouse, the whole town knows who really runnin things round here. She brought us out in the open. Called our shots. Named names. Challenged us in front of everybody. These townfolk simple people but they ain't stupid. They see what she's doin. And she gone keep right on so long as she got breath in her lungs. So now…" Lawrence mused, settling back into his chair. "We got to send a message."

At last, Hinkley's eyes met Lawrence's from across the room.

"She need to be made an example of," LeClaire sneered, rapping his finger against the tabletop. "Ain't nobody in this town go against the Klan and live to tell it. Black, white, *nobody*. And we sure as shit don't need no police or no outside help to handle our business, y'understand? This still Klan country, less you forgot. *We* are the native sons. And if we got to remind em whose hand holds the whip, then so be it."

Though Lawrence was treating him like a disobedient child, on some level, Hinkley welcomed the opportunity to wash his hands of the matter. Let it be somebody else's problem. He'd grown sick of this game. He'd just wanted things his way and like the lazy fool he was he had taken the shortest line to it. Now it had all blown up catastrophically before him. Barett just wouldn't let up about that Fordham business, so he'd snuffed him out. Now, despite being six feet underground that bastard was still tormenting him from beyond the grave. As acting Sherriff for the last thirty years Hinkley had thought he'd seen it all, but this whole thing had become more trouble than it was worth. He'd thought without her husband, Eudora Burleson would just roll over and die. And why wouldn't she? He'd cut her down at every turn, crushed her spirit in every way he knew how. He'd threatened her and intimidated her but when push came to shove and all the old tricks had fallen short, somewhere deep down, Hinkley knew he had no idea how to deal with someone willing to fight back. Willing to fight to the death.

Now, sensing his opportunity close at hand, Hinkley couldn't help but leap at it like the coward he was.

"Well," Hinkley relented, casting his eyes down at his boots, "what'll ya have me do then Lawrence?"

"*You* ain't gone do nothin," LeClaire said with disgust. "You gone walk out that door, get in your car, and head straight home.

Then you gone take a shower, sober up, and first thing tomorrow mornin you gone head into the office like you do every day. And as usual, ain't nothin gonna happen. You won't get no calls about nothin and you ain't gone hear a peep about no Eudora Burleson. All you got to do is focus on election business and don't pay it another thought."

Lost in his plans, LeClaire's eyes followed his vision as if watching a movie projected upon the screen.

"Maybe in a week or two you'll get a call to go check on her but you ain't never gone see her again. I promise you that. Her and that dead body out there gone disappear from the face of the earth like some bad dream. Like they weren't never there at all. And when people start askin bout her, you gone play the fool. Least I know you can manage that," LeClaire snorted, "you'll tell em she just up and left. Hell, she musta realized she weren't gone win after all, so she cut and run. Don't matter what the story is. The town'll talk like they always do. Fill in the blanks, make up they own excuses. But I tell you this, deep down, they all gone know *exactly* what happened to her. And I tell ya, won't nobody in this town ever make the same mistake again."

Hinkley nodded along and rubbed his exhausted eyes. Then, with a great sigh he collapsed into the chair just opposite of LeClaire's desk. As he looked down at his boots he studied the untarnished polish of his spurs.

"I'm sorry, Lawrence," he muttered, "suppose I just weren't expectin none of this, y'know? I ain't see it comin's all…maybe I'm gettin slow in my old age."

At that moment LeClaire's hand disappeared beneath the table. Hinkley's body flushed cold, but soon the hand returned above the desk with a bottle and two glasses. At the sound of the whiskey sloshing within, Hinkley's fear began to subside.

"Oh, you still got your uses ol' man." LeClaire grumbled. "You owe us. And we gone need you by the time we're through. We got big plans for this town. Have a drink with me, John. Calm your nerves. It's over now, y'understand? It's all under control."

Taking up the bottle in his hand LeClaire uncorked the lid and poured a heavy glass. Across the table Hinkley's mouth watered as the scent drifted into his nostrils. Together the two raised their drinks in a halfhearted toast. Then, Hinkley tossed it back, draining his dry in one fell swoop. That familiar warmth spread down his throat and through his belly. Finally, his hand ceased its trembling.

"So," Hinkley began, smacking his lips with satisfaction, "what y'all gonna do then?"

As LeClaire leaned back into his chair a cruel spark jumped to life in his wily eyes. Turning the question over in his mind he savored a long leisurely swig from his drink.

"We gone do what we do best, John," LeClaire said, studying the liquor swirling at the base of his glass.

"We gonna ride. And all hell gone ride with us."

Later that night, not long past the hour, on the outskirts of the Quarter, a young boy jolted awake from the burden of a fitful dream.

For a moment, lying still in the dark, he opened and closed his eyes, unable to discern any difference between the two. Finally, the boy sat up and rubbed his face before peering around the room. Down the long dark hallway across from the bed he thought for a moment he heard the approach of footsteps. He sat and listened. In the silence his belly groaned with a gnawing hunger. Shuffling over towards the edge of his creaking bedframe, he sat quietly for a minute to see if he could hear the sound again. Breathless, his feet dangled above the floorboards. The night was still, save for the tired moaning of the old and rotting house. Beside him on a rickety steel cot, his three brothers dozed on, despite the stifling temperature and the darkness that surrounded them. Inside his heart the boy felt a strange envy as he watched his brothers snore. He too wished he could fall asleep so that the unbearable night could pass quickly into morning.

But to him sleep would not come.

So, as he had done on so many sleepless nights before, the boy lowered his bare feet onto the floorboards beneath him. With ginger footsteps he padded his well-worn trail towards the window, careful not to wake his brothers or disturb his parents sleeping across the room. Before the open window, he parted the thin curtains and gazed out into the dimly lit street outside.

Often when the nights would draw out long and sleep would not come the boy liked looking at the streetlights glowing over the farm road. For all the things the house did not have, like running water or electricity, the boy loved that at this house, no matter how dark the night became, he could always look out at those few lights trailing off towards town. In their hazy bulbs he found a certain comfort that he could not explain.

Standing there, stretched out on the tips of his toes, he settled his chin upon the windowsill.

He did not know the hour but only that the moon still gleamed bright against the backdrop of a jet-black sky. He knew it must be very late for the heavens were not yet that strange shade of blue and violet that announce the arrival of dawn. Looking down again towards the street he sighed a weary sigh and watched the hovering insects beating themselves against the towering lights above.

Then, he heard it again. That strange sound once more. Like footsteps far off.

But this time they were closer. Heavy and sharp. Like iron sharpening iron. Climbing his way up onto the sill the boy turned his ear down the road. Patiently he listened as the sinister clatter became clearer with each passing second. In the approaching commotion he heard as it were the noise of thunder. All around him the airwaves rippled with that dreadful quivering ring.

He had heard this sound once before, he was certain. When his Daddy had driven steel stakes into the ground with his mighty sledgehammer. Yes, the boy was certain, that was the sound that was fast approaching. The sound of muscle and steel.

It was coming from where the road disappeared behind a veil of darkness. The boy watched with an anxious and expectant terror.

Slowly the sound drew nearer.

Then, from the blackness, they came.

White riders in the night.

Upon snorting steeds, the riders marched in formation down the road, shattering the peaceful silence of the surrounding countryside. With each slap of the horses' steel shoed hooves upon the asphalt a chilling reverberation rang out. Like death bells tolling in the night. Bound in their ceremonial white robes the riders wafted like specters drifting through the black air. In unison their voices whooped and hollered like demons sprung from the gates of hell. Bathed in the glow of torchlight, the boy counted their forms as they grew larger before him. Thirteen men upon thirteen horses. And though the riders seemed to all be one in the same, anonymous beneath their stark white robes, it was the horses the boy found himself drawn too. For he was rather fond of horses and in his unknown fear the boy could no longer bear to look upon the men. So, unsure of what to do, he counted the ponies. Shrouded under the riders' white robes he picked out a pair of painted ponies, great brown mares, and a few appaloosas trotting rank and file.

But beneath the glowing aura of the moon one horse was alight with a particular brilliance. A great pale horse. And upon him rode a man with a steadfast gaze. He did not join the others in their menacing revelry, but instead remained silent and fixed on the road before him. In his hand, he held a rifle over his lap. And though he remained still and calm there was something especially terrible about his presence.

Then, the boy remembered.

The scene came screaming back to him from the recesses of his memory. Like the recollection of a nightmare long forgotten. He could not remember the time nor the place but only that he had once stood in front of a great pecan tree and in the breeze the swaying branches called to him and so he stepped closer beneath their shade. There, he'd cast his gaze to the top of that towering tree. There, he'd seen the dangling bare feet of three boys swinging from ropes strung up high in the canopy. And though he did not know the boys by name he thought the game looked like great fun and so he had dashed over to join them, smiling from ear to ear. But just as he was about to begin his ascent his father had snatched him up and held him tight against his chest. He remembered this especially, for his father was weeping, and it was the only time he had ever seen him do so. And though his father had run very fast and held him very tightly so that his face was buried into his chest, the boy had managed to wriggle out just enough to see those strange ghosts, those white riders, disappearing just beyond the horizon. And as he'd watched their faint spectral forms vanish into the heat his father had repeated one phrase over and over. A sort of prayer perhaps, recited in some vain attempt to silence the shattering of his heart.

"You ain't see nothin son," he'd whispered through his tears, "ain't nothin there my boy. Just the trees. Just the wind and the trees and nothin else."

But now, as that terrible procession of white riders passed before his bedroom window the boy made sure to cast a watchful eye upon them. And he saw, as their thundering hooves strayed off the main drag and ventured down the unlit turnoff of Burleson Road.

Moments later, not more than a quarter mile down the way, Lawrence LeClaire held up his hand at the front of the ghastly procession. Gradually the pounding hooves came to a steady halt. At LeClaire's command a white rider approached from behind until their horses stood snorting shoulder to shoulder.

There, beneath the waning night sky, the rider awaited instruction.

With his fist still held high in the air, Lawrence sat motionless for a long while as he stared off down the road. Then, with a commanding clarity, he spoke.

"What," he began calmly, "is that?"

Swiveling in his saddle the rider beside him studied his surroundings through the holes of his hood. Out in the pasture he saw nothing but the great rolling plains and heard only the call of the bullfrog.

"Uh," the rider replied, "what's what, boss?"

With a steady hand, LeClaire pointed down the long dark road before them.

"That."

Casting their eyes down the road the riders soon spotted what LeClaire had already seen. A shambling form lurching through the darkness. The horses sensed it too. With ears cocked forward they craned their necks and shuddered beneath their masters. Behind him, LeClaire heard his mens' anxious murmurs rising as the mysterious creature plodded closer with heavy, haphazard steps.

Suddenly, a pitiful wail cried out. So miserable and haunting that even LeClaire's old steed shuffled in place, eager to break ranks. But just as Lawrence reigned in control, the form stumbled into the ravine, and disappeared beneath the cover of nightfall.

"Curtis, Gates," LeClaire snapped, "go check it out."

Spurring their horses, two riders broke away from the group and thundered off down the road with rifles at the ready. Hanging back with the others LeClaire watched as their beating hooves bore down on the unknown entity. All around the sweltering night air was tense with silence. The horses snorted, stamping their steel shoed hooves against the road.

In the distance the riders came upon their target. The horses circled, keeping a cautious distance. One rider waved back the all clear and dismounted from his horse. Working beneath the moonlight, he loaded the strange cargo upon his saddle and returned up the road.

As the men whispered amongst one another, Lawrence alone remained focused.

The moment his men came within view, he knew something was wrong. Beneath their hoods, their eyes were wide and afraid. Without a word they pulled up before him and laid bare their grisly discovery.

Lying limp across the horse's haunches, was the body of man.

His clothes were torn and stained in a crust of dried black blood. His hands seemed bound in frayed bandages that hung loose and lifeless from his fingertips. Sliding him off the saddle, the riders unfurled his body across the road as LeClaire studied him from horseback.

"Torches," he commanded as two riders brought forth their lights.

In the gentle glow of the fires, LeClaire confirmed what Hinkley had feared most. It was Francis Cockrell. Or what was left of him anyways. He had a bullet hole blown clear through his shoulder blade which had been cauterized black and crisp. His whole face was a sickly swollen mass. But it was his hands that LeClaire found most perplexing. Leaning forward in his saddle he studied them closer in the torchlight. What he had first thought to be paper-thin ribbons of gauze were in fact sheets of skin peeling away from the back of the hands. As he dismounted from the pale horse LeClaire slowly knelt beside Cockrell's body. With a gurgling gasp the man moaned. Shushing him softly LeClaire took up his hands and turned over his palms so that he could study the strange wounds more closely. As he did, he recognized the insignia immediately.

Two B's with a strike through the center.

Burleson's brand.

The hot iron had been applied with such force that it had burned straight through the tendons to the white of the bone. All around the cauterized flesh was blistered and burst as if kissed by the fires of hell itself. The thin skin still left clinging to the bone hung lifeless and gray.

In the man's haunted eyes, LeClaire understood what had been done. He was left with only one question.

"What did you tell her?" Lawrence asked calmly.

In breathless gasps Cockrell struggled to speak.

"It's ok, son," LeClaire continued reassuringly, "it's alright. We got ya now. But I need to know... What did you tell her?"

At this Cockrell's bleary eyes rolled down from the heavens. Summoning all his strength for one last breath, he spoke only a single word.

"Everything."

Before all great storms there is an eerie calm that falls over the natural world. A bracing. Even in the trees there is a tension that pulls taut among the branches, stiffening through the deeply rooted trunks. The sucking tide before the crashing of the waves. Hidden deep in their burrows and dens, all the creatures that crawl in the night cease their commotion, if only to listen to the approaching whirlwind. In every blade of grass, in every trembling stone, the earth itself quivers as if eager to expel its brewing affliction. It is a harbinger as old as time. A natural response to a nauseating symptom. A clash of particular elements, coming together at precisely the right time and place, to produce a volatile result.

A thunderous cavalcade approached the stone entrance of the Burleson property.

Riders on the storm.

Rounding the corner, past the watchful stone eyes of the Danes, the high stepping horses rumbled on in full pageantry. Mounted proudly, with puffed chests upon their saddles, the riders' white robes snapped sharply upon the wind. Like specters beneath their masks, they showed no sign of humanity. Their torches burned hot, casting a ghastly illumination down the line. The entrance was a precisely planned spectacle on display for an audience of none. But no matter.

Onwards down the gravel drive they marched. Comfortable in their approach, as if every inch of ground beneath them was theirs by birthright. Under the fell of the horse's steel shoed hooves the quaking ground announced their arrival.

Reaching their positions, the riders tightened their reigns. Without a word they fanned out with a drilled and practiced cadence.

War formation.

As the dust settled, they stood forming an arched semicircle thirty yards out from the front door of the Burleson residence. In the still and sweltering night, the low rushing of their torches flickered with evil intent.

Before them, the house was utterly still. All through the dwelling not a single light was illuminated. In every window the blinds were drawn tight. Beneath the awning hanging over the front porch there was nothing but a pitch-black void.

Mounted in their saddles the riders held steady until LeClaire made a cutting gesture through the air with the back of his hand.

Without delay a rider slid off his saddle and set to work unstrapping a ten-foot timber cross lashed to the side of his horse. Hoisting the great beam upon his shoulder he trod out heavily across the lawn and staked it into the ground. Receiving a burning torch, he stood at attention. Beneath the fading light of the moon, he looked towards LeClaire.

Seated triumphant upon his pale horse, Lawrence nodded.

With a touch of the torch, the gas drenched cross ignited with a fiery boom.

In the momentary illumination of the fireball that followed, LeClaire could have sworn he saw a ghost in the night. But as the great flaming plume rose high into the sky its illumination quickly faded to a dull glow. Still, LeClaire squinted into the darkness upon the porch, straining for a second look. Engulfed in flames before them, the cross crackled and popped. With weapons at the ready, the riders held their position, waiting for their prey to awaken to the hell that awaited her.

But then, in the blackness beneath the awning, a tiny flame sparked to life.

In the saddle LeClaire's eyes grew wide as he watched the flickering light floating through the air. It flared for a moment before fading fast into a single glowing ember. In the stunned silence that followed, the sharp clink of a lighter snapped shut sending a shudder down the line. From beneath the awning, the groaning creak of an old rocking chair. The hollow thud of boot-steps trudging across the wooden porch.

From the darkness two fiery eyes smoldered red.

Eudora Burleson stepped forth into the light.

Standing defiant before the blazing illumination of the cross they saw her truly for the first time. More predator than prey. Clad in an ensemble black as death she donned a shoulder holster strapped across her chest. Seated below her right arm, Barett's Colt .45 dangled with cruel intent. Gripped cold in her steady hands an M14 Carbine, courtesy of the United States Military. As the cigarette glowed between her lips, Dora took a deep drag. The smoke steamed from her nostrils. In her stance, her message was clear.

She would not be moved.

For a long while not a word was exchanged in the standoff, but rather an unspoken understanding. It was a dance as old as time. Combatants set face to face, awaiting the inevitable. Beneath the light of the moon, they studied one another as the infernal heat between them rose with each passing second. As Dora cast her wary eye down the line, the riders' fingers tightened instinctively upon their triggers. Tasting their hesitance on the slick night air Dora grinned a sinister smile. She was ready to die. But could they say the same? In the distance the bullfrogs roared. The cicadas screamed into the sky.

Then, just as LeClaire summoned the gall to speak it was Eudora who sounded the first words.

"Hinkley out there with ya?" she hollered towards the line. "Or did he just send the dogs?"

Twisting the reins in his grip LeClaire could suffer the indignity no longer. The audacity of this woman. Mouthing off at her own execution.

He'd hang her from the trees like the mongrel she was.

Rearing up before the fiery light of the cross the pale horse kicked its hooves and tossed its head madly in the moonlight. Pointing a fiendish finger towards her, LeClaire struck a hellish sight bathed in the ghastly glow of the flames. A masterful orator, his practiced voice boomed out across the pasture as though he were the devil himself.

"Eudora Burleson!" He bellowed, low and deep. "For the betrayal of your race and the desecration of our righteous law we have come to issue our final judgeme..."

Suddenly, a shattering pop silenced his speech.

In the ringing aftermath the metallic ping of an empty bullet casing chimed sharply against the flagstone. With a confused dread, LeClaire raised an unsteady hand and clutched at his chest. Already, a crimson river trickled down his white robes. Bewildered, he attempted to continue, but found his lungs curiously empty of breath. Then, as the cross burned before him, his limp body slid off the saddle and collapsed against the ground with a dull thud. All down the line speechless masks gazed towards their dauntless leader, lying dead upon the lawn.

"That's about enougha that," Dora muttered taking aim towards the next rider.

"Holy christ," a panicked voice cried out from the line.

As Dora squeezed off the second shot all hell broke loose beneath the early morning sky. Lighting up the yard, an ungodly firestorm of shrapnel and lead tore through the air. As the riders broke ranks, shots peppered the house, kicking up a whirlwind of shattered glass and brick dust.

Reeling upon her heels Dora crashed through the front door into the darkness of the house. Beneath a flurry of wood pulp, she returned fire as the riders scattered and dismounted from their horses. Round after round she cracked off into the mob until finally the magazine pinged a metallic tune. As the trigger clicked empty Dora wasted no time. Quickly she rolled over onto her belly and tossed the rifle. Overhead the drawn curtains fluttered aloft as the fabric was torn to ribbons in the crossfire. Slithering over shattered glass Dora moved down the long hallway towards the bedroom. In the chaos, she heard them calling to each other.

"Go round the back!"

Dora grinned madly to herself.

The fools.

Outside, just as a trio of riders made their move through the open garage, the point man felt the slight touch of a taut wire upon his ankle. Before he could look back to warn the others a savage explosion detonated. A flash of light and searing pain. In the aftermath a thick white fog billowed out from the garage over the muffled moans of dead and dying men.

Seeing their fellows cut down before them the remaining riders pushed back towards the front entryway. A point man was chosen. Soon they breached the threshold of the front door. More poured in behind. Fanning out through the dark corridors they moved between cover with weapons at the ready.

Like rats they stuck close to the walls, scurrying along with wide eyes. As the first group entered the living room the wraithlike curtains shifted eerily in the moonlight. Their hot breath stunk beneath their hoods. Taking cover behind a bookshelf, one of the masked men peered out across the room. There on the flagstone of the hallway, he spotted a strange reflection gleaming in the moonlight. Reaching out he wiped the crimson fluid against his glove and held it up for all to see.

Blood.

The discovery steeled their hearts. Turning back to the trail before him, the rider traced the bloodline down the long dark hallway until his eyes fell upon the threshold to the bedroom. There, he could just make out her silhouette in the darkness, crawling towards the back room.

But just as he opened his mouth to speak, the shadowy form levelled its arms.

"There!" he managed to cry as the first bullet tore through his chest.

Shots rang out from Dora's .45. Like mad hornets the bullets zipped through the air and buried deep into flesh. Groaning, the Klansman curled into himself and went silent. Dora's pistol clicked empty. The scent of spent gunpowder filled the air.

"SHE'S OUT!" A voice shouted.

"GET HER!" Another commanded. "SHE'S OUT! MOVE, MOVE!"

In an instant their white robes came crashing down the long corridor. Converging like the frothing whitewater of a great and powerful river they roared down the narrow gallery as a single seething mass. With every step they bore down on Dora as she crawled into the darkened recess before Barett's office. Just above her, the painting of Sir Galahad glowed in its golden frame. Beneath the sabres, crossed on guard, Dora sat with her back against the brick and gazed into the approaching onslaught.

Silent and steady, she let them come.

Storming down the hallway they rumbled past the children's empty bedrooms. The framed photos of family on the wall. The memories of a life buried and gone. They were so close now she could feel their heat. Their fury and their fear. But still she waited. Slowing before the doorway the first rider stepped boldly across the threshold. Shrouded in darkness, Eudora bided her time. Not until she saw the whites of his eyes did she rack the great bolt back and forth in its chamber.

Like a hammer the chilling sound echoed down the dark hallway. Suddenly, the riders stopped in their tracks.

But it was too late.

As Dora pulled the trigger, fire licked forth from the mighty barrel of the Browning 1917. The machine gun screamed to life in the darkness. How savagely the black steel barked shots down the tight confines of that corridor. Trapped in the choke point the riders could only fall before the buzz saw. In an instant it transformed their flesh and bone into a cloud of crimson gore. One after the other they were cut down, exposing the next man to the assault. The weapon kicked madly, stripping the plaster off the walls. Straining to hold it in place, Eudora bore down upon the trigger and focused the bucking sights upon her targets as a blinding light flashed before her. In its fiery glow she grit her teeth. Spent bullet casings chimed like a cavalcade of bells against the floor. The fabric of the ammo belt sang as it pumped round after round into the incendiary chamber. A symphony of death. In only a few moments, Dora found herself firing into a dark and smoky abyss.

Releasing her hold upon the trigger, she peeled her hands from the grip and collapsed forward against the gun. At her feet hundreds of empty bullet casings lay steaming. Before her the barrel glowed a hellish red. Like an overheated engine, exhaust billowed up from the weapon as it clicked and popped in the haze.

Taking a deep breath Dora hoisted herself up. Bracing herself against the brick wall, blood dripped from her fingertips. Wiping her hand against her trousers she drew the 1911 from its holster. Then, stepping over the sandbagged machine gun emplacement Dora studied her handiwork. The trap had worked a charm. All down the hall a trail of white robed corpses lay stacked one atop the other, disappearing off into the darkness. Here and there, their dying groans drifted up like a lazy morning mist. As Dora stepped closer, a thick fog of gun smoke swirled around her knees. Just beyond the doorway a lake of crimson trickled out across the flagstone from beneath the bodies.

Outside the first blue light of dawn was just beginning to break beyond the trees.

Her eyes fixed on the corpses lying heaped in the hall, Dora approached the bedside table and took up the telephone in her hands. Shouldering the receiver against her ear she blindly dialed a number into the rotary. In the darkness the line rang and rang and rang and rang. It must have been nearly five in the morning.

But she knew he'd answer.

Just then, a rattle sounded on the other end of the line. Against a backdrop of conversations and the crack of pool cues a raspy voice cut through the clatter.

"This Lou, how d'you do?"

"Lou, it's Dora. Lemme talk to Floyd."

"Yessuh, hold on just one minute now."

In the moments that followed Dora listened as Lou's powerful voice called out over the bar. In the distance an indiscernible country song bobbed along sadly. For a moment, Dora closed her eyes and thought of praying. But thinking better of it, she spat against the floor.

"Hello?" a grave voice finally answered.

"Floyd...it's me," she said, snapping her eyes open.

"Dora?"

"I need your help."

CHAPTER XIII

SHOTGUN WOMAN

As the long feverish night slowly gave way to a blood-tinged dawn a grave silence enveloped the Burleson property. In an hour usually reserved for the chirping activity of the starlings and warm roar of the cicadas, the pasture was shrouded with a cold disquiet.

Drifting on the damp morning air a thin veil of fog had descended upon the rolling acreage as far as the eye could see. In the almighty oak trees in the front yard, two great vultures perched patiently and set their beady eyes towards the house. There, the adobe hued brick, pockmarked with bullet holes still stood unbroken in the red glow of dawn. Licking out from the great shattered windows of the living room, the frayed curtains drifted like specters, aloft on the passing breeze. Though blood still stained the front steps of the house, not a single body remained in sight.

The early hours had been arduous and full of labors.

Though the battle was over, the war was far from won.

Just then, deep within the dark recesses of the garage a burbling growl groaned to life. The aching bones of a great metal beast creaked into motion once again. High upon their perch, the vultures' scraggly heads snapped to attention from the trees. At last, two headlamps thumped suddenly into stunning illumination.

Beneath a fiery sky, Barett's 1949 Cadillac Coupe DeVille lurched out into the early morning light. In the front seat, shrouded beneath her impenetrable black sunglasses and a haze of cigarette smoke, Dora let the wheel slip through her fingers as she eased the car down the drive.

But as she set out to fulfill her final task, a curious sight caught her eye from the passenger window. There, smoldering in the front yard the charred remains of the ten-foot timber cross still stood beneath the rising sun. Dora slammed on the brakes. The Cadillac skidded to a grinding halt.

With the engine still running Dora popped the trunk. In the treetops the wary eyes of the vultures tracked her every move. Though last night's events had consumed her entirely, somehow, she had still found the time to dress properly for a trip into town. One last hurrah as it were. Donning a crisp white dress shirt with sleeves rolled over her bandaged arms she rummaged through the trunk for a moment before quickly reappearing with a great axe in her hands. It had belonged to her father, and possibly his father before that. Long ago Edgar had spent many nights seated by the fire, whittling a rather ornate design into the pommel. A serpent coiled beneath a striking dagger.

Held now in her hands she found the symbol quite fitting.

Setting it coolly over her shoulder Dora marched out towards the yard with a cigarette pinched between her lips. Arriving beneath the towering crucifix she looked up and down its scorched and smoking remains. Before her the timber still glowed a hellish red just beneath its ashen surface. Bringing down the axe she tapped the base of the blade lightly against the totem which wobbled with a weak and hollow sound. Then, pitching her cigarette with a quick flick, she drew back with both hands. In one mighty swing she buried the blade deep into the beam, cleaving the bottom of the cross nearly in two. As the timber splintered and cracked beneath its own weight, Eudora brought up her bootheel and finished the job.

Satisfied, she returned the axe to her shoulder and marched back towards the Cadillac. Tossing the axe into the boot she slammed it shut and slid back into the driver's seat. There was still work to be done.

With the wheel gripped tight in her hands Dora pinned the accelerator to the floor. As the farmlands flanking Burleson Road snapped by out the windows, she soon saw the fated site approaching. No matter how she braced herself, the impact of that cursed intersection stung no less sharp. The black bands of singed rubber painted across the asphalt took a small piece of her every time. As the Cadillac squealed out onto the two-lane blacktop of the interstate, the sinister streaks rolled by quickly. Though never quickly enough. That old pain returned as though the wound were freshly cut. As though the tire streaks had just been left. As if they'd been seared into her very soul. How many nights had she spent since it all began, staring silently at their serpentine movement? How many times had she recounted that scene? Barett, left dead & dying in that ditch. What had they done to him in the end? Perhaps she would new truly know. In the rearview mirror she couldn't help but think as she studied their wayward recollection.

She pressed her boot deeper into the accelerator.

With the red sun now peeking out over the tree line, the curves of the Cadillac were alight with a cosmic radiance. The engine, grateful to be alive on such a fine morning, hummed a satisfied tune as it smoothly shifted into third and barreled on towards town. Outside the wind whipped through the open windows. It was a spectacular morning indeed. Gazing out at the miles flying by, in her own way, even Eudora agreed.

It was a good day to die.

As the car thundered on past the ramshackle homes of the Quarter, Eudora spied a little boy sat on his porch with his family. From a long way off he watched her, and as the Cadillac drew nearer, he stood. Recognizing it perhaps, the boy hopped down from the porch and wandered out into the yard towards the train tracks. Then, as the car passed by, he waved to her. From the cab Dora raised her hand with a half-hearted salute as her eyes met his, but only for a moment, and then she was gone. Positioned next to her in the passenger seat, the upright receiver of a Winchester M97 shotgun rattled along in time with the engine. The pump action 12 gauge had been a personal favorite of Barett's. A fine piece of machinery, as he had so lovingly called it. Not the most intricate or technologically advanced weapon of its age, but perfectly crafted for its task. The mauled and mangled bodies it had left behind on battlefields in World War I led to the German attempt to classify it as a war crime. Ironically in a world of tanks, bayonets, flamethrowers, atom bombs, mustard gas, and hand grenades, it was the trench gun that their men feared most. For all its lethal capabilities, its operation could not have been simpler or more intuitive. Point, shoot, kill. Anything caught standing before the barrel would be flayed to ribbons beneath the buckshot. One hardly to aim.

Checking the hands of the clock on the dash, Dora noted the time.

7:47 a.m.

Stomping the pedal to the floor the Caddy bucked into fourth gear and screamed down the blacktop. In the distance, the first buildings of town began to appear upon the horizon, awash beneath the blanket of a blood red sky.

Meanwhile in the heart of town, John J. Hinkley was doing exactly as he'd been told.

The night before he had showered, shaved, and gotten a good night sleep. When had awoken that morning, he was still a little drunk. But by now that was to be expected. He had spent the early hours going about his daily routine in the silence of his empty home. After stepping into his freshly pressed uniform, he poured himself a steaming cup of coffee and topped it off with a generous serving of single malt whiskey. Then, he'd combed the sparse hairs across his shining dome while humming himself a little tune.

Though he hadn't expected it, he was in a right good mood.

Last night he had received no call from LeClaire so everything must have gone off without a hitch. Just like he'd said it would. Sure, Lawrence was an ornery son of a bitch but by God the man always came through. On his way out the door the Sheriff couldn't deny that he had something of a spring in his step. With a sharp whistle he spun his keys in hand. The liquor was just hitting now. It was a fine morning indeed. All his worries had vanished into thin air just like LeClaire had promised. It was as if a great weight had been lifted off his shoulders. Surely, Eudora Burleson was dead and gone. He could feel it in the air. An inexplicable lightness.

There wasn't a person on earth who could stand up to a cavalry of Klansmen hell bent on destruction. In fact, just the thought of what they'd done to that woman put a smile on the old Sheriff's face. That old witch, he only wished he could have seen her eyes when they drove that knife into her heart.

He only wished that in her dying breath she could have known that it was him all along.

That it was he who had called the hit on Barett.

It was he, who'd arranged the men and the car.

It was he, who'd destroyed the evidence.

And it was he, who'd reap the rewards.

But done was done, and he was happy to be rid of her at last. In the end, he couldn't help but laugh at himself for all his efforts. It'd hardly been worth the trouble.

Strutting his way out towards the car Hinkley's silver spurs chimed a cheerful tune. With a heavy groan he eased his portly frame into the driver's seat and started up the engine. Taking off his hat he slicked his hairs back in the rearview mirror. The weekend was just around the corner, and he meant to spend it kicking back with a few cold brews and forgetting this whole mess ever happened. Just one more workday he thought to himself.

And by God, if this beautiful morning were any indication, it was going to be a great one.

Just a short drive from his front steps and Hinkley was already rounding the corner into the square. In many ways, the Sheriff always saw himself as sort of an unofficial herald of the day. It was a long-held point of pride. In fact, it had been a primary part of his re-election campaign.

"The first man in."

He found it gave people a certain comfort to know that just as the shopkeepers were sweeping up their front steps you could find Sherriff John J. Hinkley sitting at his desk ready to handle the business of the day. But on this morning, as Hinkley's squad car rolled through the square on its usual route, something mighty peculiar rattled the old Sheriff. Because just as he delivered his usual friendly wave to old Mr. Garland at the Wheaton Co. Feed and Seed, to his surprise, the kindly shopkeeper just backed away from the window - as though he'd seen a ghost.

Driving on Hinkley could only cock his head with a confounded expression as he passed. In the rearview he watched as old man Garland faded back into the darkness of the shop.

"What crawled up his ass?" Hinkley muttered to himself as he pulled around the corner.

The display was strangely out of character. And try as he might the Sheriff could not think of what he'd done to receive such a cold reception. In fact, the more he tried to shake this unnerving notion, the more the thought gnawed at him.

Just then the magnificent courthouse came into view beyond Hinkley's windshield and all was soon forgotten. Glowing beneath the red morning sky the towering structure seemed even more spectacular than usual. Its great roman columns rose magnificently above the thin mist atop the manicured lawns. Like some vision of Mount Olympus, where the gods and kings of old reigned for all eternity. Even as a boy Hinkley had always dreamed of working within its halls.

It said something about a man, where he worked. Hinkley had always thought so. In Wheaton, some people spent their whole lives shoveling horse shit in the same stinking stables day after day. Or stuck in some musty office swearing to themselves that one day they'd get out. But as a young man Hinkley had watched his father work himself to death while his mother drank herself to death and it didn't take long for him to figure out that kind of life just wasn't for him. He wanted open skies and all the freedom of the wild west like those tales he'd heard on the radio. Lone Ranger and the Silver Shadow. Funny enough, that was what drew him to the police in the first place. All those stories of cops and robbers. Cowboys and Indians. Shooting first and asking questions later. Not long after Hinkley became a policeman, he soon realized the world looked at him a little differently. Suppose at some point he reckoned he wasn't beholden to the law like normal folks. How could he be?

He was the law.

And the law always wins.

With a grin upon his face Hinkley parked just outside the front steps of the courthouse and killed the engine. With great care he took a moment to shine the brass badge pinned atop his breast pocket. Then, securing the gun belt beneath his belly he popped open the driver's side door and stepped out into the warm morning air.

In the square, the mockingbirds were busy flitting among the treetops and filling the sky with their sweet harmonies. On the ground, darting from one trunk to the next, chattering squirrels went earnestly about their work. The green and golden leaves of the pecan trees quivered in the breeze. The infernal heat wave that had stifled the county was just now beginning to break. As it always had, the town had survived once again. At long last, all was well in Wheaton County.

Slamming his car door shut, Hinkley placed his hat atop his head and snapped the brim between his fingers. Then, he began to lumber his way up the courthouse steps.

But just then, across the street, he caught wind of an impossible sight in the reflection of a vacant shop window.

There, drifting like an apparition across the glass, he swore he saw the chilling blue gloss of Barett's prized Cadillac. Suddenly, a pang of hot terror flashed across his face. Wheeling around on his bootheels he turned to face the street. But it was empty.

Whipping his wild eyes back towards the window he found the spectre had vanished without a trace.

"Good christ almighty," Hinkley huffed, "I must be seein thangs."

Still, he studied the desolate square with a wary eye. At first glance, he found great comfort in its silent streets. He reassured himself that everything was as it should be. Or was it? Where were the shopkeepers? Their front steps were empty. Their doors closed. The rush of hot blood once again flooded his veins. Something was amiss. Suddenly, the entire square was frozen. The birds fell silent.

The hair on the back of Hinkley's neck bristled.

The great iron hands of the courthouse clocktower tolled the top of the hour. As the deafening reverberations rang out above him, Hinkley nearly jumped right out of his skin. Seized with a rush of panic he quickly resumed his march towards the great wooden doors with haste. But just as he reached the final set of steps, he heard the unmistakable sound of a great beast approaching.

Tires crawling across asphalt.

It couldn't be.

No matter how he reassured himself, Hinkley knew there was only one way to be certain. One way to know for sure.

Finally, he mustered the courage to turn around.

It can't be, he told himself.

It couldn't be.

She was dead.

Casting up his eyes, he saw it at long last. The sinister chrome grill of the Deville leering back at him. The rumbling din of that damned engine. Inside his belly churned. His heart choked tight against his collar. Bracing himself against the handrail, Hinkley couldn't look away.

The door to the car swung open.

Eudora Burleson stepped forth.

Impossible.

Without pause Dora's bootheels began their steady approach. Cradled in her arms, the locked and loaded shotgun rattled a reckoning with every step. Behind her black sunglasses Eudora's eyes burned hot and steady just as the fresh lit cigarette smoldering upon her lips.

So great was Hinkley's shock that he remained frozen before her. Trapped like a deer in the headlights. Dauntless, she continued her measured approach. Hinkley blinked as if trying to rouse himself from some terrible nightmare. But with every feeble attempt to turn and run Eudora grew larger before him. As she tightened the gap to a few meters between them, she finally stopped with the trench gun held low at her hip.

As they stood, locked eye to eye, a welcome breeze wafted its way through the empty streets of the square. As its faint touch fell upon Hinkley's skin he was awoken from his petrified stupor. For possibly the first time in his life, he found himself at a loss for what to say. In his mind jumbled thoughts raced like rabbits darting off in every direction, each one disappearing into burrows, just out of reach. Before him Eudora stood like a statue.

"Well," Hinkley blubbered with a distinct quiver in his voice, "what? Ain't you gone say something?"

Unmoved the cigarette fumed silent upon Dora's lips. As she stoked the ember, the tip glowed a fiery red. Frozen in the cold black reflection of her sunglasses, Hinkley saw himself tiny and feeble before her.

"So, what then?" he continued, grasping for anything, "This your grand plan, is it? You mean to shoot the Sheriff in broad daylight in front the whole town? Darlin, I know you ain't that stupid to go doin somethin like that. Believe me when I tell ya, you ain't gone make it a mile outta town fore they come for ya."

Dora didn't budge. She knew a bluff when she saw one.

"Just wait," Hinkley snapped desperately, "you won't have nowhere to hide. We'll see who's laughin then. They gone come for your children! No matter where they hidin! Ya understand me?! They'll come for your head."

As Dora watched him falter before her, a knowing grin crept across her face.

At this, Hinkley's lips twisted into a stinking snarl. How dare a woman look at him as though she were his master. He could suffer the humiliation no longer. Seized with fury he grit his teeth and pulled for his pistol. Drawing in a flash he fired the first shot. But, in his panic, he'd hardly remembered to aim. Singing through the air the errant bullet zipped well past Eudora as she levelled the barrel of the shotgun at her hip. Pulling the trigger, a thunderous boom erupted, echoing out like a cannon all through the square and down the dusty back alleys beyond.

In the treetops, the beating wings of the mockingbirds snapped into flight.

On the steps Hinkley winced as a dull ache began to throb deep in his chest. Sinking back against the handrail, he slumped lazily against his side as Eudora's boots reconvened their steady approach. In the stillness, the hollow clatter of a shotgun shell rattled over the stone steps. In Dora's arms the heavy chamber racked back and forth with a mighty clack. Curling his finger around the trigger of his pistol Hinkley moved to raise his weapon but found his body incapable of obeying the command. Wheezing he fired off another round against the pavement. With a sharp whistle the bullet ricocheted off into the distance.

Suddenly, a second shearing shot rang out from the barrel of the trench gun.

Seizing the bloody stump where his shooting hand had just been, Hinkley collapsed to the ground. Like a speared snake he twisted and writhed, spitting venom and curses. At last, the steady march of Dora's boots fell silent. Upon opening his eyes, Hinkley found himself staring down the barrel of the shotgun. From its black void he felt a hellish heat upon his face. Just behind, looming like Death itself, Eudora stared down upon him. Her judgement, immovable and clear. Ejecting the spent cartridge, she racked a fresh round into the shotgun's chamber. The cigarette upon her lips flared a fiery red. Desperately, Hinkley's trembling tongue licked out across his lips. Wheezing he summoned one final breath into his lungs.

One final message.

"You'll nev-"

A third booming shot echoed out across the square.

As the fading rumble drifted off into the distance, the reverberations soon doubled back until only a humming silence remained. Flecked in droplets of fine crimson mist, Eudora turned away from the lifeless body before her. There, she drew a deep breath, motionless in the warm glow of dawn. Then, cradling the shotgun beneath her arm she removed her sunglasses and wiped the slick lenses against the bottom of her shirt.

Calmly, Dora began her measured march back towards the car. Along the way she stopped to collect each spent shotgun shell. With a methodical cadence she counted them as she placed them in her pocket. Two on the ground, one still in the chamber. With this task complete, she approached the open car door, tossed the shotgun inside, and eased herself in. Racking the car into gear, the growl of the engine soon rounded the corner and disappeared almost as quickly as it had arrived.

In the moments after, the red sun climbed higher over the trees as a cautious calm settled over the square.

Soon, certain that the coast was clear, the mockingbirds returned to their roosts just as the squirrels dared to venture down from the trees to resume their daily labor.

As the minutes passed, the crackle of gunfire echoed into a distant memory.

In the square the streets were still and quiet, save for the trickling stream of crimson blood just beginning to drip down the courthouse steps.

Across the road at the Diamond Diner, the tiny brass bell atop the door chimed a solemn tune. Venturing out tentatively from behind the door, Margie Watson surveyed the square with eyes wide and alert.

And though the scent of gunpowder faded quickly as the morning mist, the things Margie had witnessed on that fateful summer day would stay with her until the day she died.

CHAPTER XIV

LOOSE ENDS

The next afternoon, while sat at a stop light, Clyde Abbott craned his neck forward to get a better look out the front windshield. High above, the summer sun was burning with such a heat that even the blue cloudless sky felt harsh and inhospitable. Upon this backdrop, an immovable vulture hovered at staggering heights. Swaying in long lazy lines the scavenger lingered upon the wind, drifting from one invisible current to the next.

Meanwhile, down on the sizzling blacktop the chugging engine of Clyde's squad car droned on.

Dragging a sleeve across his sweaty forehead the deputy squinted into the sun until the bird finally drifted out of sight. With a heavy sigh he sank back into his seat and stared out at the sea of rippling heat waves before him. He'd been driving for what felt like weeks, but still, those strange trembling waves were always one step ahead. He shook himself to keep the sleep at bay. His dark sunken eyes were weary and red. His back ached something fierce against the metal stiff springs of the seat. Clyde reckoned it had been damn near the longest twenty-four hours of his life.

He had gotten the call around noon yesterday, while wrapping up his business at the Capitol. Though he couldn't say that the news had come as a total surprise, the timing certainly caught him on the backfoot.

In many ways he had always been expecting that fateful call. Every time the phone rang at some odd hour, Hinkley was the first man that came to mind.

In Clyde's foretelling, the scenarios had always varied but more often than not they involved drink in some way or another. Sometimes he imagined a voice on the line would tell him that the old Sheriff had wrapped his car around a telephone pole. That he'd fallen asleep at the wheel after a long night of boozing. Frankly, any possibility that ended without the loss of civilian life was about as much as Clyde could have hoped.

Of course, while he'd thought about the possibility often, he'd never chalked Hinkley up to suicide. In the end, he reckoned the old man didn't have the guts to do himself in. Just wasn't his style.

Homicide on the other hand wasn't totally out of the picture. Half the man's closest friends hated his guts. In Hinkley's world of small-town politics everybody was always twisting somebody else's arm trying to get one thing or another. You either owed somebody or they owed you and everybody was out to get their due. If you were looking for motive to commit murder, one certainly didn't have to look too far. Hinkley was the kind of man who always seemed to be rubbing shoulders with the sort of folks who'd snuff out their own first born to make a buck.

But then again, the more Clyde got to thinking, he reckoned those fellas probably didn't have the stomach to follow through with murder. They just liked the theatre of it all. Besides, for all his political posturing, Hinkley always seemed more like the kind of man to die in some roadhouse bar or dirty back alley. Shot in the back by a jilted drunk over a paltry debt, or a bad hand, or some woman he'd just met. Like all those stories about gunslingers and outlaws Hinkley had grown up reading about in ten cent comic books. All them cold blooded cowboys he loved so much. There was always some great irony in their untimely demise. As if their fates were truly penned by a hand not quite their own. Like the legend of Wild Bill Hickock, dealt the infamous dead man's hand before finally meeting his maker.

In many ways, the reality of Hinkley's demise had exceeded all expectations for the drama of his final act. A showman to the end, his legend sounded almost too buttoned up to be true. A Sheriff gunned down on the courthouse steps. Slain upon the very ground where he had sworn an oath to protect and serve. Likely by the very people he had sworn to protect and serve.

Where had it all gone wrong?

Slowly, over time. Imperceptibly Clyde supposed. Like the grass out in the pasture, one day it's clipped short and tidy then before you know it, you're swimming in it up to your hips. Seems the more you look away the more things have a way of creeping up on you. It was strange to think about it now that it was done. When Clyde had left for Austin, he half worried he might have to return for Hinkley in handcuffs. A long shot, sure, but he'd considered it. Just about the only thing he hadn't considered was returning for Hinkley in a body bag.

From the moment he got the call the young deputy's mind was moving a mile a minute. He listened to the words but couldn't believe the story they told.

Murder in cold blood.

All along the drive home he ran through theory after theory. He considered suspects and situations and tried to piece the puzzle together as the squad car sped down the interstate. But the moment he entered Wheaton County all that thinking went right out the window.

Before he'd even reached the square, Clyde was struck with the realization that already something had gone terribly wrong. There were no blockades. No police presence. Just business as usual. As his overheated squad car finally rolled up to the courthouse, having driven from Austin in five hours flat, Abbott thought he must have been seeing things.

Instead of a taped off and secure crime scene there were townsfolk milling about freely on the lawn.

Huddled beneath the shade of the trees they whispered carefully to one another and pointed towards the steps. In a hot flush of panic Abbott had feared for a moment that the body was laid out on public display. But as he rushed up the stone stairs, he realized it was even worse than he could have imagined.

They'd already moved the body.

Two young recruits, fresh out of high school. The only two officers on duty that Friday. Rookies in the truest meaning of the word. Hardly experienced enough to write out a traffic ticket. Those boys didn't know the first thing about crime scene management, let alone homicide. Instead of training them like he should have been doing, Hinkley liked to use them as errand boys. They were regulars at the liquor store, but besides that they were about as worthless as tits on a fish. By the time Abbott arrived, all that was left of the crime scene was a mop bucket. Hinkley's corpse had been moved. Drug into the courthouse, bound in tarp, and stored in a utility closet. As if that wasn't enough, the two boys had then thought it a good idea to go ahead and wash down the blood-soaked stairs outside. In their shock, they were afraid that the townsfolk would be startled by the sight of so much blood. They said they didn't know what to do. So, like the fools they were they'd sprayed down the scene with a hose before mopping everything up.

"A river of red," one young deputy had called it, his hands still stained with Hinkley's blood.

A river of red.

Above the rumbling hood of the squad car the stoplight snapped green. Rousing himself from the recollection, Clyde pressed into the accelerator. Behind him the last intersection out of town grew smaller and smaller in the rearview mirror. Soon the buildings of the main drag gave way to the gentle ebb and flow of the fields. One sweeping swath of ranch land to the next until the first crumbling homes of the Quarter came drifting into view. Here the railroad separated the interstate from the property lines. As Clyde drove on each rail pylon swooped by with a great billowing rush of wind through the open window. Just down the road a family went busily about their work beneath the shade of a mighty pecan tree. There an old man was baling hay with a pitchfork as the women worked at the wash. Even the children were working, hanging clothes on the line. Then, as if seeing an approaching twister in the distance they stopped their labor and huddled together with a peculiar urgency.

Like hares at the sight of a coyote they disappeared one after the other into their home. As he passed, Clyde realized with a certain shame it was the sight of the police car that had terrified them so. The watchful and frightened eyes of the little boy standing against the doorway told him all he needed to know.

Turning his attention back to the road before him the deputy spied a familiar sight at the top of his windshield. Craning his neck forward he saw the same great vulture soaring high beneath the sun. In lazy loops it tracked side to side at a steady pace with the car. Its eyes cast ever downward searching for its next meal. Just then, another enormous vulture came swooping into view, pulling alongside the first. Together their stark silhouettes loomed hauntingly upon the clear blue sky.

"That bodes well," Clyde grumbled to himself as he sank back into the driver's seat.

Some folks might call that superstition, others call it the jitters, but to Clyde Abbott listening to your gut was just good sense. And for a man who works with a loaded gun on his hip, Clyde reckoned that advice rang doubly true. There was a warning in those vultures. Just like there was warning in that little boy's eyes.

Setting aside his uncertainty, Clyde drew a deep breath as the turnoff was fast approaching. At last, he'd arrived.

Burleson Road.

Taking a moment to compose himself, Clyde stopped the car and double checked that his pistol was in fact locked and loaded in its holster. Then, turning the wheel down the long, lonely drive, the squad car rambled on. Soon the white barn came and went. The cropland, the bullpen, the creek. With every landmark Clyde consoled himself that everything was exactly as it should be.

Though, in the back of his mind, something about the place had changed.

He couldn't quite put his finger on it. Just something in the way the breeze drifted restlessly through the Spanish moss in the trees. For some reason it gave him that strange feeling one gets deep in the pit of their gut, when you're unwelcome upon the ground on which you stand.

Still, the squad car rolled on. Deeper into Burleson territory. High in the sky the pair of vultures trailed close. In the trees the cicadas roared, basking in the fire of the afternoon sun. Soon the fence of twisted mesquite and barbed wire gave way to the white wooden panels of the front yard.

And that's when Clyde finally saw it.

The squat orange brick set back beyond the sea of almighty oaks. Turning down the drive, Clyde studied the great stone cut Danes carved into the gates entrance. The name Burleson chiseled steadfast into the wall. Then, returning his gaze towards the house he caught sight of a lone figure sat waiting on the porch.

In the distance he could just make out her white hair, radiant beneath the shade of the awning.

But in a sudden revelation, a far more startling sight drew his eye. Because there, floating far above the house, a great wake of vultures had gathered. A teeming black mass, dozens high and dozens deep. Their great swooping wings circled wide, as if forming a sinister vortex to some hell borne twister. So extraordinary were their numbers that a strange shifting shade was cast upon the house and across the lawn. As the squad car inched down the driveway Clyde peeled off his sunglasses to get a better look. His jaw hung open. He reckoned he'd never seen so many vultures gathered in one place. They must've come from miles around.

But what had they come for?

Still reeling from the sight of the wake, Clyde took a moment to collect himself. This was no time for a wandering mind. Picking up his hat from the passenger seat, he took a deep breath, popped open the door and stepped out into the sweltering heat.

On the porch beneath the shaded awning Eudora sat coolly in a wicker rocking chair. Next to her, atop a side table, a short pitcher of tea perspired, half empty. In her hand a cigarette smoldered slow and steady. In this way the two studied each other in wary silence before Clyde began to make his steady approach.

Then, just as he was about to say hello, something must have caught his eye. Because for a brief second, he hesitated. Dora must have seen it too, for in that moment Clyde swore he saw the faintest of smiles begin to form upon her lips.

"That's quite a rifle you got there Mrs. Burleson," Clyde began, breaking the silence. "What's that, a thirty-thirty?"

Taking a slow drag from her cigarette, Dora sat back comfortably in her chair. With an easy glance she turned towards the rifle propped up against the wall a mere arm's length away. It was her father's rifle, a Marlin lever action repeater with a gold-plated receiver. Fully loaded.

"Well, ain't you perceptive deputy?" Dora said, studying the weapon. "I think you right."

"Fine rifle," Clyde said as he stepped closer, "mind me askin what it's for?"

"Shootin snakes." Dora replied with a mischievous grin.

Adjusting the hat atop his head Clyde nodded at her reply. Considering it for a moment, he cast a careful glance down either side of the house. All along the outer walls the flower beds were coated with a powdery dusting of crumbled orange brick. The entire structure was riddled with bullet holes.

"Bit of a big gun for shootin snakes, don't ya think?" Clyde said, turning back towards Dora.

"Yeah, well," Dora grumbled, "they grow pretty big round here."

As he continued up the walkway Clyde stopped short of the front steps to the porch. Perhaps, he reckoned some lines were not meant to be crossed. Deciding against going any further, he clasped his hands behind his back, careful to show he meant no harm.

"How'd your little trip to Austin go anyhow?" Dora asked. "You get things all squared up with the big bosses?"

"Oh," Clyde said, removing his hat and running a hand across his hair, "it went about as you'd expect, unfortunately. I'm sorry to tell ya, they didn't much want to hear it."

"Mhm," Dora replied beneath a cloud of smoke. "I tried to tell ya. Woulda saved you the trip."

"Weren't no problem. Just doin my job," Clyde said easily. "You uh, mind tellin me what happened to your house here, Dora?"

"What's wrong with my house?"

"Well," Clyde began cautiously, "it's full o'holes, Mrs. Burleson."

"Oh, is it?" Dora snapped, with a condescending air. "Well, boys will be boys. Least that's what your friends down at the police station told me. Y'know, I called about a day ago bout some damn fools out here drivin their trucks round the pasture, harassin me, raisin all kinda hell! Takin shots at my goddamn house!"

"You called the police? Are you sure?"

"Course, I called the police!" Dora snorted. "You just go on and check the records. I told em that's attempted murder! And y'know the answer I got? 'Oh, boys will be boys.' That's what your fine officers tol me. The nerve on y'all I swear to god I ain't never seen nothin like it in all my days."

Taking a step back Clyde surveyed the damage to the house. Everywhere the brick was pockmarked with bullet holes. The yard lay scattered with rubble. Here and there a few shattered windows still remained uncovered, though the glass and the majority of the debris had been cleared.

At his boots, Clyde noted the walkway had been swept clean. Yet, in the small spaces of grout between the flagstone the deputy noticed the faint stain of crimson. With a sudden flush his eyes snapped back to Dora.

"Well, I'm sorry you didn't get no response," Clyde offered with a measured calm. "You mind if I take a look around?"

Bringing the cigarette to her lips Dora took her time and considered her answer very carefully. Behind the black shades the deputy felt her eyes studying his every move.

"You got a warrant?"

"No," Clyde sighed admittingly, resting his hands upon his hips. "But I can get one if you'd like."

"Well, you do what you gotta do. But you ain't lookin at shit round here without no warrant," Dora replied, waving him off with one hand. "Thought the police was meant to help people. Instead, you want to go nosin round my business just like everybody else. Well, forget it then. Guess I don't need no help after all. Don't worry bout me, out here all by myself. Harassed on my own godamn property. But don't worry bout me, though. I'll be just fine."

"Of that I have no doubt, Mrs. Burleson, no doubt at all."

Overhead the vultures circled in hypnotic silence. Light as specters they drifted upon the wind. Waiting for some unknown purpose. With one squinting eye Abbott gazed up at them beneath the blinding sun. Unmoved Dora rocked patiently in the chair shrouded behind the black veil of her sunglasses.

"Well, since you obviously ain't here bout my call," Dora said after some time, "then what exactly you here for Deputy? Good company?"

Casting his gaze down from the sky, Abbott weighed how to proceed. Maybe she already knew what he'd come for. Then again, maybe she didn't have any idea at all. Curious to gauge her reaction, Clyde decided to lay it on her quick.

"Hinkley's dead."

"Good," Dora replied without hesitation. Then, shrugging off the comment like yesterday's news she took another slow draw from the cigarette. In silence she sat stone-faced as Clyde shot her a look of surprise.

"Well, what'd you expect, deputy?" she hooted. "Tears? Hell, look at me, I'm practically jumpin for joy."

As Clyde studied her, he noticed the rhythm of the rocking chair didn't skip a beat. The news had hardly fazed her at all.

"When's the last time you saw him?" Clyde continued. "If you don't mind me askin?"

"Why we had us a nice little chat at the last town hall," Dora recalled. "He called me an ol' bitch and I called him a sonuvabitch and then we shook hands and went our separate ways."

"Mhm," Clyde grunted incredulously, "and that's the last you seen him?"

"That's right."

"You sure about that?"

"Is this an interrogation?"

"No m'am, not at all," Clyde deflected, holding up his hands. "We just talkin."

"Well, y'know what, I don't much feel like talkin today Clyde. So unless you got anythin else I'll see you in your car and on your way."

Unmoved, the deputy stood before her. Taking a moment to mull over his thoughts he ground the flagstone beneath his boots before raising his gaze to meet her.

"C'mon Dora," he began, "ain't you the least bit curious bout what happened to him?"

"Not really," Dora muttered.

"Oh?" Clyde grunted with a feigned surprise. "Well, maybe that's cus... you already know what happened?"

"Clyde," Dora said, leaning forward in her chair, "there ain't an end on earth cruel enough for what that man deserved. Far as I'm concerned, so long as he's dead, he got off scott free."

"He was murdered, Dora."

Settling back into the rocking chair she resumed her steady rhythm. Though she acted as if the news were of no consequence the deputy could tell he had struck a chord. For the first time since he'd arrived, she was listening.

"Shot dead yesterday mornin," Abbott continued, "whole thing went down right in the middle of town, too. On the courthouse steps. Funny thing is, whole time I was over at the scene, I reckoned the case was bout as cut and dry as they come, y'know? Ain't take no Walter Brown to put them clues together. I mean, it ain't mystery at all, just three shots..."

Recalling the scene Clyde counted out the shots beneath his breath.

"One, two, three. Right up to the courthouse doors. Broad daylight. Openin hours. When I seen it, I says to myself, 'Clyde we gone have this thing wrapped up by lunch. Somebody saw somethin. Not a doubt in my mind. Everybody in this town knows everybody, right? So, somebody knows who done this."

Before him Dora rocked steady in her chair.

"But, I tell ya it's the damnedest thing. I start askin round the shops. Ain't nobody saw nothin. I ask round the bank. Nothin! Not one person could tell me one damn thing they'd seen that mornin. Course everybody heard the shots, but nobody went to they windows. Can you believe that? Strange ain't it? Bizarre. I mean every shop in town got a front row view of the courthouse. You'd think somebody's shootin off guns it'd draw some attention, right? But seems like everybody just had they head turned the other direction, at just the right time."

With a tired sigh Dora offered no explanation or denial, only a vague expression of weary disinterest.

"To be perfectly honest with ya," Clyde continued, running a hand against the grain of his cheek, "I ain't never seen nothin like it. Hell most the time I can't get a word in these folks be talkin so fast. Y'know how they get. Everbody's got notions. They own little ideas bout how it all went down. Every investigation I ever had in this town I spent half my time siftin through the bullshit. But yesterday, I tell ya, it was like the whole world turn upside down. All a sudden they quiet as church mice. Couldn't hardly get a statement down with all the hemmin and hawin. Just a lotta shoulder shruggin and blank stares."

For what felt like a long time after this, the two sat in a silent deadlock. Though she wore an unenthused expression on her face, Dora felt that Clyde was waiting for some kind of response from her.

"Well, I wouldn't know nothin bout it," she muttered.

"Oh, I know," Abbott said, "just thought you'd like to know is all…"

Just then the hollow sound of footsteps came trudging up from the side of the house. Soon, emerging from the garage in oil stained overalls, Floyd Thomas wiped away the sweat from his bald head with an old shop rag.

"Afternoon, Deputy," he offered with a modest nod "thought I heard somebody pull round."

"Howdy there Floyd, didn't know you were here."

"Oh, just helpin Miss Dora clean up a few things round the house," Floyd said, wiping off his hands. "takin out the trash n' what not."

"I see, well that's mighty nice of ya Floyd," Abbott replied with a smile, "always somethin ain't it?"

"Yessir, sure is," Floyd chimed agreeably.

"Ok, then," Abbott sighed, "well, suppose I'll leave y'all to it, was just getting' on my way anyhow. Got a long day ahead of me down at the courthouse. Thanks for your time, Dora. Appreciate it."

"Yeah, don't mention it."

With a tip of his hat, Clyde turned and began to walk with heavy steps back towards the squad car. As he opened the driver side door, he stood for a moment taking in the strange sight of the wake of vultures one last time. Then, removing his hat, he tossed it into the passenger seat and took a final look around the property. Out in the pasture the cattle languished idly by the fence, clustered tight into the shaded patches of grass beneath the trees. In a trance they chewed their cud and swatted their tails at the blackflies pestering their ears. From the side yard a weak little windmill squeaked soft wails as the passing breeze trickled through its blades.

On the front porch, Eudora still sat rocking in the chair with a cigarette pinched tightly between her lips. Beside her Floyd poured himself another glass of iced tea from the pitcher. He seemed to be saying something to Dora, but her gaze was long gone. Fixed off into the distance, out towards the road, as if waiting for the welcome sight of Barett to come pulling down the drive. A sight she knew she'd never see again.

Then, just as Abbott was climbing into the car, one final thought bubbled up in his mind.

"Oh, Eudora?" he called out across the yard. "Do me a favor would ya? Don't you go runnin off now. I may just be back before long with that warrant we was talkin bout."

Without so much as turning her head Eudora's voice called back.

"Well, you know me, Clyde," she hollered, "I ain't much the runnin type. Though, now that you mention it, I suppose there is a vacant seat on that county board that needs fillin."

Then very softly, as if only to herself, she continued.

"Commissioner Burleson," she muttered as the cigarette bounced upon her lips. "Well, I'll be goddamned, that's got a mighty fine ring to it."

About the Author

Beau Bernstein is a professional writer & amateur anthropologist. *Shotgun Woman* is his debut novel. Born and raised in Texas, he now lives in the majestic Pacific Northwest with his wife and two Portuguese Water Dogs. He was last spotted wandering in the forest somewhere west of the Olympic Mountains.

About the Press

Unsolicited Press is based out of Portland, Oregon and focuses on the works of the unsung and underrepresented. As a womxn-owned, all-volunteer small publisher that doesn't worry about profits as much as championing exceptional literature, we have the privilege of partnering with authors skirting the fringes of the lit world. We've worked with emerging and award-winning authors such as Frances Daulerio, Shann Ray, Heather Lang-Cassera, Amy Shimshon-Santo, Brook Bhagat, Kris Amos, and John W. Bateman.

Learn more at unsolicitedpress.com. Find us on twitter and instagram.